THE ISLAND DECEPTION

Also by Dan Koboldt

Gateways to Alissia
The Rogue Retrieval

THE ISLAND DECEPTION

Gateways to Alissia Book 2

DAN KOBOLDT

HARPER
VOYAGER
IMPULSE

An Imprint of HarperCollins Publishers

THE ISLAND DECEPTION. Copyright © 2017 by Daniel C. Koboldt. All rights reserved. Printed in the United States of America. No part of this book may be used or reproduced in any manner whatsoever without written permission except in the case of brief quotations embodied in critical articles and reviews. For information, address HarperCollins Publishers, 195 Broadway, New York, NY 10007.

Map by Dan Koboldt

Digital Edition APRIL 2017 ISBN: 978-0-06-265908-8
Print Edition ISBN: 978-0-06-265909-5

Harper Voyager, the Harper Voyager logo, and Harper Voyager Impulse are trademarks of HarperCollins Publishers.
HarperCollins is a registered trademark of HarperCollins Publishers in the United States of America and other countries.

FIRST EDITION

17 18 19 20   HDC   10 9 8 7 6 5 4 3 2 1

To Christina, the magic in my life

ALISSIA
MAIN CONTINENT

FELARA

Wenthrop

LANDOR

PIREA

Cambry

NEW KESTANI

Crab's Head

The Enclave

Bayport

CARALIS

TION

VALTERON

Valteron City

"The more time you spend lying to people, the more you think about what truth really means."

—**Art of Illusion, September 5**

CHAPTER 1

THE CALL OF MAGIC

Quinn Bradley had finally arrived.

For twenty-six years, he'd dreamed of seeing his name in the neon lights of the Las Vegas Strip. Of taking the stage at a major casino there, and joining the ranks of magic's elite. Siegfried and Roy, David Copperfield, Penn and Teller. He'd worked his ass off to get here. Designing his own tricks, performing seven nights a week, building his profile online and onstage.

Even so, as he waited in the shadowy alcove backstage, he fingered the stone pendant on a necklace under his shirt and wished he were more excited about it. Quick fingers and cleverness had taken him a long way, but he couldn't help but wonder if he'd ever have made it happen without help from CASE Global Enterprises. Kiara had made good on her promise, and suddenly Rudy Fortelli was calling—nearly panting with excitement—to tell him that a major casino had a slot open. Just a one-night engagement, but still a big deal. Quinn hadn't even asked what they were offering to pay—he'd just cashed one hell of a big check anyway.

It was the Bellagio, of course. The most iconic casino of them all, the home of Cirque du Soleil and countless other top-notch acts. He should have known. CASE Global never went in for anything but the best.

And now that includes me, I guess.

"Quinn?" a woman asked.

Her voice was quiet, but he'd know the accent anywhere. "Veena! I'll be damned."

Veena Chaudri was five-foot-two, slender, and as well-dressed as Quinn had ever seen her. Usually she was in period-matched Alissian garb, or a lab coat, but now she was a sight to behold. She'd pinned up her hair with a glittering silver barrette, and wore a silver cocktail dress with matching heels. The dress was Armani, and worth a small fortune, but Veena probably didn't even know. That made the whole thing seem effortless, and the newly official head of CASE Global's secret research initiative probably didn't even realize how good she looked.

She offered her hand, but Quinn hugged her instead.

"Damn, it's good to see you." He meant it, too. They'd only been apart a few weeks. Six months ago, he hadn't even known her. *I guess we bonded over that whole fleeing-reptilian-predators thing.*

"Likewise," she said. "And it looks like you're doing well." She gestured toward the stage, where the buzz of the audience had begun to grow.

He winked. "I'm getting by. But I'm glad you came."

"It's on business, I'm afraid."

Oh, perfect. And right before he went on, too. "Couldn't the lieutenant have just called?"

"She said you weren't answering your phone."

Damn right I wasn't. He'd been swamped getting ready for the show, and Kiara would only have added to the stress. "I'm not due back for another couple of weeks."

"Yes, well. It's a big crowd out there."

"Is it?" *Thank God.* He shook himself and rubbed his arms. "I was afraid to look." Afraid he'd see a wide field of empty seats.

"That kind of exposure makes the executives a bit nervous."

"Why? It's not like I'm high on the CASE Global totem pole." Negotiating level-ten security clearance had barely made a difference. Chaudri's had moved up as well, though, which put Quinn at the bottom by a wide margin.

"She asked me to remind you of the, uh . . ." She leaned close and lowered her voice. "Nondisclosure agreements."

He laughed. "Is that why they sent you? I thought stern intimidation was Logan's department." The big man would have said it all with a single look.

"He's otherwise occupied," Chaudri said.

"Did they find the Swedish guy?" he asked.

"Only his boat. He made the mainland, but Mendez is hot on his trail." She looked away, and grimaced.

She's worried. A pinpoint of cold uneasiness began to form in Quinn's gut. "Veena, has something happened?"

She glanced around, and bit her lower lip. "The news from over there, about my former mentor . . . let's just say it has everyone concerned."

Concerned was an understatement, if they'd sent Veena all the way up here. *Jesus.* "What's he done now?"

"You'll be briefed on-site. Kiara wants you there as soon as possible."

"I can fly down in the morning."

It surprised him a little how quickly he'd agreed. Normally, he didn't like to jump when Kiara said to, but the idea of being near the gateway again excited him. *Maybe even more than where I'm about to go on, and that's saying something.*

Chaudri's face lit up. "Really? That would be wonderful."

A chime sounded, a polite warning from the theater manager.

"That's my cue," Quinn said.

Chaudri swallowed, and the whites of her eyes showed. "I suppose I should give you some time alone. Are you ready for this?"

"To hear my name announced on the Vegas Strip?" He flashed her a grin. "Been ready my whole life."

"**A** real up-and-comer, ladies and gentlemen," said the emcee. The British accent gave it a gentry feel, like this was the House of Lords and Quinn their newest member. He fought the grin that wanted to come. He needed to focus. "Not new to the Las Vegas scene, but just revealed as the mind behind 'Art of Illusion.'"

Ah, the blog.

True to their word, the company had kept it up while he'd been away on private assignment. He felt oddly ambivalent about it. On one hand, the principles of illusion had saved his life a half dozen times in Alissia. On the other, they felt different. Before he'd taken that job, before he'd seen the other world, pulling off a perfect illusion felt like a jolt of electricity. Now, the thrill felt incomplete. It was like taking the second-best roller coaster in the park while hearing people scream on the best one.

Then again, now wasn't the time to dwell on disappointment.

"Here he is, everyone. Quinn Thomas!"

Quinn strode out into the spotlights as the emcee said his stage name. Command presence was everything in this business, so he had to own it. Big grin and wave for the audience. Enthusiastic handshake for the emcee. Deep, calming breath while he took measure of the crowd . . .

Sweet Jesus, that's a lot of people.

The inside of the theater loomed as large as a sports arena. Stained-glass windows lined the walls; brightly colored murals plastered the lofty ceilings. Even the marks were high quality. No one in the first few rows appeared visibly inebriated, which was a pleasant change. The money showed in a hundred other ways: the tailored suits and cocktail dresses. The champagne glasses. The glitter of gold and silver jewelry. This was the cream of the Vegas crop, and all here to see him.

This is my shot. He'd worked his ass off to get here. Fought tooth and nail against impossible odds— literally fought, in the past few months, at least. If he screwed up now, all of that was for nothing. And hell, part of him wondered if it *was* all for nothing.

The lights hit him.

No . . . this is totally *worth it.*

"Ladies and gentlemen," he said. The sound system carried his voice to the highest balconies, but didn't echo. Didn't even vibrate. "I've been away for six months, getting ready for the trick you're about to see tonight." That was a half-truth. In the last six months, he'd also fled from dragons, gotten himself kidnapped, and set a man on fire. *Now there's a story that might wow them as much as any illusion.* But what he'd planned *was* impressive, so pride—and a touch of ego—won out.

"But let's work our way up to that, shall we? I like to start small." He snapped his fingers and made a coin appear. A gold coin, polished to a high shine. The cameramen had instructions to zoom in for this part. "This is a five-dollar piece. Current market value, about three hundred bucks."

He walked it end-over-end across the fingers of one hand, and then the other. He flicked it up in the air. The gold sang with a lovely, high-pitched hum before he caught it.

"Sometimes when you come to Vegas, money has a way of . . . disappearing." He opened his fingers, and the coin was gone. Barely a flicker of interest from the audience. *Wow, tough crowd.*

He kept his smile on. "That's not the dream, though, is it?" He brought his hands together and rubbed them like he was trying to start a fire. "You walk into a casino, and you want to double your money." He parted his hands, and now there were two gold coins. He rubbed them together again. "Maybe you want to triple it." Now there were three, and the audience was warming up; a few of them even put down their phones. *You can never go wrong with gold.*

"Or, you bet big." He stacked the coins up on his palm. Now there were four, though most of the spectators couldn't tell. "This is the Bellagio, ladies and gentlemen. You go big." He swept his hand over the stack of coins. Now they were house casino chips. Bright yellow with red and black. A thousand bucks each. He threw them up in the air. They caught fire and burned up, leaving only wisps of smoke behind. Quinn held out his empty hands. "Or you go home."

That won him a nice round of applause. He kept them going with some up-close magic: card tricks, cups and balls, pulling a watermelon out of a hat. He used the emcee for an assistant on that last part. The guy had a British accent and the polish of a veteran showman. He and Quinn played perfectly off of one another. The audience ate it up.

"Thank you!" Quinn said. Too loud, but the sound system compensated for it. "I promised you something fantastic tonight. I promised you the call of magic."

He put one hand in his pocket, dropping eye contact with the crowd. A funny thing happened when you did that onstage. The look-away sort of drew them in.

"I've felt the call three times in my life. Once when I was a kid. Again when I started performing in Vegas. And a third time, just a month ago." That time had been different. That had been the one that really mattered.

He looked up, addressed the crowd again. "There's nothing quite like it. Tonight, I'd like to share that feeling with you. Would you like that?"

The audience cheered. Not the loud, raucous cheers of the nightclub rabble, but a steady smattering of polite applause. Everything was highbrow here.

"I thought so." He grinned. "Prepare yourselves for the call of magic." He took a wide stance, bowed his head, and held absolutely still for six seconds.

Then he relaxed, reached into his jacket, and took out his phone. Everyone roared with laughter.

Now he had them relaxed. Perfectly at ease. He punched in a command sequence. Had to put his thumb on the biometric scanner after that, to verify his identity. Kiara had insisted on that. It beeped a soft confirmation. *Three, two, one . . .*

A shock wave struck the theater as every single phone in the audience went off. Pockets vibrated and beeped. Purses buzzed. Watching how people reacted was enormously entertaining. At first, there was the panicked scramble to silence it—on the cost of the tickets alone, this wasn't an event where you wanted to be the jackass of distraction—but as they realized what was happening, they started to answer.

Hundreds of them. Thousands, probably. It was too hard to see past the spotlights on the first tier. But those in view pressed their ears to the earpiece and looked at him expectantly.

He smiled and squared himself to the crowd. "Hello there."

That was his moment. His tiny window of opportunity to offer just the right turn of phrase. To give them the magical finish to a truly unique performance. But the words failed him. Right there in the front row, a man in a suit met his eyes. Tall, light-haired, and a face that screamed Nordic heritage. He looked so much like the Swede Thorisson that Quinn had to do a double take just to be sure. No, it was a different guy. Younger, maybe. His eyes were two pools of cold lake water. Raptor Tech for certain. What the hell did they want with him now?

He'd been foolish to refuse a bodyguard. Kiara had suggested it, before he'd flown up here. That line he'd fed her about being safer in his hometown than anywhere else . . . he regretted it now. They'd sent Chaudri, but she was a goddamn anthropologist. She'd be less than useless.

The theater rippled with laughter, but he had the audience for another moment more. What was the line again? It came to him. "Sorry, wrong number!" He hung up. The audience laughed and applauded. Stood for him in ovation. Quinn made a flourish and bowed. When he thought to look again, the Nordic fellow was gone.

An hour later, he'd soaked up the applause and pressed flesh with some of the Bellagio's VIPs in a special meet-and-greet backstage. A main act was only part of the deal, when it came to Vegas casinos. They liked to have a trophy piece to trot out for their high rollers. Unsettled as he was about the appearance of Raptor Tech, Quinn was still able to put on his charming smile and make nice.

A blonde woman in a too-small black dress shook his hand. "That was incredible!" She was in her midthirties, fit and attractive.

"What was your favorite part?" He knew the answer already, but it never hurt to play the humble card.

"The ending. I swear I put my phone on silent." She let her hand linger in his. "How did you do that?"

He winked. "I can't tell you."

She pouted, gave him the puppy-dog eyes. "Please?"

"I'd rather you think me mysterious."

"How about a picture, then?"

"Absolutely."

The casino had a photographer on standby for just that. Quinn beckoned him over. The blonde cozied up to him and they posed for a couple of flashes.

"Aw, thank you!" She hugged him. Smooth as silk, she slipped a keycard into his jacket pocket. His *inside* jacket pocket, no less. She put her lips to his ear. "I'm in the tower suite."

Of course she was.

It took him half an hour to slip away graciously from the high rollers. Next up: a little face time with the theater manager. Yet another ritual of the Vegas strip. Not quite an interview, but not something you skipped, either. Quinn had some close-up magic tricks in the holster. It never hurt to impress the manager, even after a solid performance. The manager's office was up a set of stairs at the back of the stage. A stage-hand pointed him to it. He was nearly to the stair-case when the suit materialized from the shadows. At first, Quinn mistook him for security.

Then the guy stepped into the light; it brought out the sharp angles of Nordic facial features. Quinn stepped back instinctively, and damn near reached for a weapon at his belt. Except he hadn't carried a weapon in a month.

"Mr. Bradley?"

Quinn squared his shoulders in his best imitation of a Logan stance. "Who are you?" Civilians weren't allowed back here.

"My name's Carl Reiser. I work for Raptor Tech."

"I see."

"You met an associate of mine, around six months ago."

"Thorisson."

"Ah, you remember."

"He's hard to forget," Quinn said. "What about him?"

"I just wanted to know if you've seen him recently."

"Not for months."

"Are you sure?"

"I'm confused." Quinn gave him a side-look. "Are you telling me you don't know where your own employee is?"

He ignored the question. "May I ask where you've been during your recent hiatus?"

"You can ask, but I can't tell you."

"Why not?"

Quinn shrugged, and kept his pose casual. "First, because it's none of your goddamn business. Second, because there's a nondisclosure agreement."

"Isn't that a little unusual?"

"No such thing in Vegas."

Reiser stared at him with cold eyes. "I'm not sure I believe you, Mr. Bradley."

"I'm not sure I care."

They looked at each other in silence. The man wasn't entirely blocking the staircase, but he wasn't out of the way, either.

"The manager's expecting me." Quinn probably could have called for security, but that would've been a sign of weakness.

"I may have more questions for you," the man said. But he stood aside and let Quinn pass.

"I'll be sure to wait by my phone." He slid past Reiser and took the stairs at a steady pace. Halfway up, he spoiled it by glancing back. The man from Raptor Tech was nowhere in view.

He shook his head. *They must learn that at orientation.* CASE Global and Raptor Tech might be rivals, but they also had something in common: they always showed up at the worst possible time.

"No one's harder to fool than a fellow professional. We know what to look for."

—**Art of Illusion, February 18**

CHAPTER 2

COMPETING OFFERS

The Bellagio stage manager was a legendary mogul of the Vegas Strip named David Wyatt. Average-looking guy, probably pushing fifty, but he had the polish of an industry veteran. He smiled when Quinn entered, but it was the automatic kind of smile you learned to switch on at a moment's notice.

"Quite a performance, Mr. Bradley."

Quinn shook his hand. "Please, call me Quinn."

Wyatt gestured to the chair opposite his massive walnut desk. The chairs were no less luxurious: real suede, hand stitching, stuffed just enough to be cozy but not a bit more. New enough that he smelled the leather when he sat down.

"I still can't figure out how you did it," Wyatt said.

"Which part?"

"All of it."

He's just being polite. This was a guy who'd watched hundreds of performances by some of the industry greats. It was thrilling to think about who'd been in this chair.

"I'm sure you've seen some of that before," Quinn said.

"Not the phone thing." He held up his cell, a slim next-gen model in a platinum case. "This is supposed to have state-of-the-art encryption."

"Is it, now?" Quinn allowed a smile. No point telling him that CASE Global subsidiaries had made the phone, written its software, and developed that encryption. Which was only state-of-the-art outside of the prototyping labs.

"Should I get a new one?"

"Already? You only bought that last week."

"How the hell could you know that?"

Because I got Kiara to run a background check on you. Quinn shrugged. "You shouldn't worry. The security here is as good as anything I've seen." That was a lie—nothing surpassed what the company used to protect their biggest investment—but it seemed to reassure the man.

"Well, it was a good trick."

"How'd you like to see another?" Quinn produced a deck of cards and began shuffling. Two-handed, then one-handed. Riffle, cut, riffle, cut.

"That's what I wanted to talk to you about."

"Oh?"

"Look, Quinn, I've got to be honest. You were barely on our radar six months ago. Then all of a sudden the casino owners are telling me to book you."

Quinn gave a thin smile. "I guess someone put in a good word."

"I agreed to have you headline tonight. But that should have been it, even with your connections."

"Well, I appreciate the shot." He'd seen his name in the neon lights, and performed for his biggest crowd yet. It had been his dream, but somehow reaching it felt flat.

"After that performance, though, I'd be interested in having you back."

"Really? I'd enjoy that." He kept his tone casual, because this was probably just a formality. The entertainment equivalent of saying, *I'll call you*. He fanned out the cards face down on the desk. "Pick a card."

Wyatt chose one from the right-hand edge, where Quinn couldn't have glimpsed it while shuffling. That, more than anything, showed how many times he'd been around the block.

"Our main act is going on tour in about a month," Wyatt said.

Quinn swept up the remaining cards, stacked them, and had Wyatt put his card on top. He offered the deck so the man could cut it. Wyatt obliged. He reclaimed the deck, shuffled a few times, and started dealing the cards face up. It was a good excuse to cover the fact that he was holding his breath.

"What would you say to coming on board while they're gone?"

"For how long?" Quinn kept on dealing, watching for his marker card, the two of clubs.

"Six months, with an option to renew."

Quinn missed the next card. His fingers just slid away, and it stayed on top of the deck. *Damn*. It wasn't the most obvious tell, but child's play for someone like Wyatt.

He'd worked so hard for so long, just to get a shot at the Strip. The odds on an offer from a major casino had to be about one in a hundred thousand. And the Bellagio, no less. That made it one in a million.

To his credit, Wyatt offered a gracious little smile. One pro to another. He'd seen the tell, and knew what it meant.

Quinn recovered and kept dealing. *Bam*. There it was. The two of clubs, which meant the chosen card was the king of diamonds. It suited the man, too. If that wasn't a sign, he didn't know what one was. He stole a glance at Wyatt's face when his card came up, and saw nothing. Not a flicker of recognition.

Either he'd forgotten his card or he was a stone-cold fox. Or maybe the trick had gone south. The odds of that were slim, but not zero. *I can't think about that.*

"What kind of a signing bonus are we talking about?" Fifty grand was probably the average, but this was the Bellagio. The kind of acts they secured didn't come cheap.

"There isn't one."

"What?"

"I don't have the budget for it."

That was bullshit. Some of the high rollers he'd just been charming had probably lost fifty grand in the last hour alone. "I'm not sure how thrilled my manager will be about it."

"I think we both know what Rudy Fortelli will want you to say about an offer from the Bellagio."

It was Quinn's turn to smile. *Did your homework, too, didn't you?* That told him how serious the offer was. "When do you need an answer?"

"By the end of the week, at the latest. But I'd really like to know tomorrow."

Quinn kept dealing until only a single card remained in his hand. "Tell you what. If the next card I flip over isn't yours, then you get an answer tomorrow. But if it is, I take the week. And you keep my name on the sign until then."

Wyatt didn't so much as glance at the cards on the table, but he waited for two seconds. "Done."

They always fell for it. Quinn didn't flip the card in

his hand. Instead, he reached out and turned the king of diamonds face down. Wyatt's eyes widened a tiny fraction. He was one hell of a cool customer, but he gave it up. Maybe Quinn had pushed his luck too far. This was a good trick, but a manipulative one, too. No one could resist taking the bet when they'd seen their card dealt out already.

"It looks like you have your week," Wyatt said. "Don't waste it."

Quinn practically floated down the stairs from Wyatt's office. The meeting couldn't have gone better. He wasn't sure that his name would truly stay on the sign out front—it probably came down while the audience was still applauding—but that was just gravy. The offer itself was all that mattered. A contract from a major casino put him in the upper echelon of Vegas performers. And the best part was knowing that he'd earned it himself. CASE Global's connections might have landed him this performance, but no one could bully a stage manager into a contract offer. Not even them.

That was all me.

He really didn't know who to call first. Rudy, probably, though the man would be holding court at his own club by now. Drinks on the house and all that. Quinn could catch up with him later. He remembered the blonde from the VIP meet-and-greet. Why not a little extra celebration? Everything else could wait.

He hit the landing with a spring in his step. Damn near started to whistle, when he skipped around the corner and came face-to-face with the Nordic guy again.

"Jesus!" He took a step back. "You're like a bad penny, aren't you?"

"I'm sorry, Mr. Bradley."

"Listen, guy, I'm on my way to—"

The hiss of the pneumatic pistol surprised him, but not as much as the jab of pain in his midsection. He reached down and found something odd in his cummerbund—a narrow metallic cylinder about the size of his pinkie finger. The metal was cold to his touch.

He jerked it out. A numbness started to spread from his abdomen. "What the—"

"Are you all right, Mr. Bradley?" Reiser stepped forward to take Quinn's arm in a vise-like grip. "It looks like you need to sit down. My limo's just outside."

Quinn tried to refuse, but now his tongue had gone numb, too. All he managed was a faint shake of the head, which the man ignored.

A second set of arms came into view. They were slimmer, more feminine, but locked around his other arm just as tightly. Quinn couldn't even move his head up to look at her. He was limp as a rag doll while they half escorted, half carried him down a hall and toward the emergency exit.

Good, let them try that. The door had a silent alarm. Security would be all over them in about thirty seconds. A little surprising that they hadn't intervened already, in fact. There had to be cameras back here. Surely the security feed would have shown what happened.

That's when he remembered that Raptor Tech was a security company. The market leader, in fact. And the Bellagio never went in for anything but the best.

Oh, I hope I'm wrong about this.

But sure enough, the emergency exit was already propped open. They carried him outside, where a limousine sat with the engine idling. Reiser opened the door and they tossed him in.

Quinn woke up to the slow, blinding pain of a headache. He was sitting in an enclosed space. A car. The wide seats and tinted windows made this a limousine, and the faux leather said it was rented. No palm trees or neon lights scrolled past the window, only darkness. That meant they were off the Strip, probably out in the desert.

None of this information comforted him.

The couple from Raptor Tech sat across from

him, engrossed in quiet conversation. It sounded like German, or maybe Dutch. The woman's voice had a low, sultry tone to it. Only her profile was visible in the dimly lit interior. High cheekbones, sharp angular nose. She caught him looking, though, and nudged Reiser.

"Sorry about the theatrics, Mr. Bradley," he said.

"Wuh—" Quinn started. His tongue felt heavy and awkward in his mouth. "What the hell?"

"I thought it might be best if we spoke in private."

The cobwebs were starting to clear. He remembered the dart gun. It should have ticked him off, but his instincts screamed for caution. Anyone bold enough to grab him out of the Bellagio didn't give a shit about assault charges. He bit back a smart-ass remark, and just said, "About what?"

"About my colleague. Thorisson."

"I already told you, I don't know anything about him."

"Yet you were one of the last people to contact him."

Which was a mistake. He'd gotten cold feet when he first saw the gateway. When he first realized what the CASE Global really wanted him to do. And how dangerous it would be if he agreed.

"Yeah, well, he wasn't exactly up front with me," he said.

"How do you mean?"

"He failed to mention that calling him would

prompt an aerial drone attack on the company's facility. What the hell was the point of that?"

"Unfortunately, I can't remark on what may or may not have happened on a private island half a world away."

"Well, I can. The thing nearly killed everyone." He still couldn't believe that they'd managed to shoot it down. With siege machinery, no less.

"So you *were* there."

Shit. He'd given them that one for free. He played it off as best he could. "Only because your buddy Thorisson screwed me over."

"You never made contact on the island?"

"No." *We made contact, but in another world entirely.*

"Would you tell me, if you had?"

"Probably not."

"At least you're honest about that."

"I've been honest from the start, man. I wasn't kidding about the NDA. The company would make my life hell if I said anything."

"Have you considered the possibility that we could do the same if you don't?"

"Beyond assaulting and kidnapping me, you mean."

"There are worse things, Mr. Bradley. Especially when you're in bed with a company like CASE Global."

"Oh, and Raptor Tech is the paragon of virtue?" Quinn snorted. "I'll take my chances." He shoved himself up into a sitting position. They were out in the desert, all right. *Where they can make sure no one ever finds my body.*

Reiser leaned back and crossed his arms. Took a couple of calming breaths. "Look, we're not bad people. We're just trying to get some information."

"This is Vegas. You don't get anything for free."

"What about doing the right thing?"

"Ah." That old chestnut. He couldn't believe people still tried to use it on him. "So I guess you're right, and they're wrong."

"That's one way of putting it."

"I think Kiara would put it differently." He dropped the name intentionally this time. Raptor Tech almost certainly knew the names of their competitor's top brass.

Reiser did a double take. His eyes widened and his mouth fell half-open. *God, he'd be great to have in a poker game.*

"I think we might be able to—"

The limo jerked forward. The impact threw them all down to the carpeted area between the seats. Quinn ended up in a tangle with Reiser. Which made for a great excuse to check his pockets. He palmed a billfold out of one, something harder and metallic out of the other. Oh, *yes.* The pneumatic pistol. God, let it be loaded. He tucked it into a sleeve pocket.

Reiser shoved him off and grabbed the phone. "What happened?" He listened for a few seconds. "Get rid of her."

"Is it a flat tire?" the woman asked. She was prettier than Quinn expected, even with the pale scar along her jawline. It wasn't precise enough to be surgical, either. She felt his gaze, and slid back into the shadowy corner of the limo while the driver pulled over.

"Some lady rear-ended us. Driver's handling it."

They heard a man and a woman shouting outside. His voice was deep and dismissive. But hers was shrill. Indignant.

"Sounds like it's going well," Quinn said.

Whoever she was, the lady was hot about something. The sound of her voice grew louder, and then she started knocking on the window to the limousine door. "I'm not leaving until I get my apology!"

Quinn saw her face. *Oh, my God.*

It was Veena.

He slid over to the door of the limo. "Well, that's my cue."

"Get away from the door, Bradley," Reiser said.

Quinn pouted. "Aw, what happened to *Mr.* Bradley?"

"I'm serious." Reiser reached into his jacket. Then he frowned. His brow furrowed. He fumbled around, then checked the other pocket.

"I think you're looking for this." Quinn flourished, and made the pneumatic pistol appear in his hand. He leveled it casually at Reiser's chest.

"How did you—"

Quinn pulled the trigger. The hiss of the dart was

a delicious sound to hear. Reiser slumped forward. The woman never moved from where she sat. *Maybe I should shoot her, too.* But she wasn't armed, and the pistol felt like it only had one shot left.

"You know what they say, Reiser." Quinn pulled the lever on the door and threw it open. "A magician never reveals his tricks."

He stepped out, and shut the door behind him. Turned around to find the driver—a huge guy with blond hair and a buzz cut—pushing Chaudri away from the limo, back toward her car.

"Someone asked for an apology?" Quinn called.

Veena shoved past the driver. "Quinn! Are you all right?"

"Hey, Veena."

The driver looked at her, looked at Quinn, and came for him.

"Leave him alone," Veena shouted.

Bring it on, big fella. Quinn let him get within two steps. Then he raised the pistol and fired. The silver dart caught the man right in his massive chest. He glanced down at it. Then his legs gave out, and he crumpled right at Quinn's feet.

Veena's mouth fell open. "My God! What did you do to him?"

"Vulcan nerve pinch." Quinn grinned at her. "Hey, can I catch a ride?"

"The greatest threat to a pristine world is technological innovation."

—R. Holt, "Recommendations
for Gateway Protocols"

CHAPTER 3

DEAD BIRD

Paul Logan had seen a lot of drones in his career, but nothing on par with this one. Most UAVs were so fragile that a flock of starlings could knock them out of the sky. This one had taken gunfire from a .50 cal, shaken it off, and cut the gunner in half with its *own* gatling. The response time had been too quick for a human controller, too. If Bradley and his geeky friends hadn't gone old-school to shoot it down, the damn thing might have destroyed the whole compound.

He and Kiara had rappelled down the cliffs from above. Full climbing gear, too. Not taking any chances. Normally he'd have liked to bring a boat around with a full recon team, but the lieutenant wanted to keep things quiet. They still hadn't traced the source of the rogue transmission that drew Raptor Tech here in the first place.

They reached the rocky shelf where the UAV had crashed. It remained in one piece, incredibly, despite being smashed by a minivan-sized boulder. The frame must have been some new high-tensile-strength alloy. *I can't wait to get a look at this bird.*

Kiara surveyed the wreckage. "I thought it would be in worse shape."

"So did I."

When he'd been with the SEALs, "dead bird" recoveries were one of the more common missions. The numb-nuts in Congress were all about using drones to keep soldiers out of harm's way. Right up until one of them got shot down in enemy territory. Back then, drones didn't just crash, they *shattered*. You needed a shovel to pick up all the bits and pieces.

"You double-checked the satellite scans?"

"Thermals, RF, infrared, the whole nine. Everything was clean."

They cared most about the control unit, which would have the comm array and whatever scary-slick tech components that had let it reprogram incoming surface-to-air missiles. That, and a definitive ID on the maker of the bird. They knew it was Raptor Tech, but having proof in hand would give the company some serious leverage.

A thin metal flap covered the access panel for the control unit. He dug the Gerber multi-tool out of his pocket. Talk about the MVP of tools for the field soldier. This one had saved his life more times than he cared to remember.

The protective flap was stronger than it looked— just like the rest of the damn bird—but the Leatherman did the job. That's when he heard the faint click. Then a red LED flashed into life beneath the pried-up metal.

"Shit!"

"Is that thing live?" Kiara asked.

The LED began flashing, and the beep rose to a solid, high-pitched tone. Logan and Kiara shared a look of alarm. Any soldier with basic ordinance training knew what that meant.

"Take cover!" Logan shouted. He wasn't usually one to manhandle his commanding officers, but shoving the lieutenant behind a boulder seemed expedient. He threw himself down after her. The beeping became a solid tone. He squeezed his eyes shut and covered his ears.

Ka-boom! Metal and debris showered him over the boulder's rim. The explosion hadn't punctured his eardrums, thank God. It hadn't been the deep boom of C-4. More like a percussive explosion. He stood and brushed off some debris. The boulder had taken the brunt of it. Kiara was a bit wrinkled, but otherwise unharmed.

"Well, that was unfortunate," she said.

"Yeah."

"I thought you scanned it for explosives."

"I did, Lieutenant. Six different ways. Nothing flagged."

She frowned. "Maybe it's a new formulation."

"Maybe."

It only took a glance to tell them that the wreckage was beyond recovery. The control unit was totally gone, the solar panels shattered. Damn. He should have gone for those first. The engineers would've had a field day.

Say what you want about Raptor Tech, but they know how to make a good self-destruct mechanism.

The lieutenant checked her watch. "We've got about an hour until Mendez checks in."

"What about the wreck?"

"That explosion might have been a binary chemical formulation. I want trace chemicals on everything."

"I'll call in the hazmat team."

She stalked close enough to jab a finger into his chest. "And don't do that again."

"What?"

"You threw me behind that boulder like a sack of potatoes."

"Wasn't a lot of time."

"Well, I can take care of myself."

He smiled. "I never said otherwise."

Half an hour later, Logan met Kiara in MTAC for an update on the Thorisson mission. The boat he'd stolen had turned up on a neighboring island. Abandoned, of course, and nearly out of fuel. That meant he was probably still in the region. The company had shut down all outgoing telecom for that island and six others, to keep the man from contacting Raptor Tech. Because if he managed that, it would represent the biggest security breach in CASE Global's history. That's why Kiara had sent Mendez after him, rather than letting the Bravo Team member get his R & R after the rough mission through the gateway.

A bank of biometric scanners protected the door to the comm facility. Retina, voice, handprint. Logan got the green light, the door hissed open, and he heard Mendez's voice on the radio.

"Think I might have him."

I hope he really does. That bastard Thorisson had a lot to atone for. Most of Bravo team was dead because of him. The fact that he'd breached the island facility in the first place still rankled. Logan took a portable headset from one of the cubbies inside the door. High-def monitors lined virtually all of the walls. The main desk looked like the cockpit of a 737, with more switches and digital readouts than a movie soundboard. Every form of electronic communication—satellite, radio, airwave, even the fiber-optic hardline—came through here.

Kiara sat in one of the two chairs. She leaned forward. "Can you get us a video feed?"

"Already on it. Image should be coming up now," Mendez said. His burst transmitter had a range of about fifty miles, so it could get around the telecom shutdown.

An opaque rectangle opened on the main viewer. The video feed showed an open-air market—bright canopied tents surrounded by a square of cheap wooden houses. Mendez zoomed in at a pair of figures under one of the canopies. They leaned together in close conversation. One was an islander, dark-complected and shirtless. The other was a white guy.

God, let that be him. Logan moved right next to the viewscreen. The guy had a similar build to Thorisson, but the hair looked too dark.

"What do you think?" Kiara asked.

"Not sure." Logan leaned down to the mic. "Mendez, can you move around and get a better angle?"

"Give me a sec."

The screen went dark as Mendez moved. Logan watched the numbers on his GPS location, and tried not to let his nervousness show. He still blamed himself for Thorisson's escape. Not that it was anyone's fault, but Logan had made two mistakes. First, he'd let

Thorisson activate the drone. Then, he'd let the man out of his sight.

I was so eager to be back that I got sloppy. Well, lesson learned. Once they got Thorisson back in hand, Logan would put him in the brig himself.

The video feed from Mendez lit up again. Now the local's back was to him, and they could see the white guy's face. It was clear he'd dyed his hair jet-black, but he couldn't hide the pale eyes and sharp jawline.

Recognition came with a twist of cold fury in Logan's gut. "That's him."

Kiara joined him right by the viewscreen. "How did he manage to dye his hair?"

"He's resourceful," Logan said. He pushed the transmit button. "Who's the guy he's talking to?"

"A local boat captain," Mendez said.

"Damn," Logan said.

Thorisson was trying to catch a ride. If he got to the mainland, they'd never be able to keep tabs on him. Or prevent him from phoning home, for that matter.

"What do you want me to do?" Mendez asked.

"Stand by, Sergeant." Kiara stepped out to brief the executives.

Logan took the opportunity to brief Mendez on the drone recovery. "Bottom line, I'm not sure we'll figure out how that bastard activated it."

"Too bad," Mendez said. "Didn't you scan it for explosives?"

Why does everyone keep asking that? "'Course I did. We wouldn't have gone near it if there was a blip."

"Maybe they've got a new generation of Semtex."

"Will you ask Thorisson, when you get a chance?"

"Oh, sure. Because he's been so forthcoming already."

"Don't lose him. The lieutenant should be back in a minute."

She took longer than that, though. *Guess the execs are more worried about this than I thought.* When she finally pushed open the door to MTAC, her face was grim.

"What's the story?" Logan asked.

She didn't answer, but took over the mic. "Sergeant Mendez, it's Lieutenant Kiara."

"Go ahead." All business. He knew the sound of an imminent order.

"Prevent the target from reaching the boat. By any means necessary."

Logan did a double take. *Jesus, that's a kill order.*

"Say again, over," Mendez said.

"Any means necessary," Kiara said.

Logan waited until she'd released the transmit button. "Are you sure about this, Lieutenant?"

"We can't take any chances here, given what he's seen."

"He's on foreign soil. We don't have any authority there."

"Even so."

"We still haven't interrogated him."

"The executives think a capture is too risky. He's escaped us, what, three times?"

It took all of Logan's training to clamp his mouth shut. It wasn't his call. There was no point in making this any harder than it already was.

Kiara flipped on the mic. "Confirmation requested, over."

"Got the message loud and clear, Lieutenant," Mendez said.

Logan made sure to keep his face neutral. *So did I.*

"Preparation is everything. If the audience knew how much we practiced, they'd be far less impressed."

—**Art of Illusion, September 20**

CHAPTER 4

THE GREEN LIGHT

Quinn had a personal rule: he never fell for the same trick twice. The moment he boarded the plane with Chaudri, he took a sleeping pill and bagged a solid twelve hours. When he woke up, he skipped shaving and added a touch of makeup to give himself bags under the eyes. *Let them think I'm exhausted.*

When he walked into the island facility and a summons from Kiara was already waiting, Quinn could have smiled. She'd think him exhausted, but he was better than fresh. That put him, as magicians liked to say, one ahead.

He and Veena got their new security badges and made a beeline for the conference room.

"Want to tell me what this is about?" he asked.

Chaudri opened her mouth, and then caught herself. "I'd better let Kiara tell you."

They took seats as a huge black guy lumbered through the door. Paul Logan would make a decent linebacker, but became a Navy SEAL instead, and still rocked the haircut. He was frowning as he entered. Didn't even check his corners, so he didn't notice Quinn was there.

"Well, well," Quinn said. "I thought you retired."

Logan snapped his head around. He grunted, then put on a look of astonishment as he shook Quinn's hand. "Wait, aren't you that famous magician from Las Vegas?"

Quinn chuckled. "You've heard about the Bellagio, eh?"

"Heard they had a great show recently. Guy named Teller. Is that your stage name?"

Ooh, that hurts. "You're thinking of half of Penn and Teller. He's the one who never talks."

Logan scratched his chin. "Maybe you ought to look into that."

Quinn glared at him. "You'd enjoy that way too much."

Kiara chose that moment to barge in. For as long

as Quinn had known them, Logan stood up whenever the lieutenant entered the room. This time, he didn't move a muscle. Didn't even look at her. *What's that about?*

"Bradley, good of you to join us," Kiara said. "I know you must have a busy schedule."

Quinn spread his hands out, showman-style. "Never too busy for you, Lieutenant."

"Then maybe try answering your phone from now on."

Ouch. Guess I had that coming. "Look at the bright side. If you hadn't sent Chaudri, I'd be in a dark cell at the Raptor Tech headquarters right now."

"Heard about that," Logan said. "Nicely done, Chaudri."

Her cheeks colored. "I was terrified the whole time."

"I guess they really want Thorisson back," Quinn said. "So, any sign of him?" He tapped the front of his new badge, where it said *Security Level: 10.*

A cloud passed over Logan's face. He clamped his mouth shut, and raised his eyebrows at Kiara. She shook her head.

So there is a sign of him, but they're not sharing.

"Well, at least tell me you learned something from the drone we shot down," Quinn said.

Logan grimaced. "It sort of blew up on us."

"Wow. Jeez."

"Yeah," Logan said.

"Didn't you scan it for explosives?"

Logan sighed and shook his head. "Every time."

"In any case," Kiara broke in, "Raptor Tech is not your concern."

"Yeah, they shot me with a dart gun, so I'm not sure that's true," Quinn said. "But fine, what *should* be my concern?"

"Learning the nature of Richard Holt's arcane protections."

"For what purpose?"

"So that we can figure out how to circumvent them."

"All right," he said, thinking, *Good luck with that.* But hey, no point in undermining his excuse to go back. He touched the amulet that hung on a leather cord around his neck. Ever since his return, the wayfinder stone had pointed unerringly toward the secure vault that held the gateway. He was still trying to wrap his head around the implications. *Could more magic from the other world work in this one?* If it did, he didn't just want to go back. He craved it more than anything.

"The backpack is still our top priority."

"What's in that again? Hard drives?" Quinn asked.

"Hard drives with every scrap of intelligence we've compiled over fifteen years," Kiara said. "Not to mention the electronic equipment and the genetically modified crop seeds."

"And the Beretta handgun," Logan said. "We don't move until the backpack is neutralized."

He does love to neutralize things.

Kiara gave a curt nod. "The timetable isn't finalized, but Operation Checkmate is active as of this moment."

"Aw, that's our op name?" Quinn groused. "I would have liked to be consulted."

"I think it's fitting, actually," Chaudri said. "We have the same goal as any chess master."

"Which is what?" Quinn asked.

"To remove the king."

The next two weeks were beyond brutal. Every day was a new test of just how much physical punishment Quinn's body could endure. He'd moved rooms when he returned to the island facility, and used his new security clearance to request that the location not be made public. Mostly so he could avoid Logan's early-morning wake-up calls.

Unfortunately, such requests were "security matters" and so they got routed *right to* Logan. So the request was gleefully denied, and Quinn's days started at five a.m. with a ham-sized fist pounding on his door.

"Go away!" he'd shouted, the first day Logan had pulled this crap.

"Get dressed, Houdini," Logan had said. "The R & D team doesn't get moving until nine. That gives us four solid hours."

"For what?"

"Survival training."

There was no point in arguing. Logan had protested the fact that Quinn would have to spend some time traveling alone in the other world, something that virtually guaranteed to bring about his death in a gruesome fashion. Something was eating the man, too. He'd always been a harsh taskmaster, but now he was punishing Quinn like he got real pleasure out of it.

And it was past time to figure out why.

It was a morning toward the end of the first week. Might have been sixth, might have been seventh—they were already starting to run together. They were sparring in the armory, which was really just a fancy way of saying that Logan was beating the crap out of him with a blunted weapon.

Quinn made a side-handed slash at his torso. His arms already felt like lead. Logan's block nearly jolted the sword out of his hand, and spun him around enough that he couldn't see the riposte that smacked him in the thigh.

"Ow!" he shouted. "Son of a bitch, that hurt."

"If this were a real fight, you'd be bleeding out right now," Logan said.

"I'd also have run away the second I saw the size of you."

"You don't always get to pick who you fight. Now, keep your guard up this time."

"What's Mendez up to?" he asked. He needed another minute to catch his breath.

Logan's mouth twitched downward. "He's on assignment."

Here we go. Quinn sucked in a breath. "In-world?"

"None of your business."

"Hey, I'm level-ten clearance now."

"And I'm still at level 'Don't care.' "

"I don't think that's an actual security level." Maybe a different tack would help. "Well, wherever he is, I hope he's all right."

Logan's expression softened. "Me, too."

"Did he come up under the Logan learn-or-die training program, too?"

Logan smiled, but it was fleeting. "He did, but I can't take all the credit. He's a natural born soldier."

"Then I'm sure he's fine," Quinn lied. He pretended that was the end of the conversation. *Come on, give me a hint.*

Logan sheathed his sword a little too forcefully. "He's not in Alissia. I guess there's no harm in telling you that."

On assignment, but on Earth. What could that mean? The biggest threat here was Raptor Tech. What had Kiara said about them? *Not my concern.* Even as he remembered that, the pieces fell into place. Mendez must be after Thorisson. And Thorisson killed most of Bravo Team. Maybe Logan was worried what Mendez would do if he caught him.

"So—" Quinn began, but Logan waved him off.

"Enough chitchat. Let's see if your archery skills have slipped."

Quinn had been promised three solid weeks to prepare for the new mission. That was already pushing it for the R & D lab to finish his new set of equipment. So he got a bad feeling when his communicator beeped with the summons from Kiara: *Mission update. Conf room ASAP.*

"Damn." He was in the R & D lab testing out the new prototype for the elemental projector. The wrist-mounted original had saved his life a couple of times on the first mission, so he wasn't going back in without one. In fact, he had the lab making twin projectors, one for each arm. He'd been about to do the first trial run. "Guess I'll have to test it later. Just got summoned by Kiara."

Julian Miller, the R & D lab chief, waved off the disappointment. "No problem. She's the big boss."

"Can I take these with me?"

Julian scrunched up his face. "Eh, I'd rather you didn't. If you set fire to something in her office, she'll bring the hammer down on me."

Good point. Quinn started unstrapping them. "To be fair, she'd bring it down on me first. And she'd put out that fire with a look." He set them on the metal table beside Julian, careful not to point them at him or the other engineers.

"You'd better hustle. The lieutenant doesn't like to be kept waiting."

"Well, I don't like being interrupted." Quinn opened the door to the hall and strolled out. Only after it had closed all the way did he break into a jog.

She *really* didn't like to wait.

He swung into the hallway where her office was and saw Logan coming from the other way. They locked eyes and sped up. Not quite running, but hustling not to be the last to Kiara's room.

Quinn got to her door first. He slowed his breathing and strolled in at a casual pace. Chaudri was already there, buried in a report. The stress of trying to fill Holt's shoes was showing on her. Her eyes had perpetual shadows under them, and she carried a huge stack of files with her wherever she went.

Kiara looked up from her comm tablet, and her face was grim. She saw Logan come in behind Quinn, and her frown deepened.

"What's going on?" Quinn asked.

"There's been a disruption in our communications infrastructure," Kiara said.

Logan grunted. "Another UAV attack? We should be up in MTAC."

Kiara shook her head. "Our *Alissian* infrastructure."

"Impossible. We built three hundred percent redundancy into those networks," Chaudri said. "The worst storm in recorded history wouldn't knock them out."

"What about sabotage?"

Chaudri tapped a finger on her lips. "I suppose if you knew which nodes to target, and hit them all at once. But the outage would only be temporary. Less than two minutes."

"One minute forty-five seconds, actually," Kiara said. "Which would be more than enough time to tap into our network undetected."

"All of our transmissions will be encrypted, though. And we changed the keys after Dr. Holt's departure."

"After Holt's *defection*, you mean," Kiara said.

"Right." Chaudri blushed. "Of course."

"The intrusion is still a cause for concern among my superiors. Which is why we've moved up the mission timetable."

Quinn bit back a curse. "By how much?"

"We'll leave in seventy-two hours."

Son of a bitch. "Half of my equipment won't be ready by then."

"I can authorize double shifts for the whole R & D lab," Kiara said. "Whatever it takes." She turned to Logan. "Where are we with Bradley's training?"

Logan frowned. "He's coming along, but in a fair fight . . ." He raised his eyebrows and shook his head.

"Hey now, don't forget that I won a couple of those

on the last mission," Quinn said. *And saved your ass besides.*

"You never told us how you pulled that off," Logan said.

"I do better under pressure."

Logan grunted, then glanced back to Kiara. "He still needs more prep."

"We all do," Kiara said. "But Alissia will not wait."

"The fact that the gateway was discovered on an inhabited island raises the question of whether anyone has gone through before us. From their side, or from ours."

—R. Holt, "Recommendations for Gateway Protocols"

CHAPTER 5

SNOWBALLING

Quinn barely recognized the cave that held CASE Global's most valuable asset. Two new security checkpoints stood in front of the gateway airlock. The outer one had next-gen biometric scanners, which he only knew about because they also protected the door of the prototyping lab. The smell was the same, though: that wet-stone musty scent of an underground cave.

Two grim-faced men dressed in black from the company's private security division stood at attention just inside the doorway. *That's also new.* They cradled their submachine guns and made eye contact with no one. Chaudri sat in the far corner, her face hidden behind one of Holt's old notebooks. No one else had come yet.

"Where's Logan?" he asked. "Didn't think he'd be the last one here."

"He left an hour ago."

"What?"

She glanced up, probably noticing the edge of panic in his voice. "He's scouting the perimeter of the gateway cave. It's part of the new SOP."

"Oh."

"He did say something about not letting you near the gateway until he's back."

"Psh. They're lucky I'm going at all." He did have to admit, however, that being this close to the gateway was having an effect on him. Right on the other side of that portal was an entire other world. With *real* magic. And people who could wield it without illusions or sleight of hand. Quinn might even be one of them, if he could rediscover whatever it was that had happened atop those cliffs in Landor.

I need to talk to Moric. Maybe the bald magician's claims about Quinn's latent abilities weren't so far off the mark. And he wouldn't mind talking to the man's daughter, either, but for totally different reasons.

Chaudri had put down her journal and now scrutinized him. "Why *are* you going on this mission anyway?"

"I'm the only one who can get into the Enclave."

"Oh, I understand what *we're* getting out of your participation. I'm asking about what you'll get in return."

A chance to bring some real magic home. There was no putting a price on that. He grinned. "Oh, don't worry about me. A magician always ends up one ahead."

Quinn had packed his own saddlebags this time. A lot of his equipment was delicate, and he didn't want Logan's unnaturally large hands breaking something important. The last seventy-two hours had gone by in a blur. He got most of the equipment he wanted, but not all of it. And he'd barely slept at all.

I'm actually looking forward to making camp over there. That's how bad it is.

The only upside was that Logan had stopped walloping him so badly in their training sessions. Too many visible bruises would raise suspicion in the other world, especially at the Enclave. The last thing Quinn needed was Moric demanding to know who'd hurt him. He'd have a hard enough time explaining where he'd been since they parted in Landor.

An alarm sounded as a man-sized snowball trudged through the gateway from the Alissian side. Red floodlights cast the room in crimson hues. There must have been some kind of auditory challenge, and then Logan's voice boomed on the speakers. "Sergeant Major Logan, Alpha Team." He tugged off a glove and put his palm on the scanner.

The security console beeped its acceptance. *Identity confirmed.* The guard behind it reached to hit the release for the airlock.

Quinn leaned over the console and cleared his throat. "Might want to double-check that."

The guard's brow furrowed, but he was private security. And private security didn't take chances.

Quinn turned back to smirk at Chaudri, who'd looked up in surprise. "What? He's been pounding on me all week."

She smiled, and hid it behind the report she was reading.

Logan tried the door, and found it locked. He rattled it, as if he thought it might be stuck. "Door's jammed."

"Sir," said the guard into the mic. "Could you reconfirm?"

"You kidding me?"

"I need you to reconfirm, sir," said the guard.

Logan glared in the direction of the console, though there was no way he could really see through the one-way glass. "Sergeant Major Logan, Alpha Team." He jerked off the other glove and tried his other palm, then leaned down for a retinal scan. *Three for three.* There'd be no denying that one.

"Thank you, sir," the guard said.

The panel slid aside, and Logan squeezed in just far enough to shake the snow from his cloak. He spotted Quinn and his eyes narrowed.

Uh-oh. He probably should have wiped the grin off his face.

"So it's you who got cute with the IDs," Logan said.

"Well, you're always saying we can never be too careful about security."

"I'm also *in charge* of security, Bradley."

"Hey, no one's above the law."

Kiara's entrance put an end to the jabber. She took Logan's measure. "How's it look over there?"

"Like they're having a goddamn blizzard," Logan said. "No immediate threats, as far as I could tell."

"What about reptiles?" Quinn asked. They'd encountered one last time and the jury was still out as to whether or not it qualified as a dragon.

"No, none of those, either."

"It's no longer wyvern breeding season, if that's what you're worried about," Chaudri offered.

"You're *not* worried? The last one did almost eat us."

"I didn't go that far, but the immediate area around the gateway cave looks clear. No barrier, as far as I could tell."

"Well, are we doing this?" Quinn asked. *If we don't leave now, I might lose my nerve.*

"We're waiting for one more," Kiara said.

That surprised him, and he was trying to figure out what wrinkle they were adding to the mission when the door from the hallway hissed open. Another soldier strode in. He'd lost weight and looked considerably tan, but Quinn would know the owner of that easy swagger anywhere.

"Mendez!"

"Hey, Bradley." Mendez shook his hand. He gave the lieutenant a deferential nod, but didn't smile until he saw Chaudri. "Hi, Chaudri. Love the hair."

"Really? Thank you." She blushed, and checked the little silver hair clips with nervous fingers. "It's a Landorian style."

Mendez held her smile until he saw Logan. Something passed between the two men, Logan asking a question and Mendez confirming it. They stepped away to confer in low voices. Kiara didn't so much as glance at them, but as she opened a black clamshell case, she tilted her head as if trying to eavesdrop.

Five communications earbuds nestled in two inches of gray foam within. Kiara plucked one out. "These are the new comm units." She handed one to Chaudri and gave her a stern look. "Keep it in *at all times.*"

Quinn took his and looked it over. He'd spent enough time with the one from the last mission to know that this was different. "What's the new button do?"

"Long range transmission. Should work anywhere on the continent."

"What if I'm not on the continent?"

"You'll need this." She pried open a second, oblong case that held a flat, arrow-shaped piece of metal.

"A weathervane." He'd seen a few of those on top of buildings, mostly in the rural areas of Felara and New Kestani.

"It's an integrated network antenna."

"Clever." Had to admire the weathered-metal look the tech team had given it. Not shiny enough to draw attention, but not rusted enough to need replacing, either.

She fastened the case again and tossed it to Quinn. "I want this installed on the highest point of the Enclave's island."

Of course you do.

If he wanted to talk to the others at all once he got there, he'd probably need to do it, too. But there was a good possibility that would permit CASE Global to triangulate the position of the Enclave island. And that idea made him nervous.

Granted, they could probably just take the way-finder stone off him and find the island anyway, but he wasn't about to bring *that* up.

Kiara checked her watch, which was disguised as a flat copper bracelet. "It's time. It'll be Mendez, me, Bradley, then Chaudri. Logan comes last." She looked at the big man. "You know what to do?"

He nodded.

What's that about? Quinn raised a questioning eye-brow at Mendez.

Mendez shrugged, but there was no humor in it. There was no humor in any of him.

The gates and airlock opened, and he saw the gateway for the first time in weeks. The portal to another world was nestled right in the wall of the cavern. He might have imagined it, but he felt like the thing pulled him. The wayfinder trembled against his chest.

The gateway shimmered every now and then, as if it were doing funny things to the light that hit it. He'd have watched it and timed the shimmers, but Mendez and Kiara got in the way as they made their way through. *My turn.* He took the mare's reins and marched into the open airlock. He paused right in front of it. The far side was blurry, as if he were looking at it through a glass of water.

He put his head down and pushed through the void. The threshold washed over him like a warm steady rain. He stumbled through onto a smooth stone floor, and a wall of cold slapped him in the face. Even though he knew what to expect, the transition left him disoriented.

"Keep moving, Bradley," Kiara said.

He tugged his horse over to one side. Logan came through a moment later, with his mount right behind him.

Kiara had wrapped a scarf around her face so that only her eyes were visible. "Mount up, everyone."

Quinn put a hand on the pommel, kept the reins

with the other, and put one of his boots in the stirrup. Obviously that was the moment his horse chose to pivot around, leaving him to hop on one foot around in pursuit. When he finally scrambled into the saddle, he realized he was the last one.

Logan had a hand shading his eyes, as if embarrassed. "Ready, princess?"

"Damn right," Quinn said. "Tired of waiting on you."

Felara, the snow-blanketed city-state on the Alissian side of the gateway, brought a new meaning to the word *cold*. Even with the Gore-Tex boots and poly-insulated jacket, Quinn was shivering more often than not. Logan wasn't kidding about the snow-storm, either. Visibility was only about ten feet, and the snow blew every direction—sideways, down, and up—whatever it took to get under his collar and down his back.

I miss Vegas already.

His morning training sessions with Logan had helped, but horses trudging through deep snow were a whole different challenge. Keeping his saddle was still a full-time job. It didn't help that Logan had taken the lead, and the man knew only one speed.

Mendez rode twice as fast and twice as far as anyone. Half the time he brought up the rear, and the rest of it he was scouting ahead or checking their backtrail. Kiara and Logan had to remind him to eat, and to rest his horse. Quinn didn't know if he was running toward something, or from something, but something was driving him.

They pushed south for a week, three days longer than it should have taken thanks to the snow. It tired the horses faster, and made Logan's little training sessions all the more exhausting. Apparently those were still on the docket, even on this side of the gateway. Logan and Mendez drilled Quinn constantly. Even Chaudri had to participate. She'd had a few close calls on the first mission, as Logan was happy to remind her.

She stepped out of their fighting circle and bent over to catch her breath. "That's enough for me. I'm as good as I'll ever get."

Logan leaned back from Quinn's halfhearted slash. "No one reaches that point."

"You're better off spending your time on Quinn," Chaudri said.

Quinn would have argued, if it weren't for the welt on his side she'd given him in their previous melee. She fought with the longsword, and he kept forgetting the reach of the thing.

"Don't worry about me," Quinn said. "I plan to fight dirty."

"That's not a real strategy," Logan said. He brandished his sword and circled to come at Quinn's weak side.

Quinn pivoted with him. "Why not?" He didn't think to keep an eye on Mendez, until he felt the cold steel against the back of his neck.

"Because everyone fights dirty when it comes down to it," Mendez said.

Oh, hell. "Come on! That's cheating."

Mendez shrugged. "Collusion happens all the time in a real fight. It's how I've won half of mine."

"So how do I get someone to collude with me?" Quinn asked.

"The same way you get them to do anything. Lie, cheat, bribe, blackmail."

"Exactly." Logan clapped Quinn on the shoulder. "I hear you magicians are good at that stuff."

"The only thing better than a decent trick is an audience who's never seen it before."

—**Art of Illusion, October 10**

CHAPTER 6

FORK IN THE ROAD

They decided to part ways in a mountainous region called Three Corners, at the intersection of Felara, Landor, and New Kestani. The settlement there was originally a hematite mining colony, but the richest veins had run dry decades ago. Most of the village houses were deserted.

"Which way is your stone pointing you, Bradley?" Kiara asked.

"Still southeast, as far as I can tell."

She pulled up the Alissian map on her console. "Based on our position, that means you'll end up somewhere off the eastern coast. South of Pirea, certainly."

"Dr. Holt spent three months with a Pirean fishing vessel," Chaudri said. "He never mentioned any off-shore islands of any kind."

"If the Enclave doesn't want to be found, it won't be," Quinn said. He didn't add, *And the Enclave doesn't want to be found.*

"What's your plan for getting there?" Kiara asked.

"By ship. The docks at the Enclave island got regular transports. They're self-sufficient as far as food goes, but they had a lot of imports, too."

Logan grunted. "Doesn't mean a ship captain will take you."

"I think I can pass myself off as a magician." Quinn spread his fingers out and made a coin appear. An Alissian silver piece, too, with the name of some long-dead Valteroni Prime on it. He wove it across his fingers, snapped once, and disappeared it up a sleeve.

"Hey, that's pretty good!" Mendez said.

Logan frowned. "Don't encourage him."

"Logan and I will head overland to Valteron City," Kiara said. "I want daily updates from you three."

"Ooh, can I be in charge?" Quinn asked.

"Mendez is in charge."

Worth a shot.

"I want you to stick with Mendez and Chaudri

until you find a ship," Kiara continued. "Even if it means a delay in getting to the Enclave."

"I guess that's all right. Moric didn't exactly give me a timetable."

"Try not to cause any riots along the way."

He grinned. "I'll miss you, too, Lieutenant."

The way down from Three Corners to the Landorian Plateau was about as treacherous of a terrain as Quinn had ever seen. There was no road, just a narrow winding path that barely qualified as a game trail. They rode single file, with Mendez in the lead. He wanted two horse-lengths between each of them. *Never thought I'd be measuring things in horse-lengths.*

They used comm units when they needed to talk. Ninety percent of that seemed to be for Mendez to make sure that Chaudri was doing all right, in spite of her express assurances that she was.

"So what's the story with this Holt contact?" Quinn asked.

"Her name's Iridessa," Chaudri said. "Dr. Holt's journals first made mention of her almost ten years ago."

"His journals talked about a lot of people," Quinn said. He'd read many of them himself. Studious as he was, Holt had excelled at developing human assets here. *The guy missed his calling in the KGB.*

"If you look in our archives, you'll find a file on virtually all of them. Name, age, appearance, occupation. Usually a photo taken from surveillance or wrist-cameras, too."

Quinn whistled. "Sounds extensive." And by that he meant *invasive*.

"That's only the cover page. There's also a report of all interactions and correspondence with each asset, so most files contain dozens of pages."

"How many pages did Iridessa's have?"

"One. Which is unusual, given how often he mentions her in passing elsewhere in his reports."

"All right, I'm intrigued. What do we know about her?"

"Just her name and the fact that she's some kind of herbalist. No photos or physical descriptions, though those things could have been removed later."

It wasn't much to go on. "How do you know she's in Landor, then?"

"I cross-referenced all of Dr. Holt's travel routes from the seven or eight expeditions where he makes mention of her. There's only one village in close proximity to all of them."

Clever. "What did Holt talk to her about?"

"Horticulture, for the most part. They used to trade notes on the properties of local plants and things. He called her 'a fountain of information.' "

Quinn didn't miss the slight cattiness to her tone on that one. "Maybe he was sweet on her."

She was silent a moment. "There's no evidence of that in his journals."

"Well, I'm not sure it's the sort of thing he'd write down, you know?"

"I suppose that's true."

"Do you think he—" Quinn started, but Mendez cut him off.

"Let's stop for a bit. I think the horses are getting tired."

They'd taken a break two hours ago, but Quinn took the hint. "Sure, I could stand to stretch my legs."

Greenbriar was a single-inn village nestled in the vale between the mountains and the western edge of the Landorian plateau. The company's most recent census—now some five years old—put the population at around eighty. That made it a small village, even by Alissian standards. If Iridessa lived here, people would know about her. Whether they'd *share* that knowledge with three strangers who rode into town was another matter.

"What do you think is our best approach?" Mendez asked.

"We'll need some plausible reason to seek out Iridessa, if she's there," Chaudri said.

"What if you played sick?" Quinn asked.

Mendez laughed. "Come on, the old 'fake prisoner' gag?"

"What's wrong with that?"

"A little cliché, don't you think?"

Quinn spread out his hands. "I kind of figured we have a naive audience." *And besides, we need to get this show on the road.* The longer they spent searching the backwoods for Holt's contacts, the longer it would take for him to reach the Enclave.

"You'd be surprised," Chaudri said. "In any case, they might not welcome an outsider who's ill. What if it's catching?"

Guess I didn't think of that. "All right, so you're not sick. Maybe you're a fellow horticulturist."

"Mmm, go on."

"And you've heard of her, so you'd like to talk shop."

"I *have* been reading up on the herbal remedies."

Of course she had. *This might even work.* "So you're willing to give it a shot?"

She glanced at Mendez, and smiled. "Absolutely."

"So who are we going to be?" Mendez asked. "Your bodyguards?"

"I sincerely doubt a horticulturist could afford two of those," she said. "What about brothers?"

Disappointment flickered across Mendez's face. "Does it have to be brothers?"

"Why not? We're all a similar complexion."

"She's not wrong," Quinn said.

"I guess it would simplify the story," Mendez said.

"Good. Let's try the common room, then," Chaudri said.

"All right, sis—lead the way," Quinn said. "This is gonna be fun." *An Indian, a Cuban, and a magician walk into a bar . . .*

"Pireans welcome strangers with open arms, but in Félara and Landor, distrust is the rule."

—R. Holt, "Survey of the Alissian Highlands"

CHAPTER 7

WITCH HUNT

Veena took a calming breath as Mendez pulled open the battered wooden door to the village inn. This was her best lead on Dr. Holt's backpack. If it led nowhere, Kiara's superiors might change their minds about sending an anthropologist along for missions in this world. *And then I might not get to see it again.*

Or him again.

She put a hand on Julio's shoulder, ignoring his quiet protest, and slid past him into the gloomy interior. She made out a handful of other patrons, all of them sitting alone at rough-wood tables. The smell of the place said *ale* and the froth in the cloudy mugs said *cheap*.

She put on a smile and strolled up to the bar before Julio or Quinn stole her thunder. "Good evening."

The bartender was short for a northerner, maybe five-foot-five, and pudgy beneath the filthy apron. He was working the cork out of a dark green bottle, and didn't even glance up. "What'll it be?"

"I'd like to buy the next round."

"For who?"

"For everyone here. And I'd like some ale for me and my friends." She eyed the casks behind the bar, which looked downright ancient. "The best you've got."

He looked up at her and then did a double take. He forgot the bottle and sucked in his belly. Sweat glistened on his face, and dripped down into his dark beard. His eyes slid past her to Julio and Quinn, who stood a couple of paces behind. "That's going to run you ten, twelve coppers."

She untied a small leather purse, and tilted it so that half a dozen coins tumbled out on the bar. She loved the jingle of soft metal, especially gold. It wasn't quite the hard clink of copper, but a richer sound that rang like a bell. She felt Julio stiffen as every eye in the common room swung to her.

The barkeep grinned, revealing crooked teeth. "Right away." He looked past her into the gloom. "Move it, Saul! You're at the lady's table."

The husky man in question nearly fell from his

stool in his haste to get up from the largest table. He genuflected and backed away, while another bearded patron hurried forward to offer a third stool. In less than two minutes, the barkeep wiped the table with his own apron and set out three mugs of frothy ale. He stoked the fire in the hearth, which took to burning cheerily. Then he set to delivering the next round to the other patrons.

"Well, you've certainly got their attention," Quinn said.

Julio scowled. "Let's try not to draw any more, *comprende?*"

Veena hid her amusement. *He's taking his assigned role more seriously than any of us.* "I'll be fine."

"Should we make some friends?" Quinn asked.

"Enjoy your ales." Veena took a little sip and regretted it—the lukewarm ale had a strong flavor of hops—but she forced herself to take another gulp. Liquid courage. "I've got this."

She started with Saul, the man who'd vacated their table. "How's the ale?"

He nearly choked mid-sip of it, put the mug down, and wiped his mouth with his sleeve. "Good! Many thanks, m'lady."

Veena smiled. "Just Veena is fine."

"Many thanks, m'lady Veena."

He sounded younger than he looked, maybe early twenties. The beard and windburned cheeks added years.

"I was hoping to visit a friend who lives around here. Perhaps you know her," Veena said.

He grinned over his beard. "I'd like to know her."

"She calls herself Iridessa."

He furrowed his brow. "Can't help you."

Veena couldn't read faces the way Quinn did, but it sure looked like he was hiding something. *He didn't deny knowing her.* She pressed on. "I'm an herbalist myself, and hoped we might compare notes."

Saul shrugged and buried his face behind his mug of ale. So began a game of conversational cat-and-mouse with the common-room patrons. At last, Veena returned to the table with Julio and Quinn. "I think I've made some progress."

"And maybe a few admirers," Quinn said.

She felt her cheeks heating, and tried to hide them with her mug of ale. It had grown warmer and more flavorful while she made the rounds. Neither of which made it any more palatable.

"Any luck finding our mark?" Mendez asked.

"Yes and no," Veena said. "They certainly know her, and she does seem to live around here."

"So?"

She shrugged. "No one can seem to remember where."

Quinn tapped his fingers on the tabletop. "Did she move, or something?"

"I don't think that's it. See the woman by the hearth?" Veena asked.

"That's a *woman?*" Quinn whispered. His eyebrows almost leaped from his face.

"Yes."

"She's got so many knives on her, I—I guess I just assumed . . ."

"Ditto," Julio said. "Marked the knives, missed the gender."

"Obviously you both are in desperate need of a lecture on the dangers of stereotyping, but I'll save that for another time," Veena said. "She went to see Iridessa last year to handle a . . . problem."

Mendez wrinkled his brow. "What kind of problem?"

Veena's cheeks were heating again. *Please, don't make me say it.* It had been bad enough just to hear the story. "The nine-month kind."

Quinn was aghast. "You're kidding me, right?"

"She went to the herbalist to have it handled," Veena said.

"And where was that?"

"Down an old road just north of the blacksmith's place."

"That's a start," Julio said.

"But the bartender went to see her just last week for a poultice, and he took a road south by the chandler's."

Quinn shook his head. "Well, at least we know she's around."

"That might not be enough," Julio said.

Veena tried to put herself in the shoes of someone who advertised as an herbal healer in a superstitious time. In a superstitious world. She'd have to be either very foolish, or very clever. And the clever types always kept an ear to the ground. "Let's leave her a message."

"How?" Quinn asked.

She lowered her voice. "I'll give the bartender a coin, and say that a friend of Richard wants to meet her. We can come back tomorrow."

Julio drew in a quick breath. "That's a hell of a name-drop."

"People talk in small villages like this. She'll hear we were asking about her, one way or another. We should give her a reason to be curious."

Veena looked at Julio. He bit his lip, but gave her a little nod.

She got up before they could change their minds, and slid another coin across to the barkeep. Gold, this time. She shielded it from view for anyone but the barkeep, and watched his eyes light up. "If you see Iridessa, please let her know we'll be back tomorrow."

The barkeep glanced around to see if anyone else was watching. "Who's the message from?"

"Friends of Richard," Veena said.

"All right." He never took his eyes from the coin.

Veena kept her index finger on the coin. "Say it for me, please."

"Hmm?"

"Friends of Richard."

"Right, friends of Richard." He nodded, so over-eager that she nearly laughed. Maybe reading faces wasn't as hard as Quinn made it out to be.

"Until tomorrow, then." She turned hurried to the door, where Quinn and Julio were already waiting. A few of the patrons called out to her.

"Leavin' already?"

"How about another round? Our treat?"

She smiled and waved the invitations off. "Tomorrow, perhaps." They all groaned. She savored that moment, the pleading looks on their faces and the too-firm set of Julio's jaw.

"Told you that you'd made some admirers," Quinn said.

"Hush, you."

They mounted up and rode north for half an hour to find a place to camp. The ground had risen steadily since leaving Greenbriar, and most of the outlying areas were farmland. All of those lay fallow this deep into winter, which meant for good visibility. Once they'd set up a camp and set up a security perimeter, Julio kept his field glasses on the village. He marked a dozen people going in or out—and was careful not to assign any of them an assumed gender—before sundown.

"You think one of them might be our herbalist?" Quinn asked.

Veena smiled with a confidence she didn't feel. "We'll know soon enough."

The morning brought a chill that threatened the coming winter. Greenbriar and the vale around it lay hidden beneath a blanket of fog. The others were still out when Veena woke. She crawled out of her tent as quietly as she could, hoping not to wake the others.

Quinn slept fitfully, his arms moving around at random. Julio slept as quiet as death—and with his pup tent rather close to hers, she couldn't help but notice. The common room at Greenbriar probably wouldn't open for at least an hour. For the first time, Veena had a moment to simply enjoy being here on this mission, inside the very world she'd devoted her career to studying. Immersive research was proving every bit as thrilling as Dr. Holt had promised.

The fire they'd built the night before still smoldered beneath a dusting of ash. Veena poked at the coals and fed it wood to get it going again. The portable heaters in the tents kept her warm in the cold Alissian nights, but they couldn't boil water for coffee. Maybe she should bring that up with the prototyping lab.

The men both managed to stay deep in slumber right up until the coffee was ready. Veena was just pouring herself the first cup when Quinn crawled out of his tent and stretched. Julio emerged about a minute later. Not that Veena blamed him—he'd jumped onto this mission right after finishing his last assignment. Judging by the shadows under his eyes, he was still playing catch-up.

"Anything moving in the village?" Julio asked.

"Too much fog," Veena said.

The sun was coming up fast, though. By the time they'd all finished a second cup of coffee, the fog was a distant memory. And Greenbriar was already starting to wake up, too.

"Let's get down there," Quinn said.

"Do you think she got our message?" Veena asked.

Julio began saddling his horse. "One way to find out."

The whole way back to Greenbriar, Veena racked her brain for other ways they could draw the herb-swoman out, if she didn't choose to reveal herself. Nothing came to mind. They could try lurking around the inn to collect more intel, but the villagers wouldn't tolerate that for very long.

Julio insisted on riding fifty yards ahead of them, in case of ambush. Never mind that the ground was so flat in this part of Landor that they'd see other horsemen long before they approached. There was just no point in arguing with Julio when he got stiff-backed about security.

A quarter mile outside of the village, Julio's voice

crackled in their comm units. "Did we pass any signposts on the way out of town yesterday?"

"I don't think so," Veena said.

"There's one here now."

Veena shared a wide-eyed look at Quinn. They nudged their mounts forward at a decent clip.

The wooden post stood just off the dirt road. It was tall, almost to eye level when they were mounted, and pale because the bark had been shaved away. The wood itself was carved in the rune-like patterns of Alissian script.

"Oh, I've got glasses that'll read that." Quinn started rooting through his saddlebags.

"No need," Veena said. She had hers on a slender chain around her neck, and slid them into view. The lenses autofocused on the Alissian scripts, and their translations scrolled across the bottom. Veena read them and gasped, hardly able to believe that the glasses had gotten it right. "Gods above."

"What's it say?" Julio asked.

Veena looked away, and back at the signpost. The words never changed. "It says, 'Friends of Richard.'"

A faint trail led into the woods behind the signpost. The trees were sparse, leafless things here, but dense enough that they couldn't see more than the first twenty yards or so.

"Wow." Quinn chuckled. "I guess she got the message."

"A good performer owns the room the moment he or she walks in. Control the environment, or it will control you."

—**Art of Illusion, June 8**

CHAPTER 8

WHEN CHARM FAILS

The winding, almost-imperceptible trail led to a small clearing in the winter woods. Quinn about sagged in relief when Mendez took the lead. The land fell away in front of them in a sort of dell, and the trail ran right up through it to the door of a small cottage. It was no larger than any of the houses in the village, but the thatch roof looked newer. A thin line of pale smoke curled up from the chimney.

"What a quaint little spot," Chaudri mused.

Mendez held them fast while he surveyed the whole area with his binoculars. "I don't like it."

"Did you see something worrisome?" Quinn asked.

"Nothing. Just a cottage and some hitching posts. No horses, no obvious weapons."

"So what's the problem?"

"Not sure. More of a gut feeling thing."

Quinn understood what he meant. The moment they'd entered the clearing, it was like everything went stock-still. There was no birdsong. No breeze. The only sign of movement anywhere was the gentle drift of the smoke from the chimney. He took out the wayfinder stone, and the thing might as well have been an ordinary rock. The fey pull of it was gone, or at least muted, and he couldn't have guessed in what direction the Enclave might lie.

I hope that's temporary. "Maybe this is a bad idea."

"It's the best lead we have," Chaudri said.

Quinn rolled his shoulders to ease the tightness there. "We don't know *anything* about this lady. I've got a bad feeling about it, just like Mendez."

"We've spent a week getting this far," Chaudri said. "I don't want to back out now."

The thing was, Quinn really didn't want to back out, either. It was more than just wanting this part of the mission to be over with. He felt a compelling urge to ride right down to that cottage and walk inside. Maybe it was the smoke coming from the chimney. It curled up into the sky, slow and hypnotic. Beckoning him closer. Like a cobra in a snake charmer's act. He had to shake himself to keep from staring.

"I'll go," Quinn said. "I just think we should keep our eyes open, you know?"

"Count on it," Mendez said.

He nudged his horse forward at a walk, letting the animal pick its way down the trail into the dell. The sharp downward slope kept them at a snail's pace. A pace that matched that smoke drifting up to the sky.

The air felt too still, as if the entire valley held its breath. The sharp odor of wood smoke mingled with something fainter, something herbal. The complexity made him think of Jillaine, the enchanting girl he'd met at the Enclave. Well, enchanting young woman. They'd left things on . . . uncertain terms. In the end, the mission pulled him away. Much more time around her, though, and he might have said, *Screw the mission*, altogether.

The ground leveled off as they reached the bottom of the dell. Mendez dismounted, and signaled that they should do the same.

"Why are we—" Quinn started to ask.

Mendez simply pointed ahead, to where three stout wooden posts stood in a neat row. *Hitching posts*.

Quinn left his bow with the horse, but kept his sword. He had to remind himself to keep his hand away from it. The tendency to hold the grip while he walked was surprisingly habit-forming. But in New

Kestani, it signaled you were looking for a duel. Here, in this strange vale with gods-knew-what awaiting them, he didn't want to appear violent. *That's a good way to invite a crossbow bolt.*

The cottage lay about twenty yards distant, right in the middle of the dell. Still no sign of anyone, but someone had left the door open. Darkness yawned within. The windows to either side were boarded up. The air was warm down here. Quinn loosened his cloak.

Chaudri put her hand on Mendez's shoulder, and they stopped. "Hello?" she called.

Amber light bloomed in the cottage interior. A dark-haired woman appeared in the doorway. She wore a royal blue gown, which seemed as out of place as it was blinding. The shape of it followed her curves, somehow rendering them promising and mysterious at once. Quinn felt distantly aware that he was staring with his mouth wide open.

The woman took them in with a glance. "Took you long enough. Well, you might as well come in." She disappeared from view, and called back, "Leave the weapons."

Quinn glanced at Mendez, who nodded his assent. They unbuckled their sword-belts and set them on the ground outside. *It's not like I'm totally unarmed,* he thought. Then again, a woman who could hide or reveal herself with ease probably didn't feel very threatened by a couple of knives.

Mendez, God bless him, entered the cottage first. Quinn and Chaudri crowded right on his heels. Several smells hit his nose at once—the pungent aroma of fresh herbs, the musk of tanned leather, the musty smell of wet canvas. And all of that beneath the wood smoke that was strong enough to make his eyes tear up.

The woman sat in a wooden armchair beside the hearth, where a fire burned cheerily. Three other chairs sat in a semicircle facing hers. Chaudri led the way over. Ghost-like animal hides dangled from the ceiling. Quinn bumped one of these by accident. He shrank back, but too late—the hide swung ponderously over to jostle a row of wooden chimes and hand-carved talismans. All of this rang and clanked together in a deafening racket that made him grind his teeth. Veena gave him a wide-eyed look, like *Be careful.*

Quinn shook his head. *Jeez, it's not like I did it on purpose.*

She rolled her eyes and half shook her head.

They took the three chairs by the hearth, with Veena in the middle, Mendez by the fire, and Quinn uncomfortably close to all of the weird shit in the cottage interior. The chair pressed into his back, hard as metal. It didn't so much as creak when he sat down, which made it the sturdiest piece of furniture he'd encountered in this world.

"Who are you?" the woman asked. Her eyes were as dark as her hair, and her skin as smooth as a child's.

The smells and the hangings and the woman's dark eyes put Quinn off enough that he forgot to bring out his stage smile, the one that always made strangers more comfortable. *Damn.*

"My name's Veena," Chaudri said. "This is Julio, and Quinn."

Mendez managed a weak smile. Quinn found his stage training and gave her the pearly whites. "Hello."

She gave him a double take before turning back to Chaudri, more uncertain than impressed.

"You may call me Iridessa."

"Ah, what a lovely name," Quinn said.

She gave him a level look, unblinking. "That's why I chose it."

Ouch. She was not a fan of the Quinn Bradley charm. He bit back his next compliment and clamped his mouth shut.

Mendez put his hand over his face. *Hiding a smile at my expense, I'm betting.*

"So," Chaudri ventured. "I take it you've known Richard a long time."

"Depends on what a long time means to you."

Chaudri smiled. "Fair enough. Have you heard from him recently?"

"Why do you want to know?"

Quinn suppressed a sigh. The interview wasn't off

to a good start. *We've got zero leverage here.* It was her house, her invitation. Her brain that they wanted to pick.

"He's more than a friend," Chaudri said. "He's been my mentor for ten years. I'm—I'm worried about him."

Iridessa studied her for a long moment. "It's been a while. He came by half a year ago, to tell me about his foolish plan."

Quinn coughed and looked down, so that she wouldn't be able to read his face. The mystery of Richard Holt had nagged at him for months. Not just the question of how he'd managed to become the Valteroni Prime, but why he decided to defect in the first place. At last, here was someone who might able to answer those questions. *Come on, Chaudri, pry open that door.*

"I can't say I agree with it, either." Chaudri shook her head and sighed. "Men."

Iridessa barked a laugh. "Richard's as stubborn as they come."

Chaudri pursed her lips. Quinn took a breath and tried to will himself to invisibility. *She has to get this just right.*

"To be honest, I'm a little worried about him." Veena didn't have to fake the sentiment—the sincerity was written in her eyes, in the distance they held. "Did he seem . . . a little bit off-kilter?"

Iridessa didn't answer for the span of four heartbeats. Her eyebrows quirked upward. "The device he asked for was a little unusual."

"Device?"

"A white oval, about so big." She spread her arms around two feet apart. "Kind of looks like an egg."

Son of a bitch. Quinn nearly bit his tongue in half. That *device* almost put a quick, violent end to the first mission, when an invisible barrier trapped them in a confined area with a pack of wild dogs. Not to mention one hell of an angry wyvern. Logan had split the egg with his sword, but it was a close thing.

God bless her, Chaudri played it casual. "Right. The barrier."

"Do you happen to know if it worked out for him?" Iridessa asked.

Chaudri gave a thin smile. "I'm told it worked like a charm."

Quinn snorted. *There's the understatement of the year.*

"Ha!" Iridessa slapped her knee. "It's a good thing he paid so handsomely for it."

Quinn knew he shouldn't ask, but he couldn't resist. "So, what did it cost him?"

"That's none of your business."

"Right. Sorry."

He knew he was staring, but he couldn't help it. It wasn't an attraction thing, though she was certainly beautiful. No—something about the woman drew his eyes and made it painful to look away. When he did, he stole a glance at Mendez and Chaudri. They'd both fixed their gazes on her, too, like she was the most fascinating thing in the world. *So it's not just me.*

Iridessa leaned over in her chair and plucked a steel poker from the hearth. She stirred the coals beneath the fire, which already burned cheerily. The heat of it brought a sheen of perspiration to Quinn's forehead. *God, it's warm in here. Almost stifling.* Mendez must have felt like he was sitting in a furnace.

Iridessa plucked a dried sprig of some herbs out of a basket beside her chair. She tossed it in. The fire ate it hungrily, quick as flash paper. A faint perfume wafted out.

"You know, Richard said something odd to me, the last time he was here." Iridessa drew the poker in a circular motion now, tracing smaller and smaller circles in the ash on the hearth. Her lips moved between the spoken words.

"Oh?" Veena asked.

"He told me I should be wary of anyone who came here, asking after him."

Uh-oh. Holt must have warned her about them. Quinn knew he should be more alarmed by this, but he couldn't muster the concern for it. Maybe it was the smoke. It stung his eyes worse than ever, but his throat felt numb to it.

"I don't understand." Veena's voice was strained.

"In fact, he promised a handsome reward if I turned you over to him."

"I suppose we'll be on our way, then," Chaudri said. But she didn't move.

Mendez grunted in what sounded like surprise. He'd probably reached for his sword, or tried to.

Quinn would have gotten up, but his legs felt like they weighed five hundred pounds. The smoke curled around him. He couldn't help inhaling it. Each breath took away more feeling in his arms and legs.

Iridessa kept stirring the ash, stirring the ash. Quinn couldn't take his eyes off her. The smoke didn't bother him anymore. He *liked* how it smelled, and how he felt sitting here. He didn't need to leave at all. One glance at his friends confirmed this. Chaudri had a little smile on her face, and Mendez sat with his mouth open, staring into the fire.

Quinn held his hand in front of his face and turned it over. Back and forth, back and forth. An old sobriety test from his time on the Strip. Back and forth, back and forth. *Man, I've got a nice set of fingers.*

God, it was hot in here, too. He loosened his cloak a little bit. Leaned back in his chair. Started guessing what kind of animal each hide came from. Which was harder than it should be, by the way. He could have sworn one of those near the back had *scales*. It was hard to make out, though. The view was kind of fuzzy. Everything in the cottage was fuzzy.

Heh. Fuzzy. He chuckled to himself. *"Fuzzy" is a fuzzy word.*

"I think you should stay awhile," Iridessa said.

Quinn nodded, because it made sense. What was the point in rushing off anyway? *I like it here.* He liked the smells, and the crackle of the fire, and the bright orange glow it cast on everything. Even the strange animal hides and uncomfortable chairs were growing on him. The heat was the only part he didn't like. It had him sweating beneath his armor. He loosened his cloak as much as he could. *Yep, I could definitely spend some time here.*

Iridessa leaned the poker against the hearth, turned back, and smiled. "I'm sure Richard—"

She fell abruptly silent. Her eyes were fixed on Quinn. "Where did you get that?"

Quinn followed her gaze. The wayfinder stone had fallen out of his collar, and hung by his leather cord in plain view. "Moric gave it to me." He wasn't really supposed to talk about it, but what was the harm? He picked up the stone between his finger and thumb—it took a few tries to get ahold of it— and held it up. *It's a pretty little stone.* He'd never realized how pretty it was.

Iridessa gasped. "You know *Moric?*" Her voice broke as she said his name, and her eyes were wide enough to show the whites. "Who the hell *are* you?" she whispered.

"I'm Quinn." He was really enjoying this conversation. *She asks the nicest questions.* "I'm a magician, actually."

"An *Enclave* magician?"

Quinn noticed the handle to his chair was polished wood, not the cheap kind of polish, but the smooth wear from time. He rubbed it with his thumb. "This is a wonderful material." He tore his eyes away, because he felt the intensity of Iridessa's gaze. She'd asked him something. What was it again? *Oh, yeah. Enclave magician.* He grinned. "Yep, that, too."

"Gods above!" Iridessa grabbed the pail on the hearth and dashed it across the flames. Steam hissed up from the coals. She fanned it away from Quinn's face until he couldn't smell the sweet perfume any longer. Which made him a little sad. The air grew colder, too, as if a giant vacuum had sucked the heat out of it.

Anxiety marred the smoothness of Iridessa's face. "Listen." She snapped a finger in front of Quinn's nose. "Listen! I had no idea. It was an honest mistake."

He eased back away from her. The tension in her face and in her voice grated him. *She's so harsh all of a sudden.* "What was?"

"Give it a minute, and then you'll remember."

The pleasant cobwebs of intoxication lifted from Quinn's brain with agonizing slowness. Cold sobriety took their place. His heart started thumping as he started to grasp the magnitude of what had just happened. *Oh, shit.* He shook his head, fighting to remember what he'd already told her. The memories slid away, like faint dreams after a moment of wakefulness. *What the hell was in that smoke?*

Mendez cursed, and shifted in his chair. His hands fumbled at his waist, once more looking for the hilt of his sword. Chaudri's smile had fallen away. She said nothing, but her eyes glittered with a growing malice. She kept her hands on her knees, but the knuckles were white.

Quinn cleared his throat. *Oh, my God, this is awkward.* "I take it that you know Moric."

"I know *of* Moric, and that's enough." Iridessa looked away from him, and shivered. "I'd appreciate if you didn't mention this to him."

He was about to agree, but his instincts kicked in and kept him quiet. This was the first time they'd had any kind of leverage on her. "I'm not sure if you know this, but Enclave magicians look after one another."

Her eyes widened, but she managed to keep her voice level. "I'm well aware. But this was a simple mistake, and I think—"

Quinn cut her off. "You enchanted us by mistake? Hoped to claim a reward for us, *by mistake?*" He sneered with the last two words.

"Well, you never declared yourself! How was I—"

"We of the Enclave do not go around declaring ourselves." Quinn felt a little proud of himself for coming up with that on the fly. It sounded like something Moric would say. "You know that as well as I do."

She harrumphed, and looked down. "I said I was sorry."

He had her on the ropes, and she knew it. *Time to dial it back.* He sighed. "Accidents do happen. And I could probably write this off as one."

She met his eyes again, and her look was one of cold calculation. "In exchange for what?"

"Oh, I don't know—why don't we start with everything you know about Richard Holt?"

> "Militarily and technologically, we pose a far
> bigger threat to Alissians than they do to us."
>
> —R. Holt, "The Dangers of the Other World"

CHAPTER 9

ALL THINGS BARTERED

When they started in on Iridessa, Quinn was more than happy to let Chaudri take the lead.

"Let's start with how you two met," she said. "Was it here in Landor?"

"Right in Greenbriar," Iridessa said. "The innkeeper sent word that one of his patrons had taken ill. Thought it might be the blood fever."

"Was it?" Chaudri's brow wrinkled in concern.

"Almost. He had the sweats and the fever, all right. Hands were clammy, and his pupils too large."

All symptoms that can be faked, Quinn couldn't help but thinking.

"He wasn't coughing up blood, though," Iridessa said. "I made him some root tea, and we got to talking. Turned out he had an interest in herbs himself."

Quinn chuckled to himself. *Of course he did.* Holt had an interest in everything Alissian.

"How often do you see him?" Chaudri asked.

"He stops by every few months. Never stays more than a few days."

Otherwise the company might have noticed.

"I didn't realize you two were such good friends." Chaudri managed not to make it sound too accusatory.

"More like good business associates."

"What sort of business are you doing?"

"That's between me and Richard."

Time for the stick again. Quinn sighed, and started to get out of his chair. "I'm sorry you aren't willing to help us. Moric will be disappointed."

"Wait, now. Hold on." She threw up her hands in a placating gesture. "Hold on. Old habits, you know."

Thank God. His legs had been about to give out. The smoke still hadn't worn off entirely.

"Richard and I usually traded information. When he'd absorbed everything I knew about herbal remedies, we traded favors instead."

"Like the barrier egg," Quinn said.

"Yes. One of his more difficult requests."

"What did you get in return for that?" Chaudri asked.

"An old book."

"That's *it*?" Quinn was incredulous. The barrier easily ranked in the top five displays of magic he'd seen in this world.

Iridessa laughed softly, and her eyes were aglow. "Not just any book. A rare botanical reference that any herbalist would kill for."

Chaudri gasped. "Was it *Elements of Botany*?"

Iridessa's eyebrows went up. "You've heard of it."

"I thought there were only a handful of extant copies."

"Less than five in the world," Iridessa said. "I don't know how he managed it."

Mendez coughed into his hand. Pointedly. Chaudri gave him a questioning look.

"Remind me to tell you something later," he said.

So Bravo Team got it for him. Quinn shook his head. This just kept getting better and better. He couldn't resist a follow-up. "Did you make the egg yourself?"

"No."

That surprised him—he figured she'd been working alone. "Who did, then?"

Iridessa gave him a flat-eyed look that made him feel cold inside. "I'll beg Moric for mercy before I tell you that."

Quinn doubted she was bluffing, either. *Damn. I'd sure as hell like to know who can make artifacts like that.*

"Fine," Chaudri said. "I'd rather ask a different question."

"You've asked a lot already," Iridessa said.

"This is the last one. Answer it, and we'll be on our way."

"And Moric never hears of this." She pointed at Quinn. "I want your word on it."

"As far as I'm concerned, we were never here," he said. "You have my word."

Iridessa gave a sharp nod, as if to say that settled it. Quinn winked back, just to mess with her a little. *Come on, Veena, get us some intel.*

Chaudri chewed her lip, and smoothed her cloak out even though it didn't have a hint of a wrinkle. Two of her tells at once: uncertainty and discomfort. "If Richard had something valuable, something dangerous, how would he keep it safe?"

"Other than having it with him?"

"Yes. Where would he keep it?"

Iridessa pressed two fingers against her lip, and stared off at nothing for a long moment. Quinn might have been cold-reading her, but he could have sworn she knew the answer right away. *This is a performance, to make it seem harder than it is.* Her eyes gave it up the second Chaudri had said "dangerous."

"It's not a question of where," she said at last. "More like *who*. And if I had to guess, I'd say Darius Blackwell."

"Really?" Chaudri's tone had a hint of excitement.

"I'm sure of it."

"Well, then. We appreciate your time." She stood, and motioned for Quinn and Mendez to head for the door. "Give us a moment, would you?"

Mendez opened his mouth to argue. Chaudri raised her eyebrows at him. He clamped it shut. He came to his feet, steadying himself on the arm of his chair.

Quinn did the same. His legs tingled like they'd both fallen asleep. He followed Mendez in a slow retreat to the door. *I hope Veena knows what she's doing.* Then again, maybe he should be more worried about Iridessa. A woman who'd been trading favors with Holt for years was probably at the top of Chaudri's shit list.

Mendez reclaimed his sword from the ground and double-checked the blade. "Who the hell is Darius Blackwell?"

Quinn buckled on his sword-belt, surprised at how much it comforted him. "The name sounds familiar, but I can't place it."

Before he had time to contemplate it more, Chaudri and Iridessa appeared in the doorway. They shared a parting look, and smiled at one another. *What the hell is that about?*

"Thank you for your hospitality," Chaudri said. She took her sword-belt from Mendez and buckled it on.

Iridessa scanned Quinn and Mendez. Her eyes returned to the sword at Quinn's belt. Her brow furrowed. "Stay on the trail until you reach the road," she said, and then she disappeared back into her cottage.

They started back to the horses. It took all of Quinn's willpower not to look back over his shoulder.

Mendez fell into step beside Chaudri. "Please tell me you know where to find Darius Blackwell."

"No, I'm not sure where he is."

"But you know him."

"Of course." She smiled. "So does Quinn, as a matter of fact."

The memory hit him like a hammer. *Oh, hell.* "Wait a second. *Admiral* Blackwell?" The guy who'd essentially vied against Holt for the position of Prime. This made no sense. *Why would he trust a man who tried to beat him out for Valteroni Prime?*

Yet Chaudri didn't seem all that fazed. "That's him. The second-most-powerful man in Valteron."

They rode out of the vale in silence. Near the top of the ridge, the warm air dissipated into cold, and the smell of the wood smoke faded. Quinn felt the wayfinder stone shift on its cord, and clutched it tight against his chest. *Thank God.* He paused long enough to look back at the cottage. He didn't see Iridessa, which maybe was a good thing. The curlicue of smoke drew his eye, and he shuddered. *I'm definitely not going back down there again.*

Mendez checked his watch. "Damn. We were supposed to report in ninety minutes ago."

"Oh, when we were high as kites?" Quinn snorted. "That would've gone over well."

"At least we have solid intel. Let's call in." Mendez activated his comm unit.

Quinn did the same. There was a pause, then they both looked at Chaudri, who was staring back down the way they'd come.

"Chaudri?" Mendez asked.

"Hmm?" Her eyes found focus again. "Oh, right. Sorry." She found her comm unit and flipped it on.

"Three amigos to Kiara, come in," Mendez broadcasted.

Quinn chuckled. "Nice."

"You're late, Mendez," Kiara replied.

"Sorry, we were in a valley. No signal."

Quinn opened his mouth, then shut it just as quickly. *God bless Mendez for sticking to the essentials.*

"Did you find Chaudri's source?" Kiara asked.

"Affirmative," Mendez said. "She gave us a lead on where Holt might have stashed the backpack."

"I want Logan on for this, too. Stand by."

There came a soft click, and then Logan said, "I hope you have good news."

Mendez pointed at Chaudri. She cleared her

throat. "Two pieces of information, actually. First, Iridessa was the one who provided the barrier egg for Dr. Holt."

"In exchange for what?"

"An extremely rare book on botany. I'm not sure where he got it."

"We know where he got it," Kiara said.

Quinn smiled to himself. *Totally called it.*

"Any word on the backpack?" Logan asked.

"She seems to think that Holt would have left it in the keeping of Darius Blackwell."

"The admiral?" Logan scoffed. "I thought he and Holt were rivals."

"I'm beginning to wonder if that's only what Dr. Holt wanted us to believe," Chaudri said.

"The guy could be anywhere," Logan said.

"He'll be close to the fleet," Kiara said. "I want you three to proceed east to the nearest seaport. That looks to be . . . Crab's Head."

"Is that really a place?" Quinn asked. *It sounds made up.*

"It's on the east coast of Landor." Chaudri had out her parchmap, and was marking off the distance with a ruler. "Probably eight or ten days, if we go overland."

"What if you push the horses?" Kiara asked.

"We could try for a river ferry out of Landor's capital."

"That's a high-risk location," Logan said. "Strong military presence, tight security."

"Are there any low-risk locations?" Quinn asked. "Because I'd rather go to one of those, if I'm being honest."

"It *would* shave off a couple of days," Chaudri said.

"Do it," Kiara said. "We need a fix on the Valteroni fleet as soon as possible."

"Just keep your heads down," Logan said.

"I want daily updates," Kiara said with her un-mistakable tone of dismissal. "Mendez, a word in private?"

It was tempting to eavesdrop, but Quinn dropped off. He satisfied himself by listening to Mendez's half of the conversation.

"All right, you've got Mendez ... No, he's been good. Steady ... I haven't forgotten the standing order, Lieutenant ... Roger that."

He flipped off the comm, then turned to give Quinn and Chaudri the thumbs-up. "The lieutenant says nice job with the crazy-ass witch."

"Ha! Sure she does," Quinn said. "But hey, thanks for calling me 'steady.' "

"Who said I was talking about you?"

"You said 'he.' Who else would you be talking about?"

"Maybe myself. Mendez is steady. Mendez is on the ball!"

Chaudri laughed, and Mendez grinned at her.

What's that standing order, buddy? Quinn wanted

to ask. But he probably didn't want to know, and for what he had planned, he didn't want to put Mendez in an awkward position. "So, any advice on staying out of trouble in Landor's capital?"

"Well, we've got two days. That should be just enough time for me to cover all of them."

"In the short time we've been here, Alissia is largely at peace. Every observation must consider that context. War changes everything."

—R. Holt, "Summary of Alissian City-states"

CHAPTER 10

WRONG NUMBER

Logan and Kiara pressed south from Three Corners, making good time on the long ride to Valteron. They rode from sunrise to sunset, in six-hour stints, stopping only long enough to water the horses. If anyone on the road thought them an odd pair—big black guy, tiny white lady, riding together at a steady clip—they were wise enough not to say so. But the swords and crossbow probably had something to do with discouraging any casual derogatory remarks.

The animals held up well, which they damn well should for what the company paid in annual stud fees. Just for fun, Logan had pulled the pedigree on his gelding before the mission. He had stopped counting Kentucky Derby champions at six.

He couldn't complain about the pace or the weather. But the longer he spent alone with the lieutenant, the more the awkward tension grew between them. Every decision he'd made over the past two months, she'd pulled rank and overruled. He wanted personal sidearms on this mission. *Overruled.* He said Bradley needed more training. *Overruled.*

He managed to keep his mouth shut, at first. They crossed most of New Kestani without incident. Then Mendez missed his daily check-in time.

"Not like him to be late," Logan said.

Kiara put a hand to her ear, probably to flip to the backup frequency. "It could be a comms issue."

"He should have had some downtime, after Thorisson." *Or maybe not gotten that order in the first place.*

"You spent all last week telling me Bradley's more likely to hurt himself with his sword than anyone else. You want Chaudri alone with *him*?"

"Hell, no. I didn't want Bradley here in the first place," Logan said.

"We need eyes inside the Enclave, and he's our best shot."

Logan grunted. "Only if he makes it there alive."

"Which is exactly why Mendez will stick with him as long as possible."

"He needs R & R, that's all I'm saying."

Kiara hunched her shoulders. "If I could have spared him, I would. But the mission is too important."

So you said. But Logan let it drop one more time. Nothing he could do about it now anyway. "So, you going to read me in on these communications disruptions?"

"I did read you in."

"You said there was a disruption in the comms."

"Yes."

"Come on, Lieutenant. A single blip wouldn't move up the mission timetable." Not with so much at stake. That was CASE Global 101, and they both knew it. "Hell, we had two of them last month. What's different this time?"

Kiara paused. She'd either tell him the scoop, or feed him a line about insufficient clearance.

"We've lost contact with station nine," Kiara said.

Uh-oh. Station nine was a CASE Global supply cache in northern Tion. The company built a dozen such installations across the Alissian mainland in the early years of the project. Every cache held food, weapons, comm equipment, spare clothing . . . anything that Logan or other operatives might need in a pinch.

"How long ago?" Logan asked.

"Three days before we came through," Kiara said.

"You could have told me sooner."

She sighed. "I was hoping it would come back online."

For the first time, he noticed Kiara's fatigue. They'd set a grueling pace since leaving the others. *I keep forgetting that she's not a regular field operative.* He felt bad for snapping at her about Mendez.

"It's probably just a bad transmitter," he said by way of apology. The Alissian weather cycles were hell on sensitive electronic equipment. No matter how much engineering you put into them.

"Maybe," Kiara said. "It's still unusual for the primary *and* the backup to go out at the same time."

He grunted, more puzzled than concerned. The security systems in the supply caches were one of the few technology exemptions granted by CASE Global's executive team. Numeric keypad entry, pinhole surveillance cameras, self-destruct mechanisms, the works.

"Could also be a power outage, with all of that equipment." Station six had had similar problems, because the dust from the Caralissian dry season kept clogging up the solar panels.

"Here's hoping," Kiara said. Judging by her tone, though, she didn't really believe it.

They'd crossed the border that morning, and were just getting into Tion's infamous marshlands. It was like the land couldn't make up its mind between dry and sopping wet. The only reason that station nine ended up here was that CASE Global's geological surveys stumbled on a rare natural cave. Just the right square footage for a supply cache, too.

It'd be my favorite station, if it weren't for the flies. Few things felt safer than a foot of solid limestone all around you.

Virtually all of the Tioni marshlands looked identical, but Logan had kept an eye on the mileage since they crossed the border. "I think we're close. No more than a quarter mile."

"We should have the homing beacon by now," Kiara said.

The ultra-high-frequency ping had a thirty-second interval. Logan had lost count of the number of times he'd used it to find a station at night, or during a snowstorm. CASE Global comm units could pick up the beacon from half a kilometer away. Kiara's tablet had twice that range.

Logan spotted a pear-shaped boulder ahead, right next to the muck-trench that Tioni considered a road. "There. That's the landmark." The boulder's bright alabaster color helped it stand out against the Tioni marshes, where virtually everything was brown.

"Have you got anything on UHF?" Kiara asked.

Logan flipped his comm unit to the frequency, and got only static. "Nada. Smelling more and more like a power outage."

He urged his horse down the narrow trail and

around the thicket to the entrance. He dug into one of his saddlebags for a spare lithium battery, in case the keypad needed one.

His horse stopped without warning, and he nearly lost his saddle. "What the—"

The ground fell away in front of him, a steep slope that continued left and right in almost a perfect circle. The crater had to be twenty yards across, and it was right where the entrance to the cave had been. The stone walls had shattered outward, leaving nothing more than a pile of muddy rubble at the bottom where the supply cache used to be. The steel security door lay crumpled to one side of the basin, with half of it buried in the earth.

"Son of a *bitch*." He'd really been looking forward to hitting the pantry, too. "What happened?"

"Looks like the secondary blew," Kiara said.

"The remote trigger takes an executive-level passcode. Even I would have to get authorization."

"Every door has a fail-safe on the access pad." Kiara coughed and swallowed, as if relaying this information took a toll on her.

"I know that. High-voltage electric shock."

"That was the original plan . . . but the engineers were worried about the power drain."

"So?" Logan asked.

She looked away from him. "They wired it to the secondary instead."

"Are you *kidding* me?" The fail-safe was supposed

to be a deterrent, not a goddamn self-destruct. "What if some kids found it?"

"That's exactly why I didn't tell you."

"Because I'd have said, *Screw that.*" He couldn't believe her nonchalance about this. You didn't set a bomb on a keypad in a world that had never even seen a telephone. Any dumb-ass swamp-dweller might have stumbled on this and punched a few buttons, just out of curiosity.

"It doesn't matter now, in any case. The greater concern is how this installation blew."

Logan didn't agree that the *how* of it was the greater concern. When he looked at her face, though, he saw the brave show she was putting on. She clearly felt the magnitude of that error right now, that was for damn sure. He wasn't done with the ethical debate, but that could come later. "We should make a sweep of the crater, to see what's left."

She gave a sharp nod. "Let's start with the security door."

They hobbled the horses and worked their way around the crater to where the steel door lay wedged into the earth. Logan didn't even have to get close to confirm that the shape charge had blown. *Looks just like the aftermath of an IED.* He'd seen enough of them for two lifetimes.

Logan heaved the metal door over to get a look at the exterior side. Incredibly, it was in pretty decent shape. Whoever had set that shape charge really knew what he was doing. *Oh, yeah, that was me.* He thought he was putting in a self-destruct charge, a last-ditch security measure, so it hadn't bothered him. He'd done so many company install jobs that they all sort of ran together. But the biting flies jogged his memory every time.

Neon lights glowed softly on the keypad display.

"Keypad's still active. Check it out," Logan said. The last entry on the six-digit code was 090578. "Good news is the code's not even close." Hopefully that meant none of his deep-cover operatives had done this.

"It's not good news."

Logan read the numbers again, but couldn't pick out a pattern. "What am I missing?"

"That 090578 is a CASE Global employee identification number."

"Whose?"

"Who do you think?"

Aw, hell. "Holt."

"He's always had a flair for the dramatic."

And a soft spot for the natives. "Did he know about your little shortcut with the secondary?"

The corner of her lips curled downward. "Not officially."

"What the hell does that mean?"

"Because of his sentiments, I consulted with a different member of the research team before we made the change."

Of course you did. She always collected expert opinions, even when it came to civilian casualties. "Who did you get?"

"Chaudri."

"Oh, good. Because she would never tell him *any-thing.*"

"It has long been documented that observing a culture changes it, even with the best of safeguards. Our mere presence in Alissia will have ramifications."

—R. Holt, "Reevaluating Alissian Assumptions"

CHAPTER 11

DISTURBANCE

Logan hated everything about Tion. Especially the southern regions, which seemed to be one massive quagmire. The weather grew warmer as they pressed south, too, which meant that the flies got progressively worse. It wasn't too bad while they were riding, but every time they slowed to take bearings or water the horses, the flies swarmed them.

The road grew more crowded, too, which made

him nervous. Every traveler they passed could be an agent for Holt. And they passed dozens as they approached the border to Valteron. It was either that or ride behind the slowest horse cart as it trundled along, which would drive both Kiara and him crazy.

The Tioni "smart mules" were a slightly more amusing problem. The animals obeyed verbal commands—as long as the rider was polite enough—but with that cleverness came a haughty attitude. Where a normal mule naturally edged aside for the passage of a warhorse twice its size, a Tioni mule hogged the road on purpose. Like some jackass in a BMW taking up two lanes on the highway.

"Jesus," Logan muttered. "This guy is killing me."

A farmer in a broad-rimmed hat and his smart mule were plodding along, oblivious of the half-dozen riders jammed up behind him. The marsh pressed in so close to either side that there was no room to go around.

"Hmm?" Kiara asked. She was on her console again, the one made to look like an old leather-bound book. In spite of the antique appearance, the slim device represented some of the most advanced tech on either side of the gateway. The infinity cell had to be Logan's favorite feature: the next-generation battery recharged on ambient light.

The console gave her a link to Command, along with a real-time status of the Alissian communications infrastructure. She could pull up the complete research archives, including all of the maps and survey data. And those were just the functions Logan knew about. He didn't have clearance to see her tablet unless she was "incapacitated or KIA."

Just one more secret.

"What's the latest on the three musketeers?" he asked.

"They're headed for the Landorian capital to catch a riverboat."

Good. If they'd been riding as hard as Logan and Kiara had, they could use the downtime. "How's Mendez?"

"No complaints."

"He never complains," Logan said.

"A fair point."

He waited for her to say more, but she didn't. *I should check in with him later. See how he's really doing.* It's not like she'd ordered him otherwise. "So, why the hell are you sending them to a tiny port in the least-trafficked part of the east coast?"

"Why do you think?"

You don't want to know what I think, Lieutenant. He mulled it over and made his best guess. "So Mendez and Chaudri can keep an eye on Bradley?"

"And vice versa, frankly. They balance one another well."

Logan snorted. "Oh, there's no balancing Bradley."

"You kept him in line."

"Well, I'm a professional." *And I miss getting to do*

that. At least Bradley kept things interesting, and had a bright outlook.

"Mendez knows how to handle him," Kiara said. "Chaudri, too, in her way. They'll—" She cut off at the sound of an insistent buzzing from her console. She checked it, and her frown was enough to chill Logan's bones.

"What is it?"

"Southern network just went down again," she said.

"Which part?"

"Everything in Valteron, and half of Tion and Caralis."

"That's got to be, what, sixty relays?"

"Seventy-four."

Son of a bitch. "Where does this leave us?"

"Virtually no surveillance in Valteron. And comm delays while we're down there, both with Command and with the others."

"So Holt's disrupting our communications. Sounds like he's been reading up on military strategy."

She compressed her lips, in the Kiara form of a grimace.

"Unless he got some formal training I didn't know about," Logan said.

"I'm ordering an engineering team to get it back up as soon as possible."

"Really?" That surprised him. *Not like it's our first mission with less-than-perfect comms.* The delay was a pain in the ass, but manageable. "What about the mission ban?"

"I want our network fully operational by the spring."

"What happens in the spring?"

She didn't answer.

They rode while talking even less, if that was possible. It was warm enough that Logan no longer used the self-contained atomic heater in his pup tent. Truth be told, he used it as little as possible even in the colder parts. Sure, the engineers assured him it didn't leak radiation, and he was done having kids anyway, but there was no sense in taking chances.

Well, probably *done having kids.* Sharon wasn't pressing the issue with him right now—she had her hands full with the girls. But if her best friend got pregnant again, all bets were off.

They'd hit the border of Valteron soon. Enemy territory. Holt had told them in no uncertain terms to keep out. He'd probably stepped up the border control, too.

The cover identities CASE Global operatives had developed over the last fifteen years were practically legends. They had families and work histories backed by legitimate-looking documents. Not to mention the sworn testimony of paid informants.

Even Earth-side intelligence agencies would have a hard time picking out the false identities.

The problem was, Holt had consulted on every single one of them. He'd provided those finishing touches—occupational histories, connections to existing families, religion-specific marital customs—the kind of nuances that made them legitimate.

So that meant he knew the names. And he might have even alerted the authorities of other nations, too, kind of a medieval version of the no-fly list. Logan couldn't use any of his trusted aliases. Instead, he had to rely on a rush job and pray that it held up under scrutiny. *Yet another thing that pisses me off about Holt's defection. All the goddamn paperwork.*

Kiara drew rein about a quarter mile before the border crossing. A long line of impatient travelers waited for their turn to pass between two heavy stone-and-mortar towers, each about forty feet high. Logan made a quick survey with his field glasses. A spotter in each tower plus six on the ground to do the checks made for eight bogeys, all of them in the black-and-gold livery of Valteroni officials. That was normal. The men with crossbows were not. "Well, that's new."

"What is?" Kiara asked. She'd dismounted to fiddle with their straps on her mare, to make it seem like they had a real reason for stopping.

"Oh, just a bunch of soldiers waiting inside the checkpoint."

"How many combatants?"

He was already counting . . . *six, seven, eight*. "I make eight on the ground, but I'm guessing each tower has a ranged weapon, too."

Kiara had her own compact binoculars out. "It's probably just a patrol checking in. No cause for concern."

I'm not so sure. Crossbowmen were unusual in Alissia. They were easier to train, but the technology left much to be desired. The reloading time sank the crossbow as a field weapon. Unless you had well-disciplined archers, you got one massive opening salvo and that was it. Light infantry could cover the effective range of the weapon—about seventy yards, currently—in the time it took to reload. Horsemen could close the gap in half that.

Which made this even more suspicious. "I've never seen that many crossbows in one place," he said.

Kiara gave it a look with her field glasses. "You want to try skirting the checkpoint?"

"They catch us doing that, and we're in real trouble. Not even Bradley could talk his way out of that interrogation."

"That doesn't leave much of a choice," Kiara said.

Logan cursed under his breath. *Talk about a rock and a hard place.* "I guess not."

They started toward the gate. Logan played the game of watching the guards without making it obvious. He stole the occasional glimpse, though, and didn't like what he saw. In peacetime, most patrols had grizzled old veterans riding out the last few years of their service contracts. That wasn't the case here. Their youth showed in the posture, and the efficient speed of their movements as they inspected each wagon. These were soldiers in their prime. The kind you didn't waste on customs.

The waiting made it worse. Once Logan and Kiara had joined the press of bodies, it took ten minutes to get to the gate. Logan dismounted to walk his horse through—a touch of humility for the officials, and a way to look less threatening to the guards—and gestured for Kiara to do the same. *Come down off the high horse, Lieutenant.*

A liveried man waved Logan forward. He was portly, probably early forties, and had the semi-bored expression of a career government official. "Name?"

Logan slouched a bit to keep from towering over the man. "Abram Walters. I'm from Felara."

"How fascinating." The official's eyes barely flickered up from his ledger. "Purpose of your visit?"

Oh, this guy's a delight. "Looking for work."

"You might want to sell the horse."

Logan did a double take. "Sorry?"

"Your mount, Mr. Walters. The Prime is paying for horses, if you're looking to sell."

"Is he, now?"

"Handsomely."

"Well, maybe I'll pay him a visit. See if he's interested in this one."

The man laughed. "Oh, going to just drop in on the Prime, are you?" He called over to one of his colleagues. "Jensen! This one here's gonna visit the Prime."

"That a fact?" The other official looked Logan up and down. "Give him my best, will you?"

Both of them burst out in laughter, slapping their knees. Meanwhile, Kiara had a look of alarm on her face. *All right, so maybe it wasn't the best thing to joke about.*

"Are we done here?" Logan asked.

"Yes, yes." The official wheezed as he scrawled something on the ledger in front of him. "Welcome to Valteron."

Logan led his horse out of the gate, trying to ignore the obvious amusement among the Valteroni officials. *Anything to make me less threatening to the soldiers.* He stole a glance to where the crossbowmen lounged in the shadow of the towers. Most Alissian crossbows were heavy, crudely made things with windlasses as the cranking mechanism. The weapons these men cradled looked off somehow. Lighter, sleeker, and—*son of a bitch*—lever-cranked. It might seem a small thing, but a lever would let them shoot about six bolts a minute. On their own, Alissians shouldn't have made that technological advance for another couple hundred years.

Kiara got clear a minute later, and they both mounted.

"Those crossbows are a pretty big leap," Logan muttered.

Kiara glanced over, and cursed under her breath. "I think we know who to thank for that."

"I'd say there's no such thing as magic, but that
would make the world a boring place."

—Art of Illusion, March 3

CHAPTER 12

THE SLIP

The more Quinn learned about Cambry, the less he
wanted to go there.

"The King of Landor has ruled for close to two
decades," Chaudri said. "He seems to possess a strong
sense of right and wrong, and most of the kingdom
follows his lead. Even minor infractions merit severe
punishment."

"Prison time?" Quinn asked.

"More like amputation," Mendez said. "Execution's
pretty popular, too."

"They have tribunal courts in Cambry," Chaudri

said. "Government officials, merchants, and even members of the royal family have been sentenced there."

"And this is the place we're going to try to slip through to catch a riverboat?" Quinn asked.

"They run a hell of a military, too," Mendez said. "Best heavy cavalry on the continent."

"That's the part of the culture I'm least fond of," Chaudri said.

"What, just because they joust in the streets?"

"And the courtyards, and the plazas." Chaudri sniffed. "Even the market square."

Mendez grinned. "They gotta practice somewhere."

"You think we'll have any trouble?" Quinn asked. "We're just passing through."

"Crimes of which we could be accused include espionage, smuggling, and possibly fraud," Chaudri said.

Oh, delightful. "Great. And here I forgot my CASE Global get-out-of-jail-free card."

"No need to worry," Chaudri said. "The courts are quite efficient. If we're captured, we'd probably be convicted and executed before the company could task an operative."

"That *does* make me feel better."

"I'm tempted to tell you not to talk at all, Bradley," Mendez said.

"Come on, man. My charm is my best weapon."

"Not so sure the lieutenant feels the same way about that."

Quinn scoffed. "Are you kidding me? She's seen some of my best stuff."

"All right, all right," Mendez said. "You made your point. No gag orders."

"What about me?" Chaudri asked.

"You're our world expert, Veena." Mendez gave her a big smile. "You can say whatever you want."

Quinn managed not to roll his eyes. *Jeez, get a room, you two.*

They were half a day out from Cambry when they hit their first patrol. A forest of tall, densely packed conifers lined the road to either side. Mendez had the lead as usual, with Chaudri and Quinn riding side by side behind him. They rounded a blind turn and were nearly overrun by a dozen lancers in full plate armor.

"Whoa!" Mendez yanked back on the reins. Quinn's horse stopped on its own, nearly tossing him from the saddle. He scrambled to stay upright without dropping his parchmap, which he'd been perusing while they rode. Meanwhile, soldiers in bright armor parted around them, smooth as silk. Then they halted, boxing Mendez, Quinn, and Chaudri in on three sides.

One of them rode right up to Mendez and removed his helmet, revealing a wide face and the brightest orange beard Quinn had ever seen. "Good afternoon. May I ask where you're headed?"

He directed the question to Mendez, who hunched his shoulders and glanced back at Chaudri. She'd insisted on doing all the talking.

She lifted her chin and gave the man a cold look. "I'll ask you to direct your questions to me, Captain. Not my man-at-arms."

He touched his fingertips to his forehead. "Of course, m'lady. Due apologies."

Quinn slowly folded the parchmap over, to make it less conspicuous. One more fold, and he'd be able to slide it up his sleeve.

"We're headed to Cambry," Chaudri said.

"For what purpose, may I ask?"

"To catch a riverboat, and otherwise cause no trouble."

"Spoken like someone who understands our ways." The captain made to put on his helmet again, but his gaze fell to the map in Quinn's hands and he hesitated. "What is that?"

Quinn looked to Veena. Her eyes were wide with alarm. *No help there.* "Just an old map," he muttered. Like a fool, he'd failed to stash a normal scrap of parchment to swap it out with.

"I've never seen anything like it," the captain said.

"It's nothing special," Quinn said. *If I ever needed a magical distraction, it's now.* He tried to reach within himself for that power, to make a noise or a fireball or *something*, but there was nothing there. No power. No magic at all.

"May I—" the captain began, but cut off as Chaudri slumped over her saddle and fell into the arms of the patrolman beside her. "M'lady?"

He was out of his saddle in an instant, and ran forward to help the other soldier place Chaudri back in her saddle. "Water!"

Someone passed him a leather canteen, which he uncapped and brought to her lips. She drank, then coughed, and her eyes flew open. She looked around as if confused.

"What happened?"

"You fainted, m'lady," the captain said.

"Oh, how embarrassing!"

"Are you sure you're all right?"

She took a deep breath. "Yes, quite. Thank you, Captain. I'll feel better once we're in Cambry."

The man gave her a side-look, then swung back into his saddle. He glanced down at Quinn's hands, which were now empty, the parchmap having been tucked quietly up his sleeve during the chaos.

Quinn kept his eyes on Veena, with his face a mask of concern. He could feel the captain's gaze, and didn't dare meet it.

"Happy to be of service," the captain said. He replaced his helmet and took up his reins. His horse turned away, and the mounts of his patrolmen fell out of formation with it. They circled around and rode onward, leaving a cloud of dust in their wake that drifted up through the tight-pack trees.

"Nice save, Veena," Quinn said quietly.

"I prefer *m'lady*," she said.

Cambry looked more like a fortress than a capital city. It spread out in the vale below them, a great marble-colored pentagon split neatly in half by the dark blue stripe of the Loutre River. As they rode closer, the whites and grays resolved into a maze of walls and gates surrounding the city proper. Quinn hadn't imagined there was so much stone in the entire continent.

"I feel like I'm in Gondor," he said. "Where do they get all that stone?"

"Massive quarries north of the city," Chaudri said. "It's a light, porous stone similar to limestone. They bring it in one stone at a time."

"Sounds exhausting."

"It's a big part of their economy, actually. Good stone is hard to come by."

Probably because it's all been used to build this place.

Quinn took out his wayfinder stone. It still pointed east, more or less along the line of the Loutre River as it wound away from Cambry. That was good; he didn't mind sticking with Mendez and

Chaudri while their mission took him closer to the Enclave. The problem would come when that was no longer true. The lieutenant didn't seem enthusiastic about him striking out on his own. *But I'll have to do that eventually, if she wants someone working on Holt's magical protections.* That was his official reason for coming after all. And if he just happened to pick up some real magical abilities while he was working on that, so much the better.

Quinn Bradley never said no to a windfall.

The alabaster walls grew as they approached Cambry, eventually towering some thirty feet overhead by the time Chaudri led them up to the gate. It remained open despite the late-afternoon hour, but a small army of armored soldiers stood on guard. They funneled incoming travelers to one side, where an elderly man and woman sat beside a stone table taking roll.

"Let's walk the horses," Mendez said.

They dismounted and lashed their weapons to their horses. Not trying to hide them, of course, but making them appear more like cargo. Quinn hoped they wouldn't give his bow too close of an inspection. The cams alone represented a three-hundred-year leap in materials technology.

"They may ask us some questions at the gate," Chaudri said. "Keep your answers short and to the point."

"My favorite kind of answers," Mendez said.

She gave him a fleeting smile, apparently not in a

joking mood. "Quinn, don't mention the Enclave or magic of any sort."

"I wasn't planning to, but why?" Quinn asked.

"Iridessa said not to, that's why," she said.

"Really?"

"She said they're distrusting of magic in this part of Landor."

"I wondered what you two were talking about," Quinn said.

"Just follow her advice. The less attention we get here, the better." She took her horse's reins and approached the intake table.

The couple taking roll weren't as old as they'd seemed from afar. They had bone-white hair, but youthful faces with sharp, hawkish features. *They've got to be brother and sister*, Quinn thought.

"Name?" the man asked.

"Virginia Heston," Chaudri said.

"Origin?"

"New Kestani."

"Reason for entry?"

Chaudri brushed back a strand of hair from her face. "We're hoping to take a riverboat to the coast."

The man furrowed his brow, as if this didn't make sense. But he pressed on, and asked in a more formal tone, "On your oath, will you obey all Cambry laws and customs?"

"On my oath," Chaudri said.

The man looked to Quinn and Mendez expectantly.

"On my oath," Quinn said, a second before Mendez repeated it . . . *I solemnly swear that I am up to no good.*

The man gave a little nod, accepting their oaths. "On your oath, do you have coin or goods enough to pay for lodging while in Cambry?"

"On my oath," they answered.

Another nod, then another question. "On your oath, do you attest that you are not a spell-caster, woods-witch, or magician of any sort?"

Well, this just got interesting. Quinn locked eyes with the man. "On my oath," he said.

Mendez answered without a flinch, but Chaudri faltered a moment before giving her oath. At least she didn't glance at him. Quinn prayed the clerks wouldn't notice.

He glanced at the white-haired woman beside him who thus far hadn't said a word. She gave an almost-undetectable nod. Quinn held his breath.

The clerk lifted his hand toward the city interior. "Welcome to Cambry."

Quinn exhaled softly as Chaudri led them in. *That felt closer than it should have been.*

"One last thing," the man said.

They all froze. *Shit, here it comes,* Quinn thought.

"Yes?" Chaudri asked with a slight tremor to her voice.

"You'd best hurry if you hope to catch a river barge. Most have already fled downriver."

Chaudri didn't hide her surprise. "From what?"

The clerk pointed wordlessly behind them. The entire northwest horizon was dark as night, the distant mountains cloaked in a roiling mass of clouds.

A northern storm. Quinn gritted his teeth. If that caught up with them, a river was the last place they'd want to be.

Just as the clerk had warned, most of the river captains had departed ahead of the storm. The docks down by the Cambry riverfront—which were also constructed of stone—were largely empty. A single barge remained. The captain had stuck around to catch a last shipment of expensive-looking timber that was still being loaded.

He was, without a doubt, the hairiest person Quinn had ever seen. His chestnut beard was so massive and untamed that it was impossible to determine where the beard ended and the long hair began. It was all Quinn could do not to stare.

Meanwhile, Chaudri had taken the lead on negotiations, and it wasn't going well.

"I think you misunderstand, Captain," she said, allowing the first hint of exasperation into her voice. "We're only booking passage for three people. Not three hundred."

"Three people and three crap-producers," said

the captain, whose name was Benvolio. "Might as well be three hundred."

"For what you're asking, we could practically buy a riverboat of our own!"

"Couldn't sail it on your own, though." He grinned through the beard. "There's not a riverman left in town, other than my crew."

"How hard can it be?" Mendez asked.

The man gave him a hard look. "You ever worked a raft before, boy?"

Mendez stared at him, unblinking. "Damn right I have. And I'm not a boy."

The captain grunted something that might have been an apology. Then he smiled again. "You looking for work? We could use another set of hands."

Mendez seemed about to retort, but Chaudri cut him off.

"If you'll have my man working on the raft, I'm not paying his passage."

"I wasn't really offering to—" Mendez started.

"Give you a half-rate, if he's as good as he claims," the captain said.

"A third of a rate, and I want reasonable prices on the horses."

Benvolio grinned. "Done."

Both of them spat into their palms and shook. Quinn wasn't sure why he'd worried. *She's a freaking natural.*

Mendez was grumbling to himself, but Chaudri looked at him and he managed a halfhearted smile.

"We'll leave in two hours," Benvolio said. "You can leave your horses here."

Chaudri pressed a purse on him. "Here's a down payment."

"Much appreciated." He tucked the purse into a jacket pocket, but it looked like he just shoved it through his beard.

"We could use some provisions," Chaudri said.

"Go see Jacques at the Tipsy Rooster. He'll set you up." He put a broad hand on Mendez's shoulder. "*We'll* finish loading up."

Chaudri looked like she might protest, but Mendez waved her off. He probably wanted to stick around and supervise the loading of the horses anyway.

Well, as long as we have a couple of hours . . . Quinn tapped Chaudri's shoulder and beckoned with his head. "Come on, I'll buy you a drink."

The look on Mendez's face was priceless.

The Loutre River ran shallow and fast from the heart of Landor, east through Pirea, and into the Bay of Seals. Quinn wasn't a river expert, but he doubted it would be a casual float downstream. Mendez looked a little harried when he and Chaudri strolled back, both of them enjoying the warmth in their bellies brought by Landorian ale.

"How are things?" Quinn asked.

"Your mare almost wrecked his crane," Mendez said.

"She *is* a spirited one." He knew it should worry him more, but Landorian ale had a certain soothing effect on him.

"Well, the captain's pissed."

"Relax, man." Quinn put a hand on his shoulder. "You know this is a temp job for you, right?"

The super-beard himself appeared on deck, as if summoned. "Board up!"

They hurried up the gangplank onto the river barge. Quinn made the mistake of glancing down, to where the river churned and gurgled against the raft hull. *Damn, that's flowing fast.* And all that stood between him and it was a glorified pile of logs. It triggered a flash of fear and some deep survival instinct. He froze at the top of the gangplank and gripped the rail to steady himself. "Ohhhhh."

"Shake a leg, Bradley," Mendez said. "Captain wants the plank up."

"Which way to the cabins?"

"Riverboats don't have cabins. We sleep in the hold."

"With the cargo? What's he got down there?"

"Goats, mostly."

Oh, hell, no. "We're sleeping with *goats*?"

"Relax, I'm just yanking your chain. It's timber, and the captain had us stack it up so that we can sleep on top. The crew'll sleep on deck, so we should have the place to ourselves."

"What if it rains?"

"It's not going to rain."

A day later, Quinn stood on the deck when the first snow flurries fell from a shrouded gray sky.

Not going to rain, huh?

Captain Benvolio watched the clouds with a jaded eye, while little flakes lodged all over his massive beard. Finally, he swung the tiller and pointed the long, ponderous barge closer to shore. "Lock and stow it, boys!"

All of the hatches were open, and most of the poles still had to be stowed. Ropes and tools littered the deck. The crew sprang into action. Quinn jumped in to lend a hand, working his way around the edge of the upper deck to pick up the last of the loose equipment. He tossed this to the sailor manning the nearest hatch, and started winding up loose lines.

Maybe we should have asked for a discount on my ticket, too.

In the meantime, the temperature dropped by at least twenty degrees. The clouds and the snow brought twilight to midafternoon. Mendez waved to catch Quinn's eye—he was taking Chaudri below-decks. He probably wanted to carve out a little spot before all of the river crewmen got down there, which wasn't a bad idea. Quinn signaled that he'd be right there.

"Everyone below!" Benvolio bellowed.

Quinn was near the stern, so he'd be one of the last to take cover. He bent to pick up the last pole. A gray slush coated the deck. He didn't even think about how slippery that made it, until his boots slid out from under him. "Shit!" He slammed into the edge of the deck. Flailed for purchase, but couldn't find any. Then he was falling. Terrifyingly weightless.

The water hit like a freight train. Cold as ice, dark as ink. The shock of it paralyzed him. His arms and legs wouldn't move. He sank like a heavy stone. *No!* He forced his arms to move. Then his legs. Flailed against the frigid water to get back to the surface. His head broke the surface. He gulped air and tried to swim, but the current had him. The force of it swirled him away. Shouts drifted down from above, but they sounded so distant. *Too far.* He tried calling out, but got a lungful of cold dark water instead. It tasted like silt. He gagged, spluttering to clear his airway.

Jesus, I'm in trouble.

His clothes grew heavy. The water pushed him mercilessly, like a bouncer keeping riffraff out of the VIP room. The cold zapped the strength from his muscles. Fatigue set in, and it was all he could do to keep his head above the surface. The dark shape of the barge drifted farther away. The river swallowed him again.

This is it, isn't it? This is how I'm going to die. A moment of stupid carelessness. God, he was even losing the will to fight it. That's how goddamn cold the water was.

A memory popped into his head unbidden. He was back at the Enclave, perching on a rock over a fast-moving stream. One of those "exercises" to help students call on their magic when they truly needed it. He'd bombed that one, of course, as he had all the others. But that little dark-haired girl had done something when she tumbled into the water. Damn, what was it?

It's now or never. That's what it is.

He felt the pinpoint of warmth coming up from his core. A glimmer of hope. He drew his arms and legs in. Made himself into a ball while his lungs screamed for air. Then he pushed outward with everything he had. *Against* the water.

And the water fled.

It pressed back away from him, pushed by an invisible hand. Air rushed into his lungs. He could *breathe*! He stopped drifting downstream, and held fast. Heat blazed within him, like he had a fireball in his stomach. It didn't hurt.

It felt glorious.

Then a shadow loomed over him. Torches appeared over the edge. Someone was shouting his name. He didn't dare move, until he saw the pole. He grabbed it with both hands. The heat dissipated, the water flooded in. But he clung to the pole. A pair of arms reached down and grabbed him under the shoulders. They heaved him up onto deck, and Quinn found himself buried in a scratchy woolen blanket. No, not a blanket. A beard. A wonderfully thick, lustrous beard.

He tried to laugh and doubled over, retching water. The deck spun, and darkness swallowed him.

> "The best thing an entertainer can do is give someone what they came for."
>
> —**Art of Illusion, September 8**

CHAPTER 13

THE FAMILY BUSINESS

Quinn woke to the sound of hail drumming overhead, and the musty smell of horses. A soft, heavy weight pressed on his chest. Blankets. He lay under a pile of them in the ship's hold, on what felt like a stack of lumber. Mendez sat cross-legged beside him, humming something that sounded suspiciously like "La Cucaracha." *Maybe I'm still dreaming.*

He tried sitting up, but his body felt like lead. He groaned.

"Hey! Sleeping Beauty!" Mendez grinned.

Darkness cloaked much of the hold. Dim shapes squatted around gas lanterns. He couldn't seem to focus. *Christ, even my eyes are exhausted.* "How long was I out?"

"Think it's been about twenty hours."

"You kidding?" He felt like he'd barely slept at all.

"You were dead to the world, man. Veena was worried about you."

"Where is she?"

"Sneaking a little coffee out of our saddlebags."

God bless her. "She read my mind."

"Yeah, she's good at that." Mendez smiled. "So, what happened?"

"I fell overboard."

"No shit. But I mean after that."

"The water was so damn cold." Quinn shivered and rubbed his arms. "I thought I was going to drown."

Mendez glanced around and lowered his voice. "By the time I got up on deck, you were gone, man. They couldn't even see you, and the captain . . . well, his face was pretty grim. Thirty seconds later, he was pulling you up."

"I remember that part. Never been so happy to see a beard in my life."

"I don't know how you managed to get back to the barge." Mendez shook his head. "It was one hell of a magic trick."

Maybe it was better to let him think that. It would

mean fewer questions. "Well, I *am* a trained magician," Quinn said.

"You're good, but I don't know if you're that good."

"Aw, come on. I haven't even been applying myself. And you've never seen my escape act before."

Mendez laughed. "Well, there's something to look forward to."

A dark thought intruded. If Logan heard about this, he'd never let Quinn live it down. "Hey, have you made your report to the lieutenant yet?"

"Nope. I'll do that when Veena gets back."

"How would you feel about maybe not mentioning the whole falling-into-the-water thing?"

"Why not?"

"It's not relevant to our mission, is it?"

"The lieutenant doesn't like me leaving stuff out."

"Come on, man. It makes me look bad."

Mendez groaned. "It was the best part of my report!" He looked away as someone climbed down into the hold. The pocket on his jacket yawned open to reveal one of the fat Alissian gold coins the lab had minted for this mission.

Quinn plucked it out between two fingers, light-touch, and palmed it. "Can't you help me out? I'll make it worth your while." He grinned and held up the coin.

Mendez frowned. "Where'd you get that? I just had one of those."

"I know." Quinn flipped it to him so that it spun in

the air with that high-pitched metallic ring. *I never get tired of that sound.*

Mendez caught it one-handed. But when he opened his hand, it was a crude penny. "Hey!"

Quinn still had the gold coin, and now he danced it across all ten fingers. "I can do this all day."

"Maybe I'll just *take* it from you."

"Better be quick," Quinn said. He made both of his hands into fists, opened them, and the coin was gone.

Veena reappeared before he could have any more fun. "Quinn! Good to see you awake. How are you feeling?"

"Much better, actually. Just glad to be alive. And dry."

She handed him a threadbare leather canteen. "A little something to warm you up. Don't let anyone see the steam."

"Ten-four." He unscrewed the cap, careful to keep the thermal plastic bottle hidden beneath his hands. *God bless our engineers.* He lifted his hand long enough to catch the aroma. "Oh, that's wonderful."

"Good, because you've got some explaining to do."

He blew on the coffee and tried a sip. It wasn't as hot as it could have been, but the warmth riding down to his belly felt delightful. "About what?"

"Falling overboard, for starters."

He felt a spike of fear, remembering the lurch in his stomach when he went over. "I didn't realize how slippery it was."

"How did you get back?" She glanced around and lowered her voice. "Some of the sailors are saying that you *flew.*"

That was close to the mark. He knew damn well how he'd survived, and it wasn't something he was ready to share. If Kiara got word that he was manifesting real magical abilities, she might start guessing at his ulterior motive for returning to the Enclave. *I'd better keep it under wraps.* He grinned and shoved up his sleeve enough for her to see the frame of the elemental projector. "I had to use this."

"Ha! I knew it," Mendez said.

"Ohhh," Chaudri said. "Well, now I see why they'd think that."

"I know it was risky, but it was either that, or drown," Quinn said.

"How about leaving the sailing activities to actual sailors from now on?" she asked.

"Fine. I'll be happy to."

That proved a timely promise, because the captain started yelling orders a minute later. The worst of the storm had passed, and he wanted the poles manned again.

"How long until we reach port?" Quinn asked.

"When Dr. Holt took this trip, the journey was about four and a half days total," Chaudri said.

"Man, that guy sure does get around, doesn't he?" Quinn asked.

"Tell me about it," Mendez groused.

"I made a tally before we left," Chaudri said. "Dr. Holt visited every major city on the Alissian mainland at least three times in the past fifteen years."

Quinn whistled. "When did he sleep?"

"Not very often," Chaudri said. Her cheeks colored. "As far as I know, that is."

Quinn grinned. "Right. As far as you know."

"I'm not sure what you're implying."

"Not implying anything." Quinn held up his hands in apology. *Too soon to press her on it.* Besides, Mendez might just toss him overboard, and he didn't think he could produce a miracle twice.

He leaned back while Mendez and Chaudri started trading Holt stories, and toyed with the wayfinder stone. It might have been his imagination, but he felt like the pull of the Enclave was growing stronger as they pressed east.

Soon, he kept thinking. *Soon I get to start my real mission.*

For the remainder of the river journey, the crew seemed to avoid him. Everywhere he went on board, he was quickly alone. If he went belowdecks, everyone went on duty. If he came back up, everyone went on break. Chaudri assured him it was only his imagination, but he didn't buy it. All of the men and women became stony-faced whenever he was around, as if they had no feelings good or bad about him.

Captain Benvolio was the only exception. Whenever he'd see Quinn, he'd slap him on the back and say, "All right, brother?"

"All right," Quinn would say. It might not have a lot of variation to it, but at least it was conversation. Far more than he could pry out of any of the others.

"I might as well be floating down the river by myself," he complained to Chaudri, two days after the incident.

She glanced up at him, and went back to working her hair into a thick braid, intertwined with ribbon. Apparently that was the Pirean style, and she wanted to blend in. "I think you're exaggerating."

"Pay attention to the next five minutes now that I'm sitting with you, and you'll see what I'm talking about," he said.

She humored him. Five minutes later, there was no denying that everyone on Benvolio's crew somehow managed to find work on the far side of the riverboat.

"All right, maybe it's not just your imagination," she said.

"It's not like I have a contagious disease."

"Well, they're probably embarrassed."

"Why?"

"You're a passenger, and you fell overboard while working the ship."

"It was an accident. Could have happened to anyone."

"But it didn't. It happened to someone who paid to be on board."

He rolled his shoulders, but the tension remained. "I don't know."

She let the braid fall and bit her lip. "I wasn't going to tell you this, but the captain chewed them all out last night."

"While I was asleep?"

"While you were dead to the world, yes."

Damn. "Now I feel even worse."

"The best thing you can do is act normal. And not fall overboard again."

He laughed. "Oh, is that all?"

"Maybe think about spreading some coins around, before we disembark."

It was a reasonable explanation, but it didn't seem to be enough. He spent enough time in casinos to be pretty good at reading faces, and these weren't simple looks of embarrassment. There was a guardedness to their features, as if he were a black cat they didn't want to cross their path. *They suspect what I am.*

On the last mission when they'd taken a ship, Quinn had practically bragged about being a magician. He'd put on a show, in fact, and broken a foul mood that had settled over the crew. Now he'd done the opposite—tried to hide what he was—and it had the opposite effect. He was an unknown and dangerous thing to them now. That's why they gave him the look of guarded fear. The look you have when you're on a narrow sidewalk and see a couple of bangers coming down the street.

The same look, in fact, that Chaudri gave him sometimes when she thought he wasn't looking. She'd seen something. Or heard about seeing something, at least. And she didn't buy that he'd pulled it off by tech or hand-waving.

Mendez had probably told her.

I hope he didn't tell anyone else.

Pirea lay at the northeastern peninsula of the Alissian mainland, and represented the poorest of its nations. The soil and the climate were primarily to blame for that: the rocky ground was difficult to farm, and the harsh long winters only allowed for hardy, fast-growing crops. CASE Global's genetic analysis of the wheat-like plants that were farmed here had spurred a new generation of hardier crop seeds back on earth.

Quinn stood on a small outcropping overlooking the eastern seacoast. Mendez and Chaudri had gone down to the docks to see if there were any Valteroni sailors in town, but it didn't seem promising. The few ships they'd seen so far were either limping in for repairs, or headed out to the fish shoals. Which all helped Quinn realize a single important fact.

No one here has a goddamn clue where the Valteroni admiral will be holed up.

The wind blew steadily in his face, churning whitecaps atop the smoke-gray water. His wayfinder stone, too, leaned steadily toward the oceanic horizon, which was roughly southeast. How far, he couldn't tell. But they were in a port town in a nation known for its sailing abilities. If there was anywhere to catch a ride to the Enclave, it was here.

Unfortunately, he didn't really know where to start. It's not like he could go into the downtown area and start asking people where he could catch the next ship to the secret magic community. The magicians liked their privacy, and the rest of Alissians seemed to know it.

"All right, brother?"

The voice startled him, and he was surprised when he turned around to see Benvolio's heavily bearded face. "Captain! All right, I guess."

He hadn't seen the man since they disembarked. Benvolio had been so occupied yelling at his men to be careful with the wood that he almost didn't notice when Chaudri pressed a small, heavy purse into his broad hand. He paused long enough to tuck it away into the beard as he had the last one, then picked up the yelling again.

I thought that was the only goodbye we were going to get. "Listen, I wanted to thank you again for yanking me out of the water," Quinn said. "You saved my ass."

"Oh, I'm not sure it was me."

"Well, I am." Quinn laughed. "You're not easy to forget."

"I've had a few men fall into the water, over the years. Never saw anything like what happened to you."

"What happened to them?"

"Lost 'em to the river."

"Oh."

"Not you, though!" Benvolio grinned. "You're special, aren't you?"

Uh-oh. "Nah, just a regular guy."

"A regular guy would've drowned."

Quinn smiled. "And a smarter one would've stayed below, out of the way."

"Listen, you want to play coy, that's fine with me. But my brother Simeon captains a trading vessel, 'round these parts."

"I'm not sure I—" Quinn started.

"Makes *all kinds* of interesting stops, if you catch my meaning."

Oh, my God, the Enclave. He could hardly believe his luck. "Where do I find this brother of yours?"

"He's got a two-master called the *Purity*. Should be dockside by tomorrow."

"I'll look for it. Thank you, Captain." Quinn offered his hand, and they clasped arms in the Landorian style. "What's your brother look like?"

Benvolio laughed his booming laugh. "You'll know him when you see him, I'll wager."

Mendez and Chaudri got back with predictably bad news: no Valteroni vessels in the harbor, and no sailors in town.

"So, what's the plan?" Quinn asked.

"We're sitting tight," Mendez said. "Still waiting to hear back from the lieutenant."

Of course you are. Kiara probably just wanted them to stay with Quinn to keep an eye on him.

"Well, I had a little bit more luck. Benvolio's got a brother who runs a deepwater trading vessel. He seemed to think I might be able to catch a ride to where I'm going."

Mendez frowned. "I hope you didn't tell him about the Enclave."

"I'm not an idiot, Mendez. He brought it up."

"What did he say?" Chaudri asked.

"He called me special."

Chaudri giggled. "We all think you're special, Quinn."

"I'm serious. He implied that his brother makes unscheduled stops at a certain island where there were other *special* people."

"Sounds kind of vague," Mendez said.

"I don't think it could be any plainer. Trust me, that's just the way they'd want it."

Mendez shook his head. "How in the hell did you ever find that island in the first place?"

Quinn spread his hands out. "Well, I'm a magician, too. They're my kind of people."

"You're something, all right."

"Ha! Sounds like something Logan would say."

"Yeah, he gave me a few one-liners I could use to take you down a peg, as needed."

No surprise there. "Listen, you think you two will be all right if I manage to hook up with Benvolio's brother?"

Chaudri blushed, and mumbled something affirmative. Mendez grinned, and there was real happiness in it. "We'll be fine."

"Can you look after my horse for me? I won't need one until I get back."

"What about the saddlebags? I'm not sure we can keep an eye on those 24/7."

"Oh, don't worry, I'm taking those with me."

Because I've got one hell of a performance planned.

"The new ship will find the old rocks."

—**Pirean proverb**

CHAPTER 14

DIFFERENT PORTS

In spite of its, well, *colorful* name, Crab's Head was actually the fifth-largest port on the eastern seacoast, and an odd hybrid between fishing village and bustling port city. Ships were crammed in along the docks no more than a few feet apart, and no two of them were the same. Stout transport cogs bobbed low in the water beside fleet coast-cutters and deep-hulled schooners.

But this was Pirea, and so fishing vessels outnumbered the other craft ten to one. They ranged from the simple skiffs of hand-fishermen to huge three-masters that plied deep water with their nets. The smell of fish in the air was like a physical thing. Quinn hoped he'd stopped noticing it at some point, but after two days it still hadn't happened.

At least he wasn't retching anymore. *Small victories.*

Finally, a two-masted schooner coasted into the harbor. Quinn gave it a covert survey with his compact binoculars, which were disguised to look like opera glasses. Not that he planned to catch any operas in-world—he'd rather be slowly tortured by Enclave magicians—but that's how the engineers had "disguised" the equipment for in-world use. Problem was, they didn't have an opera in Crab's Head, much less opera glasses. Nor would they be the sort of thing you carried around with you and used to scan the harbor. So Quinn had to resort to quick, surreptitious glances with the binoculars, and palm them whenever someone wandered by.

He still managed to get a glimpse of the ship with them. It was the *Purity*, all right. The ship looked to be in good condition—the crew was fit, and the sails were taut as it coasted around the breakwater.

It seemed sound to him, but for all he knew it would sink before it reached the dock. Not if the captain was anything like his brother, though. *I wish I knew more about ships.*

Benvolio was still in town, waiting for the right cargo opportunity to come in. *Maybe I should have let him make the approach.* Time wasn't on his side, though—if he dallied much longer here with Chaudri and Mendez, the lieutenant would come up with some new excuse to keep them together. This little naval intelligence exercise didn't fool him. She wanted to keep him on a leash as long as possible, and maybe get a line on the location of the Enclave herself. That would make Quinn Bradley more or less expendable for future CASE Global missions to the magical community.

Not until he learned how to use some of that magic himself.

He made his way down to the docks once the crew began unloading the two-master's cargo, which was in barrels. He tried not to make any enemies among the busy press of sailors and dockworkers—every one of them had that lumbering swagger of a man looking to pick a fight. He sidestepped around a pair of crewmen carrying a barrel up off the gang-plank. *I hope Benvolio isn't playing a joke on me.* "Captain Simeon?"

"On the ship," they answered, without even looking up.

He jogged down the plank to the deck of the ship. The wood gleamed with a fresh coat of varnish, and the smell of it in the direct sunlight hit him like a brick wall. *I'll be high as a kite by the time I find him.*

The captain stood over the door to the hold, yelling instructions to his sailors as they offloaded the rest of the barrels. His curses washed over them like waves over a rocky shoreline. He had his brother's stout frame and reddish-brown beard.

Quinn did a double take. *Jesus, they could be twins.* A small part of him wondered if this was some kind of practical joke. "Benvolio?"

The captain glanced over his shoulder in Quinn's direction. "You're on the wrong ship, if you're looking for him."

The voice had a different timbre. Otherwise Quinn wouldn't have believed him. "Oh, he sent me to you, is what I was going to say."

"Is that handsome bastard still docked? Thought he'd be halfway to his next port by now."

"He's waiting for some cargo, I'm told."

"Ha! That sounds like him."

"He thought you might be able to take me where I need to go."

"Where's that?"

Quinn didn't want to say it. There were too many people around—sailors and dockworkers both—and for the first time, he wasn't sure he felt safe bringing it up. *But this guy knows. Benvolio said it.*

"An island."

"We got a lot of those around here."

Quinn lowered his voice. "This one's got seven towers." *One for each nation in Alissia.*

The captain's face had gone still, and his eyes glinted with a hint of danger. "You having a jest with me, boy?"

Something told him he shouldn't back down here. He held Simeon's eyes, and didn't smile. "I'm serious."

The captain smoothed out his beard. Benvolio had that same mannerism when he was wavering on a decision. "That sounds like a place you don't want to go without an invitation."

"Oh, you mean like this?" Quinn lifted the leather cord around his neck so that the wayfinder stone slid above his collar. It trembled and then leaned right in the direction it always had, out across the water.

Simeon's shoulders eased, and he barked a laugh. "Now there's a welcome sight. The island wasn't on my port list, but it is now."

Excitement made Quinn's skin tingle all over, but he kept his smile at a minimum. "Much appreciated, Captain. When do we shove off?"

"Morning, at tidefall."

That gave him less than a day, depending on when tidefall was. Less than a day to persuade Chaudri and Mendez—and more importantly Kiara—that it was time to part ways.

Or to sneak away.

Mendez and Chaudri had been making a slow circuit of the docks, chatting up as many sailors as they could. Few of them could recall how long it had been since they'd seen a Valteroni ship. Most of the fleet had been summoned to secure the port of Valteron

City during the civil unrest. Quinn found them just outside the dockmaster's office. They both looked exhausted.

"Any leads on the admiral?" Quinn asked.

"None so far," Chaudri said. "Everyone seems to think he's still in Valteron City."

"Maybe he is."

"Logan doesn't think so," Mendez said. "He's had his ear to the ground, and there's not a whisper of him, or the flagship."

"Dr. Holt wouldn't be so careless, in any case. He'll want the backpack as far away from him as possible," Chaudri said.

Mendez put a hand to his ear. "It's the lieutenant. Be right back." He hustled down the dock to a quiet spot where he could listen.

And where he can reply out of earshot, Quinn couldn't help but thinking. "So, what do you think Holt's up to right now?"

Chaudri smiled before she caught herself. "In addition to making Kiara's life difficult?"

"Yeah. I get the feeling he likes to have a lot of irons in the fire."

"You're not wrong." Her eyes went distant, and she chewed her lip. "If I had to guess, he's consolidating his power in Valteron."

"I thought he had that locked up, once he became Prime."

"Legally speaking, he did. There's no higher political authority in the Valteroni government. But he'll still need to get the ministers in line, and keep a close eye on the local magistrates."

"Good. That should keep him busy."

"Let's hope so. Some of the things Kiara and Logan have reported are unsettling."

"Which parts? The sabotage?"

"It's just so unlike him. He's always been a builder, not a destroyer." The worry was plain on her face, but there was something else there, too. *Sadness, maybe. Or regret.*

Quinn put a hand on her shoulder. "He's got a very different job now."

She laughed, but there was no humor in it. "I'm not sure he sees it that way. Alissia has always been his first love."

"People do crazy things to protect what they love."

She sighed. "So I'm told."

Mendez reappeared. "The lieutenant wants us to try another port. Maybe Bay of Rocks, but she said it's up to you."

"It's a little surprising that there's not a single Valteroni ship here," Quinn said. "Especially since Kiara was so insistent on sending us."

"It's a tough break," Mendez agreed. If he knew more about why she'd sent them to Crab's Head, he didn't show it.

I still haven't figured out his tells. It actually bothered him a little, but there might not be time for that. "Where's Bay of Rocks?" Quinn asked. He took out the wayfinder again. It pointed him unfailingly east.

"Almost due south of here, right at the border of Landor," Chaudri said.

Quinn bit his lip. *I have to tell them.*

Mendez pulled out his parchmap to get a bearing on it. "How long will it take to get there?"

"A few days by sea, if we can find a coast-cutter. But they don't have much in the way of storage, so it'll be tough to find one that can take three horses."

"Two horses," Quinn said.

"What?" she asked.

"I'm not going with you."

"Oh?" Chaudri asked. "Did you find the captain's brother?"

"Yeah, and get this: they're twins."

"Oh, my God, there are *two* of them?" Mendez asked.

"Gods," Chaudri corrected.

"Right, gods." He smiled and winked at her.

She *tsked* and looked away, but not fast enough to hide a little smile.

Quinn pretended not to notice. He had enough nausea to look forward to on the sea voyage. "He's offered me a ride to the Enclave island. Or possibly to dump me in the ocean just for asking. I'm not sure which."

"Sounds promising," Mendez said.

Quinn started to nod, and then paused. "Wait—which scenario?"

Mendez grinned. "I'm still deciding."

"Ha! You do that. But I think he's legit. Benvolio did right by us after all."

"He also charged us an arm and a leg to bring us out of Cambry. By their standards, at least."

"Aw, Mendez, are you worried about me? Logan would be touched."

Mendez guffawed.

Quinn cleared his throat. "The only thing is, the guy's pulling out tomorrow morning."

"So soon?" Chaudri frowned.

"Yeah. He said something about tidefall."

"That's about midmorning, this time of year."

God bless her, she was as good as Wikipedia. "Thank you! I was too embarrassed to ask him."

"I don't know about this," Mendez said.

"The Enclave is where I'll be the most useful to the team. It's why you guys brought me, isn't it?"

"Well, yeah," Mendez said. "But the lieutenant just ordered us south. We should at least run it by her."

But that might give her the chance to say no. Kiara liked certainties, not vague invitations from a man Quinn had just met. Now that he was here, tasting the salt in the air, he couldn't stand the idea of postponing his return to the Enclave. If there was anywhere in Alissia that he could learn to command real magic again, it was there. "Maybe it's better if we ask forgiveness, not permission, you know?"

"We're kind of supposed to stick together," Mendez protested.

"You mean, you're supposed to keep an eye on me," Quinn said.

"On both of you." Mendez took great care not to look at Chaudri.

Quinn saw the angle, and took it. "Come on, man. You don't need me tagging along playing third wheel while you collect intel."

"You're not a third wheel!" Chaudri said.

The lady doth protest too much, methinks. "Even so, this is my shot to reach the Enclave, and I think I should take it. The two of you will be fine alone." He drew out the last word a little.

Mendez gave Chaudri a covert glance, hesitating.

Quinn raised his eyebrows a little, guy-to-guy. *Come on, man, this is your shot, too.*

"I guess she hasn't ordered you *not* to go," Mendez said at last.

Jackpot. "See? There's no problem," Quinn said.

"I'm set to check in again tomorrow at midday."

"Fair enough. I'll be long gone by then."

"She's going to have an earful for you."

"Eh, I'm used to it." Quinn grinned. "Have to admit, I'm kinda going to miss you guys."

Mendez gripped his shoulder. "Try not to get killed before you get there, all right?"

"Relax, Mendez. As long as there aren't any fourteen-year-olds with swords along the way, I'll be just fine."

Simeon stood at the rail when Quinn made his way back to the two-master. His men were loading barrels back into the ship, and they looked suspiciously identical to the ones they'd been offloading the day before.

"Morning, Captain!" Quinn called.

"Well, well, our young man o' mystery."

Quinn had to cover a smile, because the resemblance between the brothers was simply uncanny. "Permission to board?"

The captain gave him a double take and took his measure. "Granted."

Never hurts to grease the maître d'. Respect to a captain, much like respect to a chef, always paid off.

He climbed the gangplank, bracing himself for the smell of varnish. Mercifully, it wasn't nearly as strong, and a fresh salty breeze blew in from the sea.

He'd stashed the horse at a pay-by-the-month stable. Kiara wasn't going to like the itemized receipt on that one, but he doubted the ship's captain would be as hospitable if he had *that* sort of cargo. The saddlebags converted to an integrated-frame back-pack, which he'd filled to the brim, mostly with his equipment from the prototyping lab. All of that was tucked away, under clothes and rations, out of view of prying eyes.

There was no hiding the weapons, though. He had his sword belted to one hip, his quiver on the other, and his bow strapped over his shoulder.

The captain took inventory of these in a single glance. "Is there a war I don't know about?"

Quinn winked at him. "More of a hobby, for me."

"Didn't catch your name yesterday."

"Quinn Thomas." He offered his hand.

The captain clasped his arm. His grip could crack oysters. "Can't say I'll mind having another fighting man on board, though."

Quinn didn't like the sound of that. "Something got you worried?"

"You probably wouldn't be the kind to notice this, but there's not a single ship from Valteron in harbor. Hasn't been for weeks, is the rumor."

"You don't say." *What a goddamn waste of time this was.* He couldn't wait to report that little tidbit back to Kiara.

"Well, the thing is, Valteron's sort of the unofficial patrol of the coast waters. That goes away, and things worse than sharks start turning up."

"Sea monsters?"

"Yes—the two-legged kind."

"Ah." *Pirates, then.* That was something they hadn't covered much in the briefings, but Kiara had been pretty tight-lipped about the maritime stuff. Losing your sister at sea on the maiden expedition would do that. "You think we're really in danger?"

"I'm shoving off with only half a load of cargo. What does that tell you?"

That I might have made a mistake.

"Luck counts more than it should."

—Art of Illusion, January 19

CHAPTER 15

MARAUDERS

Quinn's bad luck with sea travel didn't wait long to bite him. He got chewed out by Kiara for not briefing her first, of course, but that was expected. A day out of port, and Simeon's lookout spotted a sail on the horizon. It was moving roughly at a parallel course, but changed direction soon after. Now it would intercept their path, if they kept going.

Simeon pondered this for an hour, and then ordered a course change of his own. Six points east, which would slide them away. Quinn heard the order and wandered up to the forecastle, where the captain stood behind his steersman.

"Is there a problem?" he asked.

"We'll know in a minute," Simeon said. "What he does next will tell us his intent. He holds his course, and it was just a coincidence. He comes at us again, well . . ." He let his eyebrows say the rest.

The lookout piped up ten seconds later. "Captain! Course change on the sail."

"New heading?" the captain called.

"Six points east."

Well, shit. I knew it was too easy.

The captain ordered another course change, and then another. The two ships played cat-and-mouse for half the day. The sail drew continually nearer, and eventually resolved itself into a single-masted galleon. Simeon gave it a long survey with his brass telescope, and his lookout did the same. Quinn fought the temptation to use his opera-glass binoculars—he wouldn't know what to look for in any case, and there was no sense drawing attention.

"You mark any colors on her?" Simeon called up to the crow's nest.

"Not as I can see, Cap'n."

Simeon grunted, so Quinn took this for another bad sign.

"Second shift, axes and cutlasses!" Simeon ordered. Half the sailors made their way below to where the arms were kept.

Simeon must have seen the look on his face. "Look at the bright side. You get to practice that hobby o' yours."

Quinn shook his head. "That's not a bright side."

He ran down to the little cabin he'd been given for the voyage, which was roughly the size of a coat closet. He shut the door behind him and put his comm unit in burst transmission mode.

"This is Bradley. Got a bit of a problem here." How long did Kiara say the delay would be? He started counting and got to ten before she replied.

"Go ahead, Bradley."

"There's a ship following us."

"What kind?"

"A single-masted galleon, not showing any colors."

There was a longer delay this time. *She's probably talking to Logan.*

"I'm sorry, Bradley. We don't have any way to help you."

Logan chimed in. "Sailors fight dirty. Best stay out of the fight as long as possible."

"If they start taking prisoners, surrender right away," Kiara said. "We'll figure out a way to extract you."

Helpful as ever. "All right, I'll give it a shot. Nice knowing you."

He belted on his sword, and took up his bow and quiver. Outside his cabin, he joined the stream of men making their way to the deck, all of them armed to the teeth. Most of the sailors favored curved, single-edged swords—scimitars and sabers—but many just had a pair of daggers or fighting axes. *Why am I the only guy with a bow?*

The deck had transformed into a marine version of Thunderdome. A forest of waist-high iron barbs jutted out over the rail like metal teeth.

Quinn found Simeon at the wheel. He had a knife and sword on his belt. The handles looked well-used. "Where do you want me?"

"You any good with that bow o' yours?"

"It's the *only* thing I'm good at." Aside from the magic tech, and he'd just as soon not have to use that.

"Get up to the crow's nest. Try and pick off their helmsman."

"I'll do my best, Captain."

He'd turned away when Simeon grabbed his shoulder. "If this starts to go poorly, tell them where you're from."

"How will I know it's going poorly?"

Simeon gave a grim smile. "You'll be the only one of us still alive."

Sorry I asked.

Climbing up to the crow's nest was a terrifying experience all by itself. When he was about halfway up, the ship lurched sideways as the captain made a course change. No warning at all. His legs careened loose of the mast. He clung on with his fingertips. "Shit!"

The bow started to slide down his shoulder. He

flailed with his right leg and found a rung. *Jesus Christ!* His heart hammered in his throat. *Easy, easy.* He quested with his other leg, and managed to find the other rung. Then he clung to it and took a minute to catch his breath. *Almost died before the fight even started.*

He clambered up into the crow's nest, which was nothing more than a wooden platform with rails and room enough for two men. The lookout—a lanky kid with a pitiful attempt at a mustache on his narrow face—climbed up to join him a minute later.

Quinn smiled. "Hey, Timmers. Going to keep me company, eh?"

"Cap'n wants my eyes up top." He brandished the bow and quiver of white-fletched arrows strapped on his back. "Figure I might as well have something to do with my hands."

"You think we'll outrun them?" Quinn asked.

"The cap'n is good, but our ship's heavy and they have the wind on us."

"How long, then?"

"Half an hour. Maybe less."

Quinn loosened his arrows, checking them one at a time. The carbon shafts had the coloring to pass for light-grained wood. The self-sharpening broadheads were cast from another company alloy, and damn near indestructible. *Wish I'd insisted on the explosive ones, though.*

He'd come across those in the armory, and immediately put in a requisition for some for the mission.

Which ended up on Logan's desk, and the big man had enjoyed telling Quinn that he was more likely to "blow his own ass up" than put them to good use. *Didn't hear him complaining when I showed up at the smuggler's canyon the last time we were here, though.*

The marauders' vessel loomed closer with every passing minute. It sat higher in the water than Simeon's boat, but the sails were a patchwork of mismatched canvas. Figures crowded the deck, and weapons glinted in their hands. Sweet Jesus, there were a lot of them.

Timmers had been making a survey of the vessel with his brass telescope. He muttered a curse.

"You see something?" Quinn asked.

"Marundi."

"What?"

"They're Marundi tribesmen."

"Never heard of 'em."

Timmers turned his head to spit downwind. "Be glad of it."

"Are they bad news?"

"They're a gods-damned warrior culture."

No one told me about any warrior cultures. "From where?"

"Marundi."

"That's not very helpful."

Timmers actually grinned, though his face was tight. "An archipelago north of Pirea. They used to raid along those shores before, you know . . ."

"Pretend I don't know."

"Before Valteron built a navy."

Wonderful.

The drums of the other ship began pounding.

Drums filled Quinn's world. The beats thundered across the water as the marauders closed on the *Purity*. Simeon had to shout for his orders to be heard. The noise unsettled everyone. Quinn kept trying to gauge the distance to the ship—he'd start shooting at about fifty yards—but he couldn't concentrate.

"Going to sucker punch!" shouted the captain. "Hold fast!"

"What's a sucker punch?" Quinn asked.

"Soon as they're close enough, he'll come about," Timmers said. "Try to win the leeward side when they grapple us."

Quinn threw his bow over his arm and grabbed the rail. "What's the point of that?"

"We fight off the first attack, maybe we can cut loose and run downwind."

"Does that really work?"

Timmers shrugged.

Damn.

The captain swung the tiller around and the ship lurched in response. Suddenly they were bow-to-bow with their pursuers, and closing twice as fast.

The marauders were close enough to pick out

targets, and that also meant that Quinn got his first look at the tribesmen. They were dressed in heavy outer layers of animal skins and furs. What little skin they showed was pale, but heavily tattooed with blue-black ink. Their ears and noses were pierced with ornaments carved in dark wood. The drums were animal skin stretched over wooden cylinders. They pounded these at random with wooden sticks. The result was a cacophony, but it eventually resolved into a steady beat. And the tempo picked up slowly, like the music from *Jaws*. The dread turned Quinn's stomach to ice. It made him want to run and hide. The crow's nest offered little comfort. He felt *exposed* up here. Vulnerable.

"Get ready," Timmers said. "They're about within bowshot."

They were already in bowshot for Quinn, but he didn't say so. Timmers had a shortbow, which didn't quite have the same range. Still, the second he started shooting, the marauders would take cover. He figured it was better to have two archers unleash, rather than one. "Tell me when you're ready."

"Ready."

Quinn drew the arrow to his cheek and touched his nose to the string. The familiar movement offered a little comfort. He didn't have a shot at the steersman, so he let emotion make the call and picked out the guy hitting the biggest drum.

Thrum. Direct hit, center mass. His target—hard

to Quinn's head. Another one flew past his shoulder. "Shit! Take cover!"

He threw himself down. Timmers stood to try another shot.

"Timmers!"

He heard the wet thud more than he felt it. A warm liquid sprayed across the back of his neck. It dripped down, hot and sticky across his cheeks. Timmers gurgled and collapsed. A bolt jutted from his neck.

"Timmers! Oh, God." He tried to ease the lad down, but his body shook with tremors. His neck was fountaining bright red arterial blood. Even his medkit, tucked down below in his pack, wouldn't have made a difference. *Son of a bitch!*

Timmers flailed his arms, his eyes bulging. He tried to scream, but it came out a gurgle. Quinn was paralyzed with the shock of it. The horror of it. *I have to help.* The thought came, but no action. *Come on, Quinn, move!*

Finally, he broke out of the freeze. He caught Timmers's arms and pulled him close. "Easy, easy," he said. He looked the kid right in his eyes. Tried not to see the life gushing out of him. "It's all right, Timmers. I'm here for you." He held the boy against him until the tremors stopped. He eased back, saw that the light was gone from his eyes. He closed them with his fingertips, gently as he could. A thing that he prayed he'd never have to do again.

He laid Timmers back against the side of the crow's nest. Wiped some of the blood from his hands. *The poor kid. At least it was quick.* He looked peaceful, now that his eyes were closed. His face was slack, as if he'd simply fallen asleep. He was young. Too young to be lying here in a pool of his own blood.

Quinn cursed. The ordeal should have frightened him. Should have had him cowering on the bottom of the crow's nest, or trying to make a jump for the water. But a red-hot fury burned away all thoughts of self-preservation. His bow leaned against the side of the crow's nest, mercifully intact. He pulled his quiver to him. Nocked an arrow. He leaned over to peer between the slats of the crow's nest, and saw one of the archers on the other ship. The man had tattoos covering half his face. A wolfskin cloak hid the rest of him as he bent over to crank his crossbow.

Quinn stood and drew. The archer must have seen the movement. He looked up and grabbed a bolt to throw into the crossbow. Quinn drew a bead on him. He floated the target, the same way he'd practiced a hundred times with Logan, a thousand times back home with his grandfather. Release, follow through. The arrow buried itself just above the clavicle. The man flopped over and shuddered once.

Eye for an eye, you son of a bitch.

He heard Simeon bellowing above the din. "Break loose! Break loose!" he shouted. The sailors leaped forward to cut the ropes on the grappling hook. They were trying to break free and make a run for it.

But Quinn barely heard. He just nocked another arrow. There were only four left. *Can't think about that now.* The sailors cut the last line, and the two ships heaved apart. The marauders' vessel turned. Quinn suddenly had a view of the cockpit. And the man at the wheel of it.

He tried to draw, but the resolve was draining out of him. There was blood on his hands—Timmers's blood, and that of the Marundi—and now his arms were too shaky. He couldn't summon the strength. The navigator saw the ships break apart. He screamed wordlessly, and spun the wheel. He was going to bring them right back together. That brought the strength surging back into Quinn's arms.

Hell, no.

He took a breath, drew back. He knew he wouldn't have the strength for another shot after this one. Had to make it count. He put the sight pin right on the man's solar plexus and quick-fired. A gamble, but he knew he couldn't hold it longer. The arrow went high, hit the man's shoulder. Not a fatal shot, but it pinned him back against the ship. He lost the wheel, and it spun freely. The marauders' ship careened away.

Two more of their fur-clad sailors ran over to pull the navigator free. One of them took the wheel and started bringing the ship around.

Three arrows left, and he didn't have a clean shot.

He needed a different strategy. All he had was the elemental projector on his wrist. He'd been trying not to use it on this trip. Once the thing was spent, it was spent. He needed it more at the Enclave, to persuade them that he really had what it took to train as a student.

But I'm no good to them dead.

He dropped the bow and pulled his sleeve down. His fingers were slick with blood, so it took a minute to find the right controls. Then he hit the switch, and a ball of flame appeared over his hand. Green flame, too, a wicked and unnatural color. He could sense the men on both ships pausing, staring at him. He slid the control over and made it larger. Now it was big as a watermelon, and the heat started to sear his forearm. He reared back and hurled it at the coming ship. Right at the mainmast where the patched sail was stretched in a big, wide target.

Everything slowed down. The fireball hung in the air. It expanded as it flew, so it didn't seem to move at all. Then it struck the mast, and the flammable gel-polymer splattered like a water balloon. Flames engulfed the mainsail. The galleon began to fall back as the tribesmen scrambled to put them out.

Good, let them try that. Tossing water on a burning accelerant only made it spread faster. In seconds, the whole top half of the galleon went up like a Christmas tree. It fell away behind the *Purity*, the momentum gone, the survivors jumping for the dubious safety of the water. Simeon's men made a ragged cheer.

Quinn collapsed against the side of the crow's nest. It took him half an hour to work up the courage to climb down. Even then, it was slow and painful work. The deck of the ship was right out of a nightmare. Bodies were everywhere, and blood covered almost all the varnish. The sweet tang of it mingled with the stench of sweat and shit in the air.

Simeon stood nearby, leaning heavily against the siderail. He had a handkerchief pressed to a wound in his forehead.

He jerked his head back in surprise when he saw Quinn. "Thought you might be dead."

"No," Quinn said. He looked up at the crow's nest. "But Timmers—"

"I saw."

Thank God. He'd no idea how he was going to finish that sentence. "I'm sorry, Captain. He was a good kid."

"You and he made the difference today. Held back their second wave."

"We were lucky."

"Aye. Marundi tribesmen." He spat and shook his head. "Never thought I'd see the day. Where the hell's the Valteroni admiral when you need him?"

Where indeed?

"People are the most valuable asset to have on our side."

—R. Holt, "Investment in Alissia"

CHAPTER 16

SURVIVORS

Logan hated waiting for bad news. He and Kiara had planned to check in on human assets around Valteron City today, but the transmission from Bradley put a hold on that.

Knew we should have finished the ocean survey. They knew nothing about what lay beyond sight of shore. Didn't have a fix on the pirates' strongholds, or the Enclave island. But Kiara had never mentioned replacing the *Victoria*, and he sure as hell wasn't going to bring it up.

"What's the latest from Mendez?" he asked.

The newest member of Alpha team had been quietly tasked to track Bradley's signal as long as possible. That meant hiring a ship to shadow the *Purity* long enough to get a vector on the Enclave's island. Bradley's intel from the first mission had revised the number of magicians there by an order of magnitude. The company executives wanted a complete revamp of the threat assessment.

"He couldn't get a ship to follow the *Purity* for any amount of money." Kiara's lips twisted downward. "Apparently people were worried about piracy."

"You don't say." Logan spread out his parchmap of the continent, as he had a dozen times since morning. Based on Bradley's last known trajectory and the triangulation they got from his comm unit, the Enclave island lay roughly south-southeast of Crab's Head. That was another little detail of the mission that the lieutenant had kept from their hired magician. They couldn't get a true position fix until Bradley got the network antenna in place, but they had a vector.

How far the Enclave was, they couldn't begin to guess. Even Bradley had never gone there by boat. For all they knew, it might be a thousand leagues away.

"When's Mendez due to report again?" he asked.

"Ten minutes ago."

"He's late?"

"A little."

Logan grunted. "I'm sure he has a good reason."

"Let's hope so."

"Are you going to tell him and Chaudri about the little present Holt left for us?"

"Not until they need to know. At the moment, they don't."

I hate keeping secrets. It was part of the job, but that still made things no easier. "Still nothing from Bradley?"

She gave him the disapproving frown that officers must all learn at training school. "Don't you think I'd have told you?"

"Sorry, Lieutenant."

"You're worried about him."

Damn right I am. "He's good at thinking on his feet, but there's no talking your way out of a raid on the open water. He'll have nowhere to go."

"Then he can surrender, and we'll pick him up wherever he lands."

"*If* he lands."

"We can't do anything more for him until it plays out. We're better off putting our energy into something productive."

"Like what?" he asked.

"Figuring out a way to get close to Holt without his knowledge."

He forced his mind to the new problem and mulled it over. As it stood, there were just too many unknowns. "We need eyes inside the city. Inside the palace, if we can get them."

"All of our sources in this area have gone quiet since the last Prime died."

"*Holt's* sources, you mean," Logan said.

"That's what worries me."

When they'd stopped reporting in, Logan assumed Holt had bought them off, or begun intercepting their reports. *Maybe I jumped to that conclusion.* "You know, with all the turmoil they might have just gone to ground. Maybe they're waiting to hear from us."

"It's a possibility." She pulled up some files on her tablet and started flipping through them. She had a snapshot of the entire intelligence archive, which gave her the works: age, profession, wrist-cam photo, occupation. Over the past fifteen years, Holt had developed hundreds of sources across the mainland. Valteron alone had upward of sixty. *I hope Briannah's all right.* His adoptive mother ran an inn practically a stone's throw from the Valteroni palace. Far too close to Holt to risk checking on her.

"There's a cobbler who's given us decent intel," Kiara said.

"Last known location?"

"Tanner's Square?"

Should have guessed that. He grimaced. "That's inner city." Too close to Holt, and therefore too risky. "Got anything else?"

"Wife of a peach farmer, northwest outskirts."

A ride out to the country. He smiled. "Now you're talking."

Six months ago, the areas northwest of Valteron City were among the wealthiest in the entire nation. Orchards and vineyards dotted the rolling hills overlooking the bay. These weren't peasant farms, either: they were family estates that employed thousands of seasonal laborers. The grapes and fruit took a short wagon ride to the docks, where Valteron's trading fleet carried them to the far reaches of the world.

That was the situation before the old Valteroni Prime died. Now, half of the green, rolling hills had burned in the unrest that gripped the city. The admiral might have had something to do with that: he'd not been happy when the wealthy merchant class put forth their own candidate for Valteroni Prime, rather than backing him.

And while they screwed around, Holt slipped into the big chair.

Logan steered his horse around the charred remains of a horse-drawn wagon. Scorched lumber and iron rings marked the remains of several barrels. Whatever they'd contained, it was long gone.

"Know what I haven't figured out?" he asked.

"What?" Kiara hardly glanced up from the case file. She'd been riding with her knees for the last mile, an impressive bit of skill that she normally kept under wraps. But they had the road to themselves here. Most of the merchant elites had fled to their country, waiting to see what kind of ruler Holt might turn out to be. That was Chaudri's explanation anyway. Logan suspected that anyone who'd opposed the admiralty had gone the way of that burned-out wagon.

"How in the hell did Holt get the admiral to vouch for him?"

"Richard can be very persuasive, when he wants to," Kiara said.

"I know, but still. Seems like that much power would be pretty tempting."

"They must have had a deal of some kind. The three of them were thick as thieves, back in the day."

"*Three* of them?"

"Holt, Blackwell, and the former Valteroni Prime. They crewed a ship together in year two."

"He never told me about that." He did a mental review of the mission briefing. "Pretty sure it's not in the company records, either."

"Captain Relling gave him much more liberty than I have. Half of the time he'd just be gone for two or three months, with no reports to show for it."

Logan kept his face still, and didn't dare look at her. He could count on one hand the number of times Kiara had spoken her sister's name since they'd lost the *Victoria*. Even before that, the women had always addressed each other by rank. *Guess they weren't the touchy-feely kind of sisters.*

"What kind of ship did they serve on?"

"A trading sloop that ran the western coast. Tion, New Kestani, and Felara. The former Prime captained it, and took Holt on as a greenhorn."

"And the admiral?"

"He was the first mate."

Finally, the pieces were falling into place. "Quite the little boys' club they must have had."

"We never read much into it, because Holt had no subsequent contact with them."

"Or so he said," Logan said.

"Right. His ascension to Prime did seem too well-orchestrated to be an accident."

Logan kept half an eye on the countryside as they rode, and saw nothing to encourage him. Half of the houses were burned down or clearly ransacked, and there were few signs of life or activity. The wrought iron gates and walls of the wealthy merchants were no match for a starving populace.

Deep wagon ruts marred the dirt road that led up to the peach orchards. They crisscrossed one another at odd angles, and raised edges showed where the driver had swerved to keep on the road. Whoever they were, they'd left in a hurry. *God knows what they left behind.*

Logan gave the lieutenant a grim look. Didn't say anything, because he knew she was thinking the exact same thing. If their source had been here when all the fighting started, it didn't bode well.

The road curved right and then back to the left

through a copse of trees. When they passed these, they encountered the first signs of life. A handful of people were out in the orchards, pruning deadwood from the trees.

They were universally dirty, and moved with the slow resignation of the utterly exhausted. The manor house that overlooked the orchard's rolling hills must have been stunning at one time. Now, though, it had caved in on itself after a bad fire. The workers had tied sheets of cloth into makeshift roofs among the soot-stained ruins. He could have sworn he heard a baby crying.

Man, I miss home. It was funny how the little things made you appreciate a world with electricity and running water. How Alissians managed to get by without Diaper Genies and infant formula, he couldn't imagine.

Their hoofbeats had not gone unnoticed by the people working out in the orchards. They crept down toward the road like nervous hares. Even left their tools behind, which said something about how much fight was left in them. Four men, two women. All of them looked to be in their thirties or forties, but the past few months had probably added a few years.

A long, low hedge separated the road from the orchard proper. Logan gave the case file a quick study while the workers trudged around it. The owner's name was Portia Mandelle. Light brown hair, slender, fair complexion. She'd have been easy to spot, if she were still around. *So much for that source.* He went to put the file into archive mode.

Which is why he didn't even see the weapons come out. Kiara gave him a static burst on the comm unit, jerking him back to reality. All six were armed to the teeth. They must have stashed their weapons behind the hedge so as not to look threatening, and like a dope he fell for it. Some of them had swords, some had spears. The one that worried him was the bowman, who'd half bent his bow and held it casually at them. It didn't waste any strength, but kept the arrow taut on the bow. *The mark of a veteran.*

"Whoa!" Logan up his hands. "We don't want any trouble."

One of the women—the taller one who held a spear like she really wanted to jab him with it—stalked forward. "What do you want, then?"

"We're looking for someone." Kiara gestured at the burned-down manor house. "Do you know what happened to the family that used to live there?"

"What d'you think happened? Folks like you rode up and burned what they couldn't steal."

"Easy, now," Logan said. "We're all friends here."

"That's to be determined. You some of the admiral's men?" the woman demanded.

"No, we're definitely not with him."

"And for what it's worth, we're not both men, either," Kiara said.

The woman's expression softened from granite

to limestone. She lowered the tip of her spear and smoothed her wild-strewn hair. There was something feminine about the gesture that didn't match her persona. No, not feminine. Genteel.

Son of a bitch, Logan thought. She's *Portia gods-damned Mandelle*.

"Those are some nice horses you got," said the bowman. He had a voice like gravel underneath a boot heel. "How 'bout you climb down nice and slow, and take the long walk back to the city?"

The other workers raised their weapons again. They eyed the horses with a feral kind of hunger.

Logan made a quick threat assessment. *The bowman's the real problem.* He could probably handle the farmers, but a trained shot with a longbow could feather him before he even got five paces. The lieutenant seemed to be considering it herself. She glanced at Logan long enough that he could flash her two quick hand signals.

False. Woman. Hopefully that was enough.

The lieutenant was cool as a cucumber as she rolled her shoulders and cast an ever-so-casual glance at Portia. Only someone who knew her, who'd served with her, would make the flash of recognition in her eyes.

"Maybe I wasn't clear," Kiara said. "We're looking for Portia Mandelle."

"Yeah, and who are you?" asked the bowman.

"Some old Felaran friends."

"Felara's a long way from here, lady," he said.

But surprise had flickered across Portia's face when Kiara spoke the code words. *Old Felaran friends* was how the company's research team signed their communiqués to Portia Mandelle. How they identified themselves when they needed something from her. It was right there in the case report—Logan had seen it himself. Count on the lieutenant to play that one straight from memory.

"Jeb, you can put down that bow," Portia said. She turned to offer Kiara a nervous smile. "Cousin! I hardly recognized you."

"*You're* Portia?" Kiara asked with just the right amount of incredulity.

"Yes."

"But you don't look anything like her."

Oh, that's just cruel. But you stick a spear in the lieutenant's face, and there was going to be a price to pay.

Portia straightened to give her a level stare. "We've had a rough autumn."

"You poor thing." Kiara tilted her head. "Why don't you tell me all about it?"

"Come up to the house, and I'll make us some tea," Portia said.

Kiara dismounted, and tossed her reins to one of the swordsmen. He was so desperate to catch them, he dropped his sword instead.

Amateurs. Hell, maybe Logan could have taken them after all.

The two women walked off arm-in-arm toward the shell of the manor house. Kiara gave him a quiet signal with her right hand: *stay alert.* The other woman scurried after them, which left Logan and the other men holding the bag. Or horses, as it were.

"Well, guess I'm not invited," he muttered. He slid off the horse and tossed his reins to the other swordsman, who managed to keep his sword but ended up holding it upside down.

But Logan couldn't blame them. He knew the grit it took to get through civil unrest. How hungry it made you. How it changed you. He guessed they hadn't had a solid meal in a long time. *I should stick around to make sure they don't eat the horses.* And the orchards needed a lot of work. So he walked up to the bowman, who seemed to be the man in charge. "Looks like you got some deadwood yet to trim."

"Enough for two lifetimes."

"Can I lend a hand?" *I never turn down a little yard work.* In his line of work, he rarely got to do anything so mundane.

The bowman eyed him up and down, as if not quite believing the sincerity of the offer. He finally decided and gave a sharp nod. "Much appreciated. We'll find you some shears."

Logan watched as Kiara and Portia disappeared into the remains of the manor house. *One asset down, a hundred to go.* That was assuming the woman would

"An aura of mystery and fear surrounds Alissia magic-users; I'm certain that's exactly how they want it."

—R. Holt, "Alissian Superstition"

CHAPTER 17

THE DROP-OFF

The *Purity* was sailing blind. Quinn didn't realize this until he came up on deck and saw how thick the fog was.

"What the hell?"

Visibility might have been ten feet, if that. He stood at the center of the ship and could just make out the rail on either side, but grayness cloaked the ocean beyond. It was like they'd sailed right into a storm cloud. The air was frigid and heavy with moisture. A dew-like sheen of condensation coated everything on deck. The cacophony of sounds that he'd grown used to—sails flapping, wood creaking, men calling out to one another—were muted. Like hearing an argument in the adjoining room at a cheap motel.

The sailors went about their work as if this were perfectly normal. Not that anyone had been particularly chatty since the funerals, but still. *Shouldn't they be a little concerned?* He made his way up to the bridge. Simeon had the wheel himself, and stared off into the grayness in front of it.

"This is some serious fog," Quinn said.

"That it is." The captain glanced down at a heavy leather-bound book in front of him. He took out a silver pocket watch, glanced at it, put it away, and made a slight turn at the wheel. Maybe five degrees or so, but it was hard to tell in the fog.

Quinn bit his tongue to keep from asking what *that* was about.

The fog fell away as suddenly as it had arrived. Sunlight bloomed on the deck, and on the azure waters beneath the ship.

"Landfall!" a sailor shouted from the crow's nest.

An island lay about a mile ahead, a few points to starboard. Seven narrow, crenellated towers stood at its center. From this distance, they looked like the spires on a tall, narrow crown, and Quinn drew in a sharp breath as he recognized them right away. This was the heart of the Alissian magical community, an island that CASE Global never even knew existed until the last mission. He'd been the one to discover it, a fact that he'd leveraged like hell when the company wanted him to return. *Sure, I found it by getting myself kidnapped, but the ends justify the means.*

Simeon changed the heading, and pointed the bow even farther away from the island.

"Are we making another stop first?" Quinn asked.

Simeon laughed. "Why, you want to go back through the fog again?"

Not really. "But aren't we . . . kind of going the long way around?"

"You don't know the half of it." The captain checked his watch again, then shouted, "'Ware the boom!"

Quinn jumped over and grabbed the rail. By the time the captain gave a warning, you generally had about three seconds to get ahold of something. He'd learned that the hard way. When he looked up again, Simeon had turned past the island by about ten degrees. *Maybe he's going blind.*

For the next two hours, Simeon zigzagged them back and forth seemingly at random. Quinn could have sworn it was about midday when they'd first emerged from the fog, but the sun still hung overhead like it hadn't moved at all. At last, they rounded the rocky breakwater that protected the harbor, and the bay of the Enclave docks spilled open before them.

There she was. The *Victoria*. Even half a mile out, she was as elegant and intimidating a ship as he'd ever seen. Simeon whistled in admiration. "She's a beauty, ain't she?"

"Can't argue with that." Quinn lowered his voice. "Hey, think you can swing close for a look?"

Simeon shook his head. "The harbormaster runs a tight operation, and she's extra fussy about any ships going too close."

If only he knew. "Well, it looks like a hell of a ship. Not as nice as the *Purity*, of course, but still."

"You're a gentleman. Dead wrong, but a gentleman."

Quinn smiled to himself, and didn't push the issue.

Simeon eased the wheel in the direction of the *Victoria*. "Reckon this wind might push us a little closer all by itself."

"Wind'll do that."

Simeon ordered the sails trimmed almost all the way back, so that the *Purity* glided across the glass-like bay with barely a wake at all. Quinn put his arms over the rail, pushing his sleeve up enough to get the high-tech bracelet clear. One little button, and he could activate the tiny high-def camera. A photo of their missing ship would rock CASE Global's world. Not to mention the fact that Captain Relling was now the Enclave's harbormaster.

Then again, these revelations would also bring up uncomfortable questions about why he didn't mention this after the last mission.

God, the ship looks pristine. Not a single barnacle marred the hull, and the sails were billowing clouds of spotless white. The wrist-camera tempted him.

That was a dangerous game. He'd assured Kiara that extraneous CASE Global "visitors" would be unwelcome here, which is the only reason he got to come alone. But if she learned about the *Victoria*, all propriety and intelligence-gathering went out the doorway.

He put his sleeve back down. "Well, you got us here," he told the captain. "Might not have been the most direct route, but here we are."

"Not fast enough for you, eh?" Simeon clapped him on the shoulder. "Tell you what. Next time you pilot a ship into a harbor controlled by magicians, you can pick the route."

"You *chose* that route?"

"I like to give 'em plenty of advance notice, if you know what I mean. They weren't expecting the *Purity* for another couple o' months."

And magicians don't like surprises. "Copy that."

The first time Quinn had seen the docks at the Enclave, he'd been shocked at just how clean they were. All of the wood had been sound, not so much as stained by the salt water. That was, what, a couple of months ago? It's funny how their spotless appearance didn't even get him to look twice.

"Reef sails!" the captain shouted. The sailors jumped to obey, and the push from the wind faded.

"Three minutes, Quinn," Simeon said.

"Hmm?"

"Three minutes until you've got to jump. Best pack up!"

"Oh, crap!" Quinn flew down to his cabin. He threw on his saddlebag, then saw his sword-belt and cursed again. *Belt, then pack, then bow and quiver.* He got it all draped over his shoulders and rattled as he ran back up to the deck. He hustled over to the bridge, doing his best to ignore the amused chortles of the crewmen. The ship was still coasting, but they were a ways off from the docks yet. It might even be a quarter mile.

He panted until he caught his breath, then glanced up at the mast. "Did you put on more sail?"

"Had to. We didn't have enough to make the dock."

"You said I'd have to jump off in three minutes!"

"More like ten, I s'pose."

"Seriously?"

"I wanted to see how fast you could do it." The captain laughed—the same booming kind of laugh his brother had. Quinn did a double take. Part of him wondered if he and Benvolio *were* really the same person. He should radio back to Mendez and check to see if the riverboat captain was still in town.

"You and Benvolio are two peas in a pod."

"Think so?" He rubbed a hand through his beard, another thing that his brother did almost the exact same way. "We don't always see eye-to-eye, I'll admit. But I'm glad he sent you to me. Probably made the difference against those marauders."

Quinn nodded. He'd just as soon not think about that part of the trip. "If you don't mind, I'll say good-bye to the crewmen."

Ten minutes was just enough time to shake hands or share a joke with the sailors on the boat. After the battle, he'd taken the time to get to know every single one of them, when he could. They'd formed a kind of bond over that, and over the loss of Timmers. The lookout had been well-liked, and since Quinn had offered to fill in for him afterward, the crew had sort of taken him in as one of their own.

A few of them could write, so Quinn told them where to send a message—a name and village in Landor where the research team regularly intercepted messages—in case any of them wanted to get in touch. It would win points with the lieutenant, who'd insisted that they begin working to rebuild the intelligence network that had crashed when Holt went rogue. You couldn't do much better than sailors on a trading galley. Sea travel was still the fastest means of non-magical transportation here, so that usually put mariners a little ahead of the curve.

He gave the address to the captain, too. "I wouldn't mind hearing from you, if you get the chance."

"Might take you up on that," Simeon said. "Any

chance you'll be looking for a berth once you're done with this? We could use you."

Has to be a joke. Quinn laughed. "You offering me a job?"

The captain gave him a serious look. "Somethin' tells me you're destined for bigger things. But if they don't pan out, I'd be happy to take you on."

"I appreciate that. But I have promises to keep, and miles to go before I sleep."

"Well said."

Thank you, Robert Frost. There was nothing better than a naive audience to make someone sound like a genius. "Tell your handsome brother thanks for me, will you? If he even exists."

Simeon winked. "He'll get the message."

"The best place a magician can be? Two steps ahead of the audience."

—Art of Illusion, April 11

CHAPTER 18

THE PRODIGAL SON

Simeon might have exaggerated how little time they had before the drop-off, but he *wasn't* kidding about Quinn having to jump. The *Purity* barely slowed as it neared the dock. Then the captain started to turn it, and was shouting at his men to raise sail. *Now or never.* He held his breath, jumped, and made the dock. He had to take a knee, but he stuck the landing. The *Purity's* crew whooped and applauded. He grinned and made a mock bow. *Still got it.*

Six other vessels were moored on the long Enclave

dock, each of them an anthill of activity. Quinn's teacher Moric had assured him that the Enclave island itself was entirely self-sufficient. Still, needs and wants were two different things. The first vessel he passed was in the process of offloading dark gray burden animals. Quinn chuckled when he recognized them.

Tioni smart mules.

A pair of women in the robes and blue sashes of upper-level students were handling the heavy lifting. They stood at the edge of the dock and chanted softly, and invisible hands lifted each mule out of the hold to the dock. A never-ending line of runners—boys and girls aged about ten or twelve—took turns walking them along the docks to the shore. It created an unusual chaos on the normally serene docks.

Captain Relling's voice rose above the din. "I'm telling you, it's the *Purity*, and she's not on the schedule." She strode down the dock at the head of a phalanx of Enclave officials.

Shit. The Enclave's harbormaster was about the last person he wanted to bump into on his glorious return. One careless slip around her, one hummed tune or pop culture reference, and she'd out him for what he was: another impostor. Both of them were playing the same deception game here. He didn't know how Relling ended up working for the Enclave, but everyone at CASE Global thought she was MIA. Presumed dead.

Maybe he'd feel her out, maybe he wouldn't, but now sure as hell wasn't the time. She was twenty yards away, and the crowd on the dock parted like the Red Sea in front of her. Even the Tioni mules edged aside. *Living up to the name, as usual.*

He set his gear down on the ship that brought the mules, hoping no one would notice. One of the animals still dangled in midair because the student-magicians were busy getting the hell out of Relling's way. Even a horse might balk at such treatment, but Tioni mules expected far better. So, of course, it started to kick and bray at around head level. A few of the dockworkers moved in to pull the animal down. Quinn hopped over to join them, which conveniently put his back to Relling as she breezed past without so much as blinking.

She didn't even notice the sword.

"Appreciate the help," one of the men told him, once they'd gotten the mule settled.

Quinn reclaimed his gear and clapped him on the shoulder. "Right back at you, pal."

The Enclave island was roughly kidney-shaped, with the harbor right in the concave center. Quinn had forgotten how goddamn hilly it was until he had to climb up to it. He paused halfway up the sand-and-seashell road to catch his breath. *Why did I have to bring all of this gear?*

The view was worth it, though. Most of the trading vessels had left the harbor. The sea had gone still with the sunset, leaving the *Victoria* perfectly framed in a bowl of glass. Like a ship in a bottle. Man, what a view. He was again tempted to break out the wrist-camera. At this distance, it might have been an Alissian vessel. But no, he couldn't leave things to chance. Especially not where Kiara and the Enclave were involved.

That's when he first thought to check the way-finder stone. He took it out, and for the first time, the thing was absolutely still. But the rock still felt warm to his touch, almost contentedly so. He hoped that didn't mean it had lost its enchantment. But maybe it was simply that there was no way to find. The stone had come home.

Probably time for me to do the same.

He hoisted his pack again and marched toward the cluster of towers north of him. Now was as good a time as any to check in with the others, so he put the comm unit on burst transmission mode.

"Quinn here, checking in."

The delay was longer this time. It was a good four minutes before the earpiece crackled with their replies.

"Bradley? Thank God!" Kiara said. "I've got the others looped in, too."

"I'll second that," Mendez added.

Chaudri spoke in the background. "Is it really Quinn? Is he all right?"

"Sorry, her earpiece fell out again," Mendez said. Then in a muffled voice, "Yeah, he's fine. Guess I owe you ten bucks."

Damn, Mendez bet against *me?*

Logan chimed in last with his usual compassion. "How the hell are you still alive?"

"You trained me pretty well," Quinn said. And he had modern tech on his side, which never hurt. "Anyway, I'm at the Enclave, just thought you should know."

"We're glad you're all right, Bradley," Kiara said. "Do you still have the network antenna?"

He fumbled with his saddlebags until he felt the oblong case. "Yes. It might have gotten a little wet."

"Get that installed at a high point where it won't be noticed. But your main priority is to find out about Holt's arcane protections, and how they can be circumvented."

"It'll take some time, but I'll start right away."

"I want daily reports on your progress," Kiara said.

"Roger that. Bradley out."

Everyone in the Enclave knew Quinn by his Landorian cover identity. Apparently there was a tiny village in northern Landor—at the base of the same mountains that held the gateway cavern—where people knew his name, had grown up with him, maybe even dated him years ago. The result of this painstakingly created fiction was that the Enclave hadn't executed him, and instead had allowed him to take quarters in the Landorian tower.

That tower loomed impossibly tall overhead as he approached. The entrance was nothing more than a dome-shaped hole in the dark, polished stone. A pair of torches lit the base of the winding staircase, which seemed to be carved right out of the rock. He skipped it and went down the hall to the ground-floor room he'd been assigned when Moric first brought him here.

Probably wanted to keep me as close to the exit as possible.

The Landorian tower had proven a stroke of luck back then. Everyone here had welcomed him as a long-lost brother, no matter the charges against him and the fact that he might be dead the next day. By the time he'd won provisional acceptance into the Enclave, it felt like a second home.

He felt a strange sense of comfort when he walked in. The smell of it—sea breeze with a hint of stone—calmed him. Yet the feeling quickly faded when he got a look around inside. The normally bustling anteroom lay in injured silence. Someone poked a head out of their door down the hallway, and quickly ducked back in. *So much for a warm welcome.*

He'd cleaned out the room before he left. Now, he paused at the door, and wondered if it was still his. He knocked four times on the stout wood. Silence answered. He pushed it open a crack. Everything looked just the same as he'd left it: narrow but surprisingly comfortable bed, wooden table and chair, and a small bookshelf built right into the wall. He hurried in and set down his pack, because why not? Possession was nine-tenths of the law.

"Well, well. The prodigal student's returned," a woman said.

He knew that voice, half from the imperious feminine tone, and half from the way he snapped to attention when he heard it. "Hello, Sella."

She stood in the doorway, which was odd. He hadn't heard her boot steps on the stone-tile floor. She wore a long robe in bright purple, her favorite color. Between that and the shock of bone-white hair, he should have spotted her a mile off.

"I wasn't sure we'd see you again," she said.

"Wasn't it you who said I needed more instruction?"

"That sounds like me." She regarded him like a bird of prey.

His hands wanted to fidget, so he shoved them into his pockets. "I think I'm making progress. But it's clear I have a lot more to learn here."

"I see. And how *did* you manage to return?"

I guess there's no harm in telling her. "I caught a ride on a ship out of Crab's Head. The *Purity*."

"In Pirea." She sniffed, almost in disdain. "I'm surprised you convinced the captain to take you."

"Please don't hold it against him, because he didn't make it easy," Quinn said. "Luckily, I had this." He pulled the amulet free from beneath his shirt.

Her eyes widened. "Where did you get that?"

"It was a gift."

She pursed her lips. "From Moric."

"He wanted me to return."

"Wayfinder stones are not meant to be worn by students."

Well, I'm not taking it off. He shrugged, and put an innocent look on his face. "I just do as I'm told around here."

She softened her glare, and even forced a smile. Which was far more frightening. "It's good to have you back, I suppose. Especially after that fool's errand we were sent on by the Prime."

"Uh, thanks."

"I assume you'll be returning to class tomorrow?"

"Absolutely."

"Moric may not have been wrong when he said you have potential."

Quinn wasn't sure he agreed, but now was not a time to show uncertainty. "He does have a way of being right about things."

Her frown deepened in a way that made him glad she didn't have her walking stick with her. Well, "walking stick" was a misnomer. She used it far more for student discipline.

"I believe I can find some time for private instruction, if you thought you could use it," she said.

What is happening right now?

Sella being nice to him was as new as it was unsettling. But when in doubt, he let the Vegas instincts take over. "And spend some more time with you?" He flashed her a smile. "How could I say no to that?"

When Quinn had first come to the Enclave—back before even CASE Global knew that it existed—Moric had been a constant companion. He'd always seemed to be *around*, and because he looked uncannily like Mr. Clean, he was easy to pick out of a crowd, too. Sella's visit was a surprise, but Moric's would feel like home.

Quinn had no sooner had that thought when someone else knocked on his door. *There he is.*

But the man at the door wasn't Moric. He was taller than Quinn, clean-shaven, with long black hair pulled into a queue down his back. And he wore an embroidered cloak that was, without a doubt, the most handsome garment Quinn had seen in this world.

"You must be Quinn," he said.

"Yes." *Man, he looks familiar.* But he couldn't place it.

"My name is Anton." He offered his hand. His tone and his bearing said *regal*.

Quinn almost shook it by instinct. *Shit, they think I'm from Landor.* He locked eyes with the man, clasped his arm, and held both for a three count. "Good to know you."

Anton betrayed no hint of surprise. "Good to know you. I'm sorry we didn't get a chance to meet after your trial."

The trial in which the Enclave nearly executed him. With a little help from Moric—not to mention the tech from CASE Global's research labs—he'd managed to persuade them that he belonged here. *Now I remember where I've seen him before.* The hawk nose and high cheekbones had been among Moric's rivals on the council. The ones who'd been *against* Quinn's acceptance into the community.

So not exactly a friend.

"I was a little busy trying not to get executed," Quinn said.

"Ah, yes." Anton gave a thin smile. "An unfortunate mistake on our part. True magical power is a rare gift, not something to be falsely claimed by the common man."

"Seems a little harsh to me."

"Surely you understand the need to protect our reputation," Anton said.

He sounded like a damn mafia boss. "Let's agree to disagree."

Something flashed in Anton's eyes, but his smile never wavered. "Of course."

No, not mafia. He's something even scarier. A politician. Quinn wished he could ask where he was from, but that would be much too forward. They tried to put the past in the past at the Enclave. "So, how can I help you?" he asked.

"I thought I might help you, actually."

"Oh? How would you do that?"

"I have a great many influential friends, both here at the Enclave and elsewhere. If there was something you needed, perhaps we could assist."

"In exchange for what?"

"Nothing at all."

Quinn gave him the dubious look. *Come on, buddy. We're both pros here.*

Anton broke eye contact and spread out his arms. "Of course, there might be a time when you could return the favor. One friend to another."

And we're back to mafia. "Aww, and here I'd hoped you were just swayed by my natural charms."

Anton laughed in a quiet, princely sort of way. "There *is* something about you. I can see why someone like Moric would believe you had magical abilities."

"Are you suggesting that I don't?" Quinn held him in a stone-cold stare. Something about Anton just rubbed him the wrong way.

"I was offering you a compliment."

No, you weren't. "What about the part where I made it snow? I assume you were there for that."

Anton pursed his lips. "An impressive display, to be sure. I've yet to figure out how you did it."

"I'm good under pressure."

"I believe that. I'm certain you'll prove your ability beyond any doubt, and we'll go on to become the best of friends."

"I can't wait," Quinn said.

Anton inclined his head, acknowledging that the conversation was about to end. "Perhaps I'll offer you something right now, asking nothing in return. A bit of advice, if you will."

"I'm all ears."

"Moric's star is falling. You'd be wise to distance yourself from him."

You wish, buddy. Moric was about the only friend Quinn had in this place, and he wasn't about to distance himself. "You know, where I come from, there's an old saying about free advice."

"What's that?"

It was Quinn's turn to smile and spread out his hands. "You get what you pay for."

"It's hard to know how much a magician should share about his tricks. I like to err on the side of secrecy."

—Art of Illusion, May 9

CHAPTER 19

VISIBLE FRACTURES

After Anton left, Quinn set out to find Moric before anyone else decided to *pop in* on his Landorian quarters. If anyone knew the nature of Holt's magic protections, it was him. Whether or not he'd share that information with someone he considered a student was a harder question to answer, but Quinn had to start laying some groundwork.

The Pirean tower stood slightly away from the other six spires, much like the nation itself. Quinn hustled across the wide green space that set it apart. The lawns here were perfectly manicured, though it occurred to him that he'd never seen a single gardener or maintenance worker. It was like walking on a golf course, or a baseball outfield. Forget precious metals and fossil fuels: if CASE Global figured out a way to sell this grass on Earth, they'd make a killing.

He watched two little girls play some kind of game with a stick-and-hoop across the lawn. One rolled it, and the other would try to throw the stick through it before it fell. When her first throw missed, she made a strange little gesture with her arm, and the stick flew back to her outstretched hand like there was a string tied to it.

Hard to believe the things they take for granted here.

The Pirean tower was just as tall as the others, which is to say hundreds of feet. They didn't so much as sway in the wind, so Quinn figured that they were all the same hard unyielding stone as the Landorian tower. Yet when he got close to this one, the entire thing seemed to be made of *wood*.

"Oh, *come on.*"

He had to touch it himself to be sure. Damn, it definitely was wood. Polished smooth with the passage of time, sure, but he could feel the grain of it. How old was this place? The bones of it were more than ancient. They were deep, too.

This tower had an actual door, a wooden one

with a thick iron ring for a handle. He pulled it open, half expecting a loud groaning and creaking. Instead, the door whispered open on well-oiled hinges. *Of course.*

Despite the plain exterior, the inside was cheerily lit with glass lanterns that hung on chains from the ceiling. A cluster of men and women sat together at a long wooden table, sharing an early meal. The aroma of spicy fish and warm bread was like a siren's call. Quinn's feet carried him toward them, Moric temporarily forgotten. He couldn't have fought it if he wanted to.

"Quinn?"

Quinn turned to find a familiar face, a young fire magician he'd met his first time to Alissia. "Hey, Leward."

Leward's grin nearly split his face in half. "When did you get back?"

"Just now."

"We were just about to eat. Man, you've got great timing."

Quinn chuckled. "All magicians do."

There were six or seven people there, Pireans he hadn't yet met. Leward made hasty introductions. Then they ushered him into a chair and shoved a plate in front of him before he could so much as protest. Two whole-roasted fish as thick as cigars were the centerpiece, flanked by boiled clams and a pile of marble-sized sea potatoes. The savory spices touched his nose, and all will to resist just melted away. *Time to take a page out of Logan's book.* "I guess I could eat."

Leward found a wide serving spoon and loaded his plate for him. "I hope you can handle spicy food."

"Bring it on."

Leward scooped out a little bit of everything for him. Quinn found a spoon and dug in right away, which seemed like the polite thing to do. The food *was* spicy, but it was hot and flavorful and as satisfying as anything he'd ever tasted. *God bless the Pireans.* How was it that the poorest of Alissia's nations still managed to be the most hospitable? He pondered this while the din of soft conversation resumed around him. He could feel their eyes on him, though, while he focused on the food. Nothing hostile, of course. It felt more like the crowd in Vegas, when he'd stop by to shake some hands in the casino after a show. A feeling of *celebrity*.

After weeks of ball-busting by Logan and company, he rather enjoyed it.

"I'm glad you're here," Leward whispered finally. "We don't get a lot of visitors."

Quinn shook his head. "With food like this, I don't know why."

"Oh, you like it?"

He pointed down at his nearly empty plate. "It's the best thing I've had in a while."

Leward shrugged. "Everyone's walking on eggshells around here lately. Makes it hard to find dinner guests."

Quinn slathered a dark brown roll with butter and took a bite. The butter had a stronger flavor than he'd have liked—they got their milk from goats—but it was still heavenly. "Trust me, man, it's their loss."

"So what happened to you on the—" Leward cut himself off to make sure no one was openly eavesdropping. "On the mission? I woke up and you were gone."

Leward had been part of an Enclave contract assignment to escort Kiara's party back to Felara. That was a little bit of insurance arranged by Holt, to make sure his former colleagues got the hell out of Alissia without any detours.

"Sorry about that. Had to take care of some things." And by things, he meant the mercenaries who'd been trying to kill the rest of his team. "I'm actually looking for Moric."

"You came to the right place."

"He's around?"

"Should be here at any second." Leward gestured with his fork. "See? Told you."

A man stalked energetically into the anteroom. His head was perfectly bald, either by misfortune or choice, and smooth as a baby's bottom. He looked downright exhausted, but his smile was the kind reserved for close friends. Quinn nearly jumped up and greeted him like a fangirl, but decided to play it slow. He'd been back for hours, and no less than two other council members had found him first. *Time to have a little fun.*

He let his fork tumble to the floor, and ducked out of view to get it. Moric was pulling up a chair right across from him when he popped back into view. He wiped the fork off, took another bite, and savored the open-jawed astonishment on the bald man's face.

"*Quinn?*"

"Oh. Hey, Moric."

Moric rubbed his eyes, as if he thought it was some kind of optical illusion. "Quinn!"

"Yep, still me."

"How did you get here?"

Quinn plucked the leather cord out from beneath his shirt, and held it up for Moric to see. *No need to brandish the stone here.* He'd know what was at the other end anyway.

"Well, I'll be damned." Moric studied him for a moment. "Something tells me we need to talk."

About so many things. But Quinn gestured at the chair Moric was holding. "Let's eat first. This is too good to miss."

Quinn and Moric excused themselves toward the end of the meal to take a walk on the green outside the Pirean tower. The trees cast long shadows on the grass.

"You surprised me in there," Moric said. "I was beginning to think that you weren't coming back."

"I told you I would, didn't I?"

"Saying and doing are two different things."

Quinn laughed. "Fair enough. But I was serious about coming back. Being here, learning from you . . . it's important to me."

Moric studied his face. "There's something different about you."

More than I can possibly tell you. Quinn flashed a grin. "Think so?"

"What's happened? Tell me everything."

"Well, I finished the mission. Happy to report that everybody got home safe." As for what had happened after that, on the Earth-side of the gateway . . . well, no need to get into that.

"Excellent! Richard will be pleased."

I don't know about that. "I'm not saying it was easy. There was a moment when I wasn't sure I'd be able to save them. That I might get killed myself."

Moric gasped. "Oh, tell me you had a breakthrough."

Quinn smiled. "I called lightning from the sky. And on my way here, I did something in the water."

Moric laughed and grabbed his shoulder. "I knew it! Gods be good, I knew you had it in you."

"It's still not something I can just *do*, though," Quinn said. "Right now, if you asked me to use magic, I wouldn't be able to make a spark." Not without cheating, at least.

"Even so, Quinn, this is huge. You're a grown man coming into magic for the first time, which means that one of our fundamental assumptions about the ability was wrong. More importantly, it means I was right to expand our recruitment efforts beyond children."

"Glad I could help out."

Moric picked up on the sarcasm, but shrugged it away. "I put my reputation on the line when I sponsored you. Between you and me, I needed a win."

Quinn looked around to make sure no one else was there. A few of the Pireans had wandered out for their own stroll in the open space, but they were well out of earshot. "You want to tell me what's happened since I've been gone?"

Moric's smile fell away. "Noticed a change, did you?"

"It's not every day I have council members dropping by my chambers. Other than you, I mean."

"Who came?"

"Sella showed up before I'd even set my bag down. Anton came right on her heels."

"Anton." He said the name in a tone that lacked any emotion.

"Yeah. That guy gives me the creeps."

Moric wrinkled his brow at this expression. Maybe it hadn't translated.

"Something seems off about him," Quinn said.

"Ah."

"He walks around like he owns the place. Is he a prince or something?"

"Even if he were, that would be a thing of the past," Moric said carefully.

"Come on, man. Don't tell me you don't know."

Moric paused. "I suppose you'd have found this out on your own eventually, but he's from a family of Caralissian nobles."

Quinn laughed. "A wine baron? That is *too* good."

He'd been reading up on Caralissian wine, more out of fascination than anything. Holt had estimated that something like ninety percent of the produce grown in Caralis went to the royal vintners. The queen and her pet nobles made a killing on the wine, and the rest of the country starved. Now that he thought about it, that fit Anton perfectly.

"Remember how I said that some council members see things differently than I do?" Moric asked.

"Ah, yes. The 'friendly rivals' speech. I remember."

"In retrospect, that might have been too soft of a description. Anton and his minions are my adversaries."

"Over what?"

"The Enclave's role in Alissia," Moric said.

"I didn't think you had much of a role."

"Exactly. Our strategy has been to avoid attention and political entanglements. We have our quiet arrangements with the leaders of some nations, but little more."

to say if it was a man or a woman, because they all had long hair—tumbled over and out of view. Timmers took down someone farther aft. Quinn expected them to scatter, but the gaps in the line were filled almost right away. Someone took up pounding the drum he'd just silenced. And the marauding ship was even closer now.

Then as suddenly as they'd begun, the drums fell silent. Everyone on the deck of the marauding ship drew weapons. The captain had to throw the tiller aside, or else risk being rammed. The deck of the other ship loomed. Even in the crow's nest, it seemed so. Quinn and Timmers were shooting about three times a minute, each. The marauders seemed to have no end.

Then the grappling hooks sailed over. The mast shook as the two hulls ground against one another. Wood creaked and screeched. Then marauders were vaulting over the rail, boarding them, and the deck descended into chaos. Quinn had half emptied his quiver before he even knew it. Then it was two-thirds empty. Simeon's men were in a locked, desperate struggle to repel the first wave. The Marundi fought with a crazed fervor, screaming like wild animals. *They're insane.*

And they were starting to take notice of the archers in the crow's nest.

A crossbow bolt slammed into the mast right next

Such as Holt. "What does Anton want to do?"

"He believes the Enclave should wield its own power in Alissia. Independent of the other nations."

It honestly didn't sound that bad. "But you think it's a mistake," Quinn said.

"I think he underestimates the world's tolerance for magicians."

Quinn debated whether or not to tell him about Anton's free advice. Maybe it was too soon to go there. Moric disliked the man enough already. "Gotta be honest, I'm not sure we're going to become best friends."

Moric chuckled. "It won't be the last offer of friendship you'll receive, now that you've proven your abilities."

"I'm not sure I've *proven* them."

"Weren't there any witnesses?"

There had been a ton of them—Kiara, Chaudri, Logan, Mendez, the Swedish guy . . . not to mention the half-dozen smugglers who'd ambushed them. *Can't exactly issue a summons for them.* "Not really."

"Tell me you at least had the wayfinder stone on you."

Quinn touched his fingers to the amulet. "Yeah. I haven't taken it off since you gave it to me. Why?"

Moric paused, and looked away. "I may not have been entirely honest about what it does."

"It worked just fine to get me here. And the ship's

captain who brought me seemed to recognize it, too."

"Of course it did, that's right there in the name. And they're a sort of symbol for our people when we're on official business. But the wayfinder stone is more than that."

Quinn felt a cold sliver of dread slide down his back. "What do you mean?"

"Don't you find it curious that I was wearing it on our mission in the first place? No one knows their way back to the Enclave better than I do."

"I didn't really think about it."

"Wayfinder stones are the eyes and ears of the Enclave."

"You're talking about this, right?" Quinn held up the stone so Moric could see it.

"Indeed," Moric said. "With the right enchantment, we can see everything it's seen. Hear everything it's heard."

"You don't say." It took all of Quinn's training to keep his face neutral. *Jesus, where has that thing been?* The gateway, the island facility. The Bellagio in Vegas. Mission briefings with Kiara and the others, covering all of the intel they'd collected on the Enclave. He closed his fist around it, and didn't realize how hard until the points jabbed his palm.

"I suppose I should have mentioned that when I gave it to you," Moric said.

You think? "Eh, I wouldn't have believed you anyway." He furrowed his brow. "You know, the only thing is, when I had the breakthrough, the stone was tucked under my shirt. I don't like having it out in the open."

"Are you sure?"

"Pretty sure, yeah."

"Well, we could have a look, just to be certain."

"No!" It came out a little more forcefully than he'd intended. "It's just . . . I'd rather prove it myself. To you, and to everyone here."

Moric knitted his bushy eyebrows together. "I thought you said you couldn't do it on command."

"Not unless my life is on the line," Quinn said. "And even then, it's sort of accidental."

Moric stopped abruptly and sat cross-legged on the ground. "Let's try something."

Quinn looked around, suddenly uncomfortable. Practicing in private was one thing, but anyone could see them out here. *My lack of ability is public enough.* "Here?"

"Humor me." Moric gestured to the ground in front of him.

Quinn sat on the trampled grass.

"Remember this?" Moric held out a hand between them. A ball of blue-white light appeared above it, flickering and hissing like a wet log on a fire.

Quinn drew in a sharp breath. He'd forgotten the

thrill of seeing true Alissian magic up close. "How can I forget?"

"Go on, touch it," Moric said.

"I'm good, thanks." *It's a little hard to do card tricks with charred fingers.*

"It won't burn you," Moric assured him.

Quinn put his hand toward it, and indeed felt no heat. If anything, the ball of light cast a chill into the air around it. He waved his fingers through it once, then again. "What is it?"

"Light, without substance. As simple a thing as exists in the world." He let the ball wink out. The after-image played across Quinn's vision.

"Now, you try it," Moric said.

Quinn took a breath, and tried to will the sphere of light back into existence. Of course nothing happened. He might as well try to make the sun rise. "I don't even know what I'm supposed to be doing."

"Picture the ball of light in your mind. Open yourself to the *possibility* of creating it on your own."

Quinn could picture the ball of light, no problem. The image of it was still burned into his retina. But the deep-down warmth of magical power eluded him. *Might as well make some conversation.* "I don't suppose we got any more jobs from the Valteroni Prime?"

"Why do you ask, when you should be focusing on the task at hand?"

Quinn put up his hands in mock surrender. "I'm

focusing, I promise." Not that it would do any good. "I'm just curious, since I helped out on the last job."

"Which I'm still in trouble for. The only positive result was that you had a breakthrough."

And my friends didn't die. Quinn couldn't resist a dig. "I'm sure the Prime pays well."

"Valteron is good for it. Now, *concentrate*, please."

Quinn gave it another shot, but knew it was a lost cause. Even if he weren't exhausted, true magic just wasn't his to command. He sighed. "It's not working."

Moric nodded and stood. "You should get some rest. We'll try again tomorrow."

"I've got class with Sella in the morning. Maybe that'll help."

"That's the advanced class."

Quinn didn't like the way Moric's eyebrow went up. "So she said. Should I be worried?"

"Not at all." Moric grinned, and clapped him on the shoulder. "You're a brave man, Quinn. Don't let anyone say different."

"Port towns in Alissia are simultaneously the most dangerous and most exciting."

—R. Holt, "My Time with Tioni Cutpurses"

CHAPTER 20

BAY OF ROCKS

Veena Chaudri was in charge of her first mission ever. That's what Julio had said. *In charge.* When Quinn had been with them, they'd been a sort of committee. She'd provided the cultural input, Julio the security, and Quinn the unpredictability. Sure, Kiara had given most of her instructions directly to Mendez. But now he was letting her call the shots.

Their task was to get a fix on the admiral of the Valteroni fleet. Which should have been the easiest thing in the world, given the size of that fleet and the fact that he was in charge of it. Of course, start looking for something and that's when you can't find it.

She'd arranged passage on a shore-sweeper, the most efficient of Alissian vessels. Single-masted with a removable boom, it could switch to oar power to cut across the shallow water flats that often stretched miles beyond the Alissian shoreline. Julio was off making a report to Kiara, so Veena came up on deck and stood at the rail. They were under wind power right now, running south and almost straight downwind. The sound of the churning water under the bow, the smell of the sea, and the tickle of the wind on the back of her neck were a hypnotic combination.

"Ah, there you are," Julio called.

He joined her at the rail and put his arm around her. He'd insisted on posing as a married couple for this trip. For security reasons, of course, but he seemed to be having a lot of fun with it. Too much fun, but she didn't tell him to dial it back, either. She could feel her face heating. "Yes, here I am." She glanced around to make sure no one was within earshot. "Any news?"

"Nothing about the admiral."

That meant there was some other sort of news, but he'd deliver it in their own time. So much for spouses not keeping secrets from one another. "It's a little worrisome that the Valteroni fleet has withdrawn. They normally play a sort of policing role."

"When the cat's away, the mice'll play. As Bradley found out."

"Should we be worried ourselves?"

"Not in a shore-sweeper, no. Any ships start to hone in on us, and the captain can take her shallow."

Unless the marauders had a shore-sweeper themselves. She made a mental note to review Dr. Holt's file on Alissian piracy.

Julio took his arm away, and the place it had rested felt cold. "What do you want to do if the next port has no sign of the admiral or his fleet?"

"Then I suppose we'll head to Valteron."

"Going to turn into a regular party down there."

"We should avoid Valteron City, though. Dr. Holt will have eyes everywhere."

He grunted. "The lieutenant and Logan are working on that."

"How?"

"Trying to reclaim some of our human assets. We should be doing the same, once we've located the admiral."

"I'm not nearly as good with people as he was," she said.

"Don't sell yourself short. You can work a room as well as anyone. Even Bradley said so."

"He did?" She could feel the blush on her cheeks. "Well, I'm trying my best."

"You're much prettier than Holt. That's a good start."

"Oh, stop it," she said.

"Don't be afraid to use it. That's all I'm saying."

"All right. I'll try."

He put his arm back around her. "But not until we get off this ship, *comprende*? I got a reputation to uphold."

Veena had to admit that there were worse things than playing house with Julio. Maybe she should just live for the *moment*, rather than the man who was half a world away. She turned and smiled at him.

Of course, that's right when the lookout piped up. "Port ahead!"

Bay of Rocks was an aptly named city at the border of Landor and Pirea. Ships from both nations had free rein to dock wherever they could find room. Vessels jostled for position while they navigated the maze of rock formations for which the bay was named. Some of the delicate-looking structures were hundreds of feet tall, but only a few feet thick. How they withstood the relentless winds and battering waves was a mystery that CASE Global's consulting geologists had yet to solve.

The coast-cutter had a narrow enough profile to slip through some of the tighter gaps between the rocks. At the moment, the captain had them pointed through one that couldn't have been three feet wider than the ship itself.

"Jesus, is he going to make it?" Julio whispered.

"I hope so."

He turned away from the water. "I can't watch." His face looked a little pale, and suddenly Veena remembered why. He'd come over from Cuba on a makeshift raft at the age of twelve, and told her he'd avoided the ocean ever since. He probably couldn't swim.

"Don't worry," she said. "Coast-cutters are just about unsinkable."

He took a breath and turned back around. His knuckles were white around the rail. "How long till we get to shore?"

"Half an hour, if the wind holds."

"Why isn't he using the oars?"

"If he does that, any ship under wind power has the right of way."

"Really?"

"Rules of the water."

Even without the oars, the coast-cutter slipped through the heavy bay traffic like a slalom skier. Fifteen minutes after they'd cleared the maze of rocks, they were dockside.

"Let's get off this death trap," Julio said.

Veena *tsked* him, but let him guide her to the gangplank while the crew secured the boat to the docks. Their ship had squeezed between a wide trader's cog and some kind of longboat, with no more than a yard of space on either side. The captain certainly knew his business. She paid him twice the usual fare—an unspoken request for discretion—and then she and Julio disembarked.

There hadn't been room for their horses on the coast-cutter. They'd arrive in about a week on a trading cog whose captain had been a little too eager to take their silver. Which meant, of course, that they might not arrive at all. Julio had tagged the ship so they could track her down, if it came to that.

She stuck close to Julio as they made their way among the crowds on the dock, making mental tallies of the nationalities, genders, and occupations as best she could. It was too much even for her to keep track of, though. Not without her notebook, and Julio seemed determined to make a beeline for the shore without stopping for anything.

They'd hardly set foot on solid ground when he took her hand. "Gods, that feels good."

"Look at you, using the plural and everything."

"I'm just glad to be back on land." He pulled her in close. "Come here, you!" He wrapped his arms around her.

The sudden closeness set her heart pounding. It was so fast, so unexpected. She enjoyed it more than she should have.

Right up until he whispered, "We've got a tail."

"What?"

"Stay with me, and be ready to move when I say."

Gods above, she didn't know which upset her

more: the fact that someone was following them, or that the hug was just a cover for it. Julio's hand wrapped around hers, strong and reassuring. He led her away from the water at a ridiculously casual pace.

"Are you sure?" she whispered. She hadn't notice anything suspicious. Then again, it was crowded, and she'd always scored poorly on the company's counter-surveillance training exercises.

"One hundred percent," Julio said.

"What's he look like?"

"Dark beard, slight build, and dressed like a dock-worker. Other one's heavier, also bearded, bit of a pot belly on him."

"There are *two* of them?"

"Yep. Trying to be subtle about it, but I think they're amateurs. I made 'em too easily."

She had to remind herself to breathe. Why would anyone be following them? Julio kept her close enough that she was right up against him. With his other hand, he loosened his sword in its scabbard. The weapon was a short sword, company issue. Titanium endoskeleton, folded steel outer layer, and an edge that would never need sharpening. She had the long-sword, which would be tough to use in close quarters. She'd just as soon avoid a fight if at all possible.

"Why don't we just run for it?" she asked. "The street's so crowded, I'm sure we could lose them."

"I want to know why they're following us. Don't you?"

"Not really," she muttered.

"See that alley up ahead?"

"Yes." It was about twenty yards distant, a narrow dark space between two street-houses. Houses in Bay of Rocks bore an uncanny resemblance to the rock formations: they were narrow-framed and two or three stories tall. The clay-tile roofs were hell on the city streets, as the tiles fell to shatter on the cobble-stones with some regularity.

"I want you to walk down there," Julio said. "See if you can draw off one of them."

"And then what?"

"Then stall him, until I get back."

"Where are you going?"

"Just stall him. Stay safe." Julio gave her a little shove, and ducked into the crowd.

Veena took a breath and plunged into the alley, her boots scraping against shattered tile pieces. It was darker than it should have been for midday. She tested her sword to make sure it was loose in the scab-bard, but left it there. Let them think that she was unarmed, and less of a threat.

She was fifteen steps down the alleyway when she heard the boot steps. They crunched on the broken tile pieces just as hers had. She gave it a few more sec-onds. Then she turned. Put her hand on the sword hilt, because it was time to let the pretense drop.

The man in the alley was just like Julio had described him—dark beard, slender build. He halted in midstep when she turned around, and his eyes went to her sword.

She tightened her grip on it. "What do you want?"

"Are you . . ." He let his voice fade as he glanced left and right. "Are you *Veena*?"

She was afraid to answer. "Why do you want to know?"

"Because I've got a message for you."

She heard a sound from somewhere out on the street. A shout, and then the brief clash of steel. Then the thud of something hitting the cobblestones. *I hope it's not Julio.* "From whom?"

"From the man who worked out the timing of the coastal tides in midwinter."

Gods, that was Dr. Holt. She realized she was holding her breath, and forced herself to exhale. "What's the message?" she asked. She took two steps toward him.

The man seemed to sense her eagerness, and backed out to the mouth of the alley. Then he disappeared in a blur of arms and legs.

"Wait! It's all right!" She ran out to the street.

Julio was already on his knees over the fallen man, who lay on his back and seemed to be dazed. He hardly seemed to notice the kiss of a dagger at his throat.

"Julio, please. They're not enemies."

"How do you know?"

"Holt sent them."

"He *what*?" Julio pressed the dagger more firmly against the man.

"Easy!" She put a hand on his shoulder. "He just said he had a message."

"What kind of message?" Julio demanded. He directed this at the bearded man, who mumbled something unintelligible in reply. "What?"

"It's in my belt pouch," the man said. He started to fumble at the leather satchel at his waist.

"Don't move!" Julio hissed. He looked up at Veena and gestured with his head.

She knelt beside him and flipped open the pouch. There was nothing inside but a roll of parchment, sealed with a blob of red wax. She took it out gently, and gasped when she saw what had pressed down the seal. She recognized the ring, but she hadn't seen it since the day before Holt disappeared through the gateway. "You really did have a message from him."

She was suddenly aware that people were staring. This was too public a place. Being an innocent passerby to a mugging was one thing, but Julio looked like he might cut the man's throat then and there. No one in Bay of Rocks wanted to be witness to that.

"Please, let the man up," she said.

Julio looked at her like she was crazy, but he took a

breath and climbed off the man. He even pulled him up to his feet, and brushed him off while whispering a stern warning about "funny business."

Then he flashed a smile at the staring passersby. "No problem here. Keep walking."

They stared at him for a minute, shrugged, and moved on. No blood spilled, no big deal. It was just that kind of town.

The messenger dusted himself off and backed away a few steps. "Where's Lewis?"

"Who's that?" Julio asked.

"My friend. He was following you a minute ago."

"Heavyset guy, with breath like old fish?" Mendez asked.

"Yeah, that's him."

Julio gestured down the street. "He's taking a nap against the side of that row house. He, um, fell."

Veena wanted to know so badly what the message said, but she knew this messenger wasn't going to stick around any longer than he had to. "When did you get this?"

The man looked half-ready to bolt, and put another foot of space between himself and Julio. But he heard her and answered, "Must be a few months back. Richard's an old friend. Asked us to keep an eye out for you."

"How did you recognize me?"

"He showed us your likeness. A hand drawing, in

charcoal." The man rubbed the back of his head with one hand, looked at it, and frowned at Julio. "Told us you'd be the dark-haired beauty who answered to Veena."

She smiled. "Well, I can't argue with that."

Veena sat in a seaside tavern overlooking the Bay of Rocks, and read the letter yet another time. It was Dr. Holt's handwriting for certain—she'd read so many of his journals over the past fifteen years, she knew it as well as she knew her own. The *S* was her favorite. It started above the following letter like a lower case *F*, and glided across the line to end up twice as tall as the others.

It was coded, of course, using a substitution cipher they developed years ago. But the letters were no less lovely for it. She'd gotten good enough at the cipher that she could practically read the letter in real time.

She still wasn't sure why she'd told Julio otherwise. Maybe because he'd have insisted that she translate it for him, and the contents were only going to make him angry. Or maybe because she was still considering what Dr. Holt had said.

> *Veena,*
>
> *If you've found this letter, it means that my plan—a plan I set in motion months ago—has succeeded. I'm beyond the company's reach, and you've*

taken charge of the research team as you were meant to do.

You must think me horrible for what I've done, but if you knew the truth, you'd understand. I dare not explain it to you here. Come to me in person, and I'll tell you everything. Then you'll see that what I'm doing is in the best interest of Alissia and its people.

A war is coming, Veena. Before long, the company will be forced to show its hand, and demonstrate exactly how far they're willing to go to protect their investment. They will use you as they used me for so many years. And you could be a powerful weapon for them, because you know me better than anyone else.

Unless . . .

What if you joined our side instead? The two of us together would be a force to be reckoned with. Strong enough, perhaps, to circumvent what the company intends to do. Every captain in the Valteroni fleet is under standing orders to bring you to Valteron City. All you need to do is ask. And drop your comm unit in the sea before you arrive.

Think about it, Veena. For me. For Alissia.

Yours,

R.

The letter was dated a week after Dr. Holt had gone rogue, when Kiara and Logan were still in Vegas recruiting Quinn for the first mission. How could he have *known*? He'd written this before he'd even reached Valteron. Before the Prime had died, perhaps.

He was four moves ahead once again, and operating at a level Veena could hardly even follow.

Julio came in from the street, where he'd been having a "polite conversation" with the two men who'd delivered Dr. Holt's message. Both of them were a little shaken, particularly the one who'd been unconscious in the shadow of a nearby building.

"Are the men all right?" she asked. Part of her wished that she'd seen Julio in action. *The things he must be able to do with his hands.*

"Better now that I paid 'em off." He slid into the booth across from her, and gave the barkeep a signal that required no translation. A finger raised, and then pointed down at the table in front of him.

"Do you think they'll report back to Dr. Holt?"

"Not sure. Smart money is on them working for both of us, and hitting everyone up for more juice every time."

"Would they do that?"

He grinned. "It's what I'd do."

He had a nice smile. His mind worked in straightforward ways, and she liked that about him.

Dr. Holt didn't smile nearly as much, and his mind seemed to be everywhere at once—traversing the Landorian Plateau, or crossing some Tioni marsh on a smart mule. She'd always known that Alissia was his first love. But his words echoed in her head. *You know me better than anyone else. All you need to do is ask . . . for me.* Could he finally have room in his heart for something else? *Someone* else?

Julio was so sweet, and so strong. So *new.* Dr. Holt was anything but. *And yet . . .*

"Any luck with the note?" Julio asked.

"So far, it's a mystery." She was careful not to meet his eyes.

"You haven't cracked it?"

"No."

His eyes narrowed. "A little strange that he'd leave you a message that you can't read."

"Not as much as you'd think. He likes puzzles."

Julio didn't look convinced.

"I'll keep working on it," she promised.

"Every moment of contact with Alissian natives is a chance for them to discover our origins."

—R. Holt, "Primer on Alissian Cultural Immersion"

CHAPTER 21

INTERCEPTION

Logan had to admit, Richard Holt's dominance of Valteron was a daunting thing to behold. The man had spent fifteen years building an intelligence network that the KGB would admire. Most of his sources had unwittingly defected with him when he went AWOL through the gateway. Logan and Kiara's week-long surveillance of Valteron City had begun to explain how he'd done it.

Every morning like clockwork, a series of mounted riders left the palace by the main gate. Maybe a third of them rode across the broad plaza and down to the waterfront, where they handed dispatches to waiting coast-cutters that cast off immediately. The others rode off north or northeast along the major travel routes that led out of Valteron.

"Here they come again," Logan muttered into his comm unit. He'd gotten a job on one of the masonry crews working on the city wall. It had always been more landmark than barrier; Valteron was powerful enough not to feel threatened by its northerly neighbors. The new Prime's improvement plans were allegedly laid out in a fifty-page document that had even the city's master masons sweating like day-one apprentices.

They'd put out a call for laborers, and Logan's arms were his credentials. He didn't mind the work—it was better than sitting on his hands all day wondering what Holt was up to. And it gave him the perfect excuse to stake out the gate all day to monitor the hoof traffic. Kiara was in position on the Valteron City pier, posing as a fisherwoman and marking the colors of the message ships. She hadn't offered to flip for it.

The comm unit crackled in his year. "Logan?"

"Yes, Lieutenant?"

"You're hammering right next to the microphone."

He caught himself on the backswing. "Whoops! Sorry about that." He chuckled. "Got a little carried away."

"How many?"

He counted the riders as they went past. The message cases made them easy to pick out from the regular traffic . . . *six, seven, eight, nine.* The mounts had grown less impressive with each passing day, and these were the worst yet. He could have sworn a few were plow horses. No wonder Holt was buying horses—he'd be down to Tioni mules before long.

"I make nine, over."

Silence answered him.

"Nine riders," he repeated. "Did you copy?"

"Copy," Kiara said. "Sorry. Caught a fish."

"*Another* one?"

"The bite's on today."

"How about we trade jobs tomorrow?"

"I'll take that under consideration."

Logan had an idea of how that would go. "What's the ship count this morning?"

"Six."

"Well, he's keeping busy, isn't he?"

No response.

"Lieutenant?"

Oh, come on. "You caught another fish again, didn't you?"

"I told you the bite was on," Kiara said. "And yes, he's keeping busy. Let's find out why."

They set their ambush about a mile northeast of Valteron City. The northern route seemed to draw more of Holt's daily messengers, but it was too well-traveled. This road led primarily to Caralis, Valteron's chief economic rival. Caralissian wine was an economy all its own, and it was no accident that they only transported it by land. Shipping by sea would mean Valteron got a piece of the action. If that ever happened, it was all over.

Even so, Holt had sources everywhere. Logan figured this road was as good as any.

"I still think we should have tried intercepting a coast-cutter," Logan said. "At least those are easy to spot."

"They're also crewed with twenty able-bodied men."

He snorted. "Oarsmen. Not fighting men."

"A sea action has too many variables," Kiara said. "The wind can change, and you never know when a Valteroni patrol will stop by. Or pirates, for that matter."

But that's not the real reason, is it? Truth be told, he suspected the lieutenant avoided the ocean whenever she could, because of losing her sister to it. She'd taken the ship out of Bayport on the first mission, of course, but they were trailing Holt and knew he'd gone that way, so there was really no choice. They'd had more options this time around.

And when the lieutenant could choose solid ground over water, she would.

Logan stood atop a wooded ridge about twenty yards off the road. It curved back on itself to the south, and enough of the trees had lost their leaves that he could make out traffic on the other side. "Think I hear something."

He saw movement through the trees, but it was too slow for a courier. Even on the mounts they'd been forced to use of late. "False alarm. Just a horse cart."

Kiara stood up from where she'd been laying sprawled out near her horse. This was the medieval version of woman-with-broken-down-car, a tried-and-true classic. The idea was that a courier might pause long enough to help out. Whether it worked or not depended on the man with the message case.

The horse cart swung into view, and its driver—a farmer in homespun woolens and a straw hat—gave them a friendly wave. Judging by the empty cart, he'd done well at the city markets. No surprise there. Even with Holt's efforts, there were too many refugees and not enough food. The farmers within riding distance of Valteron City had to be making a killing.

The ones that hadn't seen their fields burn, at least.

As friendly as this one was, he didn't linger. If anything, he chivvied the tired-looking horse to pick up the pace. Not that Logan could blame him. In this part of the world, if you passed two well-armed people waiting by the road, you kept on riding and didn't look back.

He was so busy watching the horse cart that he nearly missed the cloud of dust that rose from the direction the man was headed. "Uh-oh."

"What?" Kiara demanded.

"Dust cloud to the northeast. Must be a big group."

Kiara clocked it and frowned, more in irritation than concern. "Probably just another grain caravan."

She's probably right. Wagon trains had been rolling into Caralis for months. Holt had either called in a lot of favors or emptied the treasury. Maybe both, because the food kept on coming. Judging by the look of most of the citizens, they needed it. So many of them had fled when the fighting started and probably not eaten since.

It wasn't a wagon train.

The first outriders galloped into view. The fact that there *were* outriders told Logan that this wasn't a regular caravan. One of them spotted him and Kiara, and turned on a dime to ride hard back the way he'd come. The other one loosened his sword in its scabbard, but didn't draw. Instead, he unlashed a horse bow from his saddle and nocked an arrow. He trotted away slowly, watching Logan the whole time.

These guys were pros, and that told him exactly

what was coming. *Shit.* "Gotta be a Caralissian wine train."

Guarding a Caralissian wine shipment was the highest-paying mercenary gig in Alissia. They only hired the best. Logan knew that too well, having engaged a group of them on a lonely country road fourteen years ago. Not by choice, not that it made any difference. He'd watched some of his best-trained soldiers slaughtered like cattle, and almost been killed himself. His hand tightened on his sword grip with the memory.

"Will they see us as a threat?" Kiara asked.

"They see *everyone* as a threat. These guys don't screw around."

Hooves from the southwest. *And there's the courier.* Logan didn't even have to look. The hoof beats had the cadence of a long horseman moving at speed, and Murphy's Law guaranteed he wouldn't show up until an armed party of mercenaries happened to be approaching.

"What do you want to do?" he asked.

"How long until the caravan gets here?"

"Maybe three, five minutes."

Kiara backed her horse out into the road, and positioned herself to look like she'd been thrown. She even took the clip out of her hair, so it fell in disarray around her face. She brushed it aside enough to see him. "Well? Get in position."

"Right." He ducked down into a natural hollow

that was half-concealed beneath a tangle of fallen timber. *Ten seconds.* He checked the pneumatic pistol and flipped off the safety as the courier swung into view. Kiara groaned and tried to sit up, as if still rattled by the fall. She yanked the reins without warning, and her mare whinnied in protest.

The horseman spotted her and sawed his reins. "Whoa! Are you hurt, m'lady?"

Kiara muttered something unintelligible. She came up to her hands and knees, then collapsed flat on the ground. She'd really missed her calling on the stage. The act was so convincing Logan had to fight the instinct to run and help her himself.

Now's the moment we see what kind of man he is.

The courier glanced around, lifted his reins, then sighed. He slid out of the saddle and led the horse over to her. Logan eased down into a prone shooting position, braced his arm, and took aim. *A good man, then. Sorry about this . . .*

Pfft.

The dart struck him right in the back the neck. A textbook shot. The man cursed and swatted at it like he'd been stung. He found the dart and pulled it loose. His forehead wrinkled in puzzlement. Then he collapsed like a rag doll.

Kiara was already moving, and caught him around his shoulders just before he face-planted. She grunted under the weight. Logan scrambled up and ran over to help her. They eased the man onto his back. Kiara ran over and pulled her horse clear of the road. The dust cloud of the Caralissian wine train had moved closer. If they came into view now, it wouldn't look good.

Logan took the reins of the courier's mount—an ancient roan mare that must have been called out of retirement—and pulled it over beside the others. Then he strapped feed bags on all three to keep them busy. Kiara had the messenger's case open, and pulled out eight or nine dispatches.

She cursed. "They're sealed with wax."

"There's a hot wire in the kit. Looks like a cheese slicer."

God bless the techs in the R & D lab. They'd developed an entire series of tools for document alteration in-world, all of them disguised to resemble ordinary things. The hot wire melted just enough wax seal to lift it without damaging the seal itself. That was just for starters. They could also copy the seals, color-match the ink—whatever it took.

Right now, he'd be happy just to get the damn things open quickly.

Logan hobbled the horses, then jogged over to pitch in.

For each missive, they lifted the seal, unfolded parchment, and took a few high-res images with a wrist-camera. These were synced with Kiara's tablet for translation. Logan resealed each letter while the lieutenant opened the next. Eight missives, all of them a single page of dense handwritten text. They had six done when the outriders returned. They were a quarter mile off when they showed, close enough to see the horses, but not much more than that.

Kiara glanced up. "Why don't you see what you can do to make us less threatening? I'll finish this."

"Yes, ma'am."

He hid the weapons first, because that's what the outriders would be looking for. Their swords went into scabbards on the horses. He tucked the crossbow beneath a blanket, and slid the pneumatic pistol into a concealed carry holster on his left side.

"One to go," Kiara said. "Don't forget the wine-skin."

Shit, almost did forget. He got it out of the saddle-bags, along with the other spare blanket and a some glasses. He spread the blanket out on between the lieutenant and the courier, who was still out cold. Onto this he threw a couple of plates, a hand-ful of figs, and the last of the dried meat. It wasn't Martha Stewart, but it would pass for an impromptu picnic.

Then he poured the wine into three glasses, and tucked one into the courier's hand. They'd propped him up against a tree so that it looked like he'd passed out.

Very Weekend at Bernie's.

The wine caravan swung into view, and the out-riders fell into pace beside it. Twenty mercs in total. All of them carried at least two visible weapons.

Swords were the most popular choice, but polearms and maces made their presence known as well. Not to mention the outrider with the bow. The caravan halted a hundred yards down the road. A small group detached itself and rode forward, while the others tightened the circle around their precious cargo.

Logan tried to keep casual. *If they saw us dart the courier, we're in trouble.* No amount of posturing would explain away the message copying operation. And some of these were messages to Caralis, which wouldn't bode well. At best, they'd be treated as hostiles. At worst, as enemy spies, and forcibly taken into Valteron City to explain what they'd done.

The five soldiers fanned out into a wedge formation as they approached. Three men, two women, and they never spoke a word to one another. *Like they've done this a hundred times before.*

"Morning," Logan called. He reclined against the tree, and topped off his wineglass with shaky hands. Spilled a little bit on his pants in the process, and pretended not to notice. Kiara drained her glass and held it out for a refill.

The mercenaries reined in and looked them over. Their faces were grim, but the fact that they hadn't simply ridden Logan and Kiara down was encouraging.

"We are about to bring a wagon past," said one of the mercenaries. She had a husky voice, and fin-

gered the hilt of a cavalry saber like she was itching
to use it.

"What kind of wagon?" Logan asked.

"That is not your concern."

Logan held up his hands, spilling more wine on
himself in the process. "Just making conversation."

She pointed a mailed finger at the unconscious
courier. "What's wrong with him?"

"Can't hold his wine," Kiara said.

One of the otherwise silent mercenaries snickered.
The woman in charge quieted him with a glance.
"You will not approach the caravan. You will not
touch your horses until an hour after we've gone."

Time to give a show. Logan put on his overserious
face, like the guy at the bar trying to fake at sobriety.
"We get it."

Oh, but the speech wasn't over yet.

"When we've gone, you will not follow us," the
woman said. "Nor will you tell anyone of our numbers, arms, or the time that we passed."

"Got to be honest, I'm not sure we'll even remember this conversation," Logan said.

"Enjoy your picnic." She said it like an order,
though her tone assured that it really couldn't be
followed.

They rode back to the caravan, which soon trundled into motion. The outriders thundered ahead to
scout around the blind curve in the road. The rest of

the escort gave Logan and Kiara hard looks as they rode past. The only friendly one was the vintner, a portly man who drove the wagon's horse team. He waved and lifted a mug in salute.

There was always a vintner with Caralissian wine caravans, someone who vouched for the shipment upon delivery. Logan had yet to meet a sober one. He and Kiara returned the salute. The whole caravan rumbled out of sight, leaving only a cloud of dust and the smell of horse manure in its wake. Logan watched them ride out of view, then tossed a fig into his mouth and leaned back. "Guess I've got the next hour off."

"You can't be serious," Kiara said.

"We gave them our word. What if they've got a rearguard coming up to make sure we keep it?" Logan wouldn't put it past Caralissian mercenaries to pull something like that, either. Only because it's what he'd do himself.

"I suppose it wouldn't hurt to wait. I can forward the raw scans back to command, to double-check the translations."

Logan took another drink of the wine, which wasn't as bad as he'd remembered. Certainly not anywhere near the quality of what had just been carted by, but still passable. "Yeah, take a load off, Lieutenant. You've earned it."

She cocked her head, and pressed her lips together. "No more wine for you."

They took their positions again before the courier regained consciousness. Kiara put her horse to where it had been, and backed the roan mare to a few paces behind it. Logan's was another ten paces back, as if he'd come upon this scene and stopped to help.

Then he and Kiara knelt beside the courier and pulled him up to a sitting position. The man was slow to come around. Too slow.

"Maybe we should speed this along." Logan uncapped a snifter tube and waved it near the man's nose.

He jerked upright, gasped, and looked at them wild-eyed.

"You all right there, fella?" Logan asked. "You took a nasty fall."

"Wha-what happened?"

"My horse had just thrown me, and you were kind enough to help," Kiara said.

She spoke so quietly, with such softness to her voice, that Logan about did a double take. *She's going for a goddamn Oscar today.*

"I remember that. I got . . . stung or something."

"Must have been one of these biting blood flies," Logan said. The tranquilizer darts underwent a conformational change upon impact to resemble the little insects that plagued the Alissian south. Most people would smack a blood fly on sight, since the bites sometimes caused unconsciousness. Smashing the darts made them unrecognizable. *Yet another stroke of genius by the eggheads back home.* "Damn things are merciless. I'd just come around the bend in the road, and saw you fall."

"How long was I out?" asked the courier.

"Not more than a few minutes," Kiara said.

"Gods!" The man remembered his message bag and clutched at it. He fumbled the clasps open, looked inside, and sagged with obvious relief.

"It was a noble thing you did, stopping to help me," Kiara said.

"Doesn't sound like it," the man muttered.

"Oh, hush." She tucked an emerald broach into the courier's open satchel. "A little token of my affection."

"I'm not allowed to take—" the courier started.

"I insist."

"Take it, my good man," Logan said. "My stepsister can afford it, I promise you."

"Even so." But he saw the size of the emerald, and his mouth fell open.

He just needs a little push. Logan leaned over and whispered, "It's not the first time she's given a man her token, if you know what I mean."

"I'm sure I do not." He stood, and rubbed the back of his neck in askance. The dart hadn't left so much as a scratch on him, and he'd have needed two mirrors to see it in any case. "Happy to be of assistance." He still looked a little shaken as he mounted and rode off.

"I think he bought it," Logan said. "Good call on the tracking pin."

The broach had a tiny microchip that would ping any of the comm network's towers as it passed. Not nearly as good as GPS, but it would give them a rough idea of where he went. The lieutenant had called an audible on that play, but a good one.

"So, I'm your stepsister now?" she asked.

"I thought it would help sell it. With you more a damsel in distress."

"What about the part where you called me a floozy?"

Logan winced. "I guess I got a little carried away."

"Let's skip that part next time."

"Copy that."

Kiara's tablet buzzed twice. "The translations are ready," she said.

"What did we get?"

She flipped through the translations, giving each a brief scan. "Better trade terms, and an offer of friendship for Caralis."

"That's a new leaf for them," Logan said.

Kiara grunted. "This one's an order for ten Pirean ships."

"What kind?"

"Deep-hulled transports."

Valteron already had the largest fleet, and now Holt wanted even more ships. *What the hell is he up to?*

"Skimp on the clothes and the venue and the swag, but never on the equipment."

—**Art of Illusion, March 23**

CHAPTER 22

UNCONVENTIONAL

Sella's advanced magic class was in a familiar spot: a rock-studded stream just above a two-story waterfall. Only this time the water was ice-cold, and no team of magicians waited below the waterfall to catch them if they went in. There were only two other students today: a skinny kid who talked fast (and constantly) and a dark-haired girl who'd blithely ignored both of them.

Sella showed up, walking stick in hand, and chivvied them out to rocks in the dead center of the stream. Total déjà vu. The last time he'd been here, Jillaine distracted him and he'd been swept over the waterfall.

Hopefully this lesson would end better.

He checked the wayfinder stone self-consciously as he found his balance. He'd not offered it back to Moric the night before, and wasn't planning to. If it could really do as the man said, he couldn't let it fall into the wrong hands. *I must keep the precious.*

"All of you are here because you're destined to become magicians," Sella called to them. She did something in the air in front of her, almost like sketching a little circle, and suddenly her voice boomed in Quinn's ears like she was standing right next to him. *Jesus!*

"But magic has proven stubborn for you." Sella pointed at each of them with her walking stick in a not-too-subtle gesture. "So we'll have to beat the resistance out of you any way that we can."

"Well, that sounds delightful," Quinn muttered. He'd taken a broad stone in the deeper water farther away from the falls. If he fell in, he'd at least have a shot to grab another rock before he was swept over. And he'd packed a special bit of tech that would help on the way down, too.

That would teach Sella not to use the same teaching tool twice.

"Prepare yourselves," Sella said.

The dark-haired girl snorted and rolled her eyes.

Sella frowned. "I saw that, Jade." She dipped the end of her walking stick into the stream and started muttering to herself. The water slowly rose as she chanted. Whitecaps danced atop the racing water as it threatened to flow over the stones where Quinn and his classmates were perched.

Joke's on her this time.

He'd insisted on better boots before starting this mission, and the prototyping lab had delivered in spades. The Gore-Tex inner lining of his boots was completely waterproof, and the high-friction micro-grip sole was something CASE Global developed for professional rock climbers. It would take a goddamn tidal wave to knock him off the rock. He had a couple other tricks up his sleeves, too. Literally. The next-generation elemental projector was strapped to his right forearm, and the backup was on his left.

Sella frowned when the rush of water didn't even make him flinch. She stopped her chant and moved back from the stream's banks. Victory was going to taste so sweet.

Then she produced a small, pale instrument. *What is that, animal bone?* She pressed her lips to it and blew. Quinn didn't hear anything, but it still raised hackles on his neck. "What the—"

He saw the fins first. Dark triangles sliced through the water, rushing downstream toward where he and the others perched on the rocks. They zigzagged left and right as they came, moving like predators.

Got to be an illusion.

There was no way the stream was deep enough to hold something that big. And Alissian sharks lived in salt water, as far as Quinn knew. But it was a hell of a trick. He had to give her that. Beneath the thick fins, water churned over their thick bodies like submarines coming to the surface.

That's right around when Jade started screaming. The other kid had paled and gone stock-still, as if paralyzed.

Just an illusion. Just an illusion. Quinn had seen hundreds of visual deceptions like this, and even created a few himself. That didn't make it any less convincing, though. Especially when the largest of the sharks peeled off from the others and made a beeline right for the rock where he stood.

Wham!

The impact shook his stone so hard that he almost fell. He stutter-stepped to the other rock behind him with one leg to keep his balance. *All right, so it's not an illusion.*

The shark circled him, churning the water as it came. Out of the corner of his eye, he saw Jade lose her balance and fall in. The current swept her over the falls. The skinny kid had closed his eyes and started chanting. Or maybe praying.

Quinn's shark charged at him again, and he sure

as hell wasn't going to stay on the rock it was heading at. He made a jump and landed on another one, flailing his arms wildly to keep his balance. "Whoa!" *Jesus.* That had nearly been it.

The shark shot around and hit the rock he'd just landed on. He fell to his knees to keep from tumbling off. The frigid water soaked right through his pants, and drove cold needles into his knees. *Son of a bitch!*

He worked his mind frantically, trying to remember what he'd done to save himself in the Loutre River. He'd figured he was going to die, and rebelled against that thought. Then the heat surged up from his belly, and he'd pushed the water away. The trouble was, he didn't know how to find that fire to begin with. *Maybe I have to be dying.*

And then, of course, the sharks started jumping, too. The one harassing the skinny kid shot out of the water right at him. He shouted in alarm and hopped to a nearby stone. The shark should have clipped him, but he did something with his hands. The wind roared in a tempest around him, and sent the shark spinning off over the falls.

"Yes!" Sella clapped her hands. She blew into the bone whistle again, and now the other two sharks charged at Quinn.

"Crap." He ducked aside as the closest one leaped at him. He tried copying the kid's gesture, but it had no effect. Then had to dance a two-step as the second one swept its tail across the rock. "Clever bastards, aren't you?"

All right, I'm ready to cheat. He had the elemental projectors, but fire and water wouldn't help here. The microturbine might, but probably not enough. Not for four hundred pounds of muscle and teeth. He'd push himself right into the water.

That gave him an idea. A crazy-ass idea, but he might be able to make it work. By the way the sharks had circled out at different sides on him, they were all coming for a coordinated attack. Two toothy leaps right at him, with nowhere to go.

Nowhere but up.

The sharks charged at him. Quinn found the right switches on his elemental projectors, pointed them down at the water. Crouched low on his rock. *Three, two, one . . .*

The sharks shot out of the water from both sides. He hit the turbines on max power and jumped as high as he could. He kept his arms stiff and straight down. He took off like a rocket, probably five or six feet in the air. The sharks slammed into each other headfirst. They tumbled back into the water. The current swept them over the falls.

Then the turbines sputtered and went still, and he was falling. He hit the rock hard and slammed a knee against it. *Damn, that hurts.* It kept him on the rock, though.

Sella and the skinny kid whooped and applauded.

Quinn stood to give them the prestige. "How about that?"

"A bit unconventional, Quinn," Sella said. "But certainly an improvement."

Quinn's small victory over the sharks put him on cloud nine. Yeah, he'd had to cheat a little, but the grudging compliment he won out of Sella made it all worthwhile. His mood was good enough that he decided to check in with the rest of the team during his long walk back to the Landorian tower. He made sure he was alone before putting his comm unit on burst transmission mode.

"This is Bradley, can I make my report?"

He had to wait the customary few minutes to get a reply from Kiara. "Go ahead, Bradley."

"My cover is still solid here, so I'm happy to report that I'm alive and well."

"Any insights into the nature of Holt's magical protection?"

"Not yet, but I'm working on it. I have to tread lightly." That reminded him of the encounter with Anton. "Hey, can you run a name against the archives for me? A Caralissian guy who goes by Anton. He's probably in his mid-thirties, wealthy. Some kind of a lord or something."

"Who is he?" Logan asked.

"A guy looking to give me trouble. Anything you can tell me about him would be helpful."

"We'll run the name," Kiara said. "What's the status of the antenna?"

Crap, I totally forgot. He considered telling her he'd lost it at sea, but that might raise suspicions. "I'll have to find a good spot for it. I haven't had much free time yet."

"Well, you've got your work cut out for you. Keep me posted of your progress. Kiara out."

Quinn switched off his comm unit as he jogged up the steps to the Landorian tower. He passed no one in the empty atrium. Then he got a glance down the hall, and saw light spilling from his room into the dim hallway. Which shouldn't be possible, because he'd left his door closed.

He eased up one sleeve, and slid the controls for the elemental projector. With all the people dropping in on him unexpectedly, anyone might be in there. *It would be just like Anton to wait for me in my own room.* He rounded the corner, ready to throw something nasty in the man's smug face, and startled Moric from where he stood by the window.

"Oh. Moric." *Sweet Jesus.* He shoved the sleeve hastily back down his arm. "I wasn't expecting you."

Moric spread his hands out in apology. "I'm sorry for the intrusion, but I saw you borrowed a new book, and I couldn't resist . . ."

Quinn took a calming breath. "It's all right. You startled me, that's all."

"How in the world did you get *Elements of Botany* out of the library?"

"I stopped by earlier. Old Mags was happy to see me."

Moric coughed into his hand. "I'm sorry, did you say Mags was *happy*?"

"She was delighted." The old crone could glare daggers when she wanted to, but she'd seemed genuinely pleased at Quinn's return. Even before he laid a little bottle of fancy Felaran liquor on her. *It never hurts to grease a gatekeeper.* That was Vegas 101. "She said I could borrow anything, so . . ." Quinn shrugged and gestured at the old leather-bound book. "I thought it looked interesting."

"That's one word for it," Moric said. He ran a finger down the ancient leather spine, almost like a caress. "Rare would be another. There are only a handful of copies of this book in the world."

Thanks to Holt, it's a handful plus one. But Quinn feigned surprise. "Really? I'll be careful with it, then. The last thing I want is to get on the wrong side of Mags."

Moric shook his head. "You have no idea how right you are."

Quinn tried to hide his smile. "Once you get on her list, it's a long way coming back."

The man seemed eager to change the subject.

"Speaking of which, how was your first lesson with Sella today?"

"Oh, yeah. She attacked us with sharks."

Moric nodded, as if this were perfectly normal. "Any magic?"

Quinn almost said no, because that was the truth. But if Moric talked to Sella, she'd probably mention the super-jump. *This is a delicate line.* "Mostly not," he said. "I sort of jumped, but only when the alternative was getting eaten."

Moric crinkled his forehead. "You . . . jumped?"

"Well, it was a *good* jump. A lot higher than I should have been able to on my own."

"That's something, I suppose."

"Oh, yeah, it's an impressive list." Quinn ticked them off on his fingers. "My friends didn't get killed. I managed not to drown. And today, I wasn't eaten by sharks."

Moric chuckled. "Desperation seems to bring out the best in you, and that's not a bad thing. Some of the greatest spells ever cast by Enclave magicians were brought about by desperate need."

"Even so, I'd also like to be able to use magic when my life doesn't depend on it."

"Sometimes our powers are fickle that way. Particularly with novice users," Moric said.

Ouch. He wasn't wrong, but it still stung a little. "Do you think I'll get past it?"

Moric at last tore his eyes from the book. "We'll simply have to find more opportunities to make you desperate."

"Oh, that sounds promising," Quinn said dryly.

"Something tells me that you can handle it. Just as you handled our mission for Richard's friends."

They're not his friends. "I did what I had to do. I'm just sorry it kept me away so long."

Moric's eyes widened. "That reminds me. Have you spoken to Jillaine since you returned?"

"No, I haven't had the chance."

"When we returned from that job without you, she asked a lot of questions."

"OK . . ." Quinn wasn't sure where this was going.

"I may have *implied* that you . . . well, you know."

"That I what?" Quinn asked.

"Died."

"*What?*"

"Perished."

"I know what it *means*, Moric. Why would you say that?"

Moric gave an innocent shrug. "It seemed like a good way to stave off further questions."

"You've got to be kidding me."

Moric put a hand on his shoulder and squeezed it. "Perhaps you'll drop by the chandlery and let her know that I was mistaken."

"Why can't you tell her?"

"I've a meeting with the council. Important Enclave business, I'm sure you'll understand."

"Moric—"

But the man already had a foot out the door. "I'm late already, now that I recall. Keep me posted on those lessons."

"If you want to control the game, you need to know who the players are."

—Art of Illusion, June 17

CHAPTER 23

A HINT OF FIRE

Quinn wanted to nip this Jillaine thing in the bud. The problem was that—outside of a certain stack of boulders where he'd managed to find her a couple of times—he didn't know where to look for her. Normally, she'd been the one to find him. Finally, though, he remembered that she'd mentioned making candles for the Enclave. It took him even longer to realize that the plain wooden building next to the Enclave's apiary might be the place where the candles were made. He usually gave the place a wide berth. Alissian honeybees were about the size of a large walnut. *Unnatural things.* A dozen beehives, each of them at least three feet in diameter, sat atop large wooden stands in the midst of an apple orchard. There was no fence.

Not even a damn sign. The Enclave just boggled the mind sometimes.

The sun had half dipped below the horizon when he approached the wide open door of the chandlery itself. A hundred different scents drifted out of it to greet him. Lavender, vanilla, cinnamon, wet grass, roasting meat, lemon oil . . . each one was more pleasant than the next. Half of them, he couldn't even name.

He paused outside and took a breath, centering himself. The last time he saw Jillaine, she'd kissed him, and warned him not to be away too long. But she'd also bound him so he couldn't move, so there was no telling what kind of reunion he might expect.

A chime sounded as he walked across the threshold, startling him. There weren't any wires or bells that he could see, just a pair of little stone owls on each side of the door. They were about two inches high, and faced one another. *A magic shopkeeper's bell.* He wouldn't mind having some of them on his own chambers, the way people kept dropping in.

There wasn't anyone inside. Wooden shelves lined every wall, and they were piled high with beeswax sculptures. Flowers and trees made for a little garden in the corner, while a veritable zoo of wild animals piled atop one another on the wall beside it. The largest of these was a wyvern about two feet tall, so realistic that it made him shiver. The scales were carved with such detail it was almost as good as a photograph. He moved over to the section of plant and flower candles. A fist-sized rose stood out from among these. He leaned to inhale the scent. *Her* scent. The one that she'd always used to announce herself to him.

Then a small wooden side door opened, and there she was, holding a tray full of new candles. Her golden hair tumbled in a gentle curl past her shoulders, and her violet eyes . . . well, he'd never seen eyes like those and he'd been worried he never would again. *But there they are.* She wore a sky-blue dress beneath her apron, which bore the battle scars of a thousand candle settings. It was as filthy as she was gorgeous.

"Hi," Quinn said.

Her jaw dropped, and the tray clattered to the floor. Candles spilled everywhere. A slender taper in plum rolled up to his foot. He crouched to pick it up.

"Sorry, I didn't mean to—" he began, but cut off as she threw her arms around him. "Oh."

He hugged her back, enjoying the warmth of her body against his. She let him go. Then fire bloomed in her eyes and she slapped him. *Hard.* Red sparks danced across his vision.

"Um, ow." He rubbed his cheek and frowned at her. "What the—"

"I thought you were *dead*."

As much as he wanted to throw Moric under the bus, he couldn't do it. "I guess it looked that way, from Moric's perspective. I had to leave the group."

She put her hands on her hips. "Why?"

"To finish our job." He started piling the spilled candles back onto the tray. They were different shapes—some square, others round, still others scalloped like flowers—and every one was a variation of purple. Their scents mingled in a mixture of flower and fruit aromas. "Everyone else was spent, and the people we were supposed to be protecting were ambushed." He rose with the tray full of candles—all of which had miraculously remained unbroken.

"What took you so long?" She made no move to take the tray, but began placing the candles one by one on her shelves. "The others returned weeks ago."

"I had to follow the clients through the mountains and back into Felara."

"Hmm." She took the last candle, then the tray, and set it briskly on the counter. "So, let me get this straight."

Uh-oh.

"You left this island with hardly a moment's warning," she said.

"Well, I t-told you—" he stammered.

She rolled right over him. "Then you left my

father and the others to think you'd perished, while you took a little adventure across the mainland."

Quinn held up his hands. "It wasn't an adventure."

"How would I know? I've never even been anywhere else."

That's not really my fault. "Trust me, you're not missing much." No place on the Alissian mainland could top the Enclave, in his opinion.

"And yet you were gone a long time," she said. Her voice had a chill.

"There were . . . complications. It took a lot longer than I thought."

She raised her eyebrows. "Oh, and you figured I'd still be here waiting for you."

"Well, no, I—I just wanted to let you know I'm back."

She turned away to straighten more of her candles. "And now you've done that."

He stood there for a tock more, but when it was clear she wouldn't say anything—or even look at him—Quinn stalked out the doorway. His chest hurt like he'd been punched. He wasn't done with her, not by a long shot, but a good entertainer knew when it was a bad night with a tough crowd.

Thanks a lot, Moric.

Quinn trudged back in the direction of the Landorian tower, feeling more dejected by the minute.

The worst part was the fact that Jillaine wasn't so far off with her accusations. He *had* left with virtually no warning, and he'd known at the time he wouldn't be coming straight back. Instead, Moric and the others had come back and told her he was "probably dead."

No wonder she was mad at him.

It was just after midday, the busiest time for foot traffic in the Enclave. Now and then he saw someone he recognized—an acquaintance from the Pirean tower, or one of his Landorian neighbors—but most of them were strangers. *I should work on that.* Then again, he wasn't doing very well with the people he already knew. He was halfway across the green to his home tower when a man hailed him.

"Quinn?" He wore long pants and a tailored jacket, despite the perfect ambient air temperature. *Prim* was the word for him, from the polished boots to the trimmed goatee to the dark queue of hair down his back. Almost like a kung-fu master. He carried a single ribbon-wrapped roll of parchment in both hands.

"Yes?" Quinn eyed the scroll of parchment. *I think I'm about to get served.* Did they have process servers in Alissia? He hadn't thought to ask.

"My master sends his regards." He bowed and proffered the scroll.

Quinn ignored it. Spend enough time in Vegas, and you trained yourself not to take things when people shoved them at you. "Who's your master?"

"Anton."

Curiosity got the better of him, and he took the scroll. The parchment felt thick, but smooth. It was probably the highest quality paper he'd ever encountered in this world. Anton must have some serious loot. "Thank you."

The man straightened. He didn't make eye contact, but he didn't make to leave.

"I'm guessing you want me to read this now," Quinn said.

The man coughed, polite as a British butler. "If it's not entirely inconvenient."

"All right, I guess." He untied the ribbon and unrolled it. The scroll contained a single line of elegant script, handwritten in silver ink. And virtually unreadable to someone who didn't grow up here.

"Whoops, forgot my glasses." Quinn plucked the eyeglass case from his inside pocket. Thank God for the real-time translation—illiteracy wouldn't do much for his reputation. He pointed them at the note, and the lenses showed the translation in block text.

Please join me for the evening meal.

That was the last thing he'd expected. And the last person he cared to spend time with, too. Anton's company made Captain Relling seem downright cheerful.

It was a curious kind of rabbit hole, though. Kiara would want him to see where it led. "Forgive my backward Landorian upbringing, but I don't know the polite way to accept this."

"A phrase like 'I'd be honored to accept his kind invitation' would be appropriate."

That would be a white lie, but one he could swallow. "Tell him that, would you?"

"Of course. If you'd be so kind as to make your way to the Caralissian tower, at sunset?"

Quinn smiled, and didn't have to fake this one. "I'll be there."

The moment Quinn got back to his chambers, he shut the door and put his comm unit on burst mode. "This is Bradley, checking in."

"Two days in a row. Well done, Bradley," Kiara said. "Hold on, and I'll patch in Chaudri and Mendez."

The delay lasted longer this time. "Hello, Quinn," Chaudri said.

It was good to hear her voice again. Quinn would probably never admit it to Mendez, but he'd enjoyed his brief stint as a third wheel. "Hey, Veena, how's tricks?"

"They're five by five, according to Julio. But I looked into Dr. Holt's notes for you. There's a Caralissian noble by the name of Anton. A wine baron. He's sixteenth in line for the throne of Caralis."

Of course he is. "That's him. Give me something I can use."

"Well, I'm not sure if this helps, but his family's vineyards are in disputed territory near the border with Valteron."

"What does that mean, exactly?"

"It means that two generations ago, those were *Valteroni* vineyards, and some in Valteron feel that they still should be."

That might do. "Very interesting. Thanks, Veena. You're a gem."

"Happy to help. How's the Enclave treating you?"

"Rough, but I'm working on it. Keep an eye on Mendez for me."

"Hey, I'm linked in, too," Mendez said.

Quinn grinned. "I know."

"As much as we're all enjoying the chitchat, Holt could still be monitoring our communications," Kiara said. "Any new progress to report, Bradley?"

"Not yet. Maybe tomorrow," he said. "I'll keep you posted."

"Roger that. Kiara out."

"Keep your friends close, and your fellow magicians closer."

—Art of Illusion, March 18

CHAPTER 24

DIVINATIONS

The common room of the Enclave's Caralissian tower was by far the most opulent place Quinn had seen in Alissia. He walked in and blinked, because for a moment he thought he'd been transported to the Venetian. Or maybe one of the high roller rooms at the Bellagio. His boots clicked on stone tile as he walked past the long line of torchlit sconces. The floor was polished to a high sheen. It reflected the torchlight like a mirror.

He paused at a little alcove in the wall, a shrine

with a half barrel as a centerpiece. Deep red stains in the wooden staves made it a wine cask. He could still smell the faint, light scent of fermented grapes. Four oil lamps marked the points of a compass painted on the back wall. They were shaped like little wine bottles, and embossed with gold. *Business must be good.*

The hallway opened into a broad dining room with six long rectangular tables. White tablecloths, porcelain settings. It looked like the dining room on a cruise ship. Anton sat at the head of one of these; he was the only person in the capacious dining room.

"Evening, Quinn." He rose and gestured to the seat at the far end of the table, which had a full place setting. "I'm glad you got my invitation."

"It was a bit of a surprise, I'll admit." He ignored the chair Anton offered, and instead pulled out the one right beside him. A dash of casual impropriety, as if he were a hayseed and didn't know better.

Anton's smile never left his face. He raised his hands and clapped twice. Two men in dark livery appeared out of nowhere. The fourteen-piece place setting got a quick airlift to Quinn's new spot beside Anton.

"Oh, thanks," Quinn said.

The men said nothing, but bowed and withdrew into a dark alcove to one side.

"Have you been in the Caralissian tower before?" Anton asked.

"No. But then again, I don't think I know any Caralissians."

Wait for it. Three, two, one . . .

Anton touched his palm to his chest. "Now, you can say that you do."

Quinn smiled. "I take it that Caralis is doing well. This might be the fanciest place I've ever seen." *In this world, at least.*

"Not many outsiders have the opportunity to be our guest in here. You might consider this a special privilege."

"Well, let's see how good the food is first."

Anton pressed his lips together. "Just so."

The servants appeared again, and slid silver-domed dishes in front of them. They shone like mirrors. The servants withdrew into the shadows.

Anton made a two-fingered gesture and a servant lifted his dome away.

Quinn copied the gesture, not even looking to see if anyone saw it. If this was anything like a five-star restaurant, he had his own personal attendant waiting to cater to his every whim. Sure enough, a white-gloved hand reached out and pulled the dome away.

I could get used to this.

Then he got a look at the plate, and changed his mind. Berries, grapes, and small oranges nestled in leaves of sea lettuce and spinach. Definitely a five-star arrangement, but there was no meat. Unless you counted the clams, which made an odd contrast to the rest of the ensemble.

The empty wineglass in front of him was another disappointment. He'd been secretly hoping to try some of this Caralissian wine that everyone raved about. He sighed, and armed himself with one of the three-tined forks that rested beside his plate. It had the heft of pure silver. He managed to stab one of the round fruits. While he tried it, he made sure one of the spoons made its way into his sleeve.

The fruit was firm and sweet, like a grape, but somehow less refreshing. All flash and no real substance.

Just like my host.

"I thought a meal might help us get to know one another better," Anton said. He worked the fork and knife as he spoke, slicing the lettuce into efficient squares without so much as glancing at it. "I'm curious to learn more about the Enclave's oldest student."

"What would you like to know?"

"I understand you're working with Sella."

More like, she's trying to beat the resistance out of me. "I'm in her advanced class."

"So is it safe to say you're not a full magician yet?"

Quinn stopped eating and looked at his face, to try and get a read on whether or not that was a slam. There wasn't an open sneer, but this guy had masterful self-control.

"I'm getting there," he said.

Anton smirked. "Magical power is a gift of considerable consequence. And like anything of consequence, it can only be possessed by a chosen few." He touched two fingers of his right hand to the table in front of him and slid them forward. The hackles on Quinn's arms rose. The knife beside his plate floated up into the air. It hovered about a foot above his plate, glinting in the candlelight.

"Either you have it," Anton said, and he moved his fingertips in a tight circle. The knife spun slowly around, like the hand of a clock. "Or, you don't." He tapped his fingers once. The knife dropped point-first into the table at Quinn's elbow. It stuck there in the wood, quivering.

Quinn credited his stage training for the fact that he didn't flinch. "Maybe that's true. But not everyone with a certain skill likes to show it off." He put his hands together, palms inward, and rubbed them against one another. "Some of us prefer to keep things . . . hidden." He parted his hands, revealing the spoon he'd palmed earlier.

Anton smiled in a predatory way. "If you do have an ability, I hope it's not *too* far hidden. Otherwise some might wonder if you should even be here."

Oh, that was definitely a slam. Quinn smiled anyway. "As I recall, that question was asked and answered by the council already."

"Ah, yes, your delightful Landorian snow."

"I like to bring a bit of home with me, wherever I go."

"Where is home for you, in Landor? I hope you don't mind my asking."

He goes too far. Moric had taught Quinn that much. Quinn had volunteered Landor, but such a bald question was practically an insult. Maybe it was a test, maybe it wasn't. Didn't matter. He had to show some spine. He set down his fork, and gave Anton a level stare. "I do mind, actually."

The man inclined his head. "My apologies."

Quinn let the awkwardness hang for a moment, then waved it off. "It's fine."

"I only asked because we ship wine to many parts of Landor. The capital in particular."

Quinn kept silent for a moment. He'd pushed back once; now it was time to offer a carrot. "I'm from a tiny village you've never heard of. Wyndham Down."

"Thank you for sharing that." A light flickered in Anton's eyes. He was good with his face, but he gave something up.

He already knew. It wasn't too surprising; Anton was on the council, so he probably heard it from Moric himself.

The polite thing here would be to ask something about Anton's Caralissian origins. That would cement the intimacy of the conversation, and put him at ease. And the man would obviously so *love* to tell him.

Quinn found it far more interesting to gamble instead. "So, why do you think Moric's star is falling?"

Anton's hands froze mid-cut, and he cleared his throat. "Are all Landorians so direct?"

Quinn shrugged. "Perks of being a northerner."

Anton put down his silverware and steepled his fingers. "I should think it's pretty obvious."

"Enlighten me."

"Moric lives in the past, in a time when the Enclave relied on secrecy and caution to survive."

"Those both sound pretty good to me," Quinn said.

"They're unnecessary. We are *hundreds* strong. Why should we hide ourselves, and our power?"

"What do you want to do, send out a letter?"

Anton laughed. "You've a sharp tongue, do you know that?"

Quinn allowed a little smile. "I *have* been told that on occasion."

Anton looked at him a long moment, and then picked up his knife and fork again. "So, I understand you know the Valteroni Prime."

Oh, what *a riposte.* Quinn had just forced himself to take a bite of sea lettuce, and barely managed not to choke. The leaf was far more tender than Earth lettuce, and had a faint salty taste. He chewed and wondered how to answer. Something told him it was better to be cautious. "We have some mutual friends."

"Besides Moric?"

"I think the Prime and Moric are more like business partners."

"So you're aware of the Prime's cozy little arrangement with us, I take it," Anton said.

"I'm really not. Moric was tight-lipped about it," Quinn said, hoping to pry a little information out of him.

"Really? I thought you two were close."

"As close as a student can be with one of his teachers." His relationship with Moric was a little more than that, but he needed to see where this was going.

"What if I told you that not everyone agrees about the special consideration that the Enclave gives to Valteron?"

"I guess I wouldn't be surprised. But there's not really a choice, is there?"

"There *is* a choice. Independence. Freedom from the agreements that bind us to certain nations."

Might as well play dumb. "Don't those agreements grant us protection by the Valteroni fleet?"

"Take a look around, and you'll see just how much protection they're offering us. There's not a Valteroni ship within a hundred leagues of this island."

"Is that all we get out of the deal?" Quinn scrunched up his brow. "Doesn't sound very fair."

"No, it does not. Particularly given the concessions we've made in return. Arcane protections for the Prime, and a retinue of magicians."

"He gets a retinue?" Quinn asked. That was new information. *I wish I got a retinue.*

"Some of our most talented members do his bidding. All for what, an absentee protector?" Anton shoved the plate away and shook his head. "I've lost my taste for it."

Thank God. Quinn pushed his plate aside, too. Now he could make a play on what Chaudri told him. "That's just like Valteron, isn't it? Always trying to grab what isn't theirs."

"My thoughts exactly," Anton said.

"I'd offer to help, but like you said: I'm not a full magician yet."

Anton gave him a side-look, as if measuring him anew. "Perhaps I spoke in haste. No matter your stage as a practitioner of our craft, there is always room for sound-minded individuals in our community."

The compliment made his skin crawl, but Quinn tried to be gracious. "Thanks."

"How committed are you to Moric's cause?"

The question hit like a ton of bricks, which was probably what Anton had intended. A compliment to put him off guard, then a sharp inquiry. But if he thought he was the first guy to try and throw a performer off his game in the middle of a show, he'd never been to Vegas.

"I'm not sure I understand the extent of his cause," Quinn said. "I'm more committed to the man, if I'm being honest. I owe him."

"Even if he stands in the way of what's best for the Enclave?"

Quinn paused. "That's a harder question to answer."

Anton clapped his hands three times, and the servants began clearing the table. Apparently the meal and the conversation had come to an end. "I suggest you think on it."

"Give first, take later. This is the basic principle of developing human assets."

— R. Holt, "Investment in Alissia"

CHAPTER 25

PRICE OF PASSAGE

The only good thing about the recall of the Valteroni fleet was that it bought Veena some time. The admiral was their best lead, but she and Julio could hardly collect intel this far north. Even if they found a berth on a southbound vessel, it would take a week or more to reach Valteroni shores. There were worse places to kill time than the Bay of Rocks. A brisk land and sea trade made the city a cultural hub. The seafood was outstanding. And you couldn't pick a better place to begin rebuilding the Alissian intelligence network.

They could easily burn a month here. A month to rest and replenish their supplies. To bask in Julio's attentions, which she couldn't help but appreciate. Part of her felt guilty about that. Still, as long as they were waiting, there was no harm in enjoying it. Besides, there was no need to rush her decision about Holt's invitation.

Two days later, Veena and Julio were sharing a casual breakfast on the balcony of their inn when he spotted the ship. She'd been working her way through a third bowl of winterfruit—a sweet citrus berry, damn near impossible to get this late in season—and had long since stopped watching the harbor. Ships came and went, but meals like this were meant to be savored.

"Looks like we've got a new arrival," Julio said.

Veena didn't even look up from her notebook, but she humored him. "What kind?"

"Deep-hulled two-master with a lot of sail."

That perked her interest enough to borrow his field glasses. She saw the ship, marked the size and the construction. Julio was right about the sails. There were two jibs, a staysail, main, topsail, foresail, and a broad triangular sail behind the foremast that Alissians called a "fisherman." Seven in total. She counted again to be sure, while the tension seeped into her shoulders.

"What's wrong?" Julio asked.

The gods of this world are cruel. "That's a Valteroni ship design."

"Can you make out any colors?"

She tried, but the wide swaths of canvas were in the way. "Not at this angle."

"Give it a few."

She shrugged and went back to the winterfruit, but it had lost its pleasant tang. She didn't need to see the colors.

Julio reclaimed the opera glasses, and gave her irritatingly frequent updates as the ship made anchor in the deeper part of the bay. "Looks like they're lowering a couple of tenders. Huh. This is interesting."

Veena managed not to sigh. "What?"

"Didn't see any cargo come off. Just crew, so far."

"What do you think that means?"

"Oh, I know what it means. It's shore leave time, baby!"

"Really?"

"Most definitely. Bay of Rocks has a bit of a reputation in that department."

Now that he mentioned it, there did seem to be about twice as many dockside taverns as the population-economic models would predict, even for a port city. "How exactly does one get such a reputation?"

Julio shrugged. "Cheap booze, good food, and

plenty of hook—" He coughed and glanced at her. "Uh, entertainment."

"Ah, so you're *familiar* with this kind of place, then?"

He shook his head a little too emphatically. "Me, no. Just heard a story or two."

She sniffed her disapproval.

"You don't think that I would—"

"It's none of my business."

He hunched his shoulders, and went back to the glasses. "At the rate they're rowing, those tenders will be ashore in less than ten minutes."

"Delightful." She gave up on the winterfruit. "I suppose we should head down there."

He stood, dropped a few coins on the table, and saluted the barkeep. "Ready when you are."

She slid out of the booth. "What's our plan?"

"Those sailors are looking for trouble." He gave her his wicked grin. "Let's make sure they find some."

Veena was glad to be with Julio as they pushed their way into the crowd at the docks. The two Valteroni tenders were full to the brim with crewmen, and disgorged their passengers on the gangplank like there was a fire on board. From there, they scattered in a dozen different directions, making—she assumed— for the brewhouses or less reputable establishments along the waterfront.

Veena and Julio shadowed the largest group as they trooped to a large alehouse at a near-sprint. Most Valteroni ships had a sixteen-hour shore leave, during which sailors could pretty much do as they pleased. The only requirement was that they be back to the ship by the sixteenth bell. If they weren't, the ship would leave without them. They didn't have to be sober, but they had to be on board.

So the goal of a sailor on shore leave was simple: get as ridiculously drunk as he could afford to, in the shortest possible time. The group they'd followed spilled into the broad lamplit drinking room and took over half the bar. Julio wedged himself between a pair of them and made room for Veena. Within ten minutes, they were buying drinks for two Valteroni sailors. They made small talk over the first couple of ales, and then Veena finally got down to business.

"So, where you in from?" she asked.

"North coast o' Landor," said the younger sailor, who'd said his name was Kip. He had a narrow chin and a poor attempt at a goatee. Couldn't be more than eighteen years old.

The other sailor hadn't offered his name—even after Julio bought the second round—so Veena made a mental note to call him Chinless. He'd earned it, with those jowls.

"This time of year?" she asked. "Gods, that must have been cold!"

"You don't know the half of it," said Kip. "We were

freezing our arses off most days. Barely got around Pirea before the ice took over."

"We came down from Pirea on a shore-sweeper ourselves," Veena said. "Weather's really starting to turn up there. Hope you're headed somewhere warmer."

"Back home to Valteron. Orders of the Prime and all that."

Chinless stepped on the younger sailor's foot, and gave him a dark look that said, *Don't talk about where we're headed.*

"Oh, it's all right. We're headed there ourselves, I don't mind telling you," Veena said.

Chinless relaxed a little, but still never joined in the conversation. He and Julio were well-matched in that. It was like they'd begun a contest to see who could drink the most ale while speaking the fewest words. At one point they both emptied their glasses at the same time. Julio signaled the innkeeper for two refills, and tossed the coins across to cover it. He and Chinless made eye contact, touched their glasses together. Then they went right back to drinking in silence.

"Have you been back to Valteron City this year?" she asked.

"Not since the new Prime took over," Kip said. "We were already headed north when we heard about the former one's passing, and Cap'n thought it might be a fine idea to get as far away as possible."

"Clever of him."

"He's got a sharp nose for coin. S'why we hate to go back right now."

That was an odd sentiment, for someone who'd been away too long.

Veena played innocent. "I'd have thought you'd be excited to get home again for a bit."

"Not if it means we're pressed into service."

"Gods, you think you might?"

"That's the rumor. Why else would the Prime order us home?"

Veena shrugged, but her mind was spinning. Valteron's trading fleet was massive. If Holt managed to get them under his rein for military purposes, he'd dominate the oceans. No, he'd dominate the entire *continent*, with that kind of transportation locked up. Sure, they'd lose out on trade for a while, but the Valteroni treasury could probably weather that storm. Her thoughts raced forward to these worrisome ends while Kip prattled on.

". . . just like to have something to work for, you know? If we make good time and Cap'n picks the right cargo, there's bonus pay on top of things. If we're working for the Prime, there's a flat fee and that's it. Just take these men here for this price, no negotiations. No questions asked. Not a lot of profit in that."

"I hear you," Veena said. She was listening on autopilot, but she didn't want to come across as rude.

It wasn't like Julio was going to carry on this conversation on his own. "Maybe that's not why the Prime is recalling you, though."

"We can dream, can't we?" Kip laughed. "We'll know soon enough. Got a half-empty hold right now and we're leaving port with the tide tomorrow."

The barkeep signaled last call. It was time to press a little. Veena toyed with an errant strand of her hair. "You think the captain might be willing to take on a few passengers, since you're so light?"

Kip's face grew more serious, as if he knew he'd spoken too much and wanted to fake at sobriety. "You'd have to ask him that, o' course."

"'Course. And we will." She slid a round gold coin along the bar so that it clinked softly against Kip's ale glass. "Maybe you'll put in a good word for us, eh?"

"Be happy to!" His brow furrowed. "What did you say your name was again?"

"I'm—" Alarm bells rang in her head, and she just caught herself before blurting out her real name. "Tina." She gestured to Julio. "And that's Rico."

Julio smiled in wry amusement. She had to admit, that *might* have been a tad stereotypical.

"Tina and Rico," repeated Kip. "Can't promise much, but I'll put in a good word."

Ten hours later, Veena and Julio rode over two-foot swells in a hired water taxi toward the Valteroni ship. It loomed ever larger as they grew near. This could go south in a hurry. They had all of their possessions with them, on the off chance the captain would take them on. If this glorified rowboat were to capsize, they'd probably lose all of it. But most of the sailors were already back on board. This was their only shot.

"Take us closer," Veena told the pilot.

Julio was starting to turn green. She had to ignore that, and focus on the mission.

"How close you want?" asked the man out of the side of his mouth.

He was ancient as old leather, and the plug of chewing tobacco had been in the one cheek since they'd met him. The two men working the oars turned out to be his sons. *Wide* was the word for them; it described the chins, the shoulders, even the legs. They were near-mirror-images of one another, right down to the small plugs of tobacco they were gnawing on while trying to hide it from the pilot.

"Close enough to hail them, not to catch an anchor line," Veena said. "How does that sound?"

The pilot spat over his shoulder, then looked her up and down. "Sounds like you know yer business." He smacked the starboard twin on the back of his head. "You heard the lady."

The twins weren't much for chatting, but managed to row in near-perfect unison. They had the craft in position near the Valteroni ship within minutes.

"Not bad," Julio said. He flipped a silver coin to the pilot, who caught it, bit it in the good side of his mouth, and tucked it away.

"Might say we know our business, too."

"All right, Veena," Julio said. "Work your magic."

She stood to hide her nervousness, and straightened out her dress as best she could. It was black and formfitting and a foolish thing to wear on a sea voyage. But she needed any edge she could get.

"Hello, the ship!" she shouted.

A man appeared at the rail a moment later. He wore a broad-brimmed hat studded with several large feathers. The hat looked to be made of felt. Or suede. It was about as ridiculous a thing to wear as her dress. But it also made him the captain of the Valteroni ship.

"Hello, yourself," he said.

"Any news?"

"We've been up north. You want to hear about the ice and cold?"

"Not particularly," Veena said.

"Then what can I do for you?"

This was the tip of the spear; she had to approach it just right. "We thought perhaps you might be headed toward Valteron."

The captain hesitated. "And if we were?"

"I'd like to buy passage. For my manservant, and myself."

Julio managed to keep his face neutral, though it clearly was a struggle. She'd given him advance warning about this part. It didn't take an anthropologist to recognize that a single woman stood a much better chance of gaining passage on a deepwater vessel than a married one. She'd have Julio at hand to protect her, of course, but the perception of availability might seal the deal.

He still didn't have to like it.

"Can't help you, I'm afraid," said the captain.

She blinked. "I'm sorry?"

"We're not taking any passengers."

"You're riding pretty high in the water, Captain. I'm guessing your hold is, what, half-empty?"

The captain stared at her for four heartbeats. Probably wondering how she could have guessed it. "Even so."

"We'd pay handsomely."

"I'm sure you would. Pains me to say it, but we're under strict orders." He moved back from the rail, until only the feathers on his hat were visible. They moved astern as the captain headed back to his wheel.

Orders from Richard Holt, the Valteroni Prime, Veena realized. She took a breath. It was time for plan B, and Julio would like this even less. "Perhaps it would be useful if I told you my name."

Julio's hand was on her shoulder, trying to stop her. His eyes were wide in alarm. "Don't!" he hissed.

Veena knew it was a risk, but this was the only ship headed to Valteron, and the only way to get on board. "What choice do we have?" She slid out of his grip. "It's Veena Chaudri."

The feathers went stock-still. Then the captain's head appeared again. "Did you say—"

"Veena. Chaudri," she repeated. "Can we have a berth now?"

He cleared his throat. "Anything you want, m'lady."

"One of the best things about performance magic is that there's always more to learn."

—Art of Illusion, August 15

CHAPTER 26

INTO THE FIRE

Quinn hadn't even dressed when the parchment slid under his door. The sight and sound made him jump. For more than one reason. The fact was, he'd installed a motion sensor out in the hallway, hot-linked to his comm unit, but the thing hadn't made a peep. He yanked his door open. Nothing moved in the hallway. He didn't hear any footsteps, either. *So how the hell did this parchment get here?*

He probably didn't want to know.

He found his optics, and thanked his lucky stars that he had them. The note was from Sella.

Class has moved to center island, at the amphitheater. Today only.

He sighed. Over the past few days, Sella had buried her students in mud, dangled them by their heels over the edge of a waterfall, and forced them to climb the sequoia-like trees along the island's western shore. This last one wouldn't have been so bad if Alissian tree rats weren't so damn territorial. None of these had conjured so much as a spark out of Quinn, though they'd certainly left a mark or two on his person.

And today there's a location change. This didn't bode well.

He dressed and hurried out to the Landorian tower's common room, which was just as spacious as the Pirean one, but somehow not as cheerful. Every morning, a new spread of fruits and breads would appear on the massive central table. He'd never thought to ask who replenished it, or where the food came from. *Maybe I'm supposed to be putting in on that.*

He ignored the food anyway, and made a straight shot for the ceramic kettle that hung beside the hearth. Landorian tea had a strong, slightly bitter flavor, but was the best source of caffeine on this side of the gateway. He filled one of the clay mugs about a quarter full. That was his limit. The one time he tried a full cup, he wound up with the shakes for the rest of the day.

He gave himself plenty of time to walk to the amphitheater, where the Enclave magicians had put him on trial just a few months ago. He still couldn't believe he'd managed to win them over, earning the chance to stay on as a student. The amphitheater was packed that day, too. Standing room only, which normally he'd have appreciated, if it weren't for the looming threat of execution.

Now, windblown leaves danced across the empty benches. *What the hell?* Maybe Sella had meant outside the amphitheater, not in it. He hurried across the stage and out the far side. Being alone in a wide open space made him nervous. Then he spotted her, about fifty yards south of the amphitheater. He broke into a jog and told himself it was mainly for the exercise, and not because of the lashing he'd get if he were late.

Sella stood in a circle of black dirt that he'd never noticed before. Knee-high boulders lined the perimeter, each of them flat-topped like a bench. Nothing grew inside the circle. The dirt was loose and dark, like a fresh-plowed field.

Jade leaned against one of the stones, wearing a practiced look of bored disinterest. The nameless skinny kid arrived ten seconds later, and doubled over to catch his breath. Judging by the sheen on his face, he'd run most of the way here.

"Let's get started," Sella said. "Any progress since last time?"

The skinny kid shook his head. Jade mumbled something under her breath and looked away.

Quinn refused to look at anyone.

"I take that as a no," Sella said. "Very well, then. You'll remain in this circle until I give you permission to leave."

"That sounds ominous," Quinn muttered.

"I'm sorry?"

"Nothing." He climbed over a rock bench and hopped down into the circle. The smell of char assaulted his nose. Little puffs of dirt flew up as he landed, and swirled away on the breeze. No, not dirt. Ashes.

I'm standing in a goddamn fire pit.

And Sella had already started chanting.

The flames had shot up seemingly at random. All that Quinn and the other two students could do was dance around to avoid them. Which never worked, because Sella could see them the whole time.

She was a master at psychological torture, too. Quinn saw a place near the middle of the ring where flames never seemed to touch. The second he edged over to it, a flare-up engulfed him to the waist. That was around the time that his pants started to smolder. He racked his brain to figure out a way to cheat. They were in close quarters, so the projector was out. He tried digging deep for the real magic, but found nothing. *I need a miracle.*

Jade planted her feet and held her arms out, palms facing at the ground, fingers curved just so. Her face was a mask of concentration, the most emotion Quinn had ever seen from her. She bit her lip so hard it had started bleeding. Her eyes were somewhere else.

The hair on the back of Quinn's neck stood up.

Something changed in Jade's part of the circle. Try as they might, no flames could touch her.

And they did try. Sella chanted louder, and the iridescent flames shot up around Jade. Heat rolled off them in waves. Sweat poured down the girl's face, but she held them at bay.

Quinn felt his mouth fall open. He took advantage of the brief respite to slap the smoldering debris from his pant legs. Thank God for the company's flame-proof synthetic blend, or else he'd have been a walking torch.

The skinny kid wasn't so lucky. He screamed as his right pant leg caught fire. He hopped and waved it around, which only fanned the flames.

Quinn stripped off his jacket. "Here, over here!"

The kid kept hollering and dancing around, oblivious. Quinn ran and tackled him to the ground. Then he smothered the flames with his jacket, hoping it wouldn't scorch too badly.

"Thanks!" the kid panted.

"No problem," Quinn said.

The tower of flames surrounding Jade dissipated. Quinn clambered to his feet, in case that meant the flame-torture was about to start up again.

But Sella clapped her hands. "Wonderfully done, Jade!" She hopped over one of the boulders in a surprising show of agility.

Jade fell to her knees. She was drenched with sweat, and her dark hair hung in wet strands across her face. But she looked completely unharmed, despite Sella's best efforts to the contrary. Quinn stared in amazement. *Unreal.*

The old woman knelt beside her, and they spoke in hushed tones.

"Gods, my legs are like cooked meat," the kid said.

I should ask him his name. But it was well into the awkward period to do that now. *Sella's bound to yell it at some point anyway.*

"Mine, too, but I think you got it worse," Quinn said.

"How is it that Jade's not even touched?"

"She had a breakthrough. I guess you missed it."

He whistled under his breath. "She must be a fire mage."

Quinn looked over in time to see Jade shrug and roll her eyes at whatever Sella was saying. "Yeah, that fits."

"Wealth is wastefulness."

—Tioni proverb

CHAPTER 27

GOOD FEELING GONE

Quinn spotted Anton's prim butler heading up the steps to the Caralissian tower door. "Hey there!"

The man paused midstep, but somehow adopted an elegant pose. "Yes?"

"Is Anton in? I wonder if I could have a word."

"Is he expecting you?"

"No. But I'm afraid it's a matter of some urgency," Quinn said. "And discretion." *That should pique his curiosity.*

"I'll make an inquiry." He started inside, then paused. "Quinn, was it?"

"That's right." *And I think you knew it.*

The man disappeared into the tower interior. Quinn probably should have followed him in, but where the Pirean tower welcomed visitors, something about the Caralissian tower seemed to deter them. Maybe it was the silence, or the dark interior. They might as well post a sign: *No Outsiders.*

The butler returned a minute later. "Right this way, if you please."

Anton waited in the same dining room as before, in the same seat, wearing a crushed velvet jacket in olive green. "Quinn! What an unexpected pleasure." He gestured to the chair beside him.

"I enjoyed our dinner the other night, and I've been giving our conversation some thought."

"And?"

"I'm warming to the idea of an Enclave that owes nothing to the Prime of Valteron."

"That's a welcome surprise. What changed your mind?"

"Disturbing news, I'm afraid." Quinn made certain to choose his words carefully. "The Prime is making preparations for something big."

Anton leaned forward in his chair. A hawk-like intensity pierced his causal demeanor. "What preparations?"

"Recalling his fleet, and buying more ships from Pirea. Rebuilding the wall around Valteron City."

Anton gave him a side-look. "You're remarkably well-informed."

"Well, you're not the only one who has useful friends." *And my friends knock out messengers just to get the news.* Quinn couldn't keep the smirk entirely off his face.

Anton chuckled. "Indeed." The smile faded. "Even so, one might argue that it's merely a new leader consolidating his power."

"Hmm." Quinn replayed Kiara's intelligence update in his head. *What else did she say? Oh, yes.* He adopted a casual tone. "He's buying horses."

"How many horses?"

"As many as he can get his hands on. How does *that* lend to his power?"

"It doesn't." Anton drummed his fingers on the table. "It prepares him for war. And he thinks Caralis is a plum ripe for picking."

Actually, he's working toward an alliance. That's what Kiara seemed to think, based on their intercepted communications. But if Anton saw it differently, Quinn wasn't about to correct him. "You do have pretty nice roads, I'm told."

"Thank you."

Quinn rubbed his chin and looked to one side. "All the way to the capital."

Anton kept his cool for about two seconds, then pounded his fist on the table. Somehow, even that was a kingly gesture. "This agreement with Valteron cannot stand."

"I'm not sure what we can do, though. The Prime has everything he needs from us," Quinn said. *Please, tell me I'm wrong.*

Anton dismissed this with a wave. "Enclave magicians can be recalled. Wards can be removed."

"How?"

"With a majority vote on the council."

"Will we ever get one?"

"Given what you've told me, maybe so. I believe I can convince enough members that the risks are too great."

"That sounds promising."

"But only if Moric is not around," Anton said. "They won't dare to oppose him openly."

"I think I might be able to do something about that," Quinn said.

Anton smiled, and for the first time, it looked genuine. "I knew you'd prove yourself useful. Come, let me show you what sort of luxuries lie in the wings." He clapped his hands. The butler reappeared with two bottles in hand, one hunter green, the other dark red. They were corked and sealed with drops of wax. Anton gestured at the dark red bottle. The servant produced a two-pronged tool and pried out the cork with a single, elegant motion.

"I really shouldn't," Quinn said. His legs felt hot to the touch. He only wanted to go to bed.

"Have you had Caralissian wine before?" Anton asked.

"Never." Even with the coin and jewels CASE Global had equipped him with for this mission, it would have been too expensive.

"This is going to be quite an experience, then."

"That's the rumor." *We'll see if it holds up.*

The butler filled Anton's wineglass, and then Quinn's. Not even two fingers' worth. Barely enough to fill the bottom of the glass. Then again, it did sell for its weight in gold, so it wasn't the type of thing you comped to strangers very often.

Quinn followed Anton's lead in letting the wine air out for a moment, then sniffing it. There was almost no scent at all, just a faint, fruity aroma that touched his nose only once. He tried to inhale it, but no dice. The scent eluded him like a cocktail waitress after the tip.

Anton took a sip, so Quinn did the same. It was cool on his tongue. Chill. Crisp. The coldness flowed outward, as if he'd dunked his head in water.

He smelled smoke next. Not the char of burning wood, but the dry, pungent odor of a smoke machine. He heard the sound of applause—distant, at first, and then it rose to the thunder pitch. He felt the blast of air as the audience cheered, and rose to their feet. His first standing ovation. He remembered the feeling of elation. The way it rose up in him, and set him on a path to the Vegas Strip.

All of those sensations came and went in a heartbeat, in the time it took him to savor a sip of the Caralissian wine. Sweet Jesus. Now he understood why it cost so much. It took all of his willpower not to down the rest of the glass right then and there.

He made himself wait until Anton took his second sip. Then it came again, the applause, the lights, the heat . . . all of it. He looked down at the empty glass as it faded. The disappointment felt like it would crush him into nothingness.

"Do you like it?" Anton asked.

"It's . . ." He shook his head, because the words failed him.

"No two people have the same experience," Anton said. "Often it's a vivid memory, or a hint of a dream. It depends on the drinker."

"What was it for you?"

Anton cleared his throat and looked down at the table, perhaps the first crack in composure he'd shown. "I'm not sure I—"

"Sorry," Quinn said quickly. "I just realized what a deeply personal question it was."

"Something rarely shared, even among intimate friends."

Now that he thought about it, Quinn wasn't eager to tell Anton his own experience, either. "Please, forget that I asked."

Anton nodded, and waved off the faux pas with

an elegant gesture. "How soon can you get Moric off the island?"

"I'll get back to you on that," Quinn said.

Because despite what I said, I really have no idea.

Quinn left the Caralissian tower in a woozy kind of haze. His entire body felt light, like a cloud drifting across the green spaces. He settled into a new walk he'd been working on, the slow, rolling gait of a sailor just off a ship. He added a confident swagger to it. Half sailor, half rapper. Railor. That might be the right name for it.

Nah, not smooth enough.

Even better than his taste of Caralissian wine was the possibility that Anton could sway the council to revoke Holt's magical protections. Quinn didn't know how he'd get Moric off the island to make that happen, but he'd think of something. If he pulled it off, Kiara and CASE Global would have to acknowledge how valuable it was to have him here. They might even consider letting him stay long term. *Now there's an idea that I'm warming to.*

He probably should have waited until he sobered up before checking in with Kiara, but this news couldn't wait. He tapped on his comm unit, but the thing didn't come on. He had to fiddle with it for a while to get the thing working. *Maybe I'm not in the best shape for this.* The comm unit beeped before he could change his mind.

"This is Bradley, and I've finally got something."

"Go ahead, Bradley," Kiara came back. "I've got Logan looped in, too."

"I've learned that the Valteroni Prime not only gets the magical protections from the Enclave, but also a full-time retinue of magicians to back him up. You'll want to watch out for them."

"Thanks for the heads-up," Logan said. "But maybe try and get us some *fresh* intel next time."

"What Logan's saying is that we encountered a magician in Valteron City on the last mission," Kiara said.

"All right, well, here's something you probably *don't* know. The Valteroni Prime's arcane protections can be removed."

"How?" Kiara asked.

"By the same magicians who set them up, I'm guessing. All it takes is a decision by the council, and Anton's going to help me get that."

"What about that friend of yours, the one who looks like . . ." Kiara trailed off.

"Mr. Clean," Logan offered.

"Right," she said. "I thought he was in Holt's corner."

"He's the opposition. I need to get him off the island before we vote." Quinn paused. *Here goes nothing.* "That's where you come in."

"Oh, I can't wait to hear this," Logan said.

"I'm thinking that if Holt knew you were in Valteron City, he might summon his favorite bald magician."

"It would also compromise our own security," Kiara said.

"That's why we call it a covert mission," Logan said. "Emphasis on the 'covert.'"

I knew they'd hate this idea. "Well, if you want Holt's magical protections revoked, that's what I need."

It took almost twenty minutes to hear back, which suggested a vigorous debate on Kiara's end. Finally, she came back on. "We'll see what we can do, Bradley. But you'd better make sure the vote goes the right way."

"Yeah, go out and makes some more friends," Logan chimed in. "You're always saying how you're good with people."

"I don't know that many people here," Quinn protested. "I mean, there's Jillaine, but . . ." He caught himself, but a second too late.

"Who's that?" Kiara demanded.

Shit. Shouldn't have brought her up. "Moric's daughter. She's not a council member, but I think she carries some weight."

"Work on her," Kiara said.

"Yeah, Romeo. Work your magic," Logan added with his usual helpfulness.

"Fine, I'll make some overtures," Quinn said. "Over and out."

He stopped and looked around to get his bearings. A rustle of leaves from behind made him turn around.

He was surprised to see the two men coming toward him. *Where'd they come from?* He nearly waved, but something about them felt off. They moved with the crouched-low readiness of someone about to do violence. They rushed at him the moment he saw them, which only confirmed that impression.

"What the hell?" He backed off. His mind worked frantically. *Who sent them?* Their intent was clear enough. There was no one else around, and it was past dusk. His legs wouldn't hold up if he ran. It was too dark to see if they had any weapons, but he had to assume they did.

He yanked his belt knife out of its sheath. He didn't stand a chance at hand-to-hand combat against two opponents at once. Logan had told him that much. He slid the blade between his thumb and finger. When the men were ten paces out, he wound up and threw at the right-hand one. Moonlight glinted on the blade as it spun end over end. It caught the man somewhere in his torso. He grunted and fell. The second one jumped over his fallen companion and charged right at Quinn.

If there was ever a time for magic, it was now. *No other choice.* Quinn tried to dig deep into himself and find the power that had saved his ass from the river. Knowing that if he couldn't, this guy might very well kill him. That desperation opened something in him, a crack into that tiny room of magic potential. The warmth started to flow out. Then the guy plowed right into him. They tumbled over one another onto the grass.

Knees and elbows. That was the only thing Quinn remembered from Logan's hand-to-hand fighting clinics. So he jabbed out like a funky chicken as they wrestled, catching the man's jaw with an elbow. He tried to break free and make a run for it then, but the guy hooked his leg and flung him backward.

Quinn's head slammed against the ground. His vision blurred red. His ears rang with a high-pitched tone. He shook himself and cleared up just in time to see a boot coming at his face. *Move!* He rolled away onto his hands and knees.

Time to break out the hardware. He clawed at his belt. He got the buckle loose. Then his gut exploded in pain. The bastard had kicked him. He clung to the buckle with both hands. Managed to hang on to it. The guy wound back to kick him again. Quinn flipped off the latch and shot fifty thousand volts right into him.

"Gaaahhh!" The man shook like he was having a seizure. His teeth chattered, and he went down.

Quinn jerked the electrodes out of him and hit the auto-rewind on the buckle. They zipped back into it and out of sight. The guy he'd zapped was still on the ground, and now foaming at the mouth. His eyes had the far-off look of someone whose entire world was pain.

Serves him right. Quinn's whole body hurt like hell. Especially where he'd been kicked. Well, now he could return the favor. With interest. He lifted his boot.

"Enough!" a woman shouted.

He halted mid-stomp.

A globe of light appeared over the green lawns, and brightened enough to cast everything in twilight. A woman strode toward him. The mop of white hair was unmistakable.

"Sella! Thank the gods." Quinn had never been happier to see her in his life. *Now, where was I?*

"That's quite enough!" She sounded out of breath. "What did you do?"

He put his boot down. "These guys just tried to kill me!"

She brushed past him and knelt by the guy he'd zapped. The foaming around the mouth didn't look good, and he'd stopped shaking. *Jesus, maybe I killed him.*

"He's unconscious," Sella said. "You want to tell me how you managed that?"

"I don't know . . . it all happened so fast." He had to buy some time, and figure out a reasonable explanation. "How much did you see?"

"All of it."

"Then you—wait, *all of it?*"

"Yes."

He was still reeling from this bit of information when the first attacker appeared right next to him.

"Shit!" He stutter-stepped away. "He's one of them!"

"I'm well aware of that," Sella said. Her voice was infuriatingly calm.

She knelt, and put her hand palm-down on the fallen attacker. She muttered some words. Quinn was a few paces away, but he felt the chill of fey energy from it. *A delving.*

This didn't make any sense at all. If she saw everything, why didn't she help? *She's my goddamn teacher, for Chrissakes!*

Then everything clicked at once: her casual demeanor, what she'd said, and the fact that she seemed more concerned about his attackers than her own student.

Oh, no *way*. "Did you set me up?" he demanded.

"You're in the advanced class, Quinn. We'll do whatever it takes to get rid of your block."

"Including having two guys attack me in the middle of the night."

"Would you have reacted the same way if this were staged?"

"I guess not." He *probably* wouldn't have shocked the guy.

"There's your answer."

"But I could have killed him!"

The other man, the one he'd thrown his knife at, held it up by the handle. "With this little pigsticker?

I don't think so." He flipped it over, and offered it to Quinn handle-first.

"Well, I wouldn't call it a *pigsticker*," Quinn muttered. He took it and shoved it back into its sheath.

"They were well protected," Sella said. "A normal weapon wouldn't have harmed them."

But the shocker sure as hell did. "Well, I could have had a heart attack. What about that?"

"You look healthy enough to me."

"Gee, thanks."

The unconscious guy moaned and started moving his arms. Sella sighed, and lifted her hands from him. "He'll be all right. But I'd certainly like to know what you did to him."

"I wish I could tell you."

"Do you think you could do it again?" she asked.

Quinn shook his head. *Don't tempt me.*

She'd been cold the other day, but he could get past that. Besides, he had more than just a desire to see her again: he had a goddamn mission-critical justification. *It just doesn't hurt that she's pretty.*

His advanced class with Sella didn't start for another hour. That gave him time to lay some groundwork.

In keeping with the Enclave's whimsical layout, there was a broad meadow about halfway between the residential towers and Jillaine's little chandlery. Quinn had never noticed anyone tending it, but that meadow was home to the widest variety of wildflowers he'd ever seen. There had to be magic involved. How else could desert flowers bloom right next to something that looked straight out of a rainforest? He almost didn't want to know the answer to that. Bottom line, it meant he could put together a bouquet whenever he needed one. *Something any man can appreciate.*

Chaudri had given a few briefings on the language of Alissian flowers—the subtle messages conveyed by one type or the other. Was it the most thrilling of her lectures? No. But he'd retained some basics. Better yet, he still had the scans of the book on Alissian botany that he'd taken on his last visit.

The sun was already pushing up into the sky when he got to the meadow. He felt a tad jittery because he'd had too much Landorian tea. Again. A young couple walked arm in arm down one of the paths a few hundred yards away, but otherwise he had the field to himself. *Probably for the best.* He hadn't asked anyone for permission to cut flowers.

He started with the bluebells, because he knew he'd seen them before. According to some long-dead botanist, that one meant *apology.* They grew in little clusters that were easy to spot. He crouched beside one, and snipped off a little stem with his belt knife.

Next up was the starflower: five bright-yellow petals with a white center, whose unspoken message was *thinking about you.* He burned ten minutes searching high and low for one. Apparently the Enclave residents were a thoughtful bunch. He finally spotted one right at the base of a tall cactus tree. A handful of puncture wounds later, he managed to cut it free.

The third flower was easy to find. Light pink petals, dark purple center. Like a cross between a rose and an iris. Didn't look like anyone had ever picked one, so maybe the message behind it was a little strong. *Promise.* He'd be putting it all on the line with this one.

It used to make him nervous, doing that, but the years in Vegas had hardened him. *Go big or go home.*

Twenty minutes until his class started. He jogged most of the way, and slowed up long enough to catch his breath. He skirted the beehives as best he could. The hum of the bees made him nervous. He rounded the corner of the chandlery and almost plowed into Jillaine. She stood on a stepladder, working a bright yellow ribbon into the latticework over the door.

"Good morning." He didn't have to fake the smile; it came on its own.

Her eyes flickered to him, then back to her work. "Hello."

God, I love the sound of her voice. Even with the cold shoulder. "I brought you something. Well, three things, really."

"I'm surprised you had time, with all of your grand travels and such."

"Number one." He snapped his fingers, and the bluebell appeared between them. "I'm sorry I had to leave so suddenly, and that it took so long to return."

She hesitated. Just for a moment, but it seemed to stretch on forever. But she took it, and worked it right into the latticework among the ribbon. "Apology accepted."

"Number two." He clapped his hands together, and spread them open to reveal the starflower. "I thought about you the whole time I was away."

Her lips twitched in what might have been a smile. Either this whole act amused her, or he'd not been quite right about the meaning. *Damn this flower language. That's probably the equivalent of a sympathy card.* She took it, though, so he counted that a win.

She worked it into the ribbon, and then looked back at him and quirked an eyebrow. "You said you had three things."

"Didn't I give you three flowers?"

"No."

He feigned puzzlement. "Could have sworn I did." Then plucked the pink-and-purple flower out of her boot. "Ah, here it is."

She tittered at the sleight of hand. Then she got a look at the flower, and the laugh died. He was watching her eyes, not his hand, which was why he noticed when her pupils dilated. It was a subtle thing. The stepladder wobbled precariously. He put his free hand on her hip to steady her.

"Number three," Quinn said. "I won't take another adventure without you." He hoped to the Alissian gods that he could keep that promise.

She took it with delicate, trembling fingers. She stared at it. He wanted more than anything to stay, but he'd said his piece. *Time for the grand exit.* He turned and walked away. He forced himself not to look back. He didn't need to see her face anyway. The silence said it all.

Quinn hadn't seen Moric in two days. Maybe that was a good thing, if it meant he was off the island on business. But if he wasn't, and Anton forced a vote, the whole plan would fall apart. Quinn had to know for sure. Not knowing where else to try, he figured he'd check the library, and then the Pirean tower. He strapped on one of the elemental projectors. With Sella getting cute about what qualified as a lesson, he didn't want to be caught unprepared.

As many people as seemed to live on the island, he somehow ended up alone most of the time. This part of the road ran through the middle of a small copse of Alissian lollipop trees—tall, narrow trunks and a single ball of foliage at the top—and he hadn't seen anyone else for five minutes. Which made it doubly suspicious when the strong smell of roses filled his nostrils. It was Jillaine's favorite scent, and as strong as if he'd stuck his head into a bouquet.

I don't think that's a coincidence. He came to a stop. "Are you coming out, or am I to try and find you?" he asked.

She laughed softly by way of answer. The sound came from behind him. He spun around, but saw no one. She laughed again, but this time from somewhere to the right.

It had to be some kind of concealment spell. He'd seen one of those before. How had Sella described it? Something about the light, and how he should keep still if he wanted it to work. He stalked in the direction he thought the sound had come from. If she was on the road, he'd run into her. Or she'd have to move, and he might spot her.

He'd moved about twenty yards when she laughed again, and sent another dose of her rose scent to his nose. *Yeah, yeah, keep making noise.* He'd spent his entire childhood learning woodcraft from his grandfather. Nothing on two legs could move that fast, that silently. It was like a game of Marco Polo, without the sound of water to give someone away.

He stood still for a moment, ears perked. Hell, he could hear her breathing! *She has to be close.* This concealment stuff was a damn nuisance. He shifted the metal band on his wrist, and let his fingertips brush the controls of the elemental projector. He could use that to find her, but it felt like cheating. Besides, she was suspicious enough of him as it was.

He shook his head, as if trying to clear it. "Must have been my imagination." He turned and started down the road again.

He heard the indignant scoff, but pretended not to. *Stay on target. Stay on target.*

Wham. He walked right into an invisible *something.* He was mid-step when it happened, and bounced off it like a tennis ball. He ended up in a heap in the dirt. "Son of a bitch!" So much for the graceful exit.

A shadow fell across him. "Did you fall?" Jillaine's voice was laced with honey. She chose to be visible again. Her eyes danced with amusement.

Quinn wanted to frown at her, but seeing her this close, having her *attention* for once, took the harshness out of it. "Ran into something."

"You should watch where you're going." She offered her hand, as good a confession of guilt as he'd probably get from her.

He ignored it, and climbed to his feet without any

help. He brushed himself off a tad more than necessary. "I'll get right on that." He tried not to look at her, but she drew his gaze like a magnet. Her violet eyes simply *pulled* at him.

"I hear you've taken some meals in the Pirean tower," she said.

He kept his expression neutral, though he felt a glimmer of hope. *She's been asking about me.* "They have the best food on the island. You should come by, actually. Tonight's mutton night!"

"Will my father be there?"

"I'm not sure. Now that I think of it, actually, I haven't seen him in a couple of days," Quinn said.

"Then maybe I will."

Time for one of those overtures. "Maybe we could walk there together, at the dinner hour. The chandlery's on my way." This was a bald-faced lie, but he hoped she wouldn't call him on it.

Her eyes narrowed, as if she sensed an ulterior motive. "Very well. At the last sliver of sunset."

He gave her his most innocent smile. "Until then, m'lady."

"Some tricks you just can't learn."

—Art of Illusion, March 1

CHAPTER 29

TRICKERY

Quinn practically ran to the Pirean tower, ignoring the twinges of pain from his still-tender legs.

It was early yet, so the common room lay almost empty. Leward crouched beside the hearth, where a massive haunch of mutton sizzled and crackled as it spun slowly on a spit. The smell made Quinn's stomach growl, and reminded him that he'd missed lunch. Leward moved his hands like a symphony conductor near the flames. They danced and spouted with each little movement.

It was no accident that they cooked the mutton

out here rather than back in the kitchens. The entic-
ing smell wafted out the open door, the Enclave's
version of a soft pretzel store at the mall. You
couldn't pay for better advertising than the smell of
roasted meat. In a few hours, this room would be
jam-packed with hungry Pireans and anyone wise
enough to call them friends.

Quinn took a moment to savor the sight and sound
of it. "It smells amazing in here!"

Leward's youthful face split into a grin. "Quinn!
You coming for supper tonight?"

"Wouldn't miss it for the world, buddy. Is it all
right if I bring someone?"

"It's not Anton, is it?"

"What? No. Why would I bring *him*?"

"It's common knowledge that you had dinner in
the Caralissian tower."

Quinn waved it off. "That was more of a business
meeting."

Leward gave him a flat look. "With food."

"They can't hold a candle to Pirean cooking."

"Do you mean that?"

"Trust me, it's not even close. Hey, is Moric
around? I need to talk to him."

Leward shook his head. "Haven't seen him in a
day or two."

"Neither have I. He's not on a mission, is he?"

"No, the council put a hold on assignments until
further notice."

"What for?"

"I don't know. For some reason, they forgot to tell me."

Quinn put on a puzzled expression. "Wait, aren't you running the council yet?"

Leward guffawed. "Not quite." He held out both hands toward the hearth and made a beckoning gesture. The flames leaped up to sear at the meat, which hissed and cracked in the sudden heat.

The aroma hit like a wave. Quinn's stomach was giving him actual hunger pangs. "Damn, you're good at that."

"Thanks."

"Want to do me a favor?"

"Anything."

God, I love the Pireans. Quinn pointed at the flames. "Teach me to do that."

Leward's eager smile faltered. "I'm not really supposed to interfere with the teachers—"

"Who's interfering? I just want to learn some tricks." He could do illusions all day, but that always felt like cheating. A real trick, even a small one, would make him feel like maybe he *did* belong here. That he should keep trying to learn.

"I don't know," Leward said.

Quinn made his voice casual. "I could ask a teacher, I suppose. It's just that fire is your specialty. In fact, I heard you're the best at it."

"Someone said that?"

"Absolutely." Quinn pointed at the hearth. "Now that I've seen you in action, I understand."

Leward grinned. "All right, so what sort of tricks?"

Two hours later, Quinn was beyond frustrated. "This isn't working."

"Don't give up yet," Leward said. "Here, try this." He snapped his fingers, then splayed them wide over the hearth. Blue flames leaped from the hot coals beneath it. They were in the shape of his hand, too, and mirrored his movements.

Quinn tried his right hand first. Snap, then splay. Nothing. He switched hands and tried it again, willing the flames to appear. If anything, they got smaller. "Damn."

"It's all right. A lot of people have trouble controlling fire." Leward absentmindedly waggled his fingers and brought the hearth to a steady burn again.

Never thought I'd be jealous of Leward. Quinn sighed. "What I really want to do is be able to light a candle."

"Is that all? What for?"

"To impress a girl."

Leward laughed. "You think magic will do that?"

"It works more than you'd guess, my friend."

"Not on this island."

"Come on, please? I need this."

Leward wavered, then gave in. "All right, let's try something." He put his hand beneath Quinn's so that their fingers lined up. He moved it over the hearth. The fire sprung up to follow them wherever it went.

Quinn's palm tingled—he could *feel* the power of the magic emanating from Leward's hand. "Whoa!"

"It's really something, isn't it?"

"Yeah."

"If you can feel it, you can do it." Leward let him go.

"All right." Quinn went to try it on his own.

Leward grabbed his arm. "No. Wait until you really need it, and remember that feeling."

Quinn grunted. *It's worth a shot.* "All right. Thanks, Leward."

"Anytime."

"Listen, you'll let me know if Moric shows up, won't you?"

"Did you check his room?" Leward asked.

No, because I'm a moron. "I don't know where it is."

"It's right down the hall. I'll show you, if you want."

Quinn hesitated, wondering if that might be stepping over the line. Moric was a council member. He'd never invited Quinn to visit, and he valued his privacy. *Then again, he drops by my room whenever he feels like it.* "You know what? That'd be great."

Leward made a pushing gesture over the hearth. The flames sputtered down to nearly nothing. Just enough to keep it warm. Quinn fought another spike of envy, and followed him out of the common room.

They passed the stairs and started down a long hallway lined with doors. Moric must live on the ground floor, which was good. That made it less awkward for Quinn to stop by to see him on a whim. *Better than wandering around upstairs like a peeping Tom.*

"It's up ahead," Leward said. "Second door on the right."

Quinn laughed. "Seriously?"

"What?" Leward asked.

"Nothing. It's just that he put me in the same room, in the Landorian tower."

Leward stopped in his tracks. "You've got a room on the *first* floor?"

"Why, is that a problem?"

"No, not at all," Leward said. But his eyes were still a little wide.

"Where's your room?"

"Sixteen floors up."

And they don't have elevators here, either. "Oh. Sorry. Maybe I just got lucky."

Leward snorted. "I think it takes a little more than luck to get down to the first floor. It's a luxurious privilege."

"I didn't ask for it. Hell, I didn't even know."

"I believe you." Leward started back down the hall. "But I wouldn't bring it up to the other students."

"Don't worry. Jade never gives me the time of day, and the skinny kid owes me one."

"The skinny kid?"

"Another student in Sella's class. He still hasn't told me his name, and I keep forgetting to ask."

"Ah. Well, he goes by Everett."

Quinn looked over at him in surprise. "Do you know him?"

"Better than anyone here."

Quinn recognized the facial features then. The slight chin and wide, flat nose. *How did I miss that?* "You're his older brother, aren't you?"

"By four years."

"Why didn't you say something?'

He shrugged. "I thought it might just come up in conversation."

"Well, we're usually pretty busy in class, trying not to get eaten, drowned, or burned alive."

"I guess that's true."

"Do your parents live here, too?" Quinn asked.

Leward's face fell. "They don't have the ability."

"So what, they're not allowed to visit?"

"Oh, they are." Leward chewed his lip, and dropped his eyes. "But we're from the Tip."

The Pirean Tip. That was an isolated community at the end of a narrow, north-pointing peninsula. Deeply religious and distrustful of outsiders, according to Chaudri's cultural brief. From the expression on Leward's face, Quinn guessed they weren't too thrilled to learn that he and his brother were magicians. He felt bad for bringing it up. "Sorry, man. That's got to be rough."

"We got out, which is what matters."

Quinn doubted it was easy, though. It was something to ask Moric about, once he found him. *There's a list that keeps getting longer.*

They arrived at the door, which was closed tight. Quinn knocked three times. "Moric?"

No answer from within. He knocked again, but got no answer.

"Maybe he's out," Leward said.

"I'll ask Jillaine at dinner tonight."

"Oh, she's coming? Good," Leward said. "Wait, is *Jillaine* the girl you're trying to impress?"

Quinn smiled. "She sure is."

"Wow, Moric's daughter." Leward shook his head. "You're a brave man."

"That's what they keep telling me."

> "Never underestimate the power of a small team dedicated to a greater good."
>
> —R. Holt, "Research Team: Budget Justification"

CHAPTER 30

SURVEILLANCE

Logan and Kiara lay prone on a ridge overlooking Valteron City. Winter was nearly imperceptible here; the balmy air had both of them sweating in their ghillie suits. Cleanup crews had all but erased the scars of Valteron's brief civil war. Harbor traffic was up. Refugees still flowed back into the city. CASE Global's research team estimated the population at around eighty thousand before the last Prime died. Now it was probably closer to a hundred thousand.

The heat and the crowd and the recent unrest should have turned this place into a powder keg waiting to blow. Instead, the city sprawled out beneath them looked eerily calm.

"Looks like they got the harbor cleaned up," Logan said.

Kiara's eyes were a little wider than usual. "I've never seen so many ships there at once. Look, there's a Felaran whaler. Damn, it's busy."

"A regular Hong Kong."

They'd gleaned bits and pieces of Holt's activities from people on the road. He'd doubled the size of the city watch, and given them license to use extreme force when necessary. Now they patrolled in teams of four, every man well-fed and heavily armed. Not a one had been lost under the new leadership. For the first time in recorded history, the city watch was Valteron's most coveted job.

But all of those were rumors. The company executives wanted direct surveillance. Which, among other things, happened to be Logan's specialty.

"Let's see what this bird can do," he said.

The Kite-2 unmanned aerial vehicle (UAV) was a lightweight cousin of the missile-capable drones employed in the Middle East. Solar powered, four-foot wingspan, and a surveillance technology called the Shiva Stare. Twelve high-definition cameras with independent controls provided multiple angles.

All of the parts had to be small enough to fit in a

saddlebag, so reassembly was one hell of a job. The engineers had field-tested the disassembly/reassembly process, and written a ninety-six-page manual with every step described in detail.

Which is why it took us two days to put the damn thing together. Two days of valuable op time so they could finally get a look at Holt's new seat of power.

But the drone was working, and the video feeds were transmitted via comm relay to a company outpost on the other side of the Alissian continent. Chaudri's research team could get a lot out of it. Shipping lanes, population estimates, that sort of thing. But that wasn't why they were really here, or why they'd brought the drone. They were looking for the one man who'd recognize it for what it was.

"Let's have a look at the walls," Kiara said.

"I'm on it." Logan guided the drone for a sweep of the low stone wall that bounded the north of Valteron. It was a border marker more than a defensive strategy; the city relied more on its ships and economic might for defense than anything else. Logan didn't even mark any guards along the length of it.

"Perimeter looks a little light," he said.

"Given the number of refugees he's taken in, I'm not surprised."

"Even so, he shouldn't just—"

"I think I just saw something," Kiara said. "Loop it around, will you?"

"I'd love to." Which was the truth—he loved flying

these things. The only trouble with flying million-dollar drones is that they ruined you for model airplanes.

He brought the drone around and steered it almost directly over the wall. He saw what she was talking about. "Looks like some kind of new construction."

The tower was about three stories tall and, judging by the shape of the stones, built within the last month. *How did I miss that?* There was a metal contraption on the roof. It had the shape of a shallow bowl, and looked like fine steel shined to a good polish. "What do you think that is?"

"A signaling beacon?" Kiara offered.

Logan shook his head. "Too small for that. I'll slide in for a closer look."

"No." She grabbed his shoulder, and he lurched the drone up and away. "Not until we know what it is."

"All right, no flyby." *Christ almighty, don't wreck the thing.*

"Let's move and find a vantage point for the real target."

"Roger that."

When seen from above, the schooner-shaped palace of the Valteroni Prime looked like it was crushing the city's wide swath of thatch-roofed houses on its way out to sea. That probably wasn't an accident, either—Valteron had made its fortune from dominating trade, and sea trade in particular. Land merchants from the rest of the country, and even from Tion and Caralis, all trundled their way here to have their goods shipped to distant ports.

The drone finished its current pass; a terse message appeared on Logan's screen. Command wanted another look. *They must be watching this in real time.* He banked the drone to avoid a low-hanging nimbus cloud north of the city.

"I've got some movement," Kiara said. "East wing of the palace, behind those merlons."

"Let's have a look." Logan reduced altitude and steered the drone back toward the palace.

Holt had recommended a thousand-foot hard floor for any drone flights, a height at which the small drone would resemble a large bird to any Alissians who looked up. Trouble was, it was hard to get detailed footage of anything smaller than a building at that height. Even with the Shiva Stare. And Holt himself wouldn't recognize it, which was the part of this mission they *hadn't* told Command about.

Logan dropped to about a hundred and fifty feet for a quick little pass. He'd just nudge it over the wall of the castle for a little peek, and then drop back out of sight. No harm, no foul.

"You're well below the hard floor," Kiara said.

"You want to get his attention, don't you?"

She frowned, but gave him a tiny nod. *Permission granted.*

"Making the approach." He took the UAV off its safety mode and coasted it across the city rooftops.

Someone might be able to spot it, but the thing was so little and fast that they'd never get a close look. The urban camouflage helped—the drone had a photoadaptive skin that mimicked the ambient colors around it. It couldn't disappear entirely, but it would be hard to pinpoint. *Kind of like that beast from the* Predator *movies*, Logan thought. But Holt would know the technology the second he saw it.

The drone zoomed closer to the palace, capturing a live feed from its cameras the whole time. They only had enough screen space to monitor one, but the other fifteen were recorded on the high-density drive, and also fed back to the research team back at the island facility. *And they're going to have a goddamn field day.* The company executives were reluctant to permit any surveillance technology into Alissia. The only video footage they'd taken so far was grainy stuff from pinhole cameras.

"Here we go," Logan said. He guided the drone up and over the high stone wall. *Just like clockwork.* He was so pleased with the deftness of the maneuver, he almost didn't notice what the video feed was telling him. Kiara's hand on his arm was the first warning. The camera lens refocused, and there they were. Eight men with crossbows already ranked and loaded. They were looking right at the drone, taking aim.

"Shit!" Logan said.

"Get it out of there!"

He was trying.

There was no sound, but the flicker of the crossbows and blurs of the flying bolts told the story. The camera shook violently as they struck home. The drone wasn't armored. The heavy bolts cut its airfoils to pieces. It lurched over as alarm warnings flashed red on the control unit.

"Losing altitude," Logan said. He fought with the controls, but it would have taken a magician to keep that bird in the air. The stone floor of the courtyard zoomed up as the drone fell. It crashed hard, bounced a couple of times, and ended up on its side. The video feed showed only a close-up view of the cobblestones. Then a pair of steel-tipped boots loomed large in the frame. The weight on them shifted.

Oh, no.

The screen went black. A status warning flashed: *Signal lost.*

"Well," Logan said. "So much for the drone."

"If Holt didn't know we were here, he does now."

This had better be worth it.

They were still lying in their ghillie suits trying to reconstruct what had happened when the palace gates opened. No less than two dozen horsemen charged out, riding at a gallop. They broke up into groups of four, and rode off in six different directions from the palace plaza.

"I don't think they're out for a pleasure ride," Logan said.

"Maybe he's fixed our location."

"I don't see how. He didn't have that kind of equipment with him when he went AWOL in the first place."

But it didn't mean Holt was without resources. He knew CASE Global's strategies, for one thing. Logan pulled out his parchmap of the region around Valteron City. Holt probably reasoned that they weren't in the bay, so he'd be sending these patrols to cover the major vantage points land-side. Six search parties covered a lot of ground when you cut it down like that. He and Kiara were a good half mile out of the city limits, but still.

"We need to move," he said.

"How long do we have?"

"If they're pushing the horses, probably about ten minutes until they're in visual range."

They scrambled to their feet and started packing up in a hurry—they couldn't exactly leave the control console sitting around, even with the drone destroyed. Logan fluffed up the depressions in the grass where they'd been lying prone, and Kiara obscured the most obvious boot prints. No need to talk, just the quiet efficient business of two career soldiers who knew what they were about.

Not exactly our first barbecue.

Back in the early days, before they lost Relling at sea, he and Kiara had run countless in-world operations together. You spent enough time with another soldier, and you learned how the both of you fit together into a cohesive machine. That's why he'd loved training on Alpha Team for CASE Global, once he'd left the navy. Ended up with a few new brothers-in-arms. Sure, a lot of those brothers were sisters, and the arms hadn't been used in combat Earthside for a few hundred years, but the camaraderie was the same.

They were packed up and mounted again in six minutes. A quick sweep of the land between them and Valteron City showed that Logan's hunch had been good: one of the mounted patrols was headed more or less directly toward them. They hadn't been spotted, but if they'd lingered a few minutes more, the riders might well have caught them by surprise.

"Holt's got the whole rapid response thing down. I'll give him that," Logan said. He touched his heels to the gelding and turned northeast, back toward the abandoned farmhouse they were using as a base camp.

"He should. After all, he's building an army," Kiara said.

"What makes you say that?"

"A ton of little things. The horse buying, and the crossbow upgrades. The ships from Pirea."

Logan scratched his chin. "I guess those are what you'd expect if he's mustering of forces."

"I'm certain he is, but that's not what bothers me."

"What's worse than that?"

"He *knew* to expect us today."

"That's just how he thinks," Logan said. "The guy's been two moves ahead of us since day one."

"Fine. But he had no reason to expect that we'd bring the drone, though. So . . ."

She was right about that—it had been an uphill battle with the executives to get the exemption. *Fat lot of good it did us.* "So how did he know to be waiting for it?"

"Exactly." Kiara made one last sweep of the palace with her binoculars—maybe hoping to catch a glimpse of Holt on the walls—and then spurred her horse after him. "I'd sure as hell like to figure that out."

sealed containers about the size of a large potato, disguised to look like lumps of charcoal. They wouldn't burn, though, since each one contained a garment made of CASE Global's proprietary fireproof polyblends. He broke open the one he'd marked SO, for *special occasion*, and shook it out. The shirt was light as silk, and the color of polished silver. With a couple more vigorous shakes, the wrinkles fell away. Quinn whistled. *That's a hell of a material.*

The garment technology hadn't even hit the market, but once it did, CASE Global was going to make a killing.

He tugged on his best jacket over it, a linen-and-silk job in dark gray. This was also fireproof, and customized with a number of hidden pockets. Then it was time for the breeches and riding boots to put him at the peak of Landorian men's fashion. Truth be told, he preferred the more flamboyant Kestani fabrics, but most Landorians wouldn't be caught dead in one. He strapped the elemental projector on his right arm and gave it a quick test. The thing had held up surprisingly well in Sella's class, but it was running low on juice. The backup was already about dead.

He closed up the saddlebags and shoved them under the bed, just to be cautious. He couldn't lock his door from the outside, so anyone could wander in here and poke around while he was out.

Quinn hustled to make it to his rendezvous with Jillaine. He rounded the bend and caught sight of the chandlery, just as the last sliver of sun remained above the horizon. *Right on time.* The door to the chandlery was closed, for the first time he could remember. He started to worry she'd forgotten, until he saw the glow of lamplight beneath the door. *Thank God.*

He knocked three times, and fought the sudden feeling of butterflies in his stomach. *I feel like a teenager on prom night.*

The door swept open, and he realized he'd been wrong about the lamplight. The orange glow came from hundreds of candles. Tiny flames danced on every shelf and every wall in the chandlery. Jillaine stood in the middle, and sweet Lord, she looked good. She'd done something with her hair—a bunch of ivory clips held it up in layered tresses. Her dress was the color of moonlight. It traced her form down to the waist, where it flared out to the ankles like a ball gown. Quinn was distantly aware that he was staring with his mouth wide open, but couldn't help it.

Oh, my God, it is prom night.

She gave him a shy little smile. She wasn't completely sure of herself, and somehow that made her even more attractive. She was real and she was lovely and she was *right here.* The silence stretched. He should say something. *Well, I should close my mouth, and then say something.*

"You look . . ." He couldn't even think of a word that was strong enough. Putting a word to her felt wrong. "You look like a princess."

She smiled. "Have you met many princesses?"

"I've *seen* a few of them, but not a one as lovely as you are."

She glided over and took his arm. "Shall we?"

"Oh, we definitely *shall*."

Jillaine waved a casual hand behind her as they walked out. All of the candles snuffed out at once, in a great puff of smoke. The door swung shut behind them. Quinn raised his eyebrows. *She makes it look so easy.*

"How's the candle business?" he asked.

"So *now* you're interested in what I do?"

"I've always been interested."

"So interested that you left the island," she said.

He winked at her. "But I came back, didn't I?"

She shook her head at him, but relented. "Business is slow, as it always is. That's what I get for becoming a chandler for people who can summon fire at will." She snapped her fingers, and a little pinpoint of flame appeared in the air in front of them. It drifted forward as they walked, casting a little orange glow against the encroaching twilight.

Quinn felt an odd pang of envy. "Not everyone can do that."

She gave him a sympathetic look. "Still having trouble finding your magic?"

"I know the potential is there. I just can't seem to draw on it when I want to."

She squeezed his arm where she held it. "Maybe you haven't found the right motivation."

Or maybe I have.

"So, why didn't you want to come if your father was here?" he asked.

"I'm not speaking to him at the moment."

"Oh." He let that sit for a moment. "Do you want to talk about it?"

"Not especially."

"All right. I just thought maybe I could help."

She snorted. "I think you've done enough."

"Hey now, what's that supposed to mean?"

"When my father came back and said you were . . . gone, I demanded he take me to wherever you'd been. To look for you."

"Aw, thanks," Quinn said. It was more than a little touching that she'd wanted to ride off and rescue him. *She's adorable.*

"He refused to let me do anything, because it was on the mainland." She shook her head and muttered, "Said it was 'too dangerous' for me."

"Honestly, I could have used you. You're pretty dangerous yourself."

She gave him a sharp look, like she thought he was mocking her. Finally, though, she said, "That's the nicest thing you've ever said to me."

Quinn elected not to take offense at that, even though he'd said a pile of *other* nice things to her. "Well, I appreciate that you tried."

"My father did not. Hence the silence between us." They reached the wide village green that surrounded the Pirean tower. The door was propped open, and the welcoming glow of the common room drew people from all directions, like moths to a flame. Quinn and Jillaine were no less immune. The smell and the noise pulled them through the doorway.

A crowd of friendly faces waited inside. Quinn savored the moment they turned and saw him with Jillaine. Eyebrows quirked. Elbows nudged into neighbors.

"Quinn! Jillaine!" Leward pushed through the crowd. His face was flushed, either from the exertion or the heat of his own fire pit. "Glad you could make it." He did a double take. "You look like royalty!"

"Yeah, we coordinated outfits," Quinn said. "On account of it being mutton night."

Leward grinned. "I'm glad I saved you seats." He made for the tables, beckoning them to follow.

Attaboy. Quinn took the lead. It was too tight to keep Jillaine on his arm, so he let his hand slide down to hers. And she held on, which sent a thrilling little tremor up his arm. A few of Leward's dinner pals took note of this, and gave him the nod. He grinned back at them. *Eat your hearts out, fellas.*

Leward ushered them to a couple of ladder-back chairs at one of the long tables. Quinn helped Jillaine into hers and squeezed in beside her. Two place settings—tin plates and mismatched silverware— waited for them, a far cry from the Caralissian tower,

but he couldn't ask for anything more. Leward reappeared with a massive haunch of meat, and cut
them each of a slice, *churrasco*-style.

"Looks delicious. Thanks, Leward," Quinn said.
He didn't take his own food from the platters that
were lined up in the middle of the table; in the Pirean
culture, you served your neighbors. So he found a
spoon and delivered a hefty pile of the squash medley
to Jillaine's plate, to her visible amusement. *Yeah,
that's right. I know how they do it here.*

Meanwhile, the gray-haired woman on his right
sliced off some bread for his own. Betsy was a regular,
so she knew to give him three pieces and the bowl of
honey. She glanced from him to Jillaine, then back,
and gave him a wink. All this while still in deep
conversation with the woman across from her.

"We might make a Pirean out of you yet," Jillaine
murmured.

"I do what I can." Quinn cut off a tiny corner of
the mutton. It was seared to perfection, but still so
tender that it melted in his mouth. There were five-
star restaurants back home that wouldn't stack up
against the cooking here. And nothing in either world
stacked up to the company. "So, do you—"

"Well, well. It's two of my favorite people," Moric
said. He'd appeared behind them, still in his threadbare riding cloak, looking more disheveled than
usual.

"Hey, Moric," Quinn said. "Where've you been? I was getting ready to send out a search party."

Jillaine didn't look at him, and went on as if she hadn't heard anything.

Moric frowned at her, then at Quinn. "Oh, yes. You do look *quite* concerned at the moment."

I think he just made a joke. "Well, come on. It's mutton night and we're celebrating, you know, me *not* having perished."

"For which we're all eternally grateful." Moric put a heavy hand on Quinn's shoulder and beckoned him to the door. "Could I have a word?"

"I'll be right back," Quinn whispered to Jillaine. Then he followed Moric out the door.

Moric led Quinn down the winding path that led around the green, a subtle signal for desired privacy.

"You sure you don't want to eat?" Quinn asked. "The mutton's unbelievably good." As was the company, but he didn't dare say so.

Moric chuckled. "I think you might catch more meals in the Pirean tower than I do. But I can't stay, I'm afraid."

"Everything all right?"

"I've had a message from our mutual friend, asking for some assistance."

Quinn's breath caught. "The Valteroni Prime."

"I'm headed to Valteron, and may be gone a few days."

Yes! Quinn kept his excitement under wraps. "Well, I appreciate the heads-up."

"Please keep it to yourself. The Valteroni Prime is a delicate topic right now, thanks to Anton and his minions."

Quinn felt a cold sliver of dread that Moric might know everything he'd been up to. An amateur might 'fess up to save his ass. Instead, he played it harder. "You want me to keep an eye on things while you're away."

Moric gave him a serious look. "You seem to be keeping an eye on some things already."

Uh-oh. "Luckily, I'm the kind of guy you can trust with that."

"She's my daughter. I don't trust *any* guy with *that*." Moric gave him a hard stare, and it was all Quinn could do to not tremble under the weight of it.

Surprisingly, though, Moric's face softened. "How is she?" he asked, more quietly.

"Mad at you, but otherwise fine."

"Best not to let her know that I'll be in Valteron, either."

Quinn shrugged. "If that's what you want me to do."

"I do. And there's one more thing I need from you. The wayfinder stone."

"You don't think you can find your way back here?"

"I can, but I think the Valteroni Prime may need a reminder of those I represent. If you don't mind."

Quinn couldn't refuse; he had no use for the stone now that he was here, and pushing back would only pique Moric's interest. "Sure thing." He dug the leather cord out from under his shirt and lifted it over his head. The absence felt strange. He handed it over.

Moric put it on and reached into his cloak. "Here, take this." He offered a dark-colored piece of stone.

Quinn took it, and was surprised at how heavy it was. It felt carved, but he couldn't make out the design in the darkness. "What is it?"

"A summoning statue, in case you need me while I'm away. Shatter the statue, and I'll come to you."

"Thanks." He tucked the statue into an inside pocket. "How soon do you have to leave?"

"I should be gone already. And you'd best get back to the common room. It's impolite to keep a lady waiting."

Quinn glanced back at the door to the Pirean tower, which still glowed with firelight and merriment. "Well, if you insist."

Moric stalked away across the green. Quinn waited until he was out of sight, and then made right for the Caralissian tower. The butler, whom Quinn had begun mentally referring to as Jeeves, stood at attention at the top of the stairs. He spotted Quinn, and said not a word, but beckoned him inside.

Quinn followed him to the same dining room, and waited while the man knocked. It opened to reveal Anton in his usual chair, finishing up a meal. Another place setting sat at the far end of the table, but it looked untouched.

"Sorry to drop in," Quinn said. He waited while Jeeves closed the door behind him, leaving him alone. "But I've got good news. Moric's leaving the island for a few days."

Anton dabbed at his lips with a cloth napkin, then stood. "When?"

"Now, tonight. No one else is supposed to know."

"That's good. But I'm afraid we have a slight problem," Anton said. He gestured at the empty place setting across the table. "We're still a vote short."

Quinn's heart sank. "Tell me you're kidding."

Anton shrugged. "I did everything I could, but Valteron's influence here remains strong."

I'm so screwed. Exposing the other team, lying to Moric, and now all of it would be for nothing. "There has to be something else we can do."

Anton pursed his lips. "You said that Moric left in secret."

"Yes. He wanted me to keep it quiet."

"If something were to happen to him, the Pireans would be allowed to choose a replacement."

"I don't want anything to happen to him."

"Of course not," Anton said. "But if it looked that way . . ."

"How would it look that way?"

"I'll take care of it. But we'd need to ensure the Pireans chose someone sympathetic to our cause."

"Leave that part to me," Quinn said.

Quinn hurried back to the Pirean tower, hoping Jillaine hadn't left. And that no one else had taken his place. If you left a pretty girl eating by herself in public, that was a very real hazard. No matter the time period.

He whispered a word of thanks to all the Alissian gods when he saw she was still there. Betsy'd started chatting her up about something. *Remind me to send that one some flowers.*

"Sorry about that." He slid back into his seat like he hadn't been gone almost half an hour.

"I was beginning to think you ran off again," Jillaine said.

He shook his head. "I promised you I wouldn't, remember?"

"What did my father want?" she asked.

"To hear how you were doing."

She nodded. "And what did you say?"

He took another bite of the mutton, which had remained warm despite his half-hour absence. "I said you'd tell him yourself, when you were damn well ready."

Out of the corner of his eye, he saw her little smile.

Leward turned up as Quinn finished. "How was it?"

"Best mutton I've ever had," Quinn said, because it was true.

Leward's face split into a wide grin. "Here, I'll take your plates."

"I've got it." Quinn stood and put a hand on his shoulder. "You've done enough." He gestured at Jillaine's plate. "May I?"

"Such a gentleman," she said.

He grinned, and worked his way down the hall to the common kitchen. This was a snug, stone-tiled room with ovens and roasting pits on either side. He skirted the wooden table and made his way to stone sinks on the far wall. They were already filled with warm, fragrant water. *Perfect.*

He'd just started scrubbing when he heard someone come in behind. *Probably Leward.* "I said I've got it."

"Got what?" Jillaine asked.

"Oh. I thought you were Leward." He tilted his head toward the common room. "Go enjoy yourself. I'll just be a minute."

"I don't mind helping." She slipped up beside him, warm and close and smelling of roses. He couldn't argue.

They made quick work of it. Jillaine didn't use her talents, though she easily could have. Come to think of it, most Enclave magicians didn't use their magic on mundane things. Pireans especially. Maybe it was a cultural thing.

She did, however, splash him on purpose. "Oops."

"Hey!"

"It was an accident."

It was not. But he let it slide. They finished, and set the plates and silver out to dry on the table. Laughter and the buzz of conversation drifted in from the common room. Quinn felt a touch of disappointment, because he knew he'd never spirit her away from that crowd. Not with the attention they were getting.

"It sounds lively out there. Want to hang around for a drink?" he asked.

She glanced at the door, then gestured at his soaked shirt. "But you're all wet."

He shrugged. "It'll dry."

"Hmm." She leaned closer to him and took his hand.

He didn't dare breathe.

She pulled him around the sinks and waved her free hand at the wall beside the oven. A vertical crack appeared. Stone ground against stone as it widened, revealing a dim hallway beyond.

A hidden door. He gave a low whistle. "Well, I'll be—"

Jillaine shook her head, and put a finger over her lips.

He bit his tongue. *Let no one say that Quinn Bradley doesn't know when to shut up.*

They slipped through, and the gap closed behind. She led him up a spiraling staircase. Their footsteps echoed in the semidarkness. They passed a landing, then another. On the fourth floor, she pulled him down a curving hallway. Iridescent globes hung from the ceiling every ten paces or so, and cast little pools of light on the floor. He and Jillaine ghosted through them, moving deeper into the tower. She laced her fingers into his. They were delicate little things, slender but strong. Soft as gossamer silk.

She stopped at a plain wooden door. The top half of it had been carved into a tangle of vines and roses and hidden thorns. Quinn brushed his fingers on the rough edges, marveling at the detail. It swung open silently. He followed her in, wondering if he dared to close it behind them. He wasn't brave enough, but the door closed on its own.

Jillaine snapped her fingers, and a fire sprang into life in the hearth. It was a snug one-room apartment much like his own. Narrow bed, table with two chairs. She had five times as many candles, though, and a bookshelf that would make Chaudri drool. Forty or fifty leather-bound volumes, minimum, all of them carefully lined up with each other and the edge of the shelf.

"That's a lot of—" he began. Then he realized how close she was. The words left him. She stood on her toes, pressed her lips against his. She pulled away, but held him with her eyes. The invitation was clear as day.

"It's far easier to disappear in Alissia than it is on Earth."

—R. Holt, "Ramifications of Technological Disparities"

CHAPTER 32

THE MENTOR

Valteron. For the second time in just a few months, Veena laid eyes on the most powerful nation in Alissia. For this whole mission, the distance between her and Richard had seemed almost infinite. Now it had been compressed to the size of a single city.

The Valteroni captain had kept Dr. Holt's word. They'd had their own cabins, wine and hot meals every evening, the works. The only thing not offered was proximity. Their attempts to engage the captain or crew in any sort of a deep conversation had been met with stony silence. No one was impolite, of course, but Veena got more information out of the seagulls than anyone else on the ship.

Julio was at the rail with his opera glasses when she came up on deck. She was beginning to wonder if he'd slept at all. "How does it look?" she asked.

"Crowded," Julio said.

"Is that good news, or bad?"

"Well, no one's rioting."

She took the optics and made her own sweep of the harbor. The docks were jam-packed with people, but bustling. Plenty of ships tied up and in the midst of unloading, too. The last time she'd been here, burning hulks had littered the harbor, and half the city was starving. Fast-forward a few months, and everyone looked decently fed. Content, even.

"What do you think Holt's been up to?" Julio asked.

Keeping his promises, she wanted to say. "Running a nation the size of Valteron probably keeps him busy."

Julio shook his head. "Where does he find the time?"

"I'll be sure to ask when I see him."

Julio barked a laugh. Then glanced over and saw the look on her face. "Veena, tell me you're kidding."

"He's expecting me. And the captain's going to send him word of my coming anyway."

"That's not a good reason to go running off to his palace."

"If I don't, he'll come looking for me. It's better that the meeting happen on our terms," Veena said.

"What if he takes you prisoner?"

"He won't, if I go there voluntarily. It's a matter of honor."

Julio snorted.

"Besides, he did invite me," Veena said.

"The fact that he's sweet on you isn't exactly selling me on this."

If only he were. She handed back the optics. "Look, it's the only way to find out what he's really up to. Can you say that what Logan and Kiara have been doing is more effective?"

"They're getting some intel."

"It's not enough. We both know that."

"Fine," Julio said. "But I'm coming with you."

"They might let you come as far as the palace. But not inside the walls."

"How am I supposed to protect you if I'm outside?"

"There's no safer place for me in Alissia than inside that palace. Dr. Holt gave his word." That's the part of his letter she'd told Julio about—a guarantee of safe passage.

Julio snickered. "And you think you can trust him?"

"We need to know what he's up to, don't we?" she asked.

"That's not your job."

"It's *all* of our job, and I'm the one with the actual invitation. But if Dr. Holt so much as glimpses you or Logan, we won't learn anything."

"Let me call it in," Julio said.

The moment he did that, Kiara would put the kibosh on this. Veena had no doubt. So she put a hand on his arm, not firmly, but just the fingertips. "Please, don't call it in."

He froze when she touched him. "Veena—"

"Let me do this."

He shook his head and muttered, "Logan's going to kill me."

That was as good of permission as she'd ever get. She waved to get the captain's attention. "Captain! My manservant will be getting off early."

"Here?"

"Yes."

The captain spat over the side. "Guess I can lend him a skiff and a couple of men."

"Much appreciated, Captain," Veena said.

Julio made a face. "Do I really have to get off now?"

"Why wait?"

He rolled his shoulders and looked away. "I was hoping we could, you know, spend some more time."

I wish we could. Veena had enjoyed these weeks alone with Julio far more than she'd ever have imagined. He was so kind, so attentive. So different from

Richard. "When this mission is over, we'll have all the time in the world."

"Really?"

"All we need is an excuse to break off from the group again. Think you can come up with one?"

He grinned. "Excuses are my specialty."

By the time the tender got Veena to the docks in Valteron City, a lacquered-wood sedan chair awaited her. Four bearers with long clubs hanging from their belts stood watch over it.

Veena turned to the captain, who'd insisted on seeing her ashore in person. "Did you send some kind of word that I was coming?"

"Can't say I did. But the Prime has ways of finding out what he wants to know."

"We agree on that much."

Two sailors in the bow leaped out onto the docks to make the craft fast. Veena pressed a jeweled brooch into the captain's hand. "Thank you, Captain."

He shook his head and tried to hand it back. "No need for that, miss. Just doin' my loyal duty."

"You didn't have to let us board, or feed us, or treat us well. I insist."

He let out a low whistle, grinned, and tucked the gem into his pocket. "As long as you're insisting."

A silver brooch with lab-created gemstones might

be worth a couple hundred bucks, Earth-side. Here, on a planet that knew only the real thing, it would bring a pile of silver coins if the captain knew how to sell it.

"Need me to send a couple of the boys along, just to see you safely?" he asked.

"I think the Prime might take offense if you did."

"He'll take even more offense if I don't get you there in one piece."

She threw back one side of her cloak so that he could see the sword-hilt there. "I'll be fine."

The captain's eyes went wide, and then he grinned. "Reckon I'm starting to see why the Prime takes such an interest."

He helped her mount the gangplank, then watched as she crossed to where the sedan chair waited. She climbed up, waved, and told the bearers, "I'm ready." From the corner of her eye, she watched Julio slip out of the tender as it slid back into the water. He'd changed into sailor's garb while still aboard, and blended perfectly with the crowd at the docks. He promised to shadow her to the palace and stay outside.

The bearers picked up Veena's chair without a word, and started for the shore. The docks were a hotbed of activity, but sailors and merchants and feather-hat captains alike gave the chair a wide berth. Veena took a silent tally of the ships that were tied up to the docks. Nine deep water vessels were anchored in the channel, all of them in the process of offloading crates or barrels or both. Six single-masted cutters were tied right to the docks. Their crews lounged on deck, looking bored. Waiting for something or someone.

The city proper was much as she remembered from the first mission. Just as hot, just as crowded, but somehow more relaxed. The contentment showed in the way people met one another's eyes as they passed, how they laughed and bargained and gossiped with one another. They all looked somewhat underfed, but the hard edge of hunger was gone. A few burned-out buildings still darkened the avenues and plazas, though. The scars of civil unrest were slow to fade.

Twenty minutes later, she was sweating beneath her heavy cloaks, and the ship-shaped palace of the Valteroni Prime loomed ahead. A cluster of guards challenged them at the main gate.

"Do you have an appointment?" asked the officer-in-charge. He was fair-haired and a little young for his position, probably fresh out of officer school. Gold could buy decent positions in the city guards or the military, but training always told. The uniform was as spotless as his posture was straight.

"No, I don't," Veena said. "But I think the Prime will see me."

"I'm sorry, miss. You'll have to send a letter to the clerk."

"What should I say in such a letter?" Veena asked.

"Whatever you like." He made eye contact with her bearers, and signaled them to turn it around.

She pursed her lips, as if pondering it. "I suppose it would start something like 'My name is Veena Chaudri.'"

The officer faltered in his gesturing. He looked back at her, and recognition bloomed in his eyes. "My mistake, m'lady. I believe you *do* have an appointment."

She smiled. "Wonderful."

He made a sweeping gesture toward the stairs that led up to the palace doors. "Right this way."

Four guards materialized to escort Veena into the palace. No Enclave magicians this time. Maybe he didn't see her as a threat. Or perhaps they simply had better things to do than make deliveries for the Valteroni Prime.

The guards took her to an airy meeting chamber. A dozen men and women sat around the oblong wooden table. They had the garb and self-important manner of high-level government functionaries. But Veena only had eyes for the man at the head of the table. The man who'd taught her nearly everything she knew about this world. She didn't realize how much she missed him. His face drew her like a lodestone. His smile cast warming spells on her heart, which beat far too fast for comfort.

Richard Holt held court in a disarming kind of way. He spoke in quiet tones, and infrequently, so that everyone else in the room had to watch him to avoid impropriety. His voice had a natural cadence. Veena closed her eyes and basked in the sound of it.

". . . I'm not certain I understand your hesitation. These new trade agreements will benefit everyone," he was saying.

One of his councillors coughed into a closed hand. "I can't say I like the concessions we're giving Caralis." He was heavyset, probably pushing fifty, with a brown-and-gray beard that didn't entirely cover the jowls.

"You—that is, *we*—have spurned our northerly neighbors for too long," Holt said.

"No more than they've spurned us. Why should we answer that with generosity?"

"For a single reason: to allow us to ship Caralissian wine."

"They'll never ship the wine," said the jowly man.

"They might, if we were on better terms. And given our history, I think it might be appropriate if Valteron were to make the first gesture of friendship."

He spotted her then, standing quietly behind her escort. He gave a broad smile, a true *Richard* smile. "We'll pick this up in the morning, as soon as we have a response from the Caralissian emissary."

The staff members bristled at the dismissal in his tone. Then they followed his gaze to Veena, and suddenly they were all on their feet, muttering apologies. They jostled with one another to exit by the far door. Two of them forgot their hats.

"You came!" Holt said. In six long strides he'd reached her, and took her hands in his. His gaze flickered to her escort. "Leave us."

The guards filed out, though it looked like they took up positions just outside the door as they closed it.

"Come, sit." Holt gestured to two of the recently vacated chairs at the table. He always liked to sit for a briefing. *Haste is the enemy of thoroughness*, he used to say. "I take it you received my message."

Veena took the offered chair, and marveled at how comfortable it was. The wood must be hand-carved, and the lumbar cushion felt like silk. "In Pirea, yes. How did you know I'd be there?"

"I didn't. I sent it to every port."

"*Every* port on the mainland?"

He spread out his hands. "How else could I be certain you'd receive it?"

There were six major port cities in Alissia, and easily twice that number of smaller trading centers like Bay of Crabs. The expense in couriers alone had to be exorbitant. "You never liked to take chances," she said. "Until recently, at least."

He smiled. "I only gamble when I must. When the alternative is unconscionable."

"You've kept busy, from what I hear."

He blew out a breath and shook his head. "There's just so much to do, Veena. That's why I asked you to come."

Her heart pounded in her ears. She fought to keep calm. "Valteron City seems to be doing well."

"We're recovering, but I'll soon have bigger fish to fry."

"That's exactly what the company's worried about."

He snickered. "The company. You know what the executives' problem is? They have no patience."

"They gave you fifteen years."

"And I told them it would be another fifteen before we truly understood this world well enough to best know how to use it."

"I'm not sure they have that kind of time."

He shrugged. "It doesn't matter, in any case. They have no real say here."

"I wouldn't be here if it wasn't for them," Veena said. *Neither would you*, she didn't add.

"Be that as it may, Alissia is not a farm field to be harvested when the time is most convenient. This world is a *treasure*, Veena."

"I've never said otherwise." And now that she'd seen it for herself, she never would.

"I want to make sure it stays that way." He drummed his fingers on the table. He took a breath, and looked up at her again. "I could really use some help."

"I'm not sure how I—"

He stood suddenly, and began pacing. "You'd have a position in my cabinet, as cultural minister. Complete autonomy to study this world how and where you will."

God, he's serious. And he spoke to her as a *peer*. Not that he'd talked down to her before, but they'd kept that distance so necessary between mentor and protégé. Not anymore.

"And . . . what would our relationship be?" she asked.

"You'd answer to me, certainly. Everyone in Valteron answers to the Prime."

"But we'd work closely together?"

He stopped pacing, and put a hand on top of hers. His long fingers were ink-stained, but no less warm for it. "As closely as we did before. More, even."

She worked up her courage enough to meet his gaze. His face was so animated. It was hard not to look at it and become lost. "How much more?"

His lips tightened, and his eyes grew more distant. Ever so gently, he lifted his hand from hers. "As close as two colleagues can be."

It was an odd thing how emotions could evoke physical pain. Her heart *hurt* from the disappointment. She felt suddenly chill, as if the warmth between them had dissipated. She barely heard as he made promises of the resources she'd have, the access, the intelligence network. At last, he stopped and looked at her expectantly.

"It's a fabulous offer, Richard," she said. "I'm more honored than you could know."

His smile fell away. "That sounds like the preamble to a refusal."

"It's not." She sighed, and it wasn't just for show. "I just need some time to think it over."

He smiled again. He thought he had her. "Of course. I don't expect you to agree this instant."

She paused. "Even if I wanted to say yes, I'm not sure I could get back here on my own." *Not with Julio watching me like a hawk.*

"Let me worry about that. But the sooner you decide, the easier it will be."

"I understand," she said. "And I will think about it."

"Good."

"I should probably get going."

"Yes, yes." He offered a hand, and helped her up. "I hope you'll give my best to Julio."

The remark caught her off guard, and she hesitated long enough to give away the truth. Damn. "How do you—"

"Come, Veena. What kind of Prime would I be if I didn't know what was going on right outside the palace walls?"

She closed her mouth, resisting the urge to lie. Silence was better. Her escort-guards opened the door and reentered, as if they sensed the meeting had come to an end. Or timed it, most likely. Holt was a move ahead, as usual.

But she doubted anyone would see the next one coming.

"Magicians love fire-based illusions, as our many trips to the burn unit can attest."

—**Art of Illusion, May 20**

CHAPTER 33

WITHOUT A TRACE

The interruption might have been *partly* Quinn's fault, but he preferred to blame period dress. He and Jillaine were kissing in her room. Everything was going according to plan. *And, by God, she's a good kisser, too.* Not to mention strong for her size—she had her arms wrapped tight around him. But her ball gown, as pretty as it was, became a bulky and unwelcome barrier between them.

It needed to go.

He pulled her tighter, and ran his hands down her back. It felt perfectly smooth. No buttons or fastenings. He caressed her sides, and found nothing. Maybe there *were* no fastenings. He tried to shimmy her dress down, but it didn't move. Even worse, she grabbed his wrists and leaned back.

"What's wrong?" he whispered.

She furrowed her brow and looked to the side. "I feel like there's something you're not telling me."

"Why do you say that?"

"You didn't mention my dress at all."

"What? I said it was lovely."

"And now you seem totally baffled by it."

"I'll try harder." He leaned in again.

She pushed him back. "The laces are in front."

"Oh. Thank you." *Don't have to ask me twice.* He wanted to be kissing her again.

She let him kiss her. It was glorious. Then she pulled back again. It was pure devastation.

What now?

"I'm surprised you didn't know that," she said.

He grinned. "Well, I don't wear a lot of dresses."

"This is a Landorian ball gown."

"Oh. Right." *Good to know.*

She pushed him back another inch. There was a coldness in the distance between them now. "You're not really from Landor, are you?"

Uh-oh. He was so keyed up that he didn't control his reaction. His face gave him up.

"Gods! You aren't!" she said.

Damn, I've been away from Vegas too long.

He looked down. "I thought our pasts don't matter at the Enclave."

"You told a whole story about it, at your trial."

"Well, I had to say *something*."

"And then you made that snow. Was that a deception as well?"

"You were there. Did it seem like one?"

She bit her lip. Thoughtful, and uncertain. "That's not really an answer."

Quinn regained his poker face and focused on what he knew best: misdirection. "Look, when I first came here, it wasn't by choice. Moric kidnapped me."

"He thought you'd committed a crime."

"If I didn't win the trial, I'd be executed. So I had to ingratiate myself to the crowd."

"But you live in the Landorian tower."

He spread his hands out. "I like it there." He should just claim to be Felaran, and that would be that. But he didn't trust his face to sell it. "I may have glossed over where I'm from. But I've tried to be truthful about everything else."

"Have you?" She moved away from him, a slow and careful step, but a retreat just the same. "How do I know what's true and what's false?"

That's her real question, he realized. "Everything else I've said is true. Where I came from doesn't change that one bit."

There was hope in her eyes. He thought he had her.

Then she let them fall away, and wouldn't look at him. "I think you should go."

"Come on, Jillaine."

"Please don't make me ask you again."

He sighed. This had blown up nicely in his face. "As you wish." He pulled open the door, praying fervently that she called him back.

But she didn't, and so he walked out and pulled it closed behind him. He wandered the dimly lit hallway until he found the staircase. He descended to the ground floor, and stalked through the common room. He could feel everyone's eyes on him. A few of the men wore sympathetic looks, but the women wore cool stares. Even Betsy.

Sweet Jesus, it must be written all over my face.

He shook his head and stalked out into the night. So much for the perfect plan. Moric wouldn't be gone for more than a few days, and he'd have a lot of questions when he got back. Especially if Jillaine started talking to him again. There was nothing else he could do for it until the morning, so he might as well call it a night.

Goddamn Landorian fashions.

The chandlery was open. That was the good news. Quinn approached it with the same caution he would a wyvern's cave. After the disastrous ending to mutton night, he was a fool to come back to her so quickly. But there wasn't time to give her space, not with the vote looming and Anton's plan already in motion. *I really painted myself into a corner on this one.*

He tiptoed through the doorway, hoping to make a quiet entrance, but he forgot about the owls and they betrayed him. Jillaine came bustling out of the back with an empty tray in hand, and a hopeful look on her face. She wore her customary apron over a pale yellow sundress, and had tied her hair back with ribbons of the same color. She saw him and glared. "You."

"Hello again," he said.

"Back to tell me more lies?"

Yep, I really should have given her more time. But he'd told Leward to fetch Sella, and that woman wouldn't like to be kept waiting around. He sighed. "I'm sorry. I didn't want to barge in, but . . . I think your father is missing."

She took the news with more puzzlement than concern. "How do you know?"

"No one can find him, and his place looks . . . tossed."

Jillaine's brow furrowed. "Tossed?"

"You know, messy. Like he left in a hurry."

She gave a faint shrug. "He often disappears without warning, and leaves a mess behind. You should know."

"I take your point, but this feels different."

"How?"

He tilted his head toward the door. "Why don't you come see for yourself?"

"If this is some elaborate ruse to spend time with me—"

"It's not," he promised. "I'm worried about him. Will you come?"

"Maybe we'll find him, and then I can be around *two* men I don't want to see."

"Just come on!"

She rolled her eyes, but she set the tray down, took off her apron, and followed him out.

Sella had arrived by the time they got back to Moric's chambers, and had brought a couple of council magicians with her. Both men looked vaguely familiar, but Quinn couldn't remember their names. Leward lurked beside the door, looking very much like he wanted to be somewhere else. Sella poked around a few things with her walking stick, an expression of distaste etched on her face.

Like the world's most reluctant CSI tech, Quinn thought when he saw her. "Hello, Sella."

"So, Quinn," she said. "Are you the reason I was dragged here during the dinner hour?"

He grimaced. "Sorry about that. But I think it's important."

"What's your concern?"

He gestured at the disarray in Moric's chambers. "Does this look normal to you?"

She sniffed. "I have no idea how Moric lives."

"Well, I brought someone who does."

Jillaine stepped forward. Every eye in the room went to her. She'd thrown a light cloak on for the walk over, but there was no hiding the dress beneath it. She was like a Disney princess trying to blend in with the dirty masses. Never going to happen.

Sella's walking stick hit the floor with a clatter. "Oh. Hello, Jillaine."

"Hello, Sella." She glided past the old woman at a casual pace, stepping over the walking stick as she did.

Sella held still with her back hunched until Jillaine was out of the way. Then she snatched up her walking stick like a nervous squirrel. Quinn stared in disbelief. This was the same woman who'd switched him with that stick if he showed up a minute late to class.

Maybe it was only because of the circumstances, but still. He'd never seen Sella so deferential.

Jillaine spun slowly around, taking stock of the entire room. "He hasn't been here in hours. And it looks as though someone else searched the place." She pointed to the bookshelf. "Six of his books are missing. I've never seen him drop one to the floor in my entire life."

Quinn privately celebrated with a fist-pump. *That was a nice touch with the books.*

"Is anything else missing?" Sella asked. Her tone was soft. Polite. A far cry from the pointed demands she usually made of Quinn.

"There was a little green statue of a wyvern on his dresser."

Quinn cleared his throat. "Was it made of stone, about this big?" He held his hands apart to approximate the size of the thing Moric had given him.

"Yes."

"He sort of gave that to me."

"Why would he do that?" Jillaine asked.

Better think fast. "I had a run-in with a real wyvern a while back, and told him the story . . ." He shrugged. "He said I could have it."

Jillaine's eyebrows arched as high as he'd ever seen them. "He's had that for years. I hope you put it somewhere safe."

"I did." *In my saddlebags.*

Sella waved in Quinn's direction. "Moric's always giving him things he shouldn't."

"So it would seem," Jillaine said. She said nothing more, but kept giving him a side-eye when she thought he wasn't looking.

"Do you have a way to locate him?" Sella asked.

"I can try." Jillaine closed her eyes and drew a deep breath.

Quinn had seen her do the occasional bit of magic trickery, but this was something else entirely. There was a poise and a stillness to her. And focus, too. As if nothing else in the world mattered.

The chambers grew dim all around, except for where Jillaine stood. She glowed with a fey energy. The sheer *power* of it made the air hum. Quinn took half a step back, just in case. Then she breathed out, and the light returned, and the glow around her faded. "I can't find him."

"You've no idea where he is?" Sella asked.

"No." She chewed her lip. "I'll try again later, when I'm back at the chandlery."

"If Moric *has* gone missing, it couldn't have been at a worse time," Sella said.

"Why?" Quinn asked, even though he suspected he knew.

"That's not your concern."

Jillaine took two steps closer to Sella, so that she and the woman were face-to-face. "Why is it a bad time, Sella?"

"The council is about to take a vote," Sella said.

"On what?" Jillaine asked.

Quinn schooled his face to stillness. *Come on, Sella, say it . . .*

Sella hesitated then, even though it was Jillaine asking. She looked from her face, to Quinn's, then to Leward's. "On the matter of the Valteroni Prime."

"Anyone who survives a career in an Alissian military is either very lucky or very, very good."

—R. Holt, "Assessment of Alissian Militaries"

CHAPTER 34

COAST GUARDS

Logan wasn't big on reunions, but it felt great to see Mendez. Some of the steel had left his eyes, and he'd found his laugh again. Wasn't hard to see the reason why, either. The guy lit up any time Chaudri walked into the room. He kept close to her, too, like a body-guard would.

Maybe that explains the period of radio silence.

There had been two days of it, starting with that late check-in after Mendez and Chaudri split up with Bradley. With the company-mandated daily check-ins—

yet another new policy put in place after the Holt defection—the two days were a glaring mark on the comms record. Mendez claimed they'd been on a small ship en route to Bay of Rocks and didn't have the privacy for a secure conversation. Logan didn't buy it, but he asked the lieutenant not to press the issue. Mendez deserved a little quiet downtime, after what he'd been ordered to do.

Today, he and Mendez had hired a skiff to take them out near the admiral's island. If Chaudri was right about who had the backpack, it made him the most dangerous person in Alissia other than Holt himself.

Logan found it hard to believe that Holt would keep his main piece of leverage so close to himself. The man had to know *hundreds* of people in Alissia. You'd think he'd have hidden the backpack on the other side of the continent. Instead, Holt sent them looking all over the world for a backpack he'd stashed in his own backyard.

What a goddamn chess move.

The two massive oarsmen, a father and his son, rowed with a steady, hypnotic rhythm. Their sun-leathered skin was almost as dark as his own. It wasn't like a black guy stood out on this world—skin tone ran the full spectrum here, independent of geography—but he enjoyed blending in with the locals. More importantly, they knew how to keep quiet. If they thought it odd that Logan and Mendez had brought a pile of fishing equipment but not done any fishing, they kept it to themselves. *Couple of smart fellows.*

"Think that's it?" Mendez asked. He jerked his head to the southwest, where the rocky shores of a small island shot up great gouts of white spray as the waves hit them. Beyond the rocks, the rest of it was hidden beneath a blanket of fog.

"Gotta be. This is the only island large enough to hold a structure."

No amount of their high-tech surveillance equipment could help with the fog. They'd just have to wait for the sun to burn it off. Fog was a risk you took when you ran an early-morning scouting operation, but it was also right around the traditional shift change for hired swords. Round-the-clock guards were expensive, but if anyone could afford them, it was the admiral of the Valteroni fleet.

"Want to take us around that island?" Logan asked the crew.

"Your coin, fella," said the father. He muttered something to the son, and their rhythm changed. The boat began sliding to port, smooth as could be. The sun finally chased enough fog away that they got a good look at their target. A hulking stone keep dominated the center of it. The walls had to be thirty feet tall, and each of the corners had a guard tower with two sentries.

"Yeah, I'd say we found the place," Logan said.

Mendez chuckled. "No shit."

A siege engine squatted on the roof of the keep. Four wheels, a sturdy wooden platform, and a single long arm bound by complex ropes and pulleys. Next to that was a pile of throwing stones, everything from thirty-pound rainmakers to boulders the size of a refrigerator. Sailors called those "shipkillers"—if they hit the mast or the hull beneath the waterline, that was it. Didn't matter what kind of ship you were on, not with the force those catapults could muster.

"Whoa, check out the harbor," Mendez said.

A small inlet came into view as they rounded the point of the island. There was a narrow gap, not much wider than the tiny boat they rode in now. Sheer rock faces bordered it on either side. The cove beyond grew much wider, judging by the single-master moored broadside against the keep. *Probably the admiral's personal yacht.* Too small to be the Valteroni flagship, but still wide enough to make for a tight fit coming or going.

"Only an admiral could hit that gap just right every time," Logan said. "Downright cheeky of him, isn't it?"

"Looks like the only way in, too, unless you swim it."

And I wouldn't want to try that, either. They were two-thirds of the way around the island now, and Logan had yet to see another option for landfall. Six-foot waves pounded the jagged shoreline with a constant thunder. "Man, I wish we had a chopper."

"Me, too. As long as the mangonel crew didn't see it coming."

Medieval weaponry, as it turned out, was plenty effective against the relatively fragile forms of modern aircraft. As the Raptor Tech drone pilots recently discovered back home.

"That's gonna be a tough nut to crack," Logan said.

"You said it."

Logan put his hand on the older oarsman's shoulder. "I think we're ready to head back."

"Sure you don't want to stop for a little bite somewhere on the harbor? I know a romantic little spot on the west side of the bay."

What the hell's he talking about? "We're not a couple."

The man shrugged. "Not judgin'. Just thought I'd offer."

Logan looked at Mendez. "You believe this?"

"Ridiculous," Mendez said. "I'd so be out of your league."

"Hate to break this up, but we got bigger problems," said the father-oarsman.

Logan followed his gaze, to where three sails were coming up fast from the north. The fleet ships had narrow hulls and lots of sail. *Bay cutters.*

"Can you—" Logan started, but caught himself.

The ships had to be doing fifteen or twenty knots. They broke formation as they grew near. Two to port, one to starboard. The wake from their hulls rocked their skiff from both sides. The skiff started to tip over. *Oh, shit!*

The father and son jammed their oars down into the water and steadied it, but not without a lot of cursing.

"Good work," Logan said. "You just doubled your fee." *As long as I'm alive to pay it anyway.*

Mendez gripped the gunwale so hard his knuckles were white. His face was pale, too. "Gods help me."

One of the cutters coasted in within shouting distance. A man in a blue jacket and black three-pointed hat stood in the bow. The laces on the front of the jacket were crisp, clean, and bright as driven snow.

"Shit," Logan said.

"What?" Mendez asked.

"Water patrol." In peacetime, they had charge of the traffic and shipping in Valteron City's harbor. Most were retired navy, so it made sense that they'd keep an eye on the admiral's island for him. *I should've seen this coming.*

Mendez grunted. "You know what we do where I come from?"

"Bail out and swim for Florida? Not sure that's going to work here."

"You're funny."

"All right, what would you do?"

Mendez looked away. "Nope, not telling you. Not after your cute little comment."

Damn it.

The water patrol officer chose that moment to break in. "Morning, gentlemen." He had a salt-and-pepper beard and a curved saber on his belt. The sword was the only well-worn thing on him.

"Morning," Logan called.

"May I ask what you're doing out here?"

The father-oarsman hawked and spat noisily over the side of the boat. Not directly toward the cutter, but not away from it, either. "On whose authority?"

"The Valteroni Prime."

"And here I thought it was a free ocean," the father said.

Oh, perfect. We've got an antagonizer. Logan cleared his throat. "We don't want any trouble. We're just out fishing."

He held up a spool of woven fishing line so the man could see it. Mendez pried the lid off of a wooden bucket he'd shoved under his seat. Inside were a bunch of cut-up fish that had to be a couple of days old. The stink of it hit Logan's nose, and he forced himself not to gag.

I'll bet that would *keep the coast guard away.*

The patrolman's shoulders eased down a little. "Any luck, then?"

"Can't catch a bite to save my life," Logan said.

"You know what they say. The more you need a fish . . ."

"The less you find one." The officer signaled his cutter's steersman, who began shouting orders to raise sail. The cutter got up and moving quicker than Logan could have dreamed of. He wished he could take a better look at the hull.

"If I could make a suggestion," called the patrolman. "Maybe try a different spot next time."

Logan nodded. "Understood." *Message received: stay the hell away from the island.*

"Well," Mendez said. "Guess we'll do things the hard way."

Step one, transportation. The encounter with water patrol had taught Logan that they'd need more than a skiff. That meant a galley or some kind of sailboat. But buying one of those proved a surprisingly complex procedure in Valteron. Lots of paperwork. And that was *before* Holt came to power. Logan doubted they could hire one, either. Holt would be watching for that.

Grand theft marine, it is.

Which is how he and Kiara came to be strolling along the traders' wharf in Valteron Bay, boat shopping. The city had two other wharves, but the one for the naval fleet was guarded constantly, and the fishermen's wharf never had any downtime. With this many mouths to feed, they were making a fortune. So were grain merchants, for that matter, but grain had to be grown for a season. Fish were available right now. Turns out, that's part of why Holt had recalled all of the Valteroni ships. They needed the fishermen.

Logan had charge of security, but the naval stuff was squarely in the lieutenant's department. "So, what are we in the market for?" he asked.

"A cog or a small galley. At least fifteen feet long, but no more than twenty-five. Otherwise we'll be too slow."

They passed a wooden ship that seemed to fit the bill. Twenty feet long, round hull, and four oars. The colors said it was from Pirea. No crew aboard, either. *It's perfect.* "What about that one?"

"No. It's a smuggler's ship."

Pirean smugglers? That was a new one. "How do you know?"

"Did you see how low it sat in the water?"

"Maybe it's just old."

"It's heavy, not old. That means they've got cargo aboard," Kiara said.

"I didn't see any crates."

"They're smugglers, so they don't want you to see anything. It's probably hidden under the bulkhead, or with the ballast."

Right. And we sure as hell don't want smugglers after us. That had almost put a quick, brutal end to the last mission. The wharf made a ninety-degree turn, and the lineup of watercraft began to feature more deep-water vessels.

"All right, how about the Kestani sloop over there?" Logan asked.

"Don't like the tillers on those."

"Fine, you pick one."

"I already have."

That was fast. "Which?"

"I'll give you a clue. It's flying Felaran colors."

That narrowed it down to two or three vessels. They were passing one at the moment, but it was a tiny thing with a cuddy cabin, barely enough room for Logan alone. Plus, it was chained to the dock, so that was out. Maybe it was one of the deeper-hulled sailboats farther down the wharf.

"What do you think?" Kiara asked.

"I think I don't see it."

"We just passed it."

She couldn't mean the little chained-up cuddy cabin. "You're kidding me, right? There's not even enough room on there for two of us."

"Only one person needs to be on deck. The other two can hide in the cabin."

"Gonna be tight in there."

"It's all right. You and Mendez have bunked together before."

He started to utter a curse, and coughed instead. "I sort of figured I'd be piloting."

"Oh, did you? Well, then you figured wrong."

He glanced back. "I'm pretty sure it was chained up, Lieutenant."

"That's what we want," she said.

"It'll slow us down. Might get caught."

"A ship owner who goes to the trouble to use a chain won't be watching it closely."

"Oh. Good point."

"You packed some bolt cutters, didn't you?"

He grinned. "Never leave home without 'em."

As dusk fell on the merchants' wharf, Logan slipped into the water two hundred yards west of them. They'd had no trouble scouting them during the midday rush—hundreds of sailors and merchants and dockworkers came and went, so blending in was a snap—but the wharf quieted as darkness fell. A pair of guards at the entrance took careful note of the comings and goings.

Kiara might get to pick the boat, but Logan called the shots when it came time to steal one. He could swim better than anyone on the team—which wasn't saying much for Mendez, but still—and hold his breath for over a minute. His buoyancy vest provided just enough lift to make swimming near-effortless and, more importantly, quiet. He kept his body low in the water, just enough to keep his nose over the surface. He'd be practically invisible to anyone without a flashlight or infrared goggles.

Almost a shame no one gets to see me swim. His mother told him he swam before he could walk. Spent more time in the water than on land.

He kept in the shadow of the dock, and then looped out around the hulls of ships once they turned up. It should be eight vessels to the turn, and then four more before he found the one Kiara wanted.

Except he counted *seven* vessels to the turn. How could that be? He half turned to make sure he hadn't miscounted, and he saw the gap of open dock where the Felaran smugglers had been. So, the lieutenant had gotten that one right.

Luckily, he counted three ships after the right-hand turn, and then came right to the cog she wanted. He made a sweep of the hull from the water first. It looked solid—no barnacles—and the tiller was in good shape.

Permission to board?

Granted.

He braced himself against it and unclipped the compact grappling hook from his mesh equipment belt. It unfolded like an umbrella, and locked into place with a soft *click*. Then he unwound a few loops of paracord, enough to toss the hook over the rail. It landed with a whisper, thanks to the vulcanized rubber coating on the tips. He pulled it taut, and climbed hand over hand until he reached the rail. Then he hung there for a ten-count, listening for any cries of alarm.

Nothing.

He heaved himself up enough to get a boot on the edge of the deck. Then he crouched again, listening. Still no shouts, so he dropped to the deck and took stock. The ship was nine or ten feet wide at the mast. Ropes and old buckets of long-dry tar spoke to a half-finished attempt at winterization.

Now, the chain.

He unstrapped the bolt cutters from his leg and crept to the bow. The chain was wrapped around a pair of stanchions, which complicated things. He could take the time to unwind it, but moving around an old rusty chain was just asking to get caught. A transport carrying Felaran liquor had docked at the merchants' wharf. For the past hour, it had disgorged a steady stream of inebriated passengers and crewmen. They stumbled by every few minutes in pairs or trios.

He eased into position beside the rail where the chain ran out to the dock. The bolt cutters were sharp, but the chain still resisted. He shifted to get a better angle and squeezed them as hard as he could. The link snapped without warning. He couldn't grab the ends before gravity took them. The end still attached to the ship made a faint *clink*, but the three-foot length secured to the dock swung down and clanged against it like he'd rung a goddamn bell.

Shit!

He crouched down and froze. Two figures were making their way down the wharf, and couldn't be more than fifteen yards away. One of them had a lantern, a little wick-and-oil job that cast a faint orange glow in the evening mist.

"You hear that, Bert?" asked one.

"No, whazzat?"

"Heard a sound, like a clanging."

"Where?"

"From that Felaran ship."

"So?"

"So, maybe they've got some of that Felaran liquor on there."

"You think?"

"Why don't we have a look-see?"

Damn it. Why did Logan always end up with the worst luck in this place? Bradley could waggle his fingers and stumble ass-backward into the only friendly magician in the entire world, but God forbid Logan should catch a break. *It's just unfair, that's what it is.*

He'd be in trouble if someone spotted him here. He wouldn't pass for a dockworker or sailor, not dripping wet and dressed in all black.

He should have been more cautious with the chain, but it was too late for that. He crouched in the shadows beside the rail and hoped that the two guys would move on. But no, these Einsteins decided that they should plop down ten yards away, and finish their half-full liquor bottles with their legs dangling over the side of the pier.

He checked his watch; it was a quarter to midnight. Any minute now, the wharf's security detail would do a sweep of the pier and take tally of the ships docked there. There was a chance they'd notice the broken chain. The sooner he boosted the cog and got clear, the better.

He eased down to his belly and crawled toward the stern of the ship. His back itched between the shoulder blades. He hated that feeling, the nervous tension of waiting to get caught. If they saw him and raised the alarm, it killed the whole operation.

The sailors burst out in raucous laughter. He tensed up like a nervous hare. *I'm going to have a goddamn heart attack.*

Finally, he reached the stern. The chain stretched taut from the dock to the transom cleat where it was fastened. That meant the ship was starting to drift. If it moved much more before he was ready, someone was bound to notice. He slid himself below the chain and laced some paracord into one of the links. Skip the next link, lace the next one. He tied off both ends, with a couple of feet of slack. Then he got the clippers up, and cut the link in between.

Clink.

The chain snapped apart, but the black cord held it fast. Not completely quiet, but much better than the first time.

One of the half-drunk sailors piped up. "What d'you say, Bert?"

"Huh?"

"You up for a round in town?"

"'Course. Not sure why we stopped here anyway."

They stumbled to their feet. For a terrifying moment, Logan was sure one of them would fall right into his ship. They found their balance, and he heaved a sigh of relief. Then one of them tossed his empty bottle. It thunked off the ship's deck two inches from Logan's head. He bit his lip so hard that he tasted blood. He should stay here and lay low. He should let them walk on. But the bottle was just too much. He started seeing red at the edges of his vision. Knew his temper was coming up, and couldn't stop himself.

You littering son of a bitch—

He grabbed the bottle in one hand and vaulted over the rail to the pier beyond. The two drunks were about five paces down the dock. Logan took four quiet steps, and grabbed them both by the back of the head.

"Hey—"

"What the—"

Logan scissored his arms and knocked their heads

together. They fell like rag dolls. He took a minute to prop them up against a wooden piling, and then tucked the bottle in Bert's arm. "You dropped something."

And I've got a boat to steal.

"Watch this hand over here. Ignore the one behind my back."

—**Art of Illusion, July 7**

CHAPTER 35

SEARCH COMMITTEES

The search for Moric mobilized by evening. Sella notified the rest of the council, who drummed up volunteers to do an organized search of the entire island. Every single Pirean between the ages of six and eighty turned out to help. They gathered in a circle of torches in the green by the Pirean tower. Quinn jogged over to where Sella was handing out assignments.

"That covers the outlying farms," she said. "Now we just need a couple of people to sweep the docks."

Quinn's arm shot up before she even finished talking. "I'll do it."

"That's one," Sella said.

Leward volunteered about a second later. Sella pressed her lips together on the verge of a disapproving remark, but she'd asked for two volunteers and now she had them.

"Moric's skiff is at the end of the dock. Stay away from the harbormaster's ship."

Time to play dumb. "Which one is that?"

"The biggest one there." There was a hint of condescension in her tone.

He couldn't resist taking a parting shot. "What if that's where he is?"

"It's not," Sella said.

Quinn raised his hands in acquiescence. "We'll search the rest."

"Don't dawdle."

Sella wasn't necessarily the boss of them, but Quinn and Leward hustled down the road anyway.

"What was that thing Jillaine did?" Quinn asked.

"In Moric's chambers?"

"Yes. Some kind of location spell?"

"I guess you could call it that, but it's more complicated. Sort of only works between people who are very close to one another."

"Family members, you mean," Quinn said.

"Exactly."

"Do you and Everett have something like that?"

Leward winced, and wouldn't meet his eyes.

"What, did I say something wrong?" Quinn asked.

"Well, family bonds are a very private thing."

"I'm sorry. I wasn't thinking."

Leward waved off his apology. "You couldn't have known."

"I'm the only magician in my family, so . . ." He trailed off, and shrugged uncomfortably.

"Of course." Leward was silent a moment. "I will tell you that we're working on it. It would help if Everett could get past this damn block of his."

"Has he always had it?"

"Almost as long as he's been a magician. It's kind of my fault."

"Oh, I doubt that," Quinn said. Leward didn't have an evil bone in his body.

"I made him hide his ability when we were kids."

"Why?"

"It—it wasn't safe, to be like us."

Because it was the Pirean Tip. Damn. "It seems like you wouldn't be able to hide that forever."

"Both of us? No. But one of us could."

Quinn really wanted to know how they'd made it all the way to the Enclave, but he sensed that was a story for another time. Besides, the harbor swept into view, and they had a job to do. "Well, I'm glad you're here. You guys seem like good apples."

"We seem like fruit?"

Quinn chuckled. "It's just an expression." He

counted four ships moving in the harbor, and twice that number secured at the docks. "Harbor's not too busy."

"Traffic tends to fall off before an important council vote," Leward said.

"What will happen if Moric doesn't return for it?"

"He doesn't get to vote, I guess."

Time to plant the seed. "It sounds like an important decision, though. Maybe someone can sit in for him."

"Sit in for the most powerful magician on the island?"

"I'm sure you could find someone who'd look out for Pirean interests. Someone close to him." *Someone who could break the tie in our favor.*

"I hope it doesn't come to that."

"Right. Me, too." Quinn's boots made a loud *clunk* on the docks wooden planks, and it made him self-conscious. He kept looking over his shoulder.

"Do you think Moric's really down here?" Leward asked.

"Honestly? No."

"Then why were you so quick to volunteer?"

Because the Victoria *is there, and it's a great excuse to take a closer look.* He couldn't ignore the growing urgency of Kiara's instructions for him to install the beacon, and that kind of pressure instinctively made him reach for bigger leverage. Knowing that Kiara's sister and her ship were at the Enclave gave Quinn a decent chip to play when he needed one. But uncovering how they'd come here, or why Relling hadn't returned, would hand him a crusher.

Lying to Leward felt wrong, so he settled for a half-truth instead. "I like ships."

Leward laughed. "You sure you aren't Pirean?"

Quinn allowed a smile. "Quite sure."

"I think you'd do well there."

"Thanks. I know I'd like the food." Quinn scrunched up his face. "The fishing, not so much."

"What's wrong with fishing?"

"It usually happens out in the oceans, and I'm not that great a swimmer."

"I see," Leward said.

They walked in silence toward the long line of waiting ships.

Leward cleared his throat. "You know you don't have to swim to catch the fish, right?"

Quinn snorted. "Yes, Leward." *But thanks for the vote of confidence.*

"I'm only making certain."

They made a sweep of the outer docks, going so far as to call Moric's name on occasion. Nothing. They found three sailors on the deck of a Landorian sloop, drinking and playing some kind of game with dice. Once it was clear Quinn and Leward weren't members of dock security, they extended a cheerful invitation.

"Sorry, we're looking for someone," Quinn said. Part of him wanted to accept, because he kind of missed gambling. He really should get down to the docks more often.

Well, as long as the harbormaster wasn't around. He'd given Captain Relling a wide berth since arriving, but she was probably lurking around here somewhere.

Maybe she'd taken the day off. *I can only hope.*

They neared the end of the dock, and had only three vessels to go, when they started catching glimpses of the *Victoria* through the gaps. Quinn couldn't keep from staring.

"She's a beautiful ship, isn't she?" Leward asked.

"What?"

"The big three-master you've been ogling."

"I like big ships." *And I cannot lie.*

"Sure, sure," Leward said. "Isn't that the one you were asking Sella about?"

Damn. He was more observant than Quinn realized. It was always the little guys you have to watch out for. "I'm just curious. Never seen another ship like it."

"Neither had we, when they towed it in."

"That thing was *salvaged*?"

"Two-thirds of it was underwater, from what I heard. Took five or six water mages to get it afloat."

It took every ounce of control Quinn could muster to make his next question a casual one. "Was anyone aboard?"

"Just the captain. She'd lashed herself to the wheel and was banged up pretty good."

"Wow."

Leward nudged him to make sure he was listening. "Ready for the best part?"

"All right. Lay it on me."

"She can't remember a thing."

"About what?"

"Anything. Not even her name."

Amnesia. That explained how she was still here, and not sailing back. Unless she faked it, so as not to have to answer some difficult questions. There was just no way to know.

Boots rang out against the wooden planks as someone came up behind them. Steel tips. *Oh, my God, speak of the devil.*

"You boys lost?" Relling asked.

"Evening," Leward said.

Quinn rubbed his upper lip, hoping it appeared casual, when really it was meant to make sure she didn't read his lips. "Evening."

She swiveled her predatory gaze to him. "You again? Didn't I tell you about the rules for the docks?"

Quinn mumbled something behind his hand.

"We're here on council business," Leward said. "Have you seen Moric?"

"Not since I chewed him out for letting his protégés wander around my docks. Why?"

"He's missing."

"Says who?"

"His daughter." Leward met her gaze and didn't falter. Didn't even blink.

Quinn marveled at it. *Man, where has this side of Leward been?*

Relling harrumphed. "Probably off on another of his secret missions for the Valteroni Prime, if you ask me. But I haven't seen him."

"We promised Sella we'd search the docks," Leward said.

"Looks like you've done that."

Quinn cleared his throat and tilted his head. "We'll be on our way, then."

They skirted her and power-walked back toward shore. Her steel-toed boot steps didn't resume for another half minute. Quinn could feel her eyes on his back. "Here on council business, huh?" he whispered.

Leward grinned. "What can I say? She scares me."

"I've seen scarier," Quinn said. *Like her sister.*

Quinn leaned against the wall in the corner of the Pirean common room, bone-tired and trying not to fall asleep. The search had gone through half the night, with nothing to show for it. *And only I know why.*

"Moric is nowhere on the island," Sella said. "And that puts us in a precarious position."

She sat at the head of the table. On her right was Leward, who looked like he might face-plant at any minute. Jillaine sat across from him, the model of perfect posture, but redness tinted the corners of her eyes.

No one offered any comment, so Sella continued. "Given the circumstances, we should find someone to fill his seat ahead of the vote tomorrow."

Jillaine rubbed her eyes. "What's so important about this vote?"

"I would not be exaggerating if I said it determines the future of the Enclave's place in the world," Sella said.

"Then delay it."

"If we postponed every vote for the whims of one council member, we'd never get anything done. Besides, the sooner we put this foolishness to bed, the better."

"It still seems like something my father is best suited to handle," Jillaine said.

"Which is why we're looking for him," Sella said. "Unless he reappears, however, I recommend you find someone to sit for him."

The choice was so obvious that Quinn wanted to shout it, but he bit his tongue. He was a friend and a welcome guest, but this was Pirean business. Leward perked up.

Here it comes.

"How about Quinn?" Leward asked.

Oh, no.

Sella made a face like she'd just swallowed a lemon.

Quinn was tempted to go for it for about half a second, but he couldn't risk putting himself in the spotlight. He shook his head before Sella could even reply. "Thanks, buddy, but I'm just a student here."

"It should really be someone who knows Moric well, and can act on his behalf," Sella said.

Leward rubbed his eyes. "Fine. Jillaine, then."

There was a general murmur of agreement among those packed into the common room. Quinn didn't bother to hide his grin. *I always knew he was a sharp one.*

"It's up to you how you decide," Sella said. The corners of her lips flickered upward. Anyone who was looking saw the hint of approval. "Just give me the name of your delegate to the council tomorrow morning."

Quinn schooled his face again. Based on the reaction here, they'd almost certainly name Jillaine.

Now I just need to win her back. Again.

"Some people say, 'Quit while you're ahead.' I say, quit before you lose everything."

—Art of Illusion, September 11

CHAPTER 36

PRIORITIES

Advanced magic class had been canceled, so Quinn spent most of the morning on his grand gesture. He found Jillaine out in her apiary, collecting honey from one of the hives. He really didn't want to go anywhere near it, but it was either that or miss his shot entirely.

"Hey," he called.

She half turned at the sound of his voice. "Hey yourself."

He tried to mosey in a little closer, but stopped

short when one of the bees flew past. *Damn, they're huge.* "How are you holding up?"

"As well as can be expected," she said. There were shadows under her eyes, though.

"I thought you might be hungry." He brandished the wicker basket he'd brought with him.

"You brought food?" She gave him a suspicious look.

"Consider it a peace offering."

"You can leave it inside."

That won't get me very far. The timeline was too tight to leave things to chance. "I thought maybe we could take it somewhere," he said. "You know, maybe eat together."

"Wander off to share a meal with a stranger? That's probably what happened to my father."

"I'm *not* a stranger. I'm just a guy who screwed up, and wants to make things right."

She waved her fingers beneath the hive before her, a conical basket, daubed with clay, and inverted on a wide wooden plank. There must have been a hole in the bottom, because a comb drifted out from below to settle gently in her collection pot. "Is that really what you want, or is it another lie?" she asked.

"That's what I want. And I'm guessing you could stand to take your mind off things."

She paused. "Where would we go?"

"It's a surprise." He offered his biggest, most charming smile. "Assuming you don't mind a little adventure."

She sighed. "I suppose I could use the distraction." She walked over and set the honey pot into a little cabinet on the back of the chandlery. Then she turned back to him with an expectant look.

He gestured down the road he'd just taken. "This way, if you please."

She fell into step beside him, but didn't take his arm. He tried not to let that hurt him.

Step one, get her talking. "So, how did you become a chandler?" he asked.

"Are you looking to change professions?"

"I'm just curious about what makes someone wake up and say, 'I want to make candles for a living.'"

"It's a little more involved than that. I apprenticed under the former chandler, who was called Aleria."

"How come I've never met her?"

"She's been dead five years."

"Whew." He shook his head. "Don't get in *your* way, huh?"

Jillaine gasped. "She died in her sleep, I'll have you know."

"Oh, I'm sure. But just so you know, I'm *not* a competitor."

"You're terrible," she said, but with a tiny smile.

They didn't talk about the elephant in the room. Anton had confirmed that the Pireans gave her name to the council. Moric still hadn't returned. The future of the Enclave lay partly in Jillaine's hands. Instead, they talked about candle-making and beekeeping.

She was polite, but not warm. And she still didn't take his arm. The uncovered lie hung between them like an icicle.

"Look, I'm sorry I pretended to be from Landor," Quinn said at last. "It's what I told Moric when he captured me, so I just ran with it."

"Why did you lie to him, though?"

"Honestly, I was terrified. Where I'm from, we had no idea that the Enclave even existed. Or what the magicians here might do to us." *So far, so good.* Everything he'd told her was true.

"Oh, you're from the Tip now?" she asked with a touch of scorn.

"No, not the Pirean Tip. But a place like that. When Moric offered to bring me along on his job, I thought I could go back home and change some minds."

"*That* was your grand adventure? Going home?"

"Going home was more of a duty. Coming back is the grand adventure," he said.

She gave him a dubious look. "To the Enclave."

"Well, back to *you*. The Enclave is just a bonus."

She laughed softly. "Is that the order of things?"

"Well, don't get me wrong. It's a pretty nice bonus. In fact, I'm not sure why you're so bent on leaving."

She slid her hand into the crook of his elbow. "I'm not *bent* on leaving. I'd just like to see some of the world other than our island."

The grass is always greener. "So why don't you go?"

"What?"

"Go have some adventure, before your father turns up."

"Now? It's the worst possible time."

"It's the *best* possible time."

"I have to cast my vote in the council. That's all I can think about at the moment."

He almost told her, *Screw the vote*, but without her, his entire mission would be a failure. Kiara would have no reason to let him stay on the island, if he didn't produce results. Sure, he could refuse the order to return home, but that was a decision there was no coming back from. *A decision I'd just as soon put off as long as possible.* So he made his voice casual. "I think the vote is pretty simple. Either you want to preserve the status quo, or you want to try something new."

"My father thinks our agreement with Valteron is important."

"I know." Quinn held his tongue for a moment. "But he also thinks you shouldn't leave the island."

"And that I can't take care of myself," she added.

"That's why I think you should cast your vote today, and *then* go."

Her fingers slid off his arm. He hated the cool emptiness they left behind.

"So, you said that you came back here to see me," she accused. "But now you'd like me to *leave*?"

"I want you to *be happy*." He looked away and added quietly, "Even if that means you'll be gone."

She pursed her lips and said nothing, but took his arm again.

"Besides, I might just follow you," he said. "After all, I'm a magic user myself."

A smile played at the edge of her lips. "A magic *student.*"

"I'm a person of means," he said with a hint of smugness. Then he felt his purse and feigned surprise. "Well, I thought I was."

He loosened the drawstring and shook the purse out into his open palm. Nothing came out. He gave her a side-eyed look. "Did you do this?"

"Do what?"

He shook his head. "I don't believe it. You took my jewels."

"I did no such thing."

"Then you won't mind a little search." He lifted her hand from his arm, where a dark red stone glittered. "Oh, well, look here."

She made a surprised little sound. "I have no idea—"

He held up a hand to forestall her protest. "What else are you holding?"

In short order, he found a diamond in her waistband, an emerald in her shoe, and a thumb-sized sapphire tucked behind her ear. She laughed and protested her innocence with each revelation. That was the best part of this kind of up-close magic: it was a perfect excuse to put his hands on her.

Finally, he poured the recovered gemstones back into his purse and pulled the drawstring tight. "I'm still missing a few, but I guess I can look for those later."

"Oh, you think so?"

He winked at her. "I'd sure like to try."

They came to the high point of the island, at the base of the boulder pile where they'd first met. Which would be great if she weren't wearing a gown and slippers.

"Damn," he muttered.

"What's wrong?"

"I meant for us to climb up there. I should have asked you to wear different shoes. I meant to, but I kind of . . ."

"Kind of what?"

Might as well be honest. "Kind of forgot the plan when I saw you." He shook his head. "I'm sorry." He seemed to be telling her that more and more often.

She *tsked* him and smiled. "Silly man." She closed her eyes.

Don't mind if I do. He'd just started to lean in when invisible arms wrapped around his chest. The pressure startled him. He couldn't move. "What the—"

Then he was floating, and she was, too. Rising up like a goddamn hot air balloon to touch down gently on the uppermost boulder. The pressure dissipated as suddenly as it had come. He could breathe again. Jillaine lowered herself to the boulder in a single, graceful movement, her skirts settling about her like a snowdrift.

"I was not expecting that," he admitted.

"Oh, did I scare you?"

"Maybe a little." He sat cross-legged across from her. *But like any good magician, I excel at preparation.*

Earlier in the day, he'd traded every bit of social capital for the meal inside the basket. Not that he couldn't cook himself, but he wanted a taste of nostalgia. There was pan-seared whitefish, a dark brown loaf of bread, and some kind of crustacean soup. All of it should still be warm, too. Leward had promised as much, with the enchantment he'd put on the basket.

Just don't open it until you're ready, he'd warned.

Quinn pried up the basket's lid, and a fireball nearly engulfed his face. "Gah!" He reared back and nearly fell of the boulder. *A little much, Leward.*

The fire petered out. Inside, the crockery looked unharmed, but the soup was boiling. He shook his head. "Well, I guess we should let that cool off."

Jillaine was biting her lip, probably to keep from giggling. She eyed the food. "This looks familiar."

He played it nonchalant. "Does it?"

"Where'd you learn a Pirean recipe?"

"Right from the source."

She pursed her lips. "One of your many Pirean friends."

"Not a bad guess."

"What did all of this cost you?"

He chuckled. "You don't want to know."

The food was incredibly good, but Quinn hardly noticed. It only provided a backdrop to Jillaine. Being alone with her felt hazy and warm, like a dream. They talked well into the afternoon, until the shadows of the rocks and trees stretched out below them.

"I should get back," she said finally. "The vote is at sunset."

He piled the crockery back into his basket. "What do you think you're going to do?"

"I still don't know."

He stood and offered her a hand. She took it and rose, but stumbled and lost her balance.

"Whoa!" He caught her against him.

"Thank you." She looked up at him from so close, beckoning. She closed her eyes. He leaned down to kiss her.

Then the invisible hand wrapped around him.

Oh, come on. "Again?" he asked as she floated them down to the ground like leaves falling from a tree. She spun away from him, but took hold of his arm.

"That was just mean," he said.

She giggled, and made no apology.

They walked at a brisker pace as the sun dipped down toward the horizon.

"Where do you need to go?" he asked.

"The amphitheater."

"Oh, one of my favorite places." *As long as you don't count the fire pit outside.*

They weren't alone for much longer, as a steady stream of Enclave residents flowed toward the amphitheater from all directions. Apparently the vote was a public event. Jillaine let go of his arm, which he didn't like, but he understood.

"You should probably return that basket to the Pirean tower," she said.

"Eh, I can do that later."

"What if someone needs them?"

She wants to get rid of me. That wasn't a good sign for how she'd vote, but he didn't want to press. "All right. Good luck in there."

"Thanks for the soup."

He halted and watched her walk in. Then he turned left, and made for the Pirean tower. Twilight began to fall across the island. He jogged up the steps to the tower and hurried in. The common room was totally empty, which meant that everyone had gone to see the vote. He gave the crockery a quick scrub in the sink, shoved the basket under a table, and ran back to the amphitheater. He could hear Sella's voice echoing off the walls even before he got inside.

The place was full to the brim with Enclave magicians and their families. Torches lined the wall, their flames a dizzying combination of unnatural colors. It had the feel of a medieval circus. Quinn squeezed himself on the end of the nearest bench.

". . . in exchange, the Enclave grants the Prime certain protections on his person, and a complement of young magicians to attend him in Valteron City," Sella said. She stood at the front, addressing the crowd, with an opaque circle in front of her that amplified the sound of her voice.

The sight of it brought butterflies to Quinn's stomach. *A few months ago it was me and Moric up there.*

He couldn't see Jillaine or Anton. They were probably somewhere near the front.

"A motion has been made to end this long-standing agreement." Sella gave a cool look at someone in the front row. "The council will now vote on that motion."

A murmur of anticipation swept across the crowd. Sella waited until silence returned, then held out an arm to her right. "Those in favor of rescinding our agreement with Valteron."

Anton stood up from the front row, his cloth-of-silver jacket glittering in the torchlight. He walked over to Sella's right, casual as a gentleman on an evening stroll, and turned to face the audience. Two others, an older gentleman and a matronly woman, followed and stood beside him.

Not enough, Quinn thought. It might have been a trick of the light, but he could have sworn that Sella had a little smirk of satisfaction on her face.

She held out her left arm. "Those who wish to *maintain* the agreement." The two men who'd been with her in Moric's apartment rose and walked over. Sella lowered her arms and took three steps to join them, making it three to three.

Jillaine stood from the third row, and made her way to the front. Quinn couldn't see her face. Sella looked at her and smiled.

Damn.

Then Jillaine glided over and stood with Anton's group. A collective gasp came from the audience.

"Look at that," Quinn whispered. He clenched a fist in restrained victory. *That's my girl.*

Sella looked like a deer in headlights. She recovered herself, and returned to the magic microphone. "The motion passes."

Quinn slipped off the bench and hurried out. *Take that, Richard Holt.*

It was well past dusk already, but he still had enough light to see by. The minute Quinn got clear of the crowds spilling out across the open spaces, he activated his comm unit. "This is Bradley, reporting bingo."

Kiara came back a few minutes later. "You've got Kiara and Logan. Did you say 'bingo' just now?"

"The council just voted to rescind their agreement with Valteron. In other words, bingo."

Logan came on. "How did you manage to pull that off?"

You don't even want to know. "I'm good with people, remember? And I'm a finisher. In fact, I'd like to request 'The Finisher' as my new code name."

"Denied," Logan said.

"Well done, Bradley," Kiara said. "When will it happen?"

"I assume pretty soon."

"Find out, and then sit tight. We're going radio silent for twelve hours while we go after the package," Kiara said.

The backpack. Things were about to get serious. "Understood," he said. "Be careful out there. And if you see a guy who looks like Mr. Clean, run."

"Roger that. Kiara out."

Quinn switched off the comm unit and savored the moment of his small victory. He'd never forget the look of shock on Sella's face, that was for sure. He still couldn't believe he'd managed to sway Jillaine. Maybe she would take a little adventure with him after all. *Things are looking up for Quinn Bradley.* He started humming, "Oh, Sherrie," one of his favorite songs, as he strolled back toward the Landorian tower. He even sang it a little, because it was that kind of glorious night.

He heard a sound behind him, a footfall. *Maybe that's her right now.* He smiled and looked back, but no one was there. Then he turned around and a dark figure in a hooded cloak stood before him. A wooden club slammed into his temple. Fireworks of pain exploded across his vision, and then everything went dark.

"Friendship brings more loyalty than favors. Alissians don't like owing one another."

—R. Holt, "Understanding Alissian Ethics"

CHAPTER 37

BREACH

Logan had to admit that Kiara knew how to pick a decent ship. The cog sat comfortably in the water, and the long tiller could practically turn it on a dime. He'd gotten in some practice on his way from the wharf to the rendezvous point, just in case the lieutenant changed her mind about piloting.

The fact that she'd be going along at all was a break from tradition. Kiara usually liked to let him run point on in-world operations, preferring to quarterback everything from a safe distance. Logan tried not to view her personal involvement this time as a no-confidence vote in his leadership. *Maybe it's because of the backpack.* The lieutenant had taken some heat after the first failed mission. If she came back empty-handed a second time, CASE Global might start looking for new leadership.

It took an hour to outfit the ship for the operation. The twin electric motors ran from a next-generation fuel cell about the size of a toaster. A steering rod connected both of their pivot handles to allow simultaneous operation. Logan and Mendez clamped them to the transom of the borrowed ship while Kiara and Chaudri prepped the navigation equipment. Logan didn't like bringing the anthropologist on the mission, and had shared that opinion in private earlier that day.

"Why not?" Kiara had asked. "We might need her expertise, once we're inside."

"We can use the comms for that," Logan said.

Kiara shook her head. "We may not be able to rely on those while we're in Holt's backyard."

"She's not a soldier."

"You trained her, didn't you?"

"We both know it's not the same, Lieutenant."

"Bottom line, we're going up against an unknown force, so I need all able hands," she said. Her tone signaled that the decision was final.

Logan bit his tongue. *At least we'll be well armed.* The company executives still wouldn't allow modern firearms, but pneumatics were on the table. Everyone got a 16 mm, semiautomatic tranquilizer pistol with two refill clips. The darts would drop a fully grown man in about three seconds, if that.

Logan himself had the real beauty, though: a prototype pneumatic sniper rifle from the tech lab. It had a range of eighty yards, wind permitting, and the only wide-angle scope permitted on this side of the gateway. He and Mendez had nicknamed it Slippery Pete.

There was no disguising such a weapon if it fell into the wrong hands, but he could break it down in less than twenty seconds into a bundle that looked like scrap wood. If someone captured them and there wasn't enough time to hide it, Logan had standing orders to toss it into the ocean.

They set off against the breakers at 0200, heading due south for the admiral's island. The sea was quiet except for the wind, and the splashes beneath the hull, and the quiet hum of the motors. Clouds obscured the three-quarter moon, and their destination wasn't exactly lit up with neon signs. Earlier in the day, Kiara had taken a positional fix with a laser-optic range finder. CASE Global's Automated Dead Reckoning (ADR) system did the rest: took measurements from the water and air speed sensors, integrated that with the magnetometer, and estimated their approximate distance and direction to the target. All in real time, and on Kiara's tablet. It even had a rough geomap of Valteron Bay, based on some of the preliminary coast mapping data.

The ADR was critical, because they couldn't make a straight shot for the island itself. Bow lanterns were required for any ship out after dusk, and that made their trajectory easy to watch. So they pretended to be one of the night fishermen who worked the bay—starting and stopping in a zigzag pattern, as if working their way along a line of traps.

"ETA twenty minutes," Kiara said. "Let's review the operational plan."

They'd reviewed it twice already, but Logan knew she was serious. Good thing Bradley wasn't here to roll his eyes and make a snarky comment. They went over it again, piece by piece. Then they were five minutes out. Weapons free. Mendez snuffed the lantern so they'd have some time to let their eyes adjust.

Wish we could all have IR goggles, Logan thought. He'd lobbied for that and about a dozen other things for this mission. Most of them got shot down. The company executives were nervous letting modern tech through. Especially now that they knew just how organized the world's magicians seemed to be. Granted, that was all based on Bradley's intel, which had more holes than Swiss cheese. He'd pointed this out, but it made no difference.

They'd allowed IR on exactly one optic device, and that wouldn't help at this range. The executives' casual refusals on Logan's other equipment requests rankled him more than a little. It was one thing to issue a tech ban from your two-thousand-dollar swivel chair. Another to be the guy with boots on the ground, and wishing you could see your enemies in the dark.

Logan smiled when he saw the lanterns hanging on the admiral's walls. *Talk about a lucky break.* Mendez and Chaudri both fixed on the points of light with binoculars, and made a note whenever someone walked in front of one. Which they did like clockwork, every forty-five seconds. Logan steered; Kiara monitored their progress on the ADR.

"Two minutes," she said. "Better let me skipper."

Logan moved out of the way and let her take the control rod. *Time to break out Slippery Pete.* He double-checked the cartridge, cocked it, and uncapped the scope.

"One minute," Kiara said.

Mendez and Chaudri stashed their binoculars and were checking their weapons. Logan went prone on the deck, and rested Slippery Pete's barrel on the rail. The sound of the surf hitting the rocks rose to a thunder pitch. The cliffs loomed dead ahead. The gap between them seemed smaller than he remembered. Kiara started muttering to herself.

Narrow as the cog was, they still only had about a yard of clearance on either side. If Kiara was off by more than that, the ship would hit the side of the boulders. Every sentry guarding the wall would hear them coming then, and they'd turn the passage into a goddamn shooting gallery.

Everything was silent all around them. The wind had fallen to nothing, and the hum of the electric motors became muted as Kiara cut the power. They were pretty much coasting. No acceleration meant no steering, however, so Logan said a small prayer that the lieutenant had put them on the right path. Jesus, everything had to happen just right on this mission, or they'd be in deep. He held his breath.

The rock wall to port loomed so close that he could reach out and touch it. Then even closer. The hull scraped against the rock. The sound made him hunch his shoulders. Then the ship slid free, and the wall fell away. The water opened up into a good-sized lagoon. *Thank God.*

Kiara checked her laser rangefinder. "Seventy-five yards to the wall."

Logan eased the pneumatic rifle to his shoulder. "Let's do this."

Mendez was ready. "First two targets, northwest corner."

Logan followed the wall up. It was too dark to make the targets, so he found the switch for the scope's IR mode. Kiara had gotten a tech exception for this scope only, so he might as well take advantage. He flipped it on. Two bright red blobs appeared.

There you are. He took aim, fired, pivoted, fired again. Each guard-shape flapped impotently at the dart, and then collapsed like a ton of bricks.

"Two down," Logan said. "The blood flies are a bitch tonight."

"The other pair should be about twenty degrees south," Mendez said.

Logan swiveled the scope of the rifle, but saw nothing. *Damn it, where are they?* The scope showed only darkness, and the infrared didn't do any better. "Don't see them."

"Give it a sec."

Two heat signatures bloomed out of seeming darkness. They must've been behind something. He took a breath, let half out. Pulled the trigger, dropped one. Swung over, dropped the other just as quick.

"Nice shooting," Mendez said.

Two more targets went down, and then the walls were clear.

"Gods, but you're good at that," Chaudri breathed.

Logan nodded. "Thanks." *I ought to be.* He had to admit, it felt good to be *doing* something.

"That's it for the sentries," Mendez said.

Kiara hit the throttle on the motors again. The ship lurched toward the shore. Logan broke down the pneumatic rifle, double-checked his pistol, and moved to the bow. Mendez was already there, offering some quiet encouragement to a nervous-looking

Chaudri. The whites of her eyes were showing. Mendez's were pools of darkness.

"Everyone ready?" Logan buckled on his swordbelt and cinched it tight. He'd use the dart pistol when he could, but it never hurt to bring a backup.

"Damn right we are," Mendez said. He grinned, and his teeth shone in the darkness. "Now's the fun part."

> "Alissian fighters drastically outmatch us in skills and experience. All of our technological advantages and training programs make us, at best, evenly matched."
>
> —R. Holt, "Assessment of Alissian Militaries"

CHAPTER 38

RECOVERY

Logan hated going into a building blind. The admiral's small keep probably had two or three floors and at least a dozen chambers. Not a single mason in Valteron City remembered who'd built it, or had any idea of the layout. The best they had was based on a set of plans for a smaller keep in the foothills north of the city that Chaudri dug up somewhere. The place belonged to a retired ship captain. The strong room was centrally located, on the lowest floor.

Logan hoped like hell that the admiral's place would have the same design. Otherwise it'd be a room-to-room search in a building full of soldiers. *No thank you.*

Logan signaled Mendez to take up position beside the dome-shaped front door, then tried the handle. It didn't budge. Probably barred from the inside. They had maybe eight, ten minutes before the first guard started waking up.

"We'll have to cut it," Logan said.

Mendez unshouldered a black satchel, unzipped it, and took out the plasma cutter. The fist-sized center hub snicked onto the door, about waist-high. A slim metal bar clicked into that. Logan held it in place while Mendez attached the plasma cutter. Sapphire light bloomed beneath it. Mendez swung the blade in an arc. There was no sound, other than a soft hiss. No smell, except a faint odor of char. He swung it in a full circle, thirty-six inches wide. The wood attached to the cutter slid out like a cork out of a wine bottle, except this was far heavier. Mendez strained under the weight. Logan stepped in to help. It nearly toppled both of them when it came free.

"Jesus," Logan swore quietly. *What the hell kind of wood is this?*

"Easy, easy!" Mendez whispered. They lowered it and leaned it against the wall.

"Two minutes," Kiara said.

A quarter of their op time burned already. *Damn.*

Logan slipped the safety off his pistol, gave Mendez the nod, and ducked through the hole. Mendez came through right on his heels, one hand on his shoulder, covering his blind side.

Two ingress points. One was a mudroom full of boots and rain cloaks. The other led down a torchlit corridor. Logan liked being the first through a breach, but now he gave Mendez the go-ahead. When it came to being a sneaky bastard, the Cuban had the edge.

The second Mendez took point, two men rounded a corner down the hallway. Logan raised his pistol, but didn't have the angle.

The *pfft-pfft* of suppressed fire from Mendez's pistol was a beautiful sound. Both guards slapped a hand at their necks, where crimson tranquilizer darts had bloomed. Mendez and Logan leaped forward to catch them as they fell.

Logan's burden had on a light linen uniform in some dark color, but he felt the flexible hardness of chain mail beneath. He lowered the man to the floor. Thought about confiscating his sword, but figured, *What's the point?* If they were still in the keep when the guards woke up, one guy's sword would be the least of their problems.

The corridor ended at an intersection. Identical hallways ran left and right.

"Which way?" Mendez asked.

"Don't know," Logan said. "The other keep had the strong room right here."

"Logan and Chaudri, take the left passage," Kiara said. "Mendez, you're with me."

Logan didn't hesitate, prowling down the left-hand hallway. He was on the lookout for more guards. They passed a closet, then an empty bedroom, then a small kitchen.

"Now a dining room," Chaudri whispered. "Then a coat room."

She was right on both counts. Logan paused long enough to give her a questioning look.

"I believe I have the layout now," she said. "If I'm right, we'll want the northwest corner."

"Let us know the second you find it," Kiara said. "Four minutes to go."

Logan and Chaudri crept forward as the corridor widened. There were doors on either side, all of them plain wooden jobs.

"Sleeping chambers," Chaudri said.

Logan was counting the doorways back to the hall. *Jesus, we're deep in this place.* If someone raised the alarm now, they'd never make it out.

Kiara broke in. "Got a reinforced door. This could be it."

"Chaudri thinks it's on our side," Logan said. He looked at her. She shrugged. *Might as well cover our bases.* "Try it anyway."

The lieutenant's voice barely registered. "Stand by."

He heard the creak of wood. The hiss of pneumatic pistols. Then silence.

"It's the barracks," Kiara said. Then a more muffled order to Mendez. "You sure? Count again."

Logan pressed on as he listened. Chaudri was three steps behind him. The corridor opened up into a wide, dimly lit chamber.

"Logan, there are twelve beds. But only two guards," Kiara said.

He ran the numbers in his head. *Shit.* "Two are missing."

The chamber beyond was some kind of a trophy room. Old military banners and flags hung from the walls to either side, many of them tattered or burned or both. Glass-and-steel oil lamps burned on little tables about every ten yards. Three stone pedestals stood against the far wall. One held a battered set of plate armor, another an old saber. Gods be praised, the third held a familiar canvas backpack.

"Well, look at that," Logan said. He strode into the room. He was so relieved to find Holt's leverage-cache that he forgot to check his corners.

A blur of movement was the only warning. Something slammed into his side. *A goddamn broadsword.* It would have cut him in half, were it not for the hidden armor. It still hurt like hell, and sent the pistol clattering away on the floor. Logan spun down and away. Chaudri shouted as two guards converged on her, pinning her arms to her sides.

The third man was older and still wearing a nightshirt, but holding the sword that had just hit him.

He was about six-two, solidly built, with a posture that said ex-military. His beard was longer and grayer than Logan remembered, but he was still easy to recognize. Mainly because he owned the place.

"Evening, Admiral," Logan said.

"So you *do* know whose keep this is. That makes you an even bigger fool that I thought."

"It's nothing personal." Logan drew his sword. "I'm just the repo man."

He charged and slashed out with the sword. Blackwell slid aside, deflecting it just enough. They circled one another. The admiral made a side cut at him. Logan knocked it aside and countered, though not as fast as he could. Better to hide the true speed of the lightweight sword until he was sure. His opponent leaned away from the blow. He was conserving energy. *Smart.*

Logan spared a glance for Chaudri. The two men held her arms tight, but it didn't look like they'd taken her pistol. One guy had a hand on the hilt of his dagger, but that was it. Strange that they hadn't tried using her against him. The admiral must have ordered them not to.

That would change if Logan managed to win this fight.

"Could really use some help here, Lieutenant," he muttered.

The admiral slashed at him once, twice, three times. The clang of steel drowned out Kiara's reply.

It was all Logan could do to keep the man at bay. He gave ground, retreating deeper into the chamber. Blackwell followed, moving on the balls of his feet.

Logan moved around him and lunged in, trying to lock up the admiral's blade. Then he could throw a shoulder into him, maybe knock him off balance. But Blackwell guessed his intent and twisted free, dipping his blade to gash Logan's forearm.

"Goddammit!" Logan backed off again and shook his arm to keep it from cramping. He hadn't faced someone this good in a while. Maybe ever. What would Bradley do in this situation?

Bradley would cheat like hell.

That reminded him of the dart gun. He was almost on top of it. Blackwell made a sweeping cut at him. He ducked below it, went down on one knee, and fumbled for the pistol with his good hand. He found it. He brought the pistol around, pulled the trigger . . . and nothing happened.

The admiral pounced, blade flashing in the lamplight.

Logan threw himself backward. He hit the stone floor hard, and it jogged him to a realization. *The goddamn safety's on.* He flicked it off with his thumb, rolled, and fired. Clean hit, center mass.

Blackwell clutched at his chest and collapsed on top of him. Logan leaned to the side, reaching past him, and shot the guard on Chaudri's right arm. The one on her left yanked a dagger out of his belt. He reared back with it.

"Chaudri!" Logan shouted. He didn't have a shot.

The guard stabbed downward. Or started to, when a shadow loomed behind him. Hands wrapped around his wrist. Mendez's face bore a snarl that was pure animal. He stepped on the back of the guard's knee, forcing him down. Turned the guard's knife-point toward the man's own neck.

Chaudri remembered her pneumatic pistol. "Julio, stop!" She drew it and shot the guard point-blank in the torso.

Logan exhaled. *That hurt like hell, but probably saved his life.* Mendez threw him against the wall as he crumpled.

"Where's Kiara?" Logan asked.

Mendez looked confused. "She was right behind me."

Logan ran to the pedestal and scooped up the back-pack. The material looked like old burlap, but felt like a poly-blend. Metal clinked inside of it. He held his breath and flipped open the top. There it all was. The laptop, the infrared goggles, packets of genetically modified crop seeds. Binoculars, portable generator, and even the Beretta sidearm. *This has to be it.* There weren't any other bags in the room, and they were out of time anyway. He ran back to the entrance just as Kiara appeared.

"Where were you?" he asked.

"Got sidetracked. Do you have the backpack?"

He brandished it. "Right here."

"Let's move." She about-faced and jogged down the corridor. Chaudri stood like a statue, apparently still shell-shocked from the close call. Mendez turned her around and pushed her ahead of him, but not un-gently. Logan brought up the rear, reloading his dart pistol as he followed. That should be it for the guards, but the admiral might have family here, or guests.

I hate having no intel.

Kiara led them back to the long corridor, and up it. They slipped past the half-dozen closed doors to either side. Logan checked his watch. *Twelve minutes gone.* They'd be cutting it close with the guards out-side. The keep was eerily quiet as they hustled down the long corridor to the breached front door. Through the hole, the moon's light shone on the dark waters of the tiny harbor. Just a little bit farther.

Kiara was out of the hole, then Chaudri and Mendez. Logan had one boot in and one boot out of the hole when the first bell began to ring. Not a friendly chime, either, but a deep sonorous tone that reverberated up from the ground. So much for the covert mission. He and Mendez heaved the door back into position, and freed the plasma cutter.

"Back to the ship!" Kiara said.

They flew down the stone stairs, taking them two at a time. The sound of the bell grew louder as they approached the waterline. The bell itself was in the top of the stone tower. Logan could even see the guy ringing it. He paused long enough to steady his aim, and fired. The bell ringer slumped, but of course the damage was done. Shouts of alarm came from a guardhouse a hundred yards to the south. Soldiers boiled out of it like angry bees.

None of them had ranged weapons, but in thirty seconds that wouldn't matter. Kiara, Mendez, and Chaudri leaped aboard the cuddy cabin and cut the lines. Logan jammed his pistol into the holster, put his hands on the hull, and shoved the hull away from shore. Kiara hit the throttle, and the ship shuddered into motion.

Logan checked the guards. They were fifty yards out, but coming fast. He looked back to the ship, and it was almost too far to hop on. *Crap.* He backed up three steps, ran, and jumped for it. It seemed like he was in the air forever, and just when he thought he'd make it, his boot caught the rail. He went down hard, but fortunately his momentum carried him onto the deck. Less fortunately, he landed on his wounded arm, and it exploded in a firestorm of pain.

No time for that now.

"Mendez, longbow," he said. Now that they'd been spotted, Slippery Pete was a no-go.

"On it." Mendez found the bow and quiver, nocked an arrow, and tossed Logan the crossbow.

Logan caught it with his good arm. Pneumatic pistols were fine for stealth, but when soldiers were charging you with cold steel in their hands, you had to show some teeth. Mendez drew, aimed, loosed. The arrow slammed into the guard in front with a wet *whump*. He went down, tripping up the one behind him. Logan drew a bead on the third soldier. *Clack-thrum*. The crossbow bucked, and the bolt punched through the soldier's mail in the same instance. He careened sideways into the water.

Now the ship was ten yards from shore. It'd take an Olympic long jumper to cross the gap.

Logan exhaled. Thank the Alissian gods, the admiral's men hadn't thought to use the siege engine. Then the bell started ringing again, and he cursed himself for feeling relieved too soon. He peered across the harbor and saw a broad, pale triangle ghosting toward them. *What is that?* A shadow glided beneath it, glinting with steel weapons. *Oh, hell.*

"Ship moving to intercept," he called over his shoulder. He hadn't marked it when they came in, which meant it came in after they'd arrived. Maybe that was bad luck. *Or maybe that was Holt's plan all along.* He knew they were in Valteron. If he guessed why, this wouldn't be a bad place to set a trap. *And we just took the bait.* The thought chilled him.

"I see it," Kiara said. She swung the steering rod over. The hum of the motors didn't change. They were already at full throttle.

If the other ship beat them to the cliffs, that was it. They couldn't afford a collision—no amount of high tech could drive a ship through another solid object. *It's going to be close, too.* The other ship had a wind advantage, and was already heading at the perfect angle to slide between them and the harbor mouth.

Logan wished he'd reloaded the crossbow. "Mendez, see the man on the tiller?"

"Yeah. Don't have a good shot, though. Boom's in the way."

"Can you put one right next to his head?"

"Absolutely."

"When I say."

Mendez nocked an arrow. The wind lulled as the ships and the egress point all got within fifty yards of each other. Then it gusted, and sails went taut.

"Now," Logan said.

Mendez drew to his cheek, touched his nose to the string, and let out half a breath as he took aim. The bow thrummed. The arrow thunked home, right by the helmsman's head. The man yelped and threw himself behind the bulkhead. The ship's bow wandered starboard for two glorious seconds. The sail luffed, losing wind. They fell off twenty yards before someone got hold of the tiller again.

Kiara swung the steering rod again, and the cliffs loomed up to either side. The starboard hull ground against the side, but not enough to slow them.

"Nice shooting, Mendez," Logan said.

"Learned from the best." Mendez grinned. "Well, *second* best, if you count Bradley."

Logan clutched a hand over his heart. "You wound me."

The ship glided out of the gap. Moonlight on water had never looked so good. Logan breathed for what felt like the first time in an hour.

"What do you think he's up to right now?" Mendez asked.

"Who knows? Sleeping in, flirting with pretty girls."

"So . . . the usual."

"I hate to break up this amusing conversation," Kiara said. "But we're about to be boarded."

"I must again emphasize the importance of long-term strategic thinking for Project Gateway. Impatience serves neither us nor them."

—R. Holt, "Reevaluating Alissian Assumptions"

CHAPTER 39

LOSS

When he saw how close the admiral's ship was, Logan's heart started pounding in his ears. It couldn't be more than fifty yards back. *And coming fast, too.* "How is this possible?"

"The motors only do about fourteen knots. They have the wind advantage."

Logan saw the other ship's extra sail then, round and taut with the full wind. *Damn.* "How long?"

"Thirty seconds."

He ran up to the cockpit and stashed the contraband backpack at Kiara's feet. "Keep an eye on this, will you?"

The bow thrummed as Mendez tried a shot at the helmsman. No dice. They knew about the bow, and were keeping behind cover. The ship gained on them. Logan stepped on the crossbow so he could cock it with his good arm.

"Brace yourselves!" Kiara shouted.

The ships collided with a thunder. The deck rocked beneath Logan's feet. He dropped the crossbow bolt and it rolled away. He grabbed a line to keep from tumbling over. "Can you shake them off?"

"Negative," Kiara said. "The wind's pushing them on us."

The soldiers wanted to mount a boarding party, too. Logan marked six of them. They'd piled up amidships and were already swinging grapples.

Time to take the fight to them.

He drew his sword and vaulted over the rail. He hit the deck running. Two soldiers turned to face him, and if they were surprised, they didn't show it. He charged the one closest to the rail. His opponent slashed down with a saber. Logan parried and threw a shoulder into him. He fell sprawling into the men behind him, right as they swung back their grappling hooks. They all went down in a tangle of rope and steel.

The second man skirted clear and came at Logan.

his sword already slashing. Logan skipped away. But his boot caught something on the deck, and he fell hard against the rail. The impact knocked the wind out of him. He rolled free. The swordsman pounced on him. Thrusting downward. Logan's muscles wouldn't respond.

Son of a bitch, I'm going to die at sea.

Steel flashed overhead. The swordsman went down, his neck spraying blood. Mendez again, thank God. But now three foes had found their feet and drawn weapons. They moved to surround him.

Logan tried to get up, but felt like he was moving through Jell-O. A blur shot past him. Chaudri. Her sword caught one man at the knees. He screamed, toppling over. Logan's legs finally responded. He stumbled along the rail, cutting the grappling lines as he went. A soldier threw another one onto the cog. Why were they still trying to grapple? They'd lost half their number already. They should be clearing the deck.

Unless.

God, let me be wrong.

He looked across the bay to the docks of Valteroni City. Four massive ships glided toward them on moonlit water. Galleons, by the look of them. Twenty or thirty soldiers each. The admiral must have made some kind of distress signal.

Or else it's always been a trap.

He shook his head. Better not to think about that.

"Sails ho, Lieutenant," he shouted.

Chaudri was locked in a contest with one soldier. Mendez faced two. Logan ran over to help. He tried to get the drop on the closest one, but the man jumped aside as he swung his sword. He slashed back, quick as a viper. The blade raked across Logan's chest. *Jesus, he's fast.* He retreated the way he'd come. He stumbled again, flailing his arms.

The swordsman snarled and jumped forward, slashing downward.

Hook, line, and sinker. Logan planted his feet and sidestepped. The soldier's sword found the deck. Logan chopped downward, and his blade severed the man's hands off at the wrist.

He groaned, and crumpled to the deck.

"I want everyone back on board!" Kiara ordered over the comms.

Logan slid between Chaudri and her opponent. "You heard the lieutenant."

She turned and cut the last of the grappling lines. The ships shuddered, and began to slide apart.

"Fall back!" Logan shouted.

Mendez tangled up the spear of his opponent in some of the rigging. He turned and ran toward Logan.

"Go, go!" Logan shouted.

Mendez sped up and vaulted over the rail.

Logan spun his sword and started cutting halyards. Canvas tumbled down on the deck, fouling up the opponents. "Chaudri!"

"Right behind you!" She cut the last grappling line. The deck lurched as the ships broke free.

Logan had a longer jump. By the time he climbed the rail, it was about six feet. *I can make that.*

This time his boots *just* missed the deck. He threw his arms over the rail to keep from falling. The rest of his body slammed against the hull. His bruised arm was agony.

"Hang on, Logan!" Chaudri had made it back. She worked her way along the rail toward him.

Kiara threw the tiller over, and the other ship wheeled away.

"S'OK." He ground his teeth and tried to get a foot up. He almost lost his grip. *Jesus. Maybe not so OK.*

Chaudri helped him get a foot on the deck. Mendez appeared, put him in a bear hug, and heaved him bodily over the rail. They ended up in a pile on deck. Chaudri laughed, and started to climb over the rail herself, but then something metallic clattered onto the deck. A grappling hook.

"Watch it!" Logan scrambled away and dragged Mendez clear.

The rope went taut. The hook shot back toward the rail. Chaudri grunted as it hit her. The hidden armor kept the point from skewering her, but the force of it ripped her away from the rail half a second before Logan and Mendez reached her. She tumbled into the water, flailing against the drag of the rope.

"Veena!" Mendez shouted.

Logan cursed. "Man overboard!"

"Hang tight, I'll bring us around," Kiara said. She swung the tiller. The ship started to turn. That's when Logan noticed how close the other Valteroni ships were. They towered over the cog, closing fast. Their lamplit decks swarmed with soldiers.

Logan looked at Kiara and saw the press of her jaw. *Oh, shit.*

She swung the tiller back around.

"What are you doing?" Mendez demanded.

"We can't go back for her," she said.

"*What?*"

"The backpack is more important. I'm sorry, Mendez."

"Screw that!" Mendez stripped off his cloak and jacket. "I'm going after her."

"You can't swim," Logan said.

"Then I'll see you in hell, *hermano.*"

Logan heard a soft *click* behind him. Wind brushed his cheek. A crimson dart bloomed in Mendez's neck.

Mendez mumbled something in Spanish, his eyes wide in outrage, and fell to the deck.

Logan spun on the lieutenant, who held the dart pistol with a steady hand. "What the hell?"

"We both know he'd have drowned trying to save her."

"We can't just *leave* her!" He stomped to the rail. Chaudri had wriggled free of the hook, and was swimming after them. *Not fast enough, though.* He stripped off his own jacket. "I can get to her."

"With that arm?" Kiara asked.

He looked down and saw what she saw, the mottled bruises where the admiral had hit him. "I still have to try."

He put a foot beneath the rail. Heard a click behind him. Something stung him on the back of his neck. He swatted at it, felt the hard cylinder there. *Damn it to hell.*

The world went black.

"When the spotlights are on, carelessness always costs you."

—**Art of Illusion, August 1**

CHAPTER 40

TAKEN

Quinn drifted back into consciousness through a slow curtain of pain. He tasted salt in his mouth, and the bitter tang of blood. His head throbbed. He opened his eyes. Everything was an indistinct blur of grayness. He went to rub them, but he couldn't move his arms.

"You know, I always thought there was something peculiar about you," a woman said.

Oh, no. He recognized that voice.

Captain Relling sat in a wooden chair about five yards away, tapping the wooden club casually against her open palm. He couldn't see anything other than her, but they were indoors. Some kind of small room. Rope chafed at his wrists, which were tied to the wooden chair behind his back. His ankles were bound to the front legs. *How long was I out?* Probably at least an hour. All of his joints ached.

"The polyglossia does odd things, doesn't it?" Relling said. "Trains you not to watch someone's lips when they talk." She set the wooden club across her knees and leaned over it. "Were it not for that, I'd have pegged you a long time ago."

He shook his head, which only added to the pain. He had to convince her she'd made a mistake. But the pain made it hard to concentrate. His cleverness was gone. How the hell had she *known?*

"I love Steve Perry." She sighed. "Journey was never the same without him."

Son of a bitch. Of all the things that might have outed him to one of the locals, he'd never have guessed it would be eighties music.

"It could have been a fluke, I suppose," she said. "A song with similar words might exist in this world." She held up his comm unit. "But this would be a major leap."

Oh, hell. He'd grown so accustomed to having that in his ear, he never gave it a second thought. *So much for the amnesia.* "You—" he began, but his tongue was swollen and clumsy in his mouth.

She raised an eyebrow. "Hmm?"

He tried to spit, but drooled on himself. He wiped his face on his shoulder. "You were following me."

"What better way to get to know someone?"

She looked him up and down in a predatory way, looking so much like Kiara that he barked a laugh. Or tried to, at least. It came out somewhere between a cough and a wheeze.

"I still can't figure out what you are," she said. "No one from the research team would be so careless. But one of Logan's boys wouldn't be so easy to incapacitate."

Oh, that hurts. She wasn't wrong, though. Logan was going to kill him for getting busted over a goddamn Journey song. Well, a Steve Perry song, technically speaking.

It wouldn't matter to Logan. He'd never let Quinn live this down.

Assuming I live through it anyway.

"Well, are you going to say anything?" She looked at him expectantly. "Or should I just assume that you're a spy?"

Oh, you want me to say something? He locked eyes with her. "At least I'm not a traitor."

She pursed her lips. Nodded to herself, as if unsurprised. Then she stood, and clubbed him on the head. He tumbled into darkness again.

Waking up the second time was even worse. Quinn felt like he'd been hit by a truck. *That's what I get for* *mouthing off to Kiara's sister.* He'd sure as hell found the right button to push.

"Good, you're back," Relling said. "Maybe you'll watch your tongue this time." She paced the length of the small room, the club clutched tightly behind her back. "I don't consider myself a traitor, you know."

Quinn snickered. It was the best he could manage.

"I'm quite serious. The Enclave is the reason I'm still alive."

He shook his head, and didn't look at her. He needed some time to get his wits about him. She picked up something from the floor. His belt. Damn, she must have taken it off of him. "The R & D lab has done some spectacular work. The shocker buckle used to weigh half a pound." Her fingers found the hidden catch.

He sucked in a sharp breath. He couldn't help it. Even at half charge, the shock would hurt like hell. *I'm guessing she knows how to fire it, too.*

"You've spent some time in this world," Relling said. "You must know what the storms are like here." Her eyes went distant with the memory. "Thirty-foot swells. Relentless winds whipping you from all sides. And a featureless ocean that defies your best navigation equipment."

Quinn had suffered through a couple of storms on land. He nodded. Grudgingly.

"The *Victoria* was six days out when we lost comms," Relling said. "Then the sky went black, and the wind came up. The sea tossed us around like a goddamn kid's toy."

"Sounds rough," Quinn said. He didn't feel an ounce of sympathy, but he wanted her to keep talking.

"I've seen category-three hurricanes back on Earth. They're a cakewalk compared to this storm. It nearly sank us." She paused, and looked like she'd tasted something sour. "What came after was even worse."

"Mildew?" he asked.

She poked him hard in the chest with her club. "Pirates." She spat the word. "Boarded us in the middle of the night and killed half my crew before we fought them off. Then the sky went dark *again*. The second storm tried to finish the job. The magicians found me lashed to the wheel, with a nasty head wound and no memory whatsoever."

"Seems to be working fine right now," Quinn said.

"It took even longer to return to me than the *Victoria* did to repair."

Bullshit. He didn't know much about amnesia, but it was far more common in Hollywood than it was in real life. "Why didn't you come back?"

"You don't understand. It had been *years*."

"So?"

"The Enclave magicians didn't just save my life. They gave me a home. A purpose." She looked down and away, uncertain for the first time. "I met someone."

You've got to be kidding me. He was having trouble wrapping his head around this, and the throbbing headache didn't help. But through the pain came a realization: if her loyalty wasn't with CASE Global, then he had to tread lightly. Seem nonthreatening.

Most of all, not get clubbed in the head or zapped with his own belt.

"So, it's complicated," he said. "I get that. But what do you want from me?"

"I find it best to start with the basics." She stood and took up pacing again, this time twisting his belt buckle in her hands. "Is Quinn your real name?"

"Yes." There was no point in hiding it.

"And I assume you work for CASE Global Enterprises."

"Eh, I'm more of an independent contractor."

"What kind?"

He tried for a smile, and it hurt. "What kind do you think?"

She looked at him flat-eyed. Then her lips quirked upward. "I'll be damned. You *are* a magician. But the David Copperfield kind."

Quinn didn't say anything to confirm it, but he didn't deny it, either.

"You came back for a second time." She said it more to herself than to him. Then she looked up. "This place is getting to you, isn't it?"

"Alissia?"

"The *Enclave*."

"I don't know what you're talking about." But he was pretty sure he did.

"This island has an odd effect on people. It *changes* them. I know it changed me."

Changed you into a billy-club-wielding lunatic. He couldn't deny, though, that there was something that had been pulling him back to the Enclave's island ever since he first stepped foot on it. That said, he wasn't going to give her the satisfaction of agreeing with her. "What a delightful tale," he said. "Let me go."

"Oh, that was just the warm-up. Let's move on to some real questions."

He figured an opening bet wouldn't hurt. "I'll answer three."

"You'll answer as many as I ask."

Well, it was worth a shot.

"Let's start with an easy one. Why in the hell did Richard Holt make himself Valteroni Prime?"

"*That's* your easy question?" Quinn laughed, and it hurt his lungs. "I have no idea. It caught everyone by surprise."

She opened her mouth, closed it, and made the leap. "Went rogue, did he? He always did love this place."

"Maybe a little too much."

"I told you, this place gets to you." She poked him again with the club.

"Ow!" *I thought we were past the violent part of the interrogation.*

"The company must be throwing a fit," Relling mused. "Who's in command?" She cocked her head as she asked this, as if favoring her right ear. Maybe she heard better out of it than the other, or maybe it was habit. Either way, it was a tell. This question wasn't nearly as casual as she'd made it.

He'd danced around the issue so far. But naming names was a slippery road. Once he went down it, there was no path back to vague half-answers. He looked at her and said nothing.

"Are you sure you want the hard way?" Her fingers brushed the trigger on his belt shocker. "You don't seem cut out for it."

Logan would make her beat the truth out of him. And then he probably still wouldn't say. But he was a trained soldier, and Quinn wasn't even getting hazard pay. *I overbet the pot and I don't have the cards to win it.*

All he could do now was fold with style. "I guess I'd have to say it's you," he said. "But the new and improved version."

Her eyes lost their glint for a second. *She's surprised.* Maybe she didn't expect her relationship to Kiara to be public knowledge. Something else passed over her face, and he could have sworn it was pride. Then her predatory look returned. "Why are you spending so much time with the Pireans? You claimed you were Landorian."

He tried to shrug, but his bonds prevented it. "I like them."

"And Jillaine?"

"I like her, too." He held her eyes and hoped she wouldn't press this issue.

"I suppose it doesn't hurt that she's the daughter of one of the most influential council members."

"She's plenty influential on her own. But that's not why I like her."

"Why did you come to the Enclave?"

"I think that's pretty obvious."

"Enlighten me."

He smiled crookedly. His lips were still swollen on one side. "I'm here to learn magic."

"That's not a mission objective."

"Fine. Among other things, I was ordered to put up a comm antenna."

"Where is it?"

"I haven't put it up yet."

She snorted. "Now who's the traitor?"

"I guess I'm not comfortable with the company knowing where the Enclave is. That's why I didn't sell you out the second I got here." *A decision I'm starting to regret.*

"How naive *are* you?"

"I'm not naive."

She held up his comm unit. "Every comm unit has a beacon in it that pings on the company's network. The master node has been triangulating your position since the moment you came here."

Quinn's insides turned to ice. "What master node?"

"The huge antenna outside the gateway cave." She dropped his comm unit to the floor and stomped it with the heel of her boot. "Don't know why I bother. It's probably too late."

She's right. I'm a fool.

"What are the company's plans for the Holt situation?" Relling asked.

"They're handling it," he mumbled.

"How?"

He shook his head, still not looking at her. "I'm not allowed to say."

"This puts us in an awkward position, Quinn."

He met her eyes and sneered. "Well, we wouldn't want things to be *awkward* after you knocked me out twice and tied me to this chair. So I guess I'll be on my way."

"Oh, no. I can't let you wander freely around the Enclave."

"You've no right to keep me prisoner," he said.

"And yet here we are."

"Someone will notice that I'm missing. I'm Moric's student."

She smiled. "Last I heard, Moric was missing, too."

A door banged open somewhere to the left. Lamplight flooded the room, and cast the shadow of a slim figure in sharp relief on the wall.

"He might be," Jillaine said. "but his daughter is *not*."

Quinn's mouth fell open. *Thank God.*

Relling had jumped back against the far wall. But she still had the club, hidden behind her back. "This doesn't concern you, Jillaine."

"I'll decide that for myself." Jillaine saw Quinn and hurried forward. She touched the lump on his temple. "What have you done to him?"

"He's not who he says he is."

Jillaine held his eyes for a moment. "I'm aware of that."

"In league with him, are you?" Relling stepped forward again. Her fingers flipped off the safety on the belt shocker.

"Jillaine, look—" he started.

Relling triggered the belt shocker. Jillaine shied back, but not far enough. The prongs caught her center mass. The shock hit her like a wave. Her eyes rolled back into her head and she fell down.

"You *bitch*!" Quinn shouted. He threw himself against his bindings, against his chair. Fought like an animal to get free and tear Relling apart. For all his struggling, however, all that happened was the ropes dug into his wrists and ankles until they bled.

Relling hit the retractor, and the prongs shot back into the belt buckle. "My compliments to the engineers. They've really outdone themselves."

Quinn growled at her through clenched teeth. Red rage tinted his vision. Jillaine moaned and shifted on the floor. *Thank God, at least she's conscious.* "Jillaine?"

"You *do* like her, don't you?" Relling asked. She

tossed his belt aside and retrieved her club from the chair. She patted it in her hand as she moved toward Jillaine. "Perhaps we've stumbled upon the right button to push."

Quinn's lip curled. "Let her be, or I swear to God, I'll—"

"You'll what?" Relling raised her eyebrows. "What will you do?"

He snarled wordlessly at her.

"I think you need a reminder of who's in control here." Relling kicked the chair aside and raised her club over Jillaine.

No, no, no, NO! Something snapped inside of Quinn. Heat poured into him like white-hot lava. Rage and power boiled together. They shook his body violently. He gave in to it, reached for it.

And power filled him.

He hurled it at Relling's back. A shock wave slammed into her like a hammer, hurling her against the far wall. She slumped down into a heap. He focused on his bindings next. He felt an odd detachment to it all, though it was his fury that cut through them. The ropes burned to ash and fell away. He fell out of his chair beside Jillaine. Brushed back her hair. Whispered her name.

Her chest rose and fell, but she didn't respond. The warmness of power coursed through his arms. He shaped it, and took the edge off the magic's rage. He splayed his fingers out and touched them gently to the nape of her neck. Blue light glowed beneath his fingertips.

Jillaine's eyes flickered open. She bolt upright, gasped, and clutched his arm.

He sagged in relief against her. The rage seeped out of him. The heat inside dissipated, but didn't leave entirely. A little ball of warmth remained. He stood, and pulled Jillaine to her feet. Now that the anger had gone, fatigue settled in. He could barely hold himself upright while she stumbled over to check on Relling.

"Is she dead?" he asked, his voice hoarse.

"Unconscious," Jillaine said. "What should we do with her?"

Logan would want me to interrogate her. But he probably didn't have the stomach for that. "Whatever you want." He turned and lumbered out the door.

He passed through torchlight, and saw the harbor. Whitecaps danced on the dark waters. The light came from a pair of bright-burning torches to either side of the door. The building itself was a stone structure, one story, with wooden boardwalks running left and right from where he stood. Three small cutters bobbed against the pylons right in front of him.

They weren't chained up. He could jump into one right now, and be gone before sunup. But he didn't know how to sail, and probably wouldn't be able to find the mainland even if he did. Besides, that would mean abandoning Jillaine again, and there'd be no coming back from that.

So he stood there, rubbing his wrists. Trying to piece together what had happened.

Jillaine emerged a moment later, with her hair back in perfect order. She smiled faintly, and warmth *purred* inside him. She took his hand without a word and pulled him along the docks. A lighter gray tinged the distant horizon.

"How did you find me?" he asked.

"I followed her, after she hit you over the head."

"You saw it happen?"

"From a distance."

"And you didn't think to intervene?"

She shrugged. "I can understand a woman wanting to club you."

"Oh. My. *Gods.*"

"Settle down. I rescued you eventually."

"I'm pretty sure I rescued you," he said.

He could still feel the warm glow of magic inside him. It pulsed there, waiting to be called again. He stopped and held out his left hand, palm-up. He drew the magic, remembering Leward's lesson and how it had felt on his hand. The warmth in him flowed outward, down his arm, across his open palm. A ball of fire formed above it, hissing and crackling like the Pirean hearth had. Quinn stared at it in awe. *Can it really be so easy?*

"Are you quite finished?" Jillaine asked.

He let the ball of flame dissipate, and sent the warmth away with a twinge of regret. "Sorry. I couldn't help it."

She shook her head. "Men."

Quinn's head still spun with so many thoughts at once. He'd lost his comm unit, and his cover was blown. Worst of all, the company might soon find out where the Enclave really was. And now there were no Valteroni ships patrolling its waters. "Listen, you know how I promised I wouldn't leave again without telling you?"

"It was without *taking* me, if I recall," Jillaine said.

"Fine. Whatever." He drew in a deep breath, and it hurt. *Relling must have done a number on me.* "I have to leave again. Will you come with me?"

She laughed. "Why would I do that?"

"You said you want to see the world."

"I don't need you for that."

"Probably not." He dug into his hidden jacket pocket and took out the parchmap. *Thank God I always keep this on me.* He unfolded it and held it up. "But I've got a pretty good map."

She took the parchmap in both hands. Her eyes were like saucers. "Where did you get this?" She traced the Pirean shoreline with a fingertip. It was an order of magnitude more precise than the best map in the Enclave library.

"Sorry, that's confidential." He snatched it back, folded it up, and tucked it away.

She jabbed at him with an elbow. "Let me see it!"

He stopped and faced her. *Time to lay it all out.* "Come with me, and you can see it all you want."

She looked down at the ground, chewing her lip. Then she met his eyes. "Something tells me I'm going to regret this."

"We lose ourselves to our jobs the moment we stop putting people first."

—R. Holt, "Investment in Alissia"

CHAPTER 41

INSURANCE

Logan hated the little ship's muted silence. It was the seventh day sailing north from Valteron. Comms were still out. The entire southern relay network had gone down right after they escaped the bay. Kiara had gotten off a terse update just before they lost the hotlink to command.

Another network outage, and no way of knowing how much of the network was down. The fact that it came right after they'd secured Holt's best piece of leverage couldn't be a coincidence. It was either a

Hail Mary pass to stop them, or part of some bigger plan.

And Holt was partial to the latter.

That was a long-term problem, though. The communication on the ship was no better. For one thing, the mood between Mendez and the lieutenant hadn't improved. He was a good soldier, and still following orders, but he didn't say a word more than necessary. He didn't laugh at Logan's jokes or offer any of his own.

He's back to where he was after Thorisson. Worse, maybe. In a way, Logan could understand that. It was one thing to have to kill a man—you got trained for that. It was another to lose someone you cared about. No amount of training lessened that blow.

Logan was worried about him.

The lieutenant had the tiller, which meant Mendez was at the bow. Logan sidled up and leaned over the rail beside him. "You all right?"

Mendez stared off at the water, unblinking. "I'm good, sir."

Logan grunted. He *wasn't* good, but he was talking, and that was a real improvement over the last few days. "We had some tough missions before, but I think that one takes the cake. God, I'm getting too old for this."

"Gods," Mendez corrected. He never took his eyes from the water.

Logan forced a laugh. "She would want me to say that."

"She would."

"Remember that time she made us wear those codpieces?"

A hint of a smile. "The gala down in Caralis. I don't think I'll ever forget that."

"You were blushing like a cheerleader on a third date."

"There were two hundred people there, and we were the only ones wearing them."

"You still kept it on all night."

"I kind of liked the attention."

They both chuckled, long and low. Logan sighed. *When did we stop having fun in this place?* It was well before Holt went AWOL. Sometime after losing the *Victoria*, the tone of the missions had changed. The lieutenant had changed. Mission success became far too important.

Maybe it's time to hang up my spurs. Another mission or two, and he'd have banked enough hazard pay to last for a long time.

Kiara's tablet chirped like a cricket. An Alissian field cricket, to be precise, which was smaller than the Earth version but somehow just as loud. All of their electronics had alerts and notifications based on natural sounds. Logan had them all memorized. Field cricket was the connection alert. It meant they were talking to Command again.

"What's the latest?" Logan asked.

"Bradley's comm unit went black."

"When?"

"Last night."

"Maybe he forgot to charge it," Logan said, though he didn't buy it. Bradley loved his tech, and got to carry more solar panels than anyone else because of it.

"The only good news is that he got the long-range antenna up."

"About damn time," Logan said. He tried to put himself in Bradley's shoes. What would he do if he lost his comm unit? "Maybe that's his way of asking for a ride."

Kiara went up to the bow for her full debrief. Command had her on the comm for nearly an hour, while Logan grew anxious. He couldn't put a finger on it, but something about her posture put him on edge.

Finally, she came back, though her movements were stiff. "We're ordered back to Bayport."

"What about Bradley?"

"He's back-burnered for now. We'll send a team to the beacon as soon as we can."

"Charlie Team could do it." Logan and Mendez had started their training before the current mission pulled them away. They were all ex-special-forces, culled from the latest round of military recruiting. They'd be solid.

"They're meeting us in Bayport to help secure the asset."

"They're in-world already?" Logan asked.

"The executives green-lighted them the moment they got our mission success notification."

It seemed a little redundant, but Logan figured reinforcements couldn't hurt. They'd bring new batteries for the electronics, better food, fresh horses. "I hope they brought me a gelding this time."

"You won't need one. Once we're in Bayport, I want you and Mendez on a coast-cutter headed south."

"What for?"

"New orders. Now that Bradley's neutralized Holt's protection, the executives want the threat removed."

"We already did remove the threat." Logan pointed to the hidden compartment that held Holt's backpack. "It's right there."

"Someone with Holt's knowledge is too dangerous to remain in this world. The executives want him taken out."

"Good for them."

Mendez shook his head and spat over the rail. He stomped up to the bow and didn't look back.

"Are you refusing your orders?" Kiara asked. Her tone was cold, devoid of any emotion.

Like a goddamn robot making an inquiry. "Damn right I'm refusing. I don't do assassinations. I told you that when I signed on."

"So you think we should just let Holt remain there, while he sabotages our infrastructure and bends an entire nation to his will?"

It might have been a fair point, except Logan knew the man, and had seen the changes in Valteron City. "He's doing good things. He must know he's vulnerable, now that we have the backpack. Come on, Lieutenant. That's got to be enough."

"Even if it were for me, it's not enough for my superiors. Your orders stand."

He shrugged. "Then I quit." It was the easiest thing in the world. Sharon wouldn't like the early retirement, but between his hazard pay and what they'd saved, they'd be all right.

"You're under contract," Kiara said.

"If CASE Global wants to sue me on breach of contract, that's fine with me." *We both know they won't.* A legal proceeding would compel him to disclose things the company had no interest in making public.

She didn't respond, but tapped something into her panel. A terse message. Two characters. *N. O.*

The panel whistled about ten seconds later. *Incoming video chat.*

Well, this ought to be interesting.

"You've got a call," Kiara said.

Here it came, the old dressing down from the top brass. Logan didn't give two shits about what some suit had to tell him. In fact, he was more curious than concerned. *Let's have a look at who's calling the shots.*

He gave her a see-if-I-care look, and grabbed the panel. He had to shield it from the glare of the sun on the water. And when he did that, the last thing he expected to see was his wife's face. "Sharon?"

"Hi, baby!" She smiled with those perfect white teeth.

His heart fluttered the way it always had when he saw her. He smiled back. "Hey, baby, how are you?" He glanced up at Kiara. *What the hell is she playing at?* A dread began to creep up inside of him.

"Ooh, we are great," Sharon said. "If I'd known how lovely the island was, I'd have made you bring me here sooner."

"What island?" His stomach went cold. "Are you at the *facility*?"

"Since last week. I can't believe CASE Global flew us down here."

"Neither can I." He looked up at Kiara, who was staring out at the ocean. *She can't even look at me.* "Are the girls with you?"

"School won't start for three weeks. They're having a ball."

"Aw, good. Listen, I have to get back to it." He forced a smile. "Don't have too much fun until I get back."

"No promises." She blew him a kiss. "See you soon."

The screen went blank, and he fought the urge to chuck the whole tablet into the water. "What the hell is this?"

"I thought that having your family close by would help you remember your priorities. Sharon's always wanted to see the island, hasn't she?"

And I wanted her a thousand miles away from it. "You had no right to bring them there."

"Consider it a perk. They're being treated as honored guests."

They weren't guests. They were hostages. The company had him by his soft spot, and Kiara knew that all too well. "How could you, Lieutenant?" This was brutally cold, even for her. "How many other CASE Global employees got this little perk?"

"There was a drawing for it, and only two winners."

He connected the dots, and couldn't believe how cold the picture was. "Me and Mendez."

"Yes. The whole Mendez clan. All thirty-five members."

The saddest part was that Logan should have seen it coming. *I'm such a fool.* Mendez returned from the bow wearing a grim expression.

"So, about those orders," Kiara said. "Are you still refusing them?"

Logan met her gaze, and didn't hide the fury from his eyes. He'd have gone for her right then, except she had her hand near the pneumatic pistol. And the company would still have his family. New threats assorted themselves in his head. Mendez caught Logan's eye, looked at Kiara, then back.

Gave a tiny nod. He had Logan's back, whatever happened. *Good.*

Logan put his solder's face back on. The face of cool professionalism. He let out a long breath. "Guess I'm not."

But you'd better watch your back, Lieutenant.

"The key to a good cover is mastery of the little details."

—R. Holt, "Recommendations for Gateway Protocols"

CHAPTER 42

OVERBOARD

Veena fought to keep her head above the surface, but the flexsteel armor weighed her down. She'd already given up her sword to the inky depths of Valteron City's bay. For a moment, she thought Kiara might turn the trade cog to rescue her, but the Valteroni ships descended with alarming swiftness. Almost as if they'd been crewed and ready to sail the moment their team infiltrated the admiral's complex.

So the rest of her team fled before the approaching ships, leaving Veena to fend for herself.

Now one of those Valteroni ships cast a long shadow as it loomed over her. Her arms and legs felt like lead by the time the basketball-sized cork float splashed down beside her. She grabbed on to it with both hands. It was either that, or drown.

They dragged her to the hull of the ship, and then hauled her up the side. Her arms shook with exertion. Just before she reached the top, they gave out. She'd have fallen, were it not for the arms that caught her cloak and lifted her bodily over the rail. She collapsed in a heap on the deck, coughing up seawater until she gagged. A pair of boots appeared before her. Black leather, steel tip. *An officer.*

"You must be Veena," he said.

"Yes." She coughed again, took his offered hand, and stood.

The man was middle-aged, with a short beard and ruddy cheeks. He wore the crisp white uniform and triangular hat of a Valteroni ship's captain. "I am Captain Mansfield, of the Valteroni fleet."

"Well, Captain." She straightened and looked at him with as much calm as she could muster. "You certainly took your time."

"Distraction is the magician's best friend, as long as we're not the ones distracted."

—**Art of Illusion, January 5**

CHAPTER 43

REVELATIONS

The Felaran snow was knee-deep, and Quinn's mule wasn't having it.

"Come on . . . *please?*" Quinn asked.

The animal wouldn't budge. *Goddamn Tioni smart mules.* He couldn't believe Jillaine wanted these over horses, but she'd insisted. Since she managed most of their transportation, he really couldn't argue. Without her, he'd never have found a lonely island two hundred leagues south of the Enclave, or leapfrogged half of the content to land in northern Felara.

He hated relying on her for it, but he didn't dare try the teleportation thing on his own. Even if the warm little ball of magic inside wanted him to.

Jillaine rode up beside him. "What's the problem?"

"My mule won't go."

"Did you ask him nicely?" she whispered.

"Of course," he groused.

She raised her voice. "Is that really a mule? I thought it was a courser, or a warhorse."

The mule's ears pricked up at this ridiculous praise.

"Surely a little snow wouldn't stop so strong an animal," Jillaine cooed.

The mule shook itself and plodded forward. They pressed on for another hour before Quinn started recognizing the landmarks. The gateway cave was about a quarter mile up the pass, but hidden from view by a snowcapped hill. And right outside it, the massive antenna that had tracked his movements for the past few weeks.

"It should be just over this ridge," Quinn said.

The snow was drift-deep here and powdery. The mules pushed up the last couple of steps with a bit more encouragement. The dark mouth of a cave came into view. And beside it, a dark pillar of stone that looked far more natural than it really was.

It has to look like an accident. Maybe a giant tumbling boulder from farther up the mountain. The magic within him promised that anything was possible. "Why don't we—" Quinn started began, but cut off when he saw movement. Two steps later, the rest of the shallow vale entered his vision. His jaw dropped. Siege equipment occupied most of the open space—wide mangonels, rolling catapults, and long-armed trebuchets. Dozens of figures crawled among them. Orderly ranks of soldiers filled the rest of the open space. There had to be over a hundred, and they were well-armed.

"Stop, please," he whispered to the mules.

"Who are they?" Jillaine asked. "Felarans?"

"I don't know. Maybe." But he didn't think so.

Truth was, most of the equipment was pointed *away* from the cave, so if the people in the vale were laying siege to the gateway, they were doing a poor job of it. Quinn fumbled in an inside pocket for his field glasses. He focused on the trebuchets first, then the engineers working them. Then he cut over to some of the soldiers. And it started to dawn on him . . .

They were armored, but not with clunky Alissian plate. The suppleness to it, and the freedom of movement, came from a material not of this world. Flex-steel.

I'll be damned. He shook his head. "It's begun already. And no one thought to tell me."

She met his eyes, and he saw the uncertainty there. "What's begun?"

AUTHOR'S NOTE

Dear Reader,

Thank you for reading my book! I had a lot of fun writing the sequel to The Rogue Retrieval, *and hope that you found it just as entertaining. If you did, I hope you'll keep an eye out for the third book, tentatively entitled* The World Awakening, *which should be out in 2018. If you'd like a reminder, please join my mailing list here:*

http://dankoboldt.com/subscribe

My e-mail followers get other perks, too, like free stories and some juicy contest details.

If you enjoyed my book, I hope you'll consider leaving a review on your blog, your favorite bookstore, or social media. Even a short review helps other readers find my book and decide if it's something they'd like. For a quick primer on how to write a book review, visit this page on my author website:

http://dankoboldt.com/reviews

Thanks for placing a bet on my book. It means a lot.

ACKNOWLEDGMENTS

I'm grateful to so many people for helping this book become a reality. To my wife, Christina, and our little ones (Audrey, Elliott, and Samuel), whose unflappable support allows me to keep writing. To my editor, David Pomerico, for his sharp editorial eye and continued support. To my copy editors, Christine Langone and Beth Attwood. To Caroline Perny and the team at Harper Voyager, for helping my books reach a wider audience. To my agent, Paul Stevens, for his constant support and career guidance. To my critique partners, Dannie Morin and Mike Mammay, for ferreting out my writing weaknesses.

I would never have come this far without the support of the writing community. Special thanks to my friends in The Clubhouse, Codex Writers, the Pitch Wars community, and Impulse Authors Unite.

Last but not least, I'm grateful to my readers for taking another trip through the gateway to Alissia. I hope it was everything you wanted, and more.

ABOUT THE AUTHOR

DAN KOBOLDT is a genetics researcher and fantasy/ science-fiction author. He has coauthored more than sixty publications in *Nature, Human Mutation, Genome Research, The New England Journal of Medicine, Cell,* and other scientific journals. Dan is also an avid hunter and outdoorsman. Every fall, he disappears into the woods to pursue whitetail deer with bow and arrow. He lives with his wife and children in Ohio, where the deer take their revenge by eating the flowers in his backyard.

You can find him online at http://dankoboldt.com and on Twitter at https://twitter.com/DanKoboldt.

Discover great authors, exclusive offers, and more at hc.com.